THE COMPASS SERIES

STEPHEN SANTOS

Cover design by Troy Mouer

The Compass Series

Many of us approach life holding a compass that is broken and does not move. We turn it around to make it point in a direction that suits our comfort. Yet when we find ourselves lost in life, this strategy will always fail. A compass only truly works when we choose to follow it's ability to show us the true direction we should take. You see, a big part of understanding your life and journey is being willing to move from where you are to see life from other perspectives.

Enter The Compass Series, more than a story, more than a series of books. This is an experience, an opportunity, and an introduction to a different way of living.

This series will challenge you to see your life from multiple perspectives. It will encourage you to seek understanding before conclusions. And it will push you to the limits of your comprehension of love.
If you choose to start on this journey and continue through all four compass points, your understanding and perspective of life and its purposes will never be the same.

Welcome to the journey...
that just may change your life.

Endorsements for *The Compass Series*:

"Stephen Santos opens his heart, exposes his pain and grief like few authors are able to do. He doesn't try to hide from the ugly realities that challenge his walk with Christ and seek to draw him from the path that leads to life. He is easy to read and what he says is worth reading. Do not be surprised when truth suddenly blooms before you with the beauty of a magnificent flower or when grief in a failing effort attacks the logic of your faith. In the end you will be wonderfully refreshed."

    -Charles Carrin
Author of *On Whose Authority, The Edge of Glory* and more. Co-author with R.T. Kendall and Jack Taylor of *Word Spirit Power*

"*The Compass Series* tells a story of a groom relentlessly pursuing his wayward bride --a down-to-earth, gritty and painful search for true love and a family lost. Along the way, we're filled with wisdom, struggle alongside another as she wrestles to receive love and reminded of the importance of adventure in our everyday lives. Unless we're constantly on guard, it's easy to get swept up in the tidal wave of culture that places ultimate value on the destination.
The Compass Series sets us on the path toward truth. In a sense, it begins the re-orientation process that so importantly reminds us of the value of the journey. And of the power of a selfless love that is focused on grace and surrender."

    -Troy Mouer
Mixed Media Artist (Cover Design); DefytheGray Blogger; Music, Media and Art Enthusiast; Attorney

---

"Stephen masterfully draws you into his story with profound character intuition and descriptive life twists we all can relate to. Be careful, when you pick up The Compass Series, you won't be able to put it down but you'll be better for it."

-Joshua Johnson
CEO, Mindbox Studios

"This book tells a story of love that is far too uncommon in this world. The context, however, is set in circumstances that are far too common in this world. The reader will be drawn into the unfolding drama from the very beginning as the stage is set with a shocking announcement that has the potential to wreck the life of Josh and his family. Through the developing circumstances that follow, one can't help but be challenged and filled with hope as the conclusion is reached in a gripping confrontation between good and evil. Do yourself a favor and enjoy the rewarding experience you will have in reading this book."

-Carman Niesley
Artist; Pastor; One of the greatest men I know.

"No journey of the heart is for the weak-willed. It is in the vulnerable places we find what has been hidden, wounded and lost. These vulnerable places are not an option on the path. But are they bad? Or are they the doorway to true intimacy and the deep rooted love we all long for but often doubt we deserve? May we all find ourselves knit in between the plot and pages of this story, and in so doing, find a coming home."

-Jennifer Wilhite
Song writer; Artist; Creative writer

Thank You

~To my best friend, who has walked with me through hell and highwater. Who has taught me to laugh at impending doom, and sit when I felt like I needed to run. There is no one who could take your place in my heart and life. I dedicate this book to you, not just because you are worthy of its dedication, but because I want to. Thank you, Jesus.

~To my children, each one of you are a special part of me, and I am a better man for it. Thank you for all that you have and continue to teach me.

~To my dear friend Troy Mouer, who has always believed in me beyond what was able to be seen, and who is responsible for the amazing cover design that speaks more than words to these stories and powerfully to our journey of life.

~To Benjamin and Jennifer Wilhite for your counsel and encouragement.

~To my parents whose love, support and guidance throughout my life has helped to build a strong foundation for me to continue to build upon. Thank you Dad, chapter 3 wouldn't have been written without you in my life.

~To all of my friends and family who were a part of encouragement and counsel in this project. Each of you held pieces of the puzzle and helped make this picture whole.

BOOK ONE

A man named Joshua

Prologue

Is it ok to say that I hate him?
I really do.
I hate what he has done to her, to them.
I hate what he stands for.
I hate his disguise. I can see right through it.
Why can't she see it?

We all experience pain in life. But the pain of betrayal causes a wound like a cavern. It seems it will never be able to be filled. On my worst days it seems like the flood of questions will never cease, and on my best days I use all my strength to take one more step. It is not a sharp pain, or a dull pain, it is worse. It seems almost unreal to my flesh to be able to hold the reality of all this in my hands. Why did she do this? How will I ever feel normal again? When will the pain subside? Where can I go to escape this?

I know I must seem pretty negative, but I am sharing with you an inescapable reality in my life. My wife, the love of my life, has chosen to turn her back on our covenant in order to be with him. What you will find in the pages that follow is very raw and very painful. But it is very much My story.

Chapter 1

It seems as though some memories may never be erased. I asked her to sit on our back deck and talk. I poured us both a cup of coffee, and was looking forward to digging into the recesses of her heart. I had noticed that there were things on her mind over the past few weeks that she seemed unable to share.

I reached over and took hold of her hand, but it seemed lifeless in mine. I turned to her and smiled as I looked into her wandering eyes. I told her of my love for her no matter what she was walking through. I reminded her of these past few years of our lives and the difficulties we faced throughout her sickness. A confidence rose up in my heart, as I blurted out, "You know I would walk through anything with you".

A memory flooded my mind. She laid on the hospital bed needing surgery but not strong enough to endure it. I looked into her eyes and squeezed her hand and said, "You are not quitting, I won't let you. If I need to breathe for you for the rest of your life I will, but you're not leaving me." Over the course of those years she would be what most people would call a burden to our family. But she was not to me. She was my treasure and I knew that the journey toward healing she was on, was only going to make her stronger.

It was painful at times. I had our two kids to take care of, work, a house to clean, meals to make and in the midst of all that I made it a point to be at the hospital once every day. Many nights I'd pass out before I made it to our bed. But throughout this time I never gave up on her. I just knew that she would live and that she would beat this sickness.

As we sat there in the adirondack chairs I had built for us, I became increasingly unsure of what she was thinking.

I leaned in and whispered, "You know I love you right?"

She looked at me with tears welling up in her eyes. "That's the problem," she said. "I know you love me, but I... I don't love you anymore. Joshua, I'm not sure what's going on with me, but I just know that the path that we've taken together isn't one I'm supposed to be on any longer. I feel like if I were to stay with you I would keep dying, but with... well, I really want to be alive again. Do you remember how I was before I got sick, how full of life I was? I've come to realize that I can't have that with you. I used to be free to dream and pursue life and not worry about anything. But our marriage and life and all of this that you've asked me to walk with you on has literally felt like it's killing me. Joshua, there is someone else. And this is what I want."

In a moment like that there are no words to describe the instability you feel. It's different than being turned upside down. Worse than a punch in the face or the gut. It's like someone taking you from your home where you were provided for and loved and had everything you wanted and placing you in a run down orphanage. Now known by a number, you are made to be a servant for the rest of your life, with no hope of things ever changing. You want to scream, you feel it in your bones, but it won't come out. There are no wise thoughts as to how to respond or how to handle the situation. There is only a flood, a flood of the worst kind of sick feelings you would never choose to swim in.

"Joshua, I'm so sorry, I don't mean to hurt you, I hope you can see that, but I must do this for both of our sakes."

"What about this?" I said as I pulled out from underneath my shirt a chain with her ring on the end of it.

I watched as she shuttered and replied. "That's not me anymore Joshua. I need to be away from you. Can't you see I was supposed to be free, and I just keep going through pain. I'm not saying it's your fault, but life wasn't this hard before I met you."

"That's because real freedom costs you something Bridget. You don't get anything by taking the easy path in life. You know this."

"But is there ever a point in time when it's good enough? When I can just be done with my life being such a mess? I'm so tired of fighting, and for what? There's no certainty that things will ever get better for me. I've made up my mind. And Joshua, I'm taking the kids with me."

"You what? No way! I won't let that happen." I blurted out.

"It's already written up, and he's a lawyer. They need to be with their mother. Besides, if they are with me they will have a father and a mother, and they will grow up more balanced in this world which is what we both know they need."

"What do you mean it's already written up? How long have you been planning this?"

"Joshua, it's complicated. But this is what they need."

"I don't think they need that. I actually think they need to know that love doesn't walk out, and find something more comfortable or that feels better. How could you do this? After all that we've been through, and all that I carried you through? I really don't understand you right now. It's like you forgot what love is. Ok, honestly I can deal with you leaving me, but not the kids. Please Bridget, not the kids. Did you even think about how they would suffer because of this?"

"Actually I think they will be better off in a stable home where they don't have to worry about money and if things will turn out good or bad. He's a great guy, and he loves kids. This is what they need. All the instability that you've provided for us would ruin them over time. Trust me, this is what's best for us all."

"Unfortunately trust isn't one of your strong points right now. And the whole stability thing, that's a joke. You're the one who told me when we got married that you would trust me as I led our family. So, you changed your mind on that too? Well, I didn't. Our journey together hasn't been about getting to a treasure, each step has been the treasure. We are stronger because we didn't give up no matter how difficult things got, and now... now you're bored or more interested in money and comfort than the years we've devoted to each other. Why did I do this again? Lay my heart out."

"Joshua stop!"

"It's Josh to you."

"Fine, Josh, please stop. You're making me feel bad."

"Bad? Ha, you should feel awful. You're not just sacrificing your own life, you're spitting on our covenant and potentially destroying the lives of our kids. And by the way how long have you had this paperwork written up? A court order doesn't just happen overnight. You must have been planning this for at least a month."

Her silence was all the answer I needed.

"I think I'm done talking," I said as I dumped my coffee in the grass and walked toward the door.

"Ok, well I've already packed and will come back for the kids tomorrow afternoon. I figured that way you could tell them what's going on."

"Nice, can't say I'm surprised by that one."

"Goodbye Josh. You know maybe this is my way of showing you love."

"Did you want me to thank you?" I replied as I closed the door and walked upstairs to my bedroom.

I wept that night, all night. I wasn't sure how to talk to the kids, but knew that I needed to be the one to prepare them for this very dark part of their lives. How do you hand a new life to someone, especially when it's full of pain and devoid of the dreams and normalcies they've grown accustomed to. Pain upon pain is what this feels like.

Chapter 2

I crawled out of bed early and began to make breakfast for my two treasures. The ones I would lay my life down for. Tory and Ben walked down the stairs and into the kitchen to find out what was cooking. They seemed a little surprised that breakfast was on the table ready for them. We all sat down and began to eat. They looked at me showing their concern. Tory chimed in and asked how I slept. I wasn't sure how to answer that. Is it better that they eat now and feel sick to their stomach after I break the news or hear it on an empty stomach?

"Maybe midway through breakfast is the best," I mumbled.

"What's that Dad?" asked Tory.

"I, uh, I need to tell you guys something. Um, your mother is, well, she is..."

I broke. Why did she have to do this? Why now? Why ever? For comfort. That's her reason. So that she could feel more comfortable, that's what it boils down to. She was tired of life being a journey. Well, did she really think that life was just supposed to be easy? Deep breath.

"Kids, your mom has chosen to be with another man. She doesn't want to do life with me anymore."

Forks dropped onto the table. The flood of feelings that I felt overtake me last night now washed into the kitchen and over my two dear children who never deserved this.

"Guys, I know there's a lot of questions. I will answer any that you have, but this is her decision, and the only thing we can do at this point is not give up on our lives. I'm still your dad and will always be your dad. But life now looks different. Your mom has been deceived, thinking that what would satisfy her is having all the answers and a clear path for each moment of every day. She and I are still married, at

17

least for now, but she seems to have made up her mind. I only hope that I don't lose a place in your hearts."

Through tears that streamed down her face Tory looked up and sobbed, "Dad, you will never lose our hearts, but what are we going to do?"

"Tory, Ben, your mom has informed me that she is going to have you live with her. There's nothing that I can do about that. This other man is a lawyer and has already written up the paperwork. I don't know how often they will allow me to see you guys, but I promise you, I will come and see you as often as I can."

The pain now multiplied in their hearts. I could see it. It seemed like too much. Ben slid his chair back, slamming it against the wall and ran up the stairs into his room. Tory just looked at me with those eyes. "Please Daddy, please make this stop."

"My sweet angel, I cannot stop this, but I will not leave you. We will fight this and we will not give up. Remember, we can do anything; but doing anything requires us to keep walking, even when we are in pain."

"I know Dad," she said through sobbing.

"I'm gonna go talk to Ben," I said as I stood up from the table.

As I walked up those stairs, all the ways I could approach my son and try to instill confidence into his heart ran through my mind. I knocked on the door and then pushed it open. There are so many things I wanted him to hear in this moment, but the only thing that would come out was, "I know Ben, I know this hurts. I love you Bud." I picked him up off of his pillow and held him tight into my chest as he wailed in utter pain. He put sounds to the pain that I had been feeling the whole night. Oh God, why my kids? Why do they have to endure this?

"Ben I promise you we will not be ruined by this. This is not the end of our lives and it's not goodbye."

18

"Dad, I don't want to live with mom, and especially not that guy who ruined our lives."

"I know Bud. If I had my choice, this would not be it. But if there's any chance of mom turning around, it's not going to be because we fought her. I wanted to give up on her last night. I was so angry with her and all that her decision has done to us. She doesn't really even know what she wants or needs right now. She's running toward what she thinks will make her feel better. But Ben, you and Tory may be able to turn her around."

What was I saying. I'm still just as mad as him. Do I really want her back?

"Ben, you and Tory can help her see who she really is. Don't give up on all that I've taught you. Life is not always safe and it's not always comfortable but it is full of purpose if we take enough time to see it. I love you son, and I'm so proud of you. You have always been willing to take risks, like that time we went cliff jumping at the falls."

"Oh yeah, that was awesome," he said as he wiped his tears on his sleeve. "Can we do that again?"

"Of course we can. I couldn't believe that you got right up there and didn't even hesitate. You followed me off the edge and dove right into that water. Remember, just because you live under another man's roof doesn't mean you are subject to be like him. You are my son."

"I know Dad, I still don't want this to happen though," he said with tears welling up again.

"Ben, I know. Me neither."

I helped them pack a few things and tried not to think about what I would do with all the empty space in this house. It had been a house full of relationship. Sometimes crying, sometimes intense discussion, sometimes laughter, but all the time relationship.

I watched out the window as she pulled into the driveway. The look on her face seemed to say, 'I can't wait to start on this adventure.' Little did she know that adventure looked more like chasing things that were always out of reach and being controlled by her fears that were now willing to lay dormant in order to keep her in bondage. I held Tory and Ben tight and whispered into their ears my undying love for them. I vowed to see them as often as I was allowed to, and with that the doorbell rang. I opened the door, was greeted by a "Hello Josh", and they were off, looking back with tears in their eyes.

As I closed the door the sound seemed to echo through the house and into my heart. I just have to get them back. There has to be a way for me to get them back. I walked back into the kitchen and sat down at the table. It was a mess from the breakfast I had made for the kids, but for the first time, I didn't care. I can remember when the kids were young and I longed for some down time. Some time to just sit in the quiet. But this quiet was like the constant banging of a drum in my head. I am alone. As I filled up the table with my tears I knew I needed to talk to someone. I called my dad, but all I could get out was. "Dad, I can't do this." Too choked up to tell him anything else I said I was sorry for calling and told him I'd call back later. Soon after that, I passed out from not sleeping the night before.

Chapter 3

"Huh, what's that?" I said groggily.

I feel so out of it, but I can feel the warmth of a touch on my shoulder. I raise my head off the table and give my eyes a second to focus.

"Dad?"

"Hey Son."

"What are you doing down here?"

"Hey listen, when my boy needs me, I'm here for him, and it sounded like you really needed me on this one."

I started crying again, partially because of Bridget, but also because my dad just drove 2 hours to comfort me when I needed it the most.

"Dad, I'm not sure what happened. But Bridget is gone and she took the kids and I don't know what I'm doing."

"I know Son, I know."

"How did you know? Did you really see this coming?"

"When someone goes through what Bridget went through, there's one of two choices they can make. They can either try and take control of their life and direct it toward what they think safety is, or they can surrender to the process of healing. Do you remember the last time we visited with you guys?"

"Yeah, it was a couple months ago."

"That's right, well I had a talk with Bridget while you, mom and the kids were out back. I knew then that she was holding onto her wounds as if they were a part of her. It's as if they were actually defining her. People were not built to endure those kinds of things like what she went through and when someone does go through that, there is a process that has to take place in order for them to truly heal."

"Yeah, but can't she do that here, with me? Can't I help her with that?"

21

"Well I suppose you could and some might argue that you should be the one to help her, but remember your covenant is based on each individuals decision. It's a commitment that you must choose every moment of every day. It's also a commitment that she must choose every moment of every day. Unfortunately some people don't really understand what a covenant is. They think that things will always feel great, and that the feeling will keep them in the marriage. Or they expect their spouse to make everything better that is not going right. It never seems to dawn on people that the covenant is more about them than the other person. It's kind of like standing in front of a mirror and saying to yourself, 'You will stay in this and fight no matter what'."

"So, what? I'm just supposed to tell her it's not a big deal what she did, and just give her grace?"

"Well in answer to your first question, I think deep down she knows it's a big deal, but this mountain in her life right now is far bigger and way more intimidating. It is the thing that's causing her to lose sleep at night, and wonder if things will ever be ok. You could say that she's looking at her situation from the wrong perspective. As much as it's wrong, she's choosing to order everything else in her life around dealing with this monster that seems to be at the door of her heart and since she's not sure how to get rid of it, she's running to wherever it seems the safest. I don't think she's trying to get away from you, I think she's trying to get away from it, and she just doesn't realize that you are the only chance she has at being free. This is her fight. If she's going to be free, she has to fight this thing," he says as he pushes a plate forward and rests his arms on the table.

"As far as the grace question goes. This may not be a popular opinion but I like to think of grace as the water inside of a watering can. Grace is not a cheap thing and it's certainly not a human thing. It's a very divine thing. You see, there

22

will be times when you can pour out kindness on someone and they will waste everything you have just given to them. But the true moment of grace always brings forth fruit of one kind or another. It's not just about the person who is giving the grace, it's about the one receiving it as well. The whole point of grace is to unite two parts that have been separated. Grace is a tool, a very powerful tool when used properly. There are moments in peoples lives where the weeds are surrounding them and in some instances if you were to pour out grace on them, they would just feed the weeds and become even more entrapped. But there are other moments in their lives where a drop of grace will give them the strength to grow even just one more inch, and will break them a little more free from the bondage of those weeds. Grace brings who they really are to the surface, and separates them from the lies that were defining them and keeping them held down. It's not about a person being perfect, it's not even about someone getting all cleaned up before they can have it. It was made to bring light into the dark places. Grace is like a road sign pointing in the direction of home for everyone who has blown it. Bridget needs to come home, and the best thing you can do is wait for the right moments to pour grace over her."

With that he paused and looked down at his hands folded on the table. "Son, her bad choices don't make her a bad person, but they do reveal her heart. She's very confused."

"You really think so?"

"Yeah, I do. I know how much this whole thing must hurt you, and I'm so sorry you have to go through it. I've been there myself."

"Really Dad?"

"Well not with your mother, she's got more commitment than anyone I know. That woman sticks with people through thick and thicker," he said chuckling.

"Yeah, she is so loyal," I said as I smiled thinking about how much I love my mom.

"I've experienced betrayal by those I thought I could trust the most. Some of them I trusted with my most precious secrets. You know I still love them, but it has definitely put a wall up in our relationship. But that can all be fixed in time and with their choice to come home," he smiled as he put his hand on my shoulder.

"Dad, how do I deal with the pain, it feels overwhelming and unbearable."

"Yeah, you can't change that. That shows that you really do love her. Son, sometimes people do things that really hurt us, and the only choice we have is to not allow bitterness in our hearts. It's gonna be a learning process. You are going to have to allow your heart to feel the pain, but not be led by it. It may not be easy, but I know you can do it."

"Thanks Dad," I said as I began to choke up.

"Once you figure out your schedule for seeing the kids, why don't you bring them up to the farm for a visit. Me and your mom would love that."

"I'll do that."

"Son?"

"Yeah Dad."

"I'm proud of you."

Chapter 4

The court order gave me one evening and one weekend day per week to see my children. Sunday came and I got cleaned up and ready to spend the day with Tory and Ben. I pulled up to what seemed like a small mansion and could feel jealousy surrounding me and trying to whisper its lies into my soul. It wasn't his house that I struggled with. It was what was now in it. I rang the doorbell and he answered.

"Oh hello, you must be Josh."

All I could get out was, "Where are my kids?"

"Oh yeah, they are almost ready to go." He turned around and hollered up the staircase, "Kids, Josh is here."

"They know me as Dad," I said. "Please don't forget that."

"Oh," he replied, "sure Josh. Anyways, listen, I don't want there to be any hard feelings, but there are just some boundaries we need to make sure are clear. Bridget wanted a more stable life for her and the kids. You know, more stable than you could offer. So, it's important to us that the kids aren't being forced into a certain way of thinking. Like that it's ok to not have a plan for life, or that being out of control of your life and its situations is acceptable. I was raised with a very purposeful mind and I had ways of doing things that allowed me to be in charge and in control; not out chasing dead end dreams."

"Am I hearing you right? You are not their father and you will not brainwash my kids into believing that it's somehow best to live inside of a cage that feels safe to their skin. You may have deceived Bridget for the time being, but my kids know better than to believe those lies."

"Josh, I'm sorry, I didn't mean to offend you," he said. "I can see you are upset. But this is what Bridget wants; a safer and more predictable life. I'm just doing the very thing that comes natural to me."

"You mean lying to them? Nobody can control everything that could happen to themselves, and if you're as smart as you think you are then you should know that."

Just then Tory bounded down the stairs in an outfit I'd never seen. She looked beautiful and she was smiling, thank God she was smiling. She jumped into my arms and squeezed my neck tight. "Daddy I missed you so much."

"Me too pumpkin. I'm here now."

Ben bolted through the back door of the house and came running down the hall right past lawyer man.

"Uh Ben," he said, "let's not run in the house. You remember," he pointed to a chart on the wall, "house rules."

Ben hung his head and walked out of the door and climbed in the back of my Jeep Wrangler.

"So, what do you say to a day at the river?" I asked them as I hopped in the driver's seat.

"Yeah!" they yelled.

And off we drove west on Route 44. I wanted to ask so many questions but didn't want to ruin our time together. I wanted this time to be about us and all the things that we love, not about all the pain that still seemed so fresh. I glanced back at them and noticed Tory's head down.

"What have you got there Tory?" I asked.

"Oh it's a DH15, the newest gaming system. Ralph bought it for me. He said it would keep me occupied when I got bored."

"Oh, well tell me about Ralph?"

"He's pretty busy and not around much, but he says he likes things to be in order. So as long as we stick to the layout he has, then we will run smoothly as a family."

"A FAMILY!" pause, take a deep breath, "a family huh, well ok." I still couldn't get used to the idea that my wife and children were giving some other guy the chance to have a family.

"So Ben, what do you think of old Ralph?"

"Well Dad he's ok, he's nothing like you. But it is nice knowing things ahead of time, and you know if I just listen to him it seems like I have answers for almost everything. It saves a lot of time too."

"What do you mean it saves a lot of time, Bud?"

"Well you know with us, we used to talk a lot about why we do things and how our choices affect us and others. With Ralph, he just tells me ahead of time how he wants things done and then as long as I don't ask questions we seem to be good. You know, half the time I don't know why I'm doing the things he's asking me to do but it seems like everyone is happy when I just fall in line so I guess it makes sense."

"Well Bud, I trust that you will follow your heart. You know what the right thing to do is, so just follow that and I'm sure you'll end up alright."

"Sure thing Dad. Hey do you remember how we talked about getting mom to come back? I've been trying my hardest, but I don't know Dad, she just seems so... comfortable."

"I know Bud. It may take some time for her to realize what her decision has cost her. Enough about that, let's get up to the waterfalls and have a blast today. Today is about us."

Today felt so good. We jumped off cliffs into chilly water and tried to catch fish with our bare hands. We ate fried chicken and cupcakes and when we had all finished our root beers, I announced that there was another round on me. It was as if for a moment in time my pain was all washed away. All my doubts and fears lay at the entrance ramp to the highway. Only to be picked back up on our way back to that house that held my dearest treasures in captivity.

There were so many things I wanted to say to that guy. I refrain from calling him a man because of what he's done to me and my family. Ralph. I don't even like his name. Who wants to be stolen from by a guy named Ralph? I wonder what his name even means?

As we got back the sun was just setting. Bridget was at the door as we pulled up and something in my heart stirred. God why? Why did I want her back? Why was she such a part of me, even after all the pain she's caused me?

"Hi Josh, how was it?" She asked as if she really cared.

"It was a blast. Go ahead kids, tell your mom about our adventure." They both chimed in with their stories of heroism.

"Josh, I'm so glad that you had a great time, just please next time try to stay within the times that we agreed to."

"Bridget, I didn't agree to any times, and for that matter, I haven't agreed to any of this. I've thought this whole thing was the worst idea ever, but rather than being a jerk, I've chosen to control myself and my tongue far more than anyone should have to. As far as the time goes, it's up to our kids. If they ever want to be done earlier, then that's their choice."

"Ok Josh, we'll leave that to them. Thanks for bringing them back safe."

"Sure thing."

And with that I was on my way back to our empty three bedroom house. I sat on the back deck, in the same chair in which I had received the horrific news and gazed up at the stars. Was this really what my life was going to be like? Were my kids going to recover from all this? Would I? Sometime around midnight I crawled into an empty bed and shortly after, found my pillow soaked with tears. Someday this will pass, right?

Chapter 5

It's been three months since she said goodbye. Although I would love to say that time has flown by, my mind fills up most moments with the sum of all that I've lost. Time has not healed me yet. I wonder if it ever will.

I pick up Tory and Ben today. I can't wait to see them. They are the light in my life right now. I have a full day planned. We are headed up to Grandma and Grandpa's house.

Ben has become quite the artist. He can paint almost anything I ask him to. The other week I asked him to paint me a picture of a peacock. It was breathtaking, looked just like the real thing. And Tory, well, she loves to read. So, I write her letters constantly. Sometimes while we are driving somewhere I will look in the rear view mirror and catch her reading one of my letters. It's so funny, that I'm right there in the car with her, and she still wants to read those things. But I don't care, I know it's because she loves me. Sometimes I ask her questions and find her just staring out the window. It's as if she's lost her ability to hear me. Sometimes her heart feels miles away. I try to find out what's going on inside of her, but it almost feels like she's put a wall up between us. I asked her about it once. She told me that Ralph always says, 'When we are vulnerable, then we are weak, and when we are weak, we get hurt.' I think she is probably trying to avoid pain at all cost because of all that she's already experienced. That really sucks for me. I may be the only one for her to be vulnerable with and because of the little time we actually get to spend together, my voice seems to be growing more and more dim.

Well here I am again, opening up the door of my Jeep and the pain of my heart. Bridget answers the door. "Hi Joshu... I mean Josh. Um, the kids are just finishing breakfast, do you want to come in?"

"I should probably wait out here, you know, I don't want to upset Ralph and his rules."

"It's ok, he's at the gym getting in his daily workout. Come on in."

As I stand beside the table next to the kids and see Bridget in her chair, I flashback to our home. It's so surreal. I can smell it and taste it. It's like I've been transported back in time. What happened? Everything in me wants to break down right here, to get down on my knees and beg her to come back to me. To tell her all the things that she is and remind her of all that we are together. To remind her of all of our dreams and plans and hopes. We had a purpose in life together. But now what? I pull myself together.

"Josh, can I get you anything? Coffee?"

"No thanks, I'm fine."

"You know Josh, I've been thinking about the kids and some different things and I was wondering if you would be interested in being more involved? You know Ralph is such a great provider, but he is so busy with work. With his schedule, he can't make it to a lot of the things that the kids are doing. I was wondering if you would want to help out with taking the kids to some of the extracurricular activities I had been wanting to get them involved in?"

"Well, like what?"

"Well, Ralph thinks it would be good for them to get a well balanced approach to life, so things like sports and dance and maybe some elective courses that the college is offering for younger kids."

"That sounds interesting. What are the courses about?"

"Well, there's one on maintaining your wealth that he really wants them to take, and another one on making your dreams happen. Oh, and another one on debating skills. He really feels like the younger that we train our kids to have and use these basic life skills, the further they'll get in this world."

"I don't know Bridget, I'm not sure I want my kids to be so focused on wealth or making things happen, or even learning ways to sound right even when they're not. None of that seems like it's helping them to be real. But if they want to play sports and dance, I'll definitely help with those things."

"I don't understand you Josh, why is it so hard for you to just change? You know, to be what people want you to be, or at least, what could've kept us together?"

"So, I'm to blame for you leaving?"

"Well, yes. In some ways. If you would've just provided a safe place for us, a place where I didn't have to worry about the things I was worried about, then I wouldn't have felt like I needed to go look for it somewhere else."

"Whatever happened to choosing not to worry about things, or fighting off the fears that come against you?"

"Josh, you know just as well as I do that whether you worry or not, there are still bills that need to be paid, people who get sick and things that were outside of our financial reach."

"Yeah, but life is more than just paying bills. It's more than a feeling of safety."

At this she began to cry. This whole time I thought her calloused heart was impenetrable. But I could tell those words pierced deep. She knew she had walked out on love to chase after comfort, but she dreaded going back to the process of healing and freedom.

"Do you really believe that you can't be touched by calamity? Do you really think that what Ralph offers you is more stable than a devoted love that will hold onto you while you're on your deathbed? Bridget, my love, wake up!"

There I let it out. My heart, out in the open again. I just couldn't hold it back any longer. I long for her to be back in my house, in our house.

I bought that house two years after Bridget and I moved into town. It was run down and needed to be gutted.

I practically tore it down and rebuilt it. I remember each day speaking to that house and telling it about what it would hold someday. I would say, "House, you are going to protect my family someday. Ceilings, our joy will bounce off of you and fill us up again. Walls, you will witness true love. Windows, you will show us displays of divine beauty. And doors you will welcome our guests into peace and kindness and generosity." I loved that house. Sweat and tears, and even some blood were mixed into its craftsmanship.

I had worked for my dad in his construction business when I was young and continued on my own years later. I loved learning how to build things well. And had no problem with things taking a little bit longer in order for them to look just right. After it was finished, Bridget and I moved all of our things out of our apartment and into our new home. It was our house, and we had poured ourselves into every room. I encouraged her to decorate it however she thought best. She's so creative. She picked out bright colors and simple accents. It became a display of our love in no time. How I love that house. But not as much for what it is, as for what it held. I have a mountain of memories from our times together within those walls. Intense conversations, calm and cool nights, heated moments, and the thrill as we locked eyes. Passion was no stranger. Well, until we found out about her sickness.

I don't blame her for wanting a way out, or a quick fix. I've found those same thoughts passing through my mind on a dark night when it seemed like the weight of the world was on my shoulders. Having to walk through those pain-filled years was supposed to build in her a resilience, not a weakness. I think it was just too much time hanging out on that limb, and not being sure if each day was her last. Not sure if she should tell her children for the tenth time each day that she loved them and was so proud of them.

Throughout those years I saw the sickness control her life like a sadistic torture machine. If only I could've taken that from her, I would have. It was awful. In the beginning the doctors told her that if she could survive all the treatments and surgeries she would end up becoming immune to this disease. They explained that it was a very rare disease and because it was already in multiple locations in her body, it could at any moment overtake her whole system. As long as they acted quick and continued with the procedures, she would be free of it. They also told her that if everything went well that her body would actually create an antibody that could be extracted and used on others stricken with this disease.

None of us expected the length of the fight. We grew weary after the first three months, but were determined to continue. After the first year, she wanted to give up and die, and at moments I would've let her. To watch the one you treasure go through agony and what seems like torture is a pain no lover should have to bear. We hung on by a thread through year two and then we saw the light. Her body was finally making a turn for the better and the tumor that they had discovered, which was causing her so much pain, was finally able to be removed.

I remember bringing in her favorite meal from our favorite Italian restaurant downtown. We had a candlelight dinner right there on her hospital bed. It was the first real food she'd had since we started the treatments. She could feel her strength coming back and it was as if she had a new body. She knew she was different. Something had changed. But those years did their damage. She was afraid. Fearful of the instability of life. She had been healed of a physical disease, only to be overtaken by an emotional and spiritual one. And now here we stand in Ralph's kitchen, the place where she feels safe, and I feel sick to my stomach.

33

My words rang through the open floor plan. I wondered if Ralph had videocameras or microphones throughout the house. I didn't really care if he did. I would want him to see and hear this. She stood there in silence, I guess she thought that I would either go find someone else or change who I was to try and win her back. She never figured that I was this much of a solid rock. The one that needed to stay the same.

I could see it in her eyes. She was replaying the moments of those three years of hell she had endured and seeing my face in every moment. Until now, she had only seen herself and what she had carried. She missed the fact that with all that she carried through those years, I had carried her.

"I have to go, and uh get ready, Josh. Uh, have fun with the kids today, I have to go," she stammered.

With that she ran up the stairs. As Tory, Ben and I headed out the door, I could hear her sobbing. I knew then that there was still a chance and hope flooded my heart.

Chapter 6

"Tory?" I said.

"Yes Dad?"

"Do you think mom is happy?"

"Yeah, I guess so. Well, what does it mean to be happy? I mean she got what she wanted, so I guess if that's what makes you happy, then yeah, she's happy."

"Are you happy?" I pried a little bit further.

"Dad, I haven't been happy since mom got sick. I think being happy is for people who have everything they want and never have to worry about anything. That's what mom always tells us, and I think that's why she's with Ralph, because she doesn't need to worry about anything. Supposedly he has more money saved up than that guy Robert, the retired doctor that used to live down the road from us. Well, we're not really allowed to spend it, and we haven't ever seen it, but he talks about it a lot. I can see how mom likes that about him. I guess I kind of like that about him too. He just feels safe."

That cut deep. Would my own daughter choose a life of so called comfort over true love? What is wrong with this world? I spent so much time and energy giving our kids a home full of love and acceptance. I was so purposeful about building them up. And in what seems like an instant they are questioning it all.

(handwritten margin note: ↗ would I, God? No)

"Got it, thanks Tory."

"Hey Bud, how are you doing back there?" Ben is gazing out the window, he seems lost in his thoughts.

"Good Dad. How are you?"

"I'm fine Ben, what's on your mind?"

"A lot."

"Go ahead, spill the beans."

"Well, I thought I knew what life was supposed to look like before, and I liked how it looked, but now things seem so different and I guess I kind of like some of the differences. Ralph seems like a good enough guy, and sometimes when he tells me about what he thinks my future will be like, it sounds really good to me. I mean, things were great with all of us, but when I hear what I could be and how much money I could have, and how things could go the way I want them to, man, that just sounds so nice. Especially after all that's happened. I like the idea of not having to go through all that junk."

"But Ralph caused all that junk!" I lower my tone, and take a deep breath. "Bud, we all have our own choices to make in life and we will only answer for ourselves. It's up to you to search out truth, not just what feels good or seems like a good path. You have to figure out whether or not what seems like it's right is actually a path of truth. You are such a special boy. When you were born I looked at your mother and said, 'He's going to be such a free spirit.' I knew it when I peered into your eyes. You have always been the one to cut a new path through the forest and to play a new song that's different than what anyone else had even thought of. But I'm pretty sure if you take the path of least resistance you will lose that part of you. Your heart was made for adventure and for pushing limits. You have actually helped our family quite a bit to see the joy in every part of life. Even when mom was sick, you were the one who told us all to dress up in costumes on Christmas and bring the celebration to the hospital. Mom always said that was her favorite day in the hospital. Just don't forget who you are Ben."

With that he gazed back out the window at the passing trees. "Ok Dad, I won't."

As we pulled onto Grandma and Grandpa's dirt driveway, the familiar smell of lavender and citrus trees came through the window of my Jeep. Some people don't appreciate that smell like I do. I like to describe it as 'joyful summer'. I have so many fond memories from being up here on this farm. It is such a sweet and surreal place.

My parents have always carried wisdom as if she were a close friend. I have called them over the past months more times than I can count. Most of the time weeping for Bridget and the kids, wondering what to do next. My dad constantly reminded me that a war is not won overnight and that perseverance and love will always outlast any evil that comes against us.

I often wonder about Ralph, what he's like and what makes him tick. You know he seems like a nice enough guy. It's not like he is beating my kids or Bridget. It seems like they are well taken care of, but I can't get over all the ways they are changing, and the change doesn't seem good. So for now I guess I'm ok with saying he's evil, along with some other nicknames I came up with. I wonder if people miss the things that are really damaging because of how subtle they are.

I remember this time when a guy in our town started to print counterfeit money. Nobody was the wiser for two months. In fact, he was practically giving money away to people, and he was gaining so much fame and friends in such a short time. Everyone started to think that he would make a great town mayor. He offered to build a new community park and so many other things to help our town.

Then one day it was all uncovered. They found the printing machine in his basement and everyone who thought they were rich because of what they got from him now realized they had less than before. It took our town a while to recover from that. Well, I guess we never really recovered. The town became closed off after that. It was as if they were ashamed that they were deceived, so they became even more guarded toward outsiders and even toward insiders. That was during the time my dad was the mayor and after that they even began to question him in some of his decisions.

They asked him to resign soon after that and elected some guy that didn't seem very qualified, but told them that with his set of guidelines they could avoid this ever happening again.

In fact, that's when Tory was born. Our first child, a beautiful girl. I knew it when I saw her, she had a lot of justice in her personality. There is a right and there is a wrong with Tory. Of course, she always seems to get to decide which is which, but she's determined to not be on the wrong side. I often wondered if that situation in our town had any sort of link to her personality.

As I step up onto the porch, the floorboards of rough cut cypress creak under my weight. Some people would think that a porch isn't supposed to make that kind of noise. But that noise is earned. This porch has held years of deep conversations and gallons of tears. I think that the things in life that go through the hardest times, have the most beautiful sounds. As I knock on the wooden screen door I can hear it echo down the hallway.

"Are those my little treasures?" I hear coming from the kitchen, and then the sound of wood chairs sliding away from the table.

"Hi Dad, hi Mom"

"Grandma, Grandpa!" yell the kids.

Big hugs all around as everyone is happy to feel the embrace of love once again. It feels safe here. Even though Bridget isn't here, this feels like home. In fact it feels the closest to home I've been in quite a long time.

"Come on in, come on in," Dad says with an, 'I've got a surprise for you', look on his face.

As we follow them into the living room, I'm intrigued. There on the coffee table are two boxes very intricately wrapped. One for Ben and one for Tory.

"Well go ahead kids. They are for you."

Ben and Tory ran to the table and began unwrapping. Ben got his opened first. As a parent there is nothing like watching your kids receive gifts, especially when they've been through a hard time. I'm so grateful when these things happen. Ben has a blank stare as he looks at his new treasure. I'm trying to see what it is, but can't from where I'm standing.

"What is it Ben?" I ask.

He looks up at me and pulls out what looks like a small sword made out of wood. It's hand crafted and beautiful.

Grandpa pipes in. "Ben, we know how you love to paint pictures and we are so proud of you for doing that. I was thinking a while back about how I love your pictures and how I believe they will touch people's hearts in such a powerful way. Go ahead pull off the handle of the sword."

Ben gently pulled the handle away from the sword to reveal what was a perfect placement of horsehair bristles. It was a handmade paint brush.

"Ben, this is a gift so that you will always remember that you have a gift. Your grandma and I are so proud of you."

I saw tears begin to well up in his eyes. This was not some cheap plastic toy that he had seen on a commercial. It was not something he would play with for a month and then forget he had. This was a true gift that would last his lifetime. This was a treasure.

Over in the corner, Tory sat and looked over the beautiful leather cover of what seemed like a large book.

"What is it Tory?" I asked.

She smiled at me and looked at Grandma, "Thank you Grandma, but what is it?"

"Well Dear, your dad told me how you love when people write you letters, so I decided that I would make a book for you to keep all those letters in. That way you can organize them just the way you want, and if you ever need help with it, you can just call me and ask. Tory, the way you connect through reading and writing is such a gift. However, it can also keep you from communicating face to face with people. Always keep the relationship ahead of the knowledge you enjoy gaining. If life becomes only about knowledge, then a very necessary part of you will die. Keep your heart open, even when it hurts."

"Thank you so much Grandma, I love it. I can't wait to start putting my letters in it."

With that Grandpa clapped his hands and announced that the fishing was great down at the lake and that we should start moving if we were going to eat fish for dinner. We all grabbed a fishing pole and headed down to the lake.

As we sat there on the edge of the lake, casting and reeling our lines back in, I wondered if Bridget had any desire to come up here with us. She loved mom and dad and often would tell me how she felt like they were the parents she missed having. I think one of the hardest things for her about leaving me was that she wouldn't be able to come up to this place. I'm sure mom and dad would be cordial if she came around, but it would probably be a little awkward.

Ben wanted to go back up to the house and paint something, so I told him I would head up there with him. Tory kept on fishing trying to catch up to Grandpa's score, while Grandma scolded Grandpa and told him to let her win.

Chapter 7

On the way back to the house Ben looked over at me. "Dad?"

"Yeah Bud?"

"I've got a problem. Well maybe it's not a problem, but Tory and me, we are fighting a lot. She keeps telling me that I should be like Ralph, and that someday a woman is only gonna want to marry me if I'm like him, and she goes on and on, and I don't want to be like him. I feel like I'm in a cage with all his rules, but sometimes it feels good to follow his advice. Like the time he told me that I should use my money for something I really wanted. You see, there is this boy at school and his family is pretty poor and I noticed his shoes were worn out. I had fifty dollars that I had saved up for this new video game I really wanted. Well, I was telling mom about it and Ralph overheard me. And he began telling me that I shouldn't worry about the other kid. He said that this kid's parents just needed to get their lives together and that a handout wouldn't help them to do that. He said that since I earned that money I should reap the benefit of it and be able to buy the game if I wanted to. Dad, it made so much sense to me, and so I went out the next day and bought the game. That boy is still wearing those shoes, and I can't bring myself to look at him."

"Wow Bud, I'm so sorry. That sounds rough. I love your heart in wanting to help that boy. Let me ask you this. If you helped that boy, how would it have made you feel?"

"Probably really good."

"Ok, well how do you think it would've made the boy feel?"

"Probably pretty special."

"Yeah, I think so too. So, do you think you feel better after buying the game than if you would've bought the boy some shoes?"

41

"Probably not. I mean, I got what I wanted, but.."

"Hey maybe it's not too late. Do you really like that game?"

"Actually, I've only played it once and it's nothing amazing."

"Well, how about I buy that game from you and you can have the money you had paid for it to do what you'd like with. We'll call it a do-over."

"Really, I can do-over stuff like that?"

"Sometimes you can Bud."

"Thanks Dad. But what do I do about Tory? She just makes me so mad sometimes with all the stuff she tells me I'm doing wrong. It sometimes feels like she doesn't like who I am. Like just the other day I decided to go for a ride on my skateboard and I had this great idea to have Penny, our dog, pull me around the neighborhood. Well, everything was going great until Penny saw a cat and took off running. I ended up in the bushes and Penny almost got hit by a car. Ralph was so mad at me and Tory was right there beside him. I already felt awful but they made me feel like a complete idiot. I just wanted to do things a little different; I thought it was a great idea. And I knew flying down the road would be awesome. But they just couldn't let it go. Tory even told some kids at school about my adventure, but she ruined the whole story, and made me look stupid. Honestly Dad, I would do it again if I had the chance. Before I fell, it was the coolest ride ever."

"I love that about you Ben. You are such an adventurer. It's okay that Tory doesn't understand that. She sees life differently, but that's why it's so powerful when you guys choose to love each other even though you have your differences. It's like looking at a quarter. Here, come stand in front of me. What do you see when I hold up this quarter?"

"I see heads."

"What if I told you that you were wrong, it's actually tails?"

"Well, that's not what I see."

"Right! We are both looking at the same quarter and yet we are seeing it from different sides. We are both right and yet our perspectives could actually divide us if we are only focused on what we see. Now, come over here next to me. Watch as I turn the quarter both ways. See? We really are both right on most things. Sometimes one of us might need a little adjustment, but the key is to not let a difference in perspective turn us against each other. Don't give up on Tory. She may never go dog-boarding, but that's not the thing that makes you guys close. It's your commitment to love each other no matter what."

"Got it, Dad."

"You know Ben, the fact that you long for those moments of ecstasy where you can feel the adventure well up in your soul is such a wonderful thing. But don't mistake those moments for a deep connection to life. Life doesn't always feel that way, and if you find yourself so focused on experiencing those moments, I'm afraid you might find yourself running in the wrong direction. I'm not sure if this all makes sense. I just want you to remember that every puzzle piece of life makes it a blessing. Not just the mountain-top experiences. Those experiences will happen on their own, you don't need to chase them. Enjoy receiving every puzzle piece with a thankful heart and a teachable perspective."

"I think I understand. Hey Dad?"

"Yeah Bud?"

"Do you think you and Mom will ever get back together?"

With that, a slight pain hit my chest. "I don't know Bud, why do you ask?"

"I just kind of think that she misses you."

"Did she say that? Or are you just thinking that?"

"Well the other night before I went to bed, I overheard her crying downstairs. Ralph was out and as I walked down the stairs I saw her looking at pictures of our family vacations. Once she saw me on the stairs, she stuffed them under a pillow. I asked her what she was doing, but she said she wasn't doing anything and then told me I should get to bed. I really think she might be rethinking all of this."

"Well Bud, if that's true, then time will tell. But I'll be honest, as much as I still love your mother, I'm more concerned with you and Tory right now. I don't want you guys to lose who you really are."

As we reached the house, Ben ran inside to pour out his feelings on another canvas with his new paint brush and his new perspective on the gift he's been given.

Chapter 8

I decided to take a walk to the cabin where Bridget and I began our married life. As I stepped up onto the front porch the feelings and memories came upon me like a deep breath I couldn't fully take in. I walked through the kitchen where I used to make coffee for her while she was still fast asleep in the early and crisp mornings. I made my way into the bedroom and sat on the edge of the bed I had built for us. I felt overwhelmed with loss as I looked over at our old bookshelf in the corner. There I saw a book that must have fallen out of the back of the bookshelf and was now just barely visible. I walked over and picked it up. As I brushed off the dusty cover, I realized what it was. I had written a love story to Bridget when we were still dating. This was it. I laughed as I opened the handmade leather bound book. In an instant the passion that had come over me back then, was reawakening. "God, I don't want to go there," I mumbled as I began to weep. I couldn't help but turn those pages one by one that seemed to add fuel to my desire to be with the love of my life. I still remember what led me to write that book for her.

We were young, and she had so much life in her. I loved her with all of my heart, but I didn't have concrete plans as to where I was headed in this world. She, on the other hand, had a plan, a purpose and a desire to be free from uncertainty about things. She kept dragging her feet when I would ask her about our future. She knew where I stood on life, but she was consumed with this desire to have everything figured out ahead of time.

Sometimes we plan out our lives because we are afraid. We have every kind of insurance because of 'just in case'. But I was already free from fear. I refused to worry about things, and I was ok with the ways that life changes direction. She figured she needed to control her life so that nothing was left in the air. I know why she did this, but I also knew she would always be nagged by the fears of her childhood unless she followed me. She knew deep down her desire was to live with me, but she kept wondering how she would function in this kind of reality? She used to always tell me she thought I lived on a cloud somewhere, and she was trying to make things work down here in the real world.

I wrote this book to her to help her see how real I was, how I understood pain and how well I knew the path to freedom. I wanted so badly to represent what our lives would be like if she would marry me.

I paged through the beginning, which was all about my past before I met her, and how I had dreamed of her and how there were key things in my life that pointed to her. I remember the feelings of loneliness in this one story. I was always excited as a boy, so full of wonder at this world. Sometimes I felt like the whole world was mine and yet at other times, I felt like nobody even cared about me.

It was my seventh birthday and my mom was bringing a cake into school. I was so excited, hoping that maybe today some of the kids would want to be friends with me. Well, everyone came and devoured the cake, but as soon as they were finished eating they went right back to what they were doing. Not even one 'Happy Birthday Josh'. The teacher had to force everyone to join in on the Happy Birthday song. I was crushed. I wanted friends to play with. I wanted to feel loved and for the kids to know me, but it seemed like they were all busy with their own things. Those are the kind of moments that can really damage you. Thankfully my dad is awesome. After we talked through all that I was feeling and he instilled his wisdom into my sorrow-filled heart, I knew I could make it another day.

I flipped through another few pages and found the story of when I first saw Bridget. It's actually a funny story. It was my dad who met her first. He came home from town one day and said, "Son, I think I found your wife." What dad does that? I was sure I had to see her for myself. So, the next day I went into town to the grocery store where she worked and, let's be honest, words can't really do those moments justice. I picked up a couple apples and a loaf of bread and walked up to her line. It just so happened to be the longest checkout line, but this was the first time I didn't care. One of the cashiers two lines over tried to signal me to come to her lane, but I quickly averted my eyes and went down for a shoe re-tie. You know, there's nothing wrong with re-tying your shoes in advance of them needing it. It's about being prepared for anything that could happen. If I have to chase a thief down the road to reclaim a stolen purse, I need to know that my Chuck Taylor's are not going to come all untied. Anyways, it worked and the other cashier found another customer to offer her services to.

By the time my bread came to a sudden halt on that conveyor belt that seemed to be pulling my heart strings closer to Bridget, my palms had already soaked the pockets of my jeans. "Uh, hi," I said with the most confident voice possible at that moment.

She looked up and smiled at me. "Hello Joshua."

What??? She knew my name? This girl is amazing. How do you respond to that? Any control I had over my coolness was suddenly gone.

She smiled again. "So, I talked with your dad yesterday, he said you would be stopping by today. He even gave me this picture of you," she said as she giggled.

"He what?" This tops the level of embarrassment that can come from a family member's actions.

She smiled, "Yeah, he is such a sweet man."

"I'm afraid to ask what else he told you."

"All good things," she looked down with a smile still spread across her face. "So, did you really want to buy the bread and apples?"

47

"Uh, well, no, but I will."

"Listen, I go on break in five minutes. How about you just buy the apples and we'll eat them at the picnic table outside."

"Ok, I'll be out there!"

The next five minutes seemed to drag on so slowly, but the moment she stepped through those sliding doors was divine. We spent the next thirty minutes laughing about the whole situation. I mean, my dad had actually told her that he thought she was made for me. That's gutsy. She didn't seem to mind though. This was a new start for her in life. She told me that moving here and getting this job was like a do-over for her, and that she could use a good friend. She still loved home, but she knew she would only go so far if she stayed where she was. Over the next months, I would see her as often as I could. She was such a good friend. When I talked about how I lived life on the farm and the simplicity of life, I could tell she longed for that in her own life.

We lived up here on my parents property for the first year of our marriage. I built us this little cabin back in the woods just up from the lake. It was a place of refuge for us. A place where our intimacy grew strong and she learned so much of who I really am. I tried to show her the depths of my love and commitment, as much as is possible for newlyweds. We would wake up with the sun and drink our coffee on the front porch with our feet up on the railing. The ducks would swim circles looking for breakfast while we sat back and tried to take it all in.

She loved my dad. When she saw him on his morning walk around the lake, she would kiss me on the cheek and run down to meet him. They would walk around the lake and she would ask him all about life. She longed for the love and wisdom only a father could bring. It seemed as though she grew more in that first year than the previous twenty-three years of her life.

Then came the day when it was time for us to move into town. Our one bedroom apartment was smaller than our cabin and the view much less appealing. But it was ours, and we had committed to pursue our love above all else. She went back to work at the grocery store and quickly got promoted to a manager position. I was so proud of her. Every morning I reminded her of why she was there and the amazing things she brought into that store.

She really is so amazing.

Oh yeah, so I forgot about the end of this book. I wrote her a song and included the lyrics on the back cover. I wonder if I can remember the tune? That's right!

Love is fought for everyday
Many will leave and few will stay
I will stay with you
And formulas I cannot find
For our two hearts in real time
Our answer is fight it through

And let God be our witness
And may our words live through
All of life before us
Baby, this is my I Do

Though feelings shift and moods will sway
And life will hand us what we must take
Faith and love will be our stay
On the good and through the bad
When all of life feels so sad
These arms will carry you

As the waves bow down today
And the sun sets its seal in every shade
Our Father joys in the covenant being made

And the Son sees his love displayed
While the Spirit dances on this place
My love into one we are being made

I sang this to her on our wedding day. Since then she's asked me to sing it whenever things have gotten tough or confusing in our lives. I offered to sing it to her that night on our back deck before she told me she was leaving. That's the first time she refused. I wonder if she would let me sing it to her now?

Chapter 9

I can hear Tory, Mom and Dad walking up to the house. By the sound of their excitement, I imagine we're having fish for dinner. I look at the book in my hands and hold it tight. 'I should give this to Bridget', I think as I stand up to walk out of the cabin and back toward the house.

I sit down in Dad's favorite leather recliner while Mom is sitting with Tory and Ben in the living room admiring Ben's painting.

Dad hollers from out back, "Come out here Joshua, give me a hand cooking these fish."

"Sure thing Dad." He knows just how to cook fish. He used to always tell me, 'Josh, the longer you can wait, the better it will taste'. I think that's wisdom for a lot of life.

As I step out the back screen door and over to the grill, he puts his arm around me.

"I'm so proud of you son."

A smile spreads across my face. I've said this countless times to Ben. There is a power in these simple words coming from a father to his son. Even more so when it doesn't feel like there is much for him to be proud of.

"I lost her dad."

"Joshua, you cannot control someone else, you and I know that so well. You didn't lose her, she just lost her way. But don't worry, she'll find it again."

"Dad, this hurts like hell, being separated from her."

"I know Son, it never should have happened, but it shows that there were still places in her heart that weren't given to you. Maybe this is the very thing that will weed out those untouched places. Maybe this is what will allow her to truly be given to you and to be healed from the pain in her past."

"Dad? I hate him."

"I know. It makes sense that you would. I'm sure that even this Ralph fellow didn't used to be like this. We all have countless opportunities and choices we get to make in life. Some people choose to follow what they think is best for them; some choose what is best for others. No matter what motives are behind your choices, you are the only one who is responsible for your choices. I know your heart is probably trying to tell you to move on and forget about Bridget, but I think this situation is the opportunity to reveal what your personal commitment is to her.

"I don't understand. You really think she deserves another chance?"

"Son, it's never been about what a person deserves. You see, love steps over the boundaries of good and evil, over the borders of right and wrong. It raises itself higher than any human intellect or emotion, far above any standard or equation that rules this world. And it especially pours itself out on situations like these. You know how when you are starting to feel like you need some time away, you come out here and go up to that special spot by the waterfall?"

"Yeah, it's like a restart button. When I come back down, it's like I see everything with fresh eyes."

"Well, I think Bridget just needs some time like that. She's gotten so turned around with her sickness and all, she's forgotten her need to take a break. To recalibrate, if you will. She's become so focused on having answers for everything that it's caused a rift between you and her and damage to the kids. Tory and Ben have always seen things differently, but since this all happened they've almost become enemies. I can see it Josh and it breaks my heart. Tory has become very closed off and self sufficient, and Ben is struggling so much with confusion over what is and isn't true. In some ways, I think Ben is further along in relating to people, but Tory seems to be way more grounded in life. They need each other Josh, just like Bridget needs you. Don't worry, time will heal this. You just stay focused on each moment being a purposeful one for your kids. Now that I've said all that, let's eat."

"Sounds good Dad."

Some people never had a dad in their lives. It's really sad. I have the greatest dad ever. I would gladly share him with anyone.

That night we laughed, ate fresh-caught lake trout, and drank homemade root beer. It was just the kind of day we needed.

As I look into the rear view mirror, I see Ben looking out the window at the stars in the sky. He looks lighter, more free. I glance up at the stars and notice Orion's belt. I heard this story about Orion once. I'm not sure if it's true but it's a good one. The story goes that Orion did something that the Greek gods didn't like, so they put him up in the sky and told him that in order for him to be freed from being up there he would have to kill the bear. The Bear is a constellation that is always on the other side of the sky. He has this opportunity to get free, it's a way out of his prison, but it always seems impossible to accomplish. As much as he moves through the sky, the Bear moves the same amount at the same speed.

I wonder if Bridget feels like that, like it's impossible to gain her freedom again. Like she has hurt me too much for me to forgive her and take her back. It makes sense that she would feel that way.

Honestly, part of me wants her to feel that way. It's not because I want her to feel the pain. I just want her to recognize all that she has sacrificed and how much it has cost her. I gave up my life for her. I wonder if she realizes how much it cost me?

Marriage is such a funny thing. Two very different people make an agreement that they are no longer going to be independent and that now they will rely on and serve each other. It's as if they leave behind how good they were alone in order to be amazing together. But that doesn't happen overnight. We were married for fifteen years and obviously still learning about this whole love thing.

As we pull into the driveway, I see Bridget through the front window, as she hops up and runs to the door. The kids are both asleep so I help her carry them up to their beds and kiss them goodnight. As I go to pull the front door closed behind me, she stops me.

"Josh, um, thanks."

"For what?"

"For being such a good dad. I guess I forgot how amazing you were with them. I don't know, I am just really grateful that you are still in their lives."

"You're welcome, Bridget. Actually, I have something I wanted to give to you."

"Sure, what is it?"

I walked back to the Jeep and pulled out the book I had made for her years earlier. "I found this behind the bookshelf in the cabin. It's yours. I mean, I wrote it for you, so I don't think it would be right for me to keep it."

I could see her biting her lip to try and stop the tears from pouring out of her eyes.

"Josh, I can't take that."

"Sure you can. It's still true, all of it."

"I don't deserve that. I'm not who you thought I was."

"A wise man told me tonight..."

"You mean your dad?" she said smiling through tears that were waiting to fall.

"Yeah, my dad. Anyway, he said that I couldn't judge based on what someone was doing or even how they were living, but on what I believe is the truth in their heart. Bridget, what's in this book is what I believe is true. It's not possible for me to take my heart back once I've given it away. Trust me, some days I wish I could just to stop the pain, but I can't. So, I'm left in this place where all I really want is to be

54

free and I can see what it would take, but the Bear is on the opposite side of the sky."

"You lost me on that one."

"I know. I've been thinking a lot and it probably doesn't all make sense. I guess what I'm trying to say is that my ability to pour out my love is only hindered by your ability to receive it. My hand is on the handle of the pitcher of my love and it is ready to pour, but I will not waste a drop into the dirt. I will wait until you are ready to receive it."

Maybe that was too much.

The door closed abruptly and I could hear her weeping on the other side of it.

"Go away, you don't deserve this and I don't know how I could possibly earn your love again. Can't we just be happy the way we are?" she pleaded through the door.

I sat down with my back against the door. "Can you be happy with the way we are? Bridget, it feels like you only want the parts of me that benefit you. But the parts that cost you something or make you feel uncomfortable, you shy away from. Every aspect of our relationship is meant to bring joy to you, even the tough parts."

This is the first time I've been able to share my heart with her like this. This pain actually feels good.

"No Josh. I can't, I won't do this. Our kids have been too damaged as it is. I'm not coming back."

With that I left quietly. Tonight wasn't about things being healed, it was about planting a seed in her heart that not even she could keep from growing. As I pulled away, I heard her calling my name and saw her opening the door to look for me. But it just wasn't time yet. There's a time to embrace and a time to turn away. Knowing the time for things is so tough with all these feelings we have. I would have loved to hold her in my arms tonight, but she would've believed that it was okay for her to have both me and Ralph. No! I have to stay strong. It's her choice, but I won't muddy the waters. She must leave him if she is going to choose me.

Sleep never sounded so good. My body and mind and emotions are ready for a break. I'm not sure if I feel like crying or singing, but something feels very different.

Chapter 10

I can't help but wonder what's in store for this week. I feel like I'm in one of those moments where you know something is going to happen, but you don't have any real tangible reason to believe that anything will. It's like when you are outside and you breathe in and can taste the rain before one drop hits the ground. Something is going to happen this week, I just don't know what.

I decided to write another letter to Tory, it seems to be the only way to know that she will hear me. I tell her all the things I love about her, all the things I love about Ben and ask her to try and love him just as I do. It's so tough to see brothers and sisters that are so powerful together get so stuck on differences. They end up crucifying each other over the silliest things.

Mankind is funny like that. If there was a black guy, an asian guy, a white guy, and a hispanic guy stuck on an island and a pack of wolves was trying to kill them, they would fight alongside each other with no problem. But put them in any city and they can only see their differences. I wish Ben and Tory could see their need for each other over their differences.

It wasn't like this before. When we were all together, I would lift up each of them and praise their strengths and show them how they helped each other become strong in their own weaknesses. But now, with my limited time with them, it seems I can only break down a couple of the many walls they've built between each other. As I finish writing this letter to Tory, I feel this nudge to write to Bridget. Most of the time it's hard to know what's emotion and what's wisdom. But just because I write it, doesn't mean I have to give it to her, right?

My Dearest Bridget,

I cannot begin to explain the feelings I have endured over the past months. It seems I've felt the deepest of pain in my bones, and yet at other times a peace that a mind could not understand. I'm not going to tell you it's been easy without you. Although you seemed to leave in an instant, I could feel the walls you were building in your heart years ago. Your eyes seemed to always be looking for what was next and many times right past me. I did recognize it, but I guess I just hoped there would be some radical breakthrough for us instead of this season of separation.

I don't even know what to tell you about where I'm at now or what I think about any possible future for us. I just know I talked to this wise man last weekend, yes my dad, and he told me that love was easy enough to give when it didn't cost us anything. *But the truest love is the one that lays itself down knowing that enduring through the pain is what will make it shine the brightest.* I don't know if that really makes sense to you, but I want you to know that all of this has not stifled my love for you. It has purified it. It has caused it to become like a lighthouse, calling out to you in the midst of your storm. Warning you of danger and showing you where true safety is.

Sometimes the things we think we need are really just the debt of fear. Fear can be such a devouring monster in our lives. It can steal so much from us. If you really love living with Ralph, then I will leave you to your choice. But if your choice of him has anything to do with trying to satisfy your fears, I'm shining my light right now and yelling, 'Don't do it Bridget! It will only leave you shipwrecked.'

I hope you are not offended by my boldness. I do not wish to cause you more pain. I just want to see you in true freedom. You would not believe how absolutely breathtaking you are when you are dancing in freedom, consumed by love. I remember the moments when I've witnessed this in your life, and it's those moments that remind me why I chose you. I don't care about you being perfect all the time, I just want to see you dance in freedom once again.

With a deep longing for his bride,
Joshua

Wow, that felt good. Maybe that's the key for me. Even if I don't give her what I write, it at least allows me to get out all that I'm working through. If I had a Therapist, he would probably pat me on the back right now.

Chapter 11

So, I gave her the letter. You don't pour your heart into something like that just to put it in your sock drawer. That was two days ago and I haven't heard from her since. I pick up the kids tomorrow for our day out. I decided I would take them rock climbing down by the old railroad bridge. It has been a few years since I climbed, but recently with all the time I have I began to get back into it. Plus it's a great way to get conversation going. "Might I remind you, you are thirty feet up right now, if you don't talk, I'll drop you." Well, whatever works, right?

My kids are both so different, but one thing they know is that they can count on me to always catch them. It's not just about the years I spent climbing and setting up climbs. It's also about character. I think character is shaped and refined in seasons like the one I'm currently walking through. Any Joe Shmoe can walk into a room and talk about his character and integrity. But true character and integrity are revealed during the hardest of situations. It's in the fire that you begin to see who a person really is. I think this is why most people try to avoid uncomfortable circumstances at all cost. They figure if they just stay out of those situations then their character will stay intact. Maybe they should make it a point to not avoid the fiery situations, but instead use them to grow stronger and more real.

The garage door is open as I pull up and I don't see Ralph's car in the garage. Interesting. I walk up to the front door and knock. The door flies open and two bundles of intense happiness bolt out the door and into my arms. I think this is what heaven feels like.

"Are we going, are we going?" Ben blurts out.

"We sure are, I have everything loaded up and the rocks are calling our names." Bridget walks to the door as if the cloud that I've seen her wearing for the past months has suddenly started to move away from her by the wind of sanity.

"Hey Josh, I hear you are taking them climbing."

"Yeah, to the old railroad bridge, where we used to climb."

"I love that place. The view from the top is amazing," she said almost hinting as if she wanted to go with us.

"Where's Ralph?" I ask.

"Oh, he's gone on a business trip for the weekend. So, I'm just here getting some down time."

"Oh okay, well if you wanted to come with us, there's room and enough food for you."

"Oh, I'm not sure if I..."

"Come on Mom," pipes in Ben.

"It would be nice to get some fresh air. Alright, if you're sure it's ok."

"It's more than okay. Besides this way I'll have someone to belay me."

"You sure you trust me with your life?" she asked.

"More than you trust yourself." I said as I watched a slight smile form at the corner of her mouth and spread across.

"Yeah, you're probably right. Well, let me get changed and I'll be right out."

"Ok, we'll be in the Jeep," I said.

Did that really just happen? I couldn't believe it. I wanted to do some karate kick dance moves on the way to the Jeep, but certainly didn't want anyone to see me.

"Dad," said Ben. "Can you believe this? It's great! Mom's coming with us, maybe this is our chance?"

I tried to stay cool and calm. I could hear Tory in the back seat sigh. I knew she had already given up hope on me and Bridget ever getting back together. She figured this was her lot in life and she just needed to accept it.

"I know Ben. This will be a really fun day, but let's not put any pressure on mom. Let's just show her love and an awesome relaxing time."

"Sure Dad." Ben said, trying to hold back his excitement.

I didn't want him to know that I was hoping for more out of this than he was. Deep down I knew that Bridget's return to me had nothing to do with what I did. It was completely up to her. I had been consistent in my love. I had already made my desires known. I chose to live unoffended by what she did to me and the kids. The ball was not in my court. It was her choice alone and all I could do is wait.

As we hiked to the base of the cliffs, we sang our goofy songs that we had all sung growing up. About trees that could talk and bunnies that could sing. At one point, I glanced over to see Bridget singing quietly along. We used to have so much fun as a family. I opened up the cooler and asked Tory to start making sandwiches for everyone while Ben and I went to set up the ropes.

"Is there anything you want me to do?" asked Bridget.

"Just stand there and look.... I mean, uh no, just relax down here."

Brilliant Josh, probably a little too much. I did, however, catch that sideways smirk she used to give me.

As Ben and I set up the climb, I caught myself looking down at her every once in a while. Why did my heart long for her so badly? I didn't just want the physical relationship we had, although that would be nice. I didn't just want the friendship we had. There's something you can only find in a marriage. I know there's a lot of debate on people living together and having these "committed" relationships without being married, but one thing that's impossible to have without a covenant made between two people, is intimacy. It's like this thing that forges two people into one. It takes two separate things and joins them and makes it impossible

62

for them to become separate again without a whole lot of pain, agony and scars. It makes more sense now than it ever has before. I was made to have another part that fit me. I found her and I was whole but now I feel broken. But I've never been a quitter and I don't plan on giving up hope now.

"Tory, you make the best outdoor turkey and cheese sandwiches of anyone I know."

"Thanks Dad. I'm here to serve."

"Thank you Dear, but just remember you are not a servant, you are my daughter, my treasure." I could see her breathe in those words. There have been so many times over the past year I tried to speak these things to her, but her own beliefs of her worth and position just kept overshadowing my words. This time I actually watched her catch those words and embrace them inside her soul.

"Thanks..." she replied.

This is my perfect little angel. I still remember the day we found out we were having a girl. I thought, surely this will be my sweet little princess who can do no harm; but Tory came out holding a firecracker. She was so strong-willed and determined. I wouldn't have had it any other way, but I often wondered if her soft side was the equivalent of 80 grit sand paper.

I walked over to her and pulled her into my arms. She began to cry for just a moment, until she realized that this was vulnerability, and she quickly wiped the tears from her eyes. With a tear smudged straight-face she said, "Thanks Dad, that was very nice of you to say that."

"You're welcome Tory."

I turned to Bridget and Ben, "Are you guys ready to climb? Who's up first?" Ben jumped right up and shoved the last bite of his sandwich into his mouth.

"I am, I am," he mumbled.

We ran through a couple of climbs for everyone. I was surprised at how well they all did. They remembered everything I had taught them. It had probably been a couple years since our last climbing trip and this had so many sweet memories attached to it for me. There's something about the trust and friendship that is built between people who climb together.

As Bridget clipped into the rope, I saw her glance back at me. It was as if I could hear her thoughts, 'I know you hold my life in your hands while I'm up there. And I know my actions deserve you letting me go, but I know you never would'.

She did great. She always was a natural on the rocks and so free. It's funny that as scary as it is being forty plus feet up in the air, she was more afraid of not having enough money and not knowing how she was going to get better when she was sick. Those fears have so many possible answers, so many ways that things can turn out. But up there, way up high on a rock, if you fall and your rope doesn't hold you or the person belaying you doesn't catch you, you die. I think it boils down to control and what we can actually see. When we feel like we have some control over a situation we are able to deal with the fear of it easier. But when it seems like it's out of our hands or we can't see a possible outcome, we really have a problem with resting through the process.

"You're up Josh." Bridget says.

"Ok, well let's see what the old man can do. Are you sure you're good to go Bridget?"

"Yep, just like the old times."

Oh how I wish that were true. But it's not like the old times. With every good feeling I feel around her, there are ten painful ones that jump right in.

I can't say that was the best climbing I've done, but it felt so good to be way up there. And the view today was amazing as I looked down and saw her watching me and smiling. When I got unclipped from the rope, I went over to the high-five's awaiting me and then patted Bridget on the arm, "Thank you for coming with us."

She recoiled immediately and put her hand over her arm.

"I'm so sorry, I didn't mean to overstep a boundary."

"No, no it's fine, just.. it's fine."

Well, I'm not sure what I did there, but that's a bummer. The rest of the car ride home was painfully silent. How could things go from seeming so full of hope and love to this silence. As we pulled into the driveway she turned to me and said, "Josh, I'm sorry. It's just that I hurt my arm and that was a sensitive spot that you touched."

"Oh, I had no idea, did you hit it on the rock?"

"Uh, no it... I ran into something at the house last week and since then it's just been sensitive, but it's not a big deal. I just didn't want you to think that I was offended by your touch."

"Oh, ok, thanks for letting me know. You sure there's nothing I can do to help? Can I see it?"

"No, no it's almost healed. Thanks again for an amazing day Josh, I've missed that kind of fun."

"You're welcome Bridget. I had a lot of fun too."

I helped her get the kids, who were fast asleep in the back of the Jeep into their beds and said my goodbyes at the door.

Chapter 12

a few days later...

I decided to surprise Tory with some flowers this morning. I've always tried to be intentional about showing my love for her, but it seems that there's not a lot of things that I can do or say that penetrate the walls she's built up in her heart. I know she loves me. I can see it in her devotion to the values I've taught her while she was growing up, but I just wish things with her could be like they were before.

We used to go for walks in the morning together. She was my early riser, very different from Bridget and Ben. In the cool of the morning, we would walk through the trails behind our house and talk about all sorts of things. Sometimes we didn't even use words. Communication is funny that way. Just being next to someone communicates a world of words to them and then there's those things that we can't even find words for. It's all funny, it's like we ourselves are the communication and the words are just one outflow of it. *wow! Incredible Insight!*

That's why I despise the texting thing. It limits my interaction with someone to letters on a screen. I wonder if you could track how many friendships were broken apart because of a text message that was misunderstood? That would be an interesting statistic.

Well, here I am again at this familiar door that I honestly think is ugly and probably highly over-priced. With flowers behind my back, I knock on the door with my signature knock and wait for the door to open. Ralph opens the door, he looks like he just woke up. I want to ask him if he has a right side of the bed that he can get out of, but I refrain.

"Hi Ralph, is Tory here?"

"Uh yeah, what are you doing here?"

"Just wanted to talk to my daughter, Ralph."

"I'll get her, wait here."

"Sounds like a good plan." I've found that being just a little sarcastic with Ralph has done miracles for my emotional healing. Not enough to get punched in the face, but just enough to know that if a film crew were here, they'd be getting some great material.

Tory shows up at the door, "Hi Dad, this is a surprise, what's up?"

"Oh just this." Pulling the flowers from my back, I shove them in her arms and yell, "Sneak Attack!" Then I run to my Jeep and drive away. I glance back, and see her standing at the door with flowers in her hand and a smile spread across her face.

When the kids were little we used to love to surprise each other. Bridget never liked us saying "BOO!" and scaring each other. So I created a safe phrase that could be used instead. Sneak attack can happen at anytime and for any purpose. You, as the bringer of the sneak attack, decides what will be the surrounding circumstances. However, the one thing you have to remember when planning a sneak attack is that you, as the sneak attacker, do not always get to control the outcome. But in this situation, I'm pretty sure the outcome was exactly what I had hoped for.

As I looked up I saw Bridget watching me out of the upstairs window. She looks more beautiful in the morning than at any other time of the day. It isn't over. I keep telling myself this every day. It is not over until the day I walk away and throw the towel in, or some lady with poor eating habits belts out an unfamiliar tune. It's not over.

My dad used to say to me, 'How do you do something impossible?' Then he'd look me in the eye and continue, 'Don't walk away until you've done it. Son, perseverance isn't for the people wanting comfort, it's not for those spoiled kids, or even the people with big muscles. It's for the ones who have a heart like a lion. Fierce and determined. You know how you get a heart like that? You refuse to give up in the small things. You persevere through those and then pretty soon the small things become bigger things and on it goes, till you're up in front of a mountain and you really need that mountain to move. The good news is if you've done your work well and persevered before you got to that mountain, it will have heard of you and will realize that it doesn't stand a chance. And it will gladly move out of your way.' *love this!*

Don't get me wrong, I don't always feel like persevering. I have my off days just like the next guy, but I think we always have the choice to either stay down and snuggle with our feelings or kick them to the curb and stand back up. I've had to stand back up a lot of times over this past year. Sometimes I feel all bloodied and bruised when I stand back up, like I can barely hold my own weight. But I make it as long as I refuse to give up.

Chapter 13

three days later...

I could hear the phone ring as I sat on the back deck admiring the sunrise. I walked in and answered it. "Hello?"

"Hi Daddy."

"Hey Tory, how are you doing?"

"Good Daddy. I want you to take me on a date tonight, that is if you're not busy."

"Wow honey, I would love that."

"Great. I want to go someplace fancy. With lots of gourmet choices on the menu. Of course I will only want the mac'n cheese, but it's still good to have choices. And they must have a plethora of dessert options."

"Honey, where did you learn the word plethora?"

"Dad, I am a well-educated woman. Plethora is in my vocabulary."

"Okay Tory," I said with a laugh. "But you are still my little princess. Do you have any other requests? Did you want me to make sure there is no rain tonight?" I heard her giggle on the other end of the line. She is such a sweet girl. Sometimes distant, but so sweet.

"No, that will be all. And please pick me up at 5:30 sharp."

"I can do that. Did you clear this with your mother?"

"Yes I did. Uh Daddy?"

"Yes Tory?"

"I'm really excited."

"Me too sweetie, thanks for calling."

Well that certainly is interesting. I wonder what she's up to?

I arrived at 5:28 and knocked on the door. Bridget answered and smiled at me.

"Hi Josh, she is so excited about this. Thanks for doing this it means a lot to m... to her."

"Sure thing Bridget, I'm just looking forward to spending time with her. What's that on your neck?"

She pulled her shirt up over what looked like a bruise and said, "Oh nothing Josh, it's just an accident I had the other day."

"You mean the one from your arm, when we were climbing?"

"Uh yeah, I think that's the same one."

"Bridget? Are you okay?"

"Yes Josh, I'm fine, just a little clumsy these days. Well, have fun on your date."

Tory bounded down the stairs all dolled up in a beautiful gown and shiny shoes. She looked so beautiful. It was hard to believe how much she had grown up in the last year. Time really does fly.

"You ready Sweetie?"

"I was born ready Daddy."

"Hey, that's my line," I said with a smile.

"I know, it's a good one," she smiled.

"Alright, off we go to a restaurant fit for a princess."

We arrived at the finest restaurant in our small town, Annabella's. Tory picked a table outside. When we sat down I noticed that she had brought the book Grandma had given her.

"Well Tory, I'm very excited to be here with you. Is there a specific reason why you wanted to go on a date? Or was this just for the fun of being together?"

"Daddy, I'm sorry I've been afraid to open up to you. I don't even know all the reasons why. I began to believe that things were never going to work out for me and that I would always be stuck in a place I didn't want to be. I even began to get mad at you because I felt like you should have rescued us from all this. So, I'm sorry. I realized when we went climbing how amazing it was to be a family again. I don't think Ben and I fought at all that whole day. We've been fighting a lot lately."

"I've heard."

"Yeah, I figured he told you. It's just that I really started to believe that if we just went along with all the stuff Ralph was telling us that everything would smooth itself out; but it hasn't, and honestly, things have just gotten worse. It's pretty bad."

"What do you mean, Tory?"

"I don't know Daddy, it's just not what mom or us expected it to be. Ralph is sometimes pretty bossy and mean."

"Like how so?"

"Daddy, I shouldn't talk about all this. Mom says it's our bed and we need to lie in it. I don't even know what that means, but I don't think I should talk about it."

"Tory, look at me, if you guys are in danger, I need to know about it." With that she broke down in tears and put her head on the table.

"He tells us what to do all the time and then threatens us when we won't do it just the right way. He yells constantly, and just recently he..."

"He what, Tory"

"He hurt mom."

That's where the bruises came from. I should've known it. She was acting so weird both of those times. I can't believe this.

"Tory, are you telling me the truth?"

"Yes Daddy, but please don't tell anyone I told you."

"Does he know you came out with me?"

"No, Mom said it would be our secret."

"Where is he right now?"

"Um let's see, it's Thursday night, so bowling league. He goes and bowls from 5:00p.m. to 8:00p.m."

71

"Let's try and enjoy our dinner without thinking about all of this." I say trying to change the pit in both of our stomachs into something not near as sickening.

"Ok Daddy, I'm so sorry."

"Tory, there is nothing for you to be sorry about, none of this is your fault. Let's talk about something else. Hey, how was your soccer game this last week?"

"Good, I scored two goals. The coach says we may get to play in the championship game if we keep playing like we are."

"Wow, that's great honey. I can't wait to see your next game. It's Tuesday, right?"

"Yep, Tuesday night. We play the Skyhawks. They're undefeated so far. I'm a little nervous."

"You're gonna do great, I know it."

Tory dug into her Mac'n Cheese and I into my Portabella Ravioli. It's funny that I would think I could just turn a switch and forget about all this new found information about my beloved family. I'll be honest, I was about to flip a table over and storm out of the restaurant. But I figured it's best not to make a scene at the only fine-dining in town. I may need them again sometime in my life.

"So Tory, why did you bring the book?"

"Oh yeah, well, I've been thinking about how I don't really talk to you a whole lot anymore and I had this idea. I want this to be our book. See look, I already started. I put your letters in on this side of the page and then on the other side I wrote back to you. So I was thinking that if you wanted to, we could hand the book back and forth and I could start writing how I'm feeling in here also. What do you think?"

"Wow honey, that's the best idea ever. I love it and I would be honored to do that with you."

"Great, it's your turn to take the book. For the past week I've been writing back to all your letters from before and I'm finally caught up."

"This is wonderful. I can't wait to write more. But why now?"

"You know when you sneak attacked me the other day?"

Jesus saw!

"Yeah that was a good idea, huh?"

"It wasn't just a good idea Daddy, it was the best idea! I realized in that moment that my daddy loved me and wanted my heart. That you didn't just want the amazing things about me, but all the things about me. Daddy, do you really love me, even when I'm a brat?"

With tears now welling up in my eyes I said, "My darling Tory, I love you even when you choose not to love me. You are a part of me and I can't unchoose that."

"Thank you Daddy. Daddy? How are you so good at loving even when people hurt you? I don't feel like I could do that. I mean, out of all of us you seem to be doing the best and you're alone most of the time. You don't have any distractions like us. Whenever we are feeling down, Ralph buys us something or gives us a project or puts on a movie. He says that feeling sad about our life is a waste of time, so we just need some help to forget our feelings. It's kind of like what you say about handling our feelings. Most of the time it works."

"That's funny, that is kind of what I say, except I tell you not to live by your emotions. It sounds like Ralph wants you to try and sweep your emotions under the rug and forget about them. But that doesn't really make you stronger, it just teaches you how to wear masks. You see Tory, the world loves to wear masks. The average person would rather be someone else because they are so caught up on the appearance of things. I can not change who I am from the outside in, it has to start with my heart and then all the other stuff naturally follows. Hey, the next time you are sad, go up to your room and shed some tears on your pillow. Then when you feel like you've gotten it all out, remind your emotions that they are a part of your life to help you, not control you."

"That is pretty different from what Ralph tells us to do, huh?"

"Yeah, quite a bit. Oh look, it's almost seven o'clock. We need to get you home since it's a school night."

"Ok, thanks Daddy, everything was perfect tonight."

"You're welcome honey, thank you."

Chapter 14

How in the world am I going to talk to Bridget about this? I mean, she needs help, she can't stay in that environment, she can't keep our kids in that environment. As we pull up to the house I feel sick nervous. There are different types of nervous, but this is the one that makes you feel like you might need to visit the bathroom before you deal with the thing that is making you nervous. Tory and I walk up to the front door. She pulls me down to eye level and puts her hands on my cheeks.

"I love you Daddy," she says just before giving me a kiss. "Thank you for not giving up on us and leaving."

"I will never leave you Tory and I will never turn my back on you."

The door opens and Bridget is standing there with a strange look I don't quite understand.

"Hi Bridget, thanks for arranging this, we had a great time." Tory squeezes between us and heads upstairs to bed.

"Goodnight Daddy, love you," she hollers from the stairs.

"Love you too sweetie," I reply.

Bridget looks up at me and I can tell something is on her mind.

"Bridget, what is it?"

"Nothing Josh, thanks for taking Tory out."

"Yeah sure, we had a blast. It's like I have my Tory back. She opened up to me just like the old days on our morning walks. What a blessing that was. Bridget, can I ask you something?"

"Sure Josh, what is it?"

"What are the bruises on your arm from?"

"I told you already Josh, just me being clumsy."

"Bridget, please if you need help, I can help, just don't stay in a bad situation. Not for yours or the kids sake. Please, I can help; but you need to choose."

"Josh..."

Just then the door opened a bit further to reveal Ralph standing there.

"Hi Josh, what are you doing here?"

"Oh, Hi Ralph, I was out with Tory and we just got back."

"Josh, if I'm not mistaken tonight is not one of your nights to spend time with the kids."

"No Ralph, it certainly is not. Tory asked me if I would take her out, and I understand that according to that paperwork you gave me, that if a child should request a visit outside the times stated, they will be granted the request. Yeah, I read it over just to make sure that there wouldn't be any issues."

"Well, there is an issue. We need to know these things ahead of time Josh, poor communication causes things to fall apart."

"Ralph, I'm pretty sure Bridget knew about this and didn't have a problem with it. Please don't mistake your role in my children's lives. And don't call control, communication."

Well, that didn't sit well. I don't think he's used to people talking back to him. He slammed the door right in my face. I could hear him starting to raise his voice at Bridget and then quiet. I walked back to my Jeep and pulled out of the driveway.

Defeated. I feel a little bit defeated right now. Not like the battle was lost, just postponed while my enemy seems to have the advantage. Yeah, I think it's okay to call Ralph my enemy. That's actually probably a lot better than the other names I call him when no one is around.

I glance back at the house as I shift into first gear. What! This is too much. He's yelling at her in the family room. It's like I'm watching this whole thing in slow motion. Now he's flailing his arms around. I must have really ticked him off. It's probably time I intervene. He just shoved her onto the couch. I can't believe this guy. I jump out of my Jeep and walk toward the front door. It's as if I'm gaining momentum with each step I take. I feel like a train gaining speed, preparing to barrel through any obstacle. As I step up to the door, I kick right above the handle, which sends the door flying open.

The sound of it all must have startled Ralph a little bit because he came hesitantly over to the door to see what happened. His demeanor changed from anger to fear in an instant.

As soon as he saw me he yelled, "I'm going to call the cops on you. You're going to jail for this. You can't break someone's door down," he said with anger rising in his tone.

"You're not calling anyone. I have you abusing Bridget videotaped on my phone, do you really want that on the headlines in the morning?"

"Get out of my house Josh, before someone gets hurt."

"There have already been too many people getting hurt in your house, Ralph."

I turned to Bridget, "Can I take the kids with me?"

She nodded in agreement.

"You're not taking my kids anywhere" he yelled.

"They are not your kids Ralph, and if you try and stop us, the headlines will expose you to the whole city."

I had him and he knew it. I turned to Bridget.

"You can come with me if you want, it's your choice."

"Bridget!" Ralph said with a controlling tone. "If you leave me you are leaving who you really are. This is all that you ever wanted: the shopping trips, the freedom to make your life the way you want it, not wondering where the money will come from, and of course being free from your panic attacks. You will throw all that away and I won't take you back."

"Ralph, let me speak with Josh alone."

"But..."

"Ralph, I need to speak with Josh alone," she said firmly.

We stepped outside the door that now was not closing the whole way.

"Josh," tears began to well up in her eyes. "I am responsible for so much pain. For all this time I thought pain only happened to me. I feel like there are two roads for me and neither one of them seems easy. I think I know which is the right one. But I can't leave yet. I'm not ready."

"But what if he hits you again, or worse?"

"Josh, I don't understand it all, but I'm not ready yet and I'm not going to be back and forth with my choices. I'm not sure how to help you understand."

"Understand what? I've shown you nothing but love, but in the times when things were tough and uncomfortable you actually believed that somehow my love stopped. Yes, I didn't always have three months of cash saved up for our bills, but we're still here. We've always had enough. And look at you, you're better. I told you that you would get better and you are. Bridget, what does it take for my bride to understand what true love is?"

"Josh, I'm just not ready."

"Okay," I replied. It wasn't okay though. What is it going to take for her?

"I just need some more time," she said.

I should know this. It's not always about having the right answers in front of you that brings about a heart change; it's about the right moment. Nobody likes waiting, do they? I wonder if waiting is actually the thing that brings out the truth in people's lives more than anything else. We are

78

Wow! profound!

always trying to do things faster and slow down time, but what if we slowed our lives down and used time to our advantage. What if we looked at time as a pair of binoculars that allowed us to see further and bigger pictures than we could with only our eyes. We would have to get really good at sitting in the same place for awhile, but I wonder how that would change our lives?

"Bridget, we'll be up at my parents."

"Ok, Josh. I'm so sorry. It seems like I've messed everything up again."

"Well, then you're the only one who can clean it up. If you want my help, you know where I will be."

"Thank you Josh, I'll get the kids packed up."

We stepped back into the house and Bridget walked upstairs to get the kids. As I began trying to put pieces of the door back together Ralph stepped around the corner.

"You know Josh, this is really stupid. You're gonna regret all of this."

"Ralph, I'm not scared by your intimidation and I'm not going to be controlled by your manipulation. Don't you ever wonder what it would be like for you to be free? Free from all the ways you try to control your life and the lives of others?"

"Ahhh, shutup!" he yelled.

"Let me make one thing very clear. If you hurt Bridget, I will be back and I'm positive you don't want that."

"Ha, Josh you don't have the guts or the ability to take Bridget from me."

At that I stepped up right in front of him. Eye to eye.

"Do not question my abilities, for in just a short time all that you've stolen from me will be mine once again and what is left to you will be your loneliness and bad choices."

He shrunk back, knowing he couldn't stop his upcoming defeat. But I know in his mind he was strategizing how he would postpone it as long as possible.

"Fine Josh, have it your way."

"I will, Ralph," I said.

Tory and Ben came running down the stairs with their backpacks on.

"Dad we're going to Grandma and Grandpa's?" Ben yelled.

"Yeah Bud, go ahead and hop in the Jeep."

Ralph stepped forward, "No way, you can't take them up there. It's too... far away and we don't have a good way of contacting you up there." He looked at Bridget, "You can't let them go up there."

"Ralph, I can't change that. I'm sorry," she said.

He stormed off into the kitchen sulking at the obvious loss of his control over my family. Now it was just Bridget who was left there, and who knew how long it would take her to come around completely.

"Goodbye Bridget, you know where to find me if you need anything."

I was almost half waiting for her to start walking to the Jeep and leave right then with us. But I also know Bridget. She's determined to get what she thinks she needs and she has to first understand her need before she'll make a decision to move. Again with the whole timing thing.

"Thanks Josh."

"The next time you see me, you can call me Joshua."

"Ok," she said, as tears began to stream down her face.

Chapter 15

As I climbed into my Jeep I couldn't help but wonder what lay ahead. <u>Sometimes you feel like you just can't get traction in life, and then all of a sudden you have a foot that sticks and you are climbing again.</u>

It's a beautiful drive during the day, but you should see it by night. The stars are brilliant pressed against the dark blue canvas. The moon is a quarter crescent giving off just enough light to take the edge off of the darkness.

There's plenty of time for me to think about all that just happened. Both kids are passed out in the back and it's a couple hour drive up to my mom and dad's farm. After the highway, none of the roads are paved, so it can be a little bumpy and difficult to navigate if you are not familiar with the way to go.

There is only one road that leads to their farm, but if you don't know the way, it is easy to get turned around or lost on roads that branch off in other directions. In some places the road is pretty rough and narrow and at other's it is windy and can feel like you are going in circles. But it has become like second nature to me to get to their place, and tonight I have precious cargo in my back seat that really needs the refreshment that comes from being up there.

The coolest part about the trip is that you have to go from the valley, where the town is located, up through the mountains and to the other side of the range. Most people don't even know that my parents live up there. It's a hidden treasure for sure.

I consider it an honor to provide a safe place where my kids can find rest, even in the midst of the tragedy they've been through over the last year. I look through my rear view mirror at them sleeping in the back seat. It's as if nothing is wrong, like they could wake up and forget about the nightmare they just lived through. This could all just have been a bad dream. I wish it were. But they do look so strong. So much stronger than they did before. I'm sure they feel worn, but something has grown inside of them through this. I can see it. Something has changed for the better.

My thoughts race back to Bridget. I wonder how she is. I hope she's okay; that he hasn't hurt her anymore. I meant what I said. I'm not a violent person by nature, but I have a very low tolerance for him and what he's done to my family.

I wonder what she's thinking about right now. I don't doubt that she still loves me and still wants to be with me, but she still just seems so confused.

It was like the perfect storm. The perfect time for her to be misled and deceived. That's exactly what it was, lies that convinced her that she would be happier if she was more comfortable; more content if she had things that seemed stable; and free from pain if she had in her possession more money. She began to look more with her feelings than with truth and she got swept away so quickly. I still remember the depression that she was in after being healed. On one hand she was happy that she was now healed, but on the other hand she was deeply wounded by the fear of whether this could happen again. It was as if all she had thought about life got turned upside down and she no longer knew what and who to trust.

So, when Ralph stepped in and looked stable to her, it seemed like the right thing. That's why you never make a decision when you are feeling depressed. Eat cake, ice cream or chocolate, sure. But don't make decisions. It's like trying to decide which direction to go on a mountain when the fog is covering everything around you. That's the best time to stay where you are and rest until it clears up. Then once the fog moves away and exposes what's around you it's much more productive to move and it's a lot easier to keep from getting lost.

82

Chapter 16

It feels so good to be up here. Waking up to the smell of mom cooking breakfast is the best. And the sunrise, wow, it is breathtaking. There is only one thing that would make this better. But it's just not time for her to come back yet. As much as I think I understand, it still doesn't feel right.

Tory and Ben are already outside. I can hear them giggling as they feed the baby goats. Dad has always had this special relationship with animals. He tries to keep as many as mom will allow him, up here on the property. He's been known to take care of injured animals and nurse them back to health.

There was a sparrow that was up in the tree out back of the house and he used to go out in the morning and play his harmonica for the mom and her eggs. He'd play all sorts of songs for them. The day that they finally hatched he was so excited. He ran back in the house and grabbed his harmonica. As he started to play for them, he noticed they all started moving around and then, before he knew it, they hopped right out of the nest trying to get to him. Thankfully he was close enough and not one of them hit the ground. He caught them and placed them back in the nest. After that he decided to put the harmonica away until they had learned to fly. Mom and I still tease him about that one.

It's funny how someone who knows so much and sees such a big picture on life, is so captivated by the simplest of accomplishments. You should have seen him when I learned to ride a bike as a kid. You would've thought I won a gold medal in the Olympics. But I guess that's where the world learns what celebrating life is all about. I think that when you pour your heart into something and finally accomplish it, the feeling you get when someone celebrates you is more than a feeling. It's like a seed that in time can grow into a tree. It can actually change who you are. I don't celebrate my kids to make them feel good about who they are. I celebrate them so that they will become the glorious things I see in them that they don't yet understand. It's kind of like paving a road for them, so that the next time they take that journey, it's easier for them to get where they are going. It's this place of confidence that they find themselves in that feels more natural each time.

I should probably get out of bed and start my day. There's not really a whole lot on my schedule up here. Mostly just spending time with Ben and Tory and making sure they are okay after last night. Thankfully, they didn't realize all that was going on downstairs.

Kids are resilient, but that doesn't mean I want them to experience unnecessary pain. Some pain is necessary in life. It has a purpose and I'm okay with that. But as a father I do everything I can to guard my kids from the unnecessary stuff.

"Now this is breakfast! Thanks Mom," I say walking into the kitchen.

"Tory, Ben, come on and eat!" she hollers through the screen door.

"Coming Grandma," they respond in unison.

"So Honey, how are you feeling this morning?"

"Good Mom. Thanks so much for this. The kids have been wanting to come back up to the farm for some time now."

"You are always welcome here dear. How do you think Bridget is doing?"

"You know Mom, I've seen what seems like a change of her heart, but it just doesn't seem like it's strong enough yet to make her move. Do you remember when my friend John died in that accident at the mill?"

"Yes I do Honey. We all miss John so much."

"You know it took me so long to forgive his boss and ever go up to the mill again. I used to always meet him on lunch breaks and we'd go throw rocks into the river. I could

84

tell him anything and all I ever felt was accepted and loved. He was such a good friend to me. Anyways, I was so upset when he died. It took me years till I went back up there and when I finally did, I just sat there on the edge of the river chucking rocks and talking to him like he was still there. Then I looked down right beside me and saw a seedling that must've just popped through the soil. I remembered what he used to tell me about life and that sometimes it seems like things will never change and we feel just plain stuck. It's at those moments that we get to decide what kind of person we will be. Will we believe that there is sunlight right on the other side of our next move or will we just stay where we are, sulking in the difficulties and hoping someone digs us out? He was such a good friend. After seeing that seedling and remembering his words, I felt free from the sorrow of losing him. But I don't think I would be free had I not gone up there, and I don't think I could've gone up there any earlier than I had. It's almost like there's a perfect timing for healing, and sometimes we just find ourselves in that place and before we know it, we're better."

"Well Dear, I think you are right. I hope that Bridget finds herself in that perfect timing soon. We miss her a lot up here. I miss having a daughter around to cook with me and laugh about all the funny things your father does."

"I bet you do Mom, I bet you do," I laugh.

"Dad, do you mind if we take the four wheeler out for the day?"

"Sure thing Joshua, what are you guys up to?"

"Well, I was thinking today would be a good day to get lost and then find our way back."

"That sounds magnificent," he says with a smile.

I slide a compass across the table to Tory and one to Ben. "Here you go guys. Today we're going to learn how to make it back home no matter where you find yourself."

"Awesome," yells Ben.

"Are you sure about this?" says Tory.

These are my kids. I love them so much. So different in the way they interact with me and the world. I wouldn't trade them for anything.

"Ben, yes it is awesome, and Tory yes I am sure. Now pack up a backpack with a change of clothes in case we need them and a jacket in case it gets cold. Mom, do you mind putting a lunch together for us? We should be back before dinner."

"Sure thing, Honey," she says with a smile.

Chapter 17

We all climb on the four wheeler and I show them a map of the surrounding area.

"Now pay attention. There are landmarks all around us. If you can remember the landmarks and find them on your map, you'll be better off. But even if you get turned around, your compass will show you the right direction. First we'll do a practice run."

We head up and over the first ridge, then cut east along a valley floor and across a small creek. I am trying to disorient them a little so that I can be sure they know what they need to do before I give them the real test. I pull over by the bottom of a rock face I used to call, Old Faithbuilder.

"Alright guys, here's the map. It's your job to get us back to Grandpa's meadow. I'm just the driver, so I will only be taking directions from here on out."

Tory reaches for the map right away. I can't say I'm surprised by that! Ben is watching my eyes to see if I will give any hints as to which direction it may be. He gets that from his grandmother. She seems to be able to figure out what people are thinking simply by watching them.

"Ok, we have to go Northeast to get back, right Dad?"

"Sorry Tory. I'm just the driver, you tell me where to go and I'll go there." This is good, it's one of those times when you are so excited about the outcome that you can hardly wait through the process.

"Ok driver, go that way," Ben says as he points to a steep incline that I'm not sure the four wheeler can make it up.

"Ben, that can't be it," says Tory. "There's no way we can make it up that way."

"If you have a better idea feel free to let me know, but my instincts tell me it's that way."

"Here, look at the map," she says trying to show him some logical path.

"Tory can't you just trust me?"

"You mean trust your 'instincts'?"

"Yeah, I know we have to go that way."

"You want me to just trust how you feel about where we are at? I've got two words for you Ben, dog and skateboard."

"Why you little..."

"Guys, I know I'm just the driver, but might I interject for just a moment?"

"No!" they responded in unison.

"Nice, well I forgot to mention that I'm also a wonderful counselor. So, you might find that both of you have a key to this puzzle, but if you fight, you will probably end up going in circles and not gaining any ground. Just saying."

"Alright Tory," said Ben. "I know this is the direction we need to go. So, if we can't go that way, what do you suggest?"

"Well if you will just look here on the map, I think we need to follow the creek north till it opens up and then look for a way to get over the ridge when it's less steep. We need to go that direction, surprisingly you are right, but we need to find a way that we can actually drive on without dying."

"Alright Tory, I will trust you."

That's enough to let a father who has feared for the well-being of his children know that they will be just fine.

"Alright, so where to?" I say with an, 'I'm just here to help' smile.

"That way Dad, just follow the creek," says Tory.

We made it back to the meadow with only a couple hang-ups. They were so excited to see what they had accomplished together.

"It's not even lunchtime Dad. We blew your test out of the water."

"Well Ben, that actually wasn't the test. That was the training for the test. Hop back on, there's another place I want to show you."

This time we ride over the ridge and head up through the forest and then out past a wilderness area that they've never seen before. We are about six miles from the house now and it will take them about four hours to get back if they are able to work together and keep moving. I stop the four wheeler and hop off.

"Here we are," I say.

They look a little hesitant as they search for a sign of some familiarity.

"Dad? This seems pretty far from the house," says Tory with obvious concern in her voice.

"It's a little farther than you guys have ever been before, but I know you can handle it. You proved it by... I believe the words were, 'blowing my test out of the water', right Ben?"

"Well driver, you wait there while Ben and I look at the map."

"Tory, there's something else you need to know. I won't be driving you this time."

"Yes, I get to drive. This is awesome!" shouts Ben.

"Not exactly what I meant Ben. You guys are on your own getting back to Grandma and Grandpa's. It may seem like a pretty big thing I'm asking you to do. But remember, I would never ask you to do something that I didn't absolutely know you could do."

"Daddy?" Tory asks with hesitance in her voice.

I knew this was coming, this is the hard part of these situations.

"Yes honey?"

"I don't want to be alone. What if something happens?"

"Tory, there will always be 'what if's,' but we can't let those things stop us. You guys are going to do amazing. I have no doubt about that. Remember, your mission is to stay together and find your way back without letting it separate you. I'll see you back at the house. I love you guys."

As I started driving away I saw Tory drop her backpack and slump down on the ground. This is tough parenting. But what this will build in them is priceless. I drive back to the house and park the four wheeler in the shed as dad walks out from the house.

"How does that feel?" he asks with a smile.

"It hurts a little, but I know they'll do fine."

"I know they will too," he says.

"I'll be back in a few hours," I say as I turn to head back into the woods.

"Son, I'm proud of you, you're a good man."

"Thanks Dad, I learned what it means to be good from you."

I tighten up my backpack and start jogging toward Tory and Ben. Although I won't let them see me, I plan on being right there for them through their hike. I want them to experience all of the emotions that they wouldn't feel if I were right there beside them. But I also want to keep them safe, whether they can see me or not.

There's nothing like running through these woods. Something of freedom comes alive in me when I'm all alone out here. I wonder if the animals feel free. Probably a lot more free than we do. They're not tied to a cell phone or emails. They don't have to prepare their food or think about making it to the bathroom on time. That might be nice. Okay, keep running. I should make it to them in about 40 minutes. I just need to make sure they don't see me.

Yes, there they are. I think if I just hide behind these rocks, they will pass me and I can follow them just out of sight. I feel like a sniper, getting ready to hit my target with bullets of wisdom, teamwork and good character. <u>These are the moments that allow the knowledge you receive into your mind to form into a bedrock of foundation in your life.</u> I think I'm more excited about this than they are. Well, judging by the look on Tory's face, yeah, I'm definitely more excited than her. "You are not a victim to your circumstances, Tory." I whisper, hoping that somehow my words will ring in her mind.

"Ben, this can't be the way. I told you the directions when dad left us. Now we are all messed up because you thought you felt like this is the way we should go. I never should have trusted you."

"Tory, seriously. All your hate talk is not doing us any good."

"I just wish mom was here. She would make dad come pick us up."

"She would also make you stop being so mean to me." Then Ben started to yell out loud. "Mom, Mom, we could really use your help out here. I mean, Tory could really use your help out here."

Ouch, she just slugged him in the arm.

I smile as he reaches over and puts his punched arm over her shoulder.

"Tory, remember what dad said? When we work together we are unstoppable. We've never really worked together on anything before, but let's just keep trying. Don't worry we'll find our way. Dad wouldn't have left us unless he truly believed we could do this."

"Oh yeah, maybe this is payback for us going and living with mom. Maybe he just wants us to feel what it felt like for him."

That one stung. This is one of those times that I would love to peek out over the rocks that are hiding me and say, 'Look Tory, I'm right here. See, I will never leave you and I will never turn my back on you. I'm right here.' But I can't. It would only take away from what she is desperately in need of. To walk through this, each step of the way, her and Ben, with no ability to see me or the end.

These are the moments that will show whether or not they truly trust me. It's so easy to trust when you can see how it will all work out, but when you feel like they feel right now is when your level of trust in someone or something really shines forth.

They keep walking. In about two miles they should be able to recognize some of the landscape.

I keep my distance just to make sure that there's no chance of being seen but still close enough to hear them talking. Overall they are doing really well. They're going the right way, they've just never been here before. I can see fear trying to get at Tory. It's the same fear that whispers about the unknown to all of us in tough situations. Ben seems to be doing good at the inability to know exactly where they are; but I can tell he's getting tired of hearing her complain and is even starting to get ahead of her a little bit.

"Come on Tory, try and keep up." Ben yells back to her.

"I'm trying, but this is hard, and I'm tired."

"We just need to keep moving. We'll make it. I think I know where we are now."

"Really, how?"

"It just feels like I've seen this place before."

"There you go with your 'just feels like' again. Ben I need something concrete, something I can see on paper."

Ben reaches the top of the ridge about 20 steps ahead of her.

"Ok Tory. Here's your piece of concrete paper."

"What? What does that mean? What do you see?"

"Come see for yourself."

They stand there for about five minutes, taking in the beautiful view of the river below. I watch as they point to different spots on the river and retell the stories and memories from each spot. It's the same river that we used to swim in every summer. The cliffs that lined it's northern banks are where we used to look our fears in the eye and jump into the chilly pools of mountain fresh water only to climb back out and do it again. They know this river, and they now can see where they are. They're not back to the house yet, about another mile, but I can see the confidence on them as they realize they are okay and this test will soon be over.

The rest of the way they seem lighter. They are joking with each other and I even hear them devise a plan to have Ben hide his arm in his shirt and tell me that a bear attacked them and bit it off. Sounds like something I would've done at his age. I can't help but laugh. I head up and around another crossing of the river so that I can be there waiting for them when they get back to the house. This was a great day. I can't wait to see them with their earned confidence.

As they crest the hill into the meadow I'm relaxing in my hammock chair. I love this thing. Whoever invented these was a genius.

"Dad," ben yells.

"Hey Bud," I sit up and act surprised to see them. "So how was it? Oh no Ben! Your arm, did you get attacked by a bear?"

Taken back by my immediate response to his arm not being visible, he responded, "Uh yeah, we just ran into some trouble."

93

"Trouble?" Tory spurted out. "Yes, a bear bit off his arm Dad, all because you weren't there. That's not trouble, that's like... double trouble."

Ben couldn't hold it in and neither could I. We burst out laughing, and after a minute Tory joined in.

"But seriously Daddy, why did you just leave us there? We could've gotten hurt, or even killed out there."

"Tory, come here. I want to show you something."

"I don't think you could show me anything that would make me feel different than I already do."

"Just come over here."

I reached into my pocket, pulled out my phone and opened up my pictures. I turned the phone around to show her a picture of herself with her arms up in the air and Ben about ten feet in front of her shaking his head.

"What is this from? How did you?" Tory said with shock.

"I knew you were following us, ha. Dad, that was a good one," laughed Ben.

"Tory, don't you remember that I told you I would never leave you or turn my back on you? I meant that."

"I guess I forgot that. It just felt like you were nowhere around." Waw! God.

"I know it did, but I'm really proud of you guys, even through some rough patches when it would've been easy to part ways, you guys kept going together and stuck it out. And look, you made it. How does it feel to pass the test?"

"It feels pretty good," Ben said smiling.

"Yeah, pretty good Daddy," said Tory as she wrapped her arms tightly around me.

"Let's go get some dinner. I'm hungry and I'm sure you guys are too."

"Yes sir," they both replied.

Chapter 18

Tory and Ben went right to bed after dinner. I imagine they were pretty tired after our excursion. My dad and I are sitting here on the back porch again, having one of our heart to hearts. We talk about the way the world is going, and how if we controlled everything, what we would do to fix all the mess. We laugh a lot, and I of course cry when he talks about all the things he loves about me, the kids, and Bridget.

"I can feel it in my chest. She's coming back," he says as he sweeps his gaze across the star filled sky.

"I think so too Dad, I just don't know how long I'm going to have to wait," I begin to cry.

"Son, don't worry about trying to understand the times of the seasons, just be ready."

"Do you think I need to do anything more? Like maybe send her flowers or a note, or just drive down there to make sure she's still okay?"

"It sounds like you've already done so much. You've laid your life down for her. I think now is the time to wait. The ball is in her court now and she knows that. She'll come when it's the right time."

"Yeah, you're probably right."

"Well Son, it's time I get some sleep. Rest is a privilege and I intend to enjoy it."

"Goodnight Dad, I love you."

"Love you too, Son. And hey Joshua, I'm proud of you," he says with a smile.

Hearing him say that never gets old.

There's Orion, bright and shining right smack dab in front of me. There's nothing like looking at the stars from up here. Absolutely beautiful. They feel so close, like I could touch them.

You know that feeling you get when every muscle in your body relaxes and you just know that this is the place out of any place in the world that you would choose to stay in, if you could. It's like a feeling, but somehow deeper.

I've never felt more feelings like that than when I was with her. We've been through so much. There's actually this weird thing that happens to people who are married where they start reading each other's minds, and sure enough one of you gets mad at the other when they can't read your mind. And you even start looking alike and doing things the same way. Then before you know it you're like one person that can do superhuman amounts of work.

Like raising a child, which is actually quite a miraculous thing. I know they have a lot of statistics out there, but how about statistics of parents who died from the amount of labor involved in diaper changes and cleaning up the same toys 12 times in one day.

I often wondered as I was growing up if I could be a Navy SEAL. After we had Tory and Ben and I went through daddy boot camp, I knew I could make it. It's one thing to wake up to a drill sergeant yelling at you to get dressed and go on a hike in the dark, and a complete different skill set to wake up to blood curdling screams, that you have to endure until you change a diaper full of poop all the while trying not to get poop on your hands. And then when the baby wipe slides off your hand and you end up with poop under your finger nail, you now have to hold baby in one arm while trying to wash your hand that is soiled using only that hand. That's worse than trying to figure out a Rubik's Cube that your kid rearranged the stickers on. Oh yeah, and this is while baby is still letting out blood curdling screams because the poop was only half the problem. Baby wants her bottle. And yes, you are doing all this while not fully awake and exhausted from staying up to clean up the same toys for the twelfth time that day. I sometimes think that if the SEALs had an honorary degree, then I should definitely be an honorary Navy SEAL. Well, that season of life is now over for me. No more diaper changing or bottles at midnight. But boy do I miss those sweet moments of snuggling a little child that fits in your arms. Or the looks they give you that say a thousand words, even before they can speak one.

Well, I need to get to bed. It was such a good day. My kids grew so much in those few hours. That makes a dad's heart glad.

Chapter 19

days later...

Time has gone by so fast up here. We wake up with the sun, enjoy breakfast and conversation, and then fill up the rest of the morning with helping out around the farm. We all seem to find our own way to spend the afternoons. Sometimes we go swimming down at the lake, and other times we find a quiet spot to read. Inevitably I end up falling asleep in my hammock chair while reading. Usually I'm awakened by the sound of the kids laughing as Grandpa is spraying them with the water hose. This is really good for us, we all needed this time away from the town.

My thoughts still return to her constantly throughout each day. It's been five days since the kids and I came up here. I can even see a change in them. There's a freedom that they're experiencing being up here. But I don't doubt for a moment that a huge part of their freedom has come because of what they just walked through in life. Something that could have been so crippling has built in them a strength that seems impossible to obtain in any other way. Yesterday my dad told me that he thinks I should finish my book. I asked him what book he was talking about?

He said, "you know that book you had written for Bridget before you two were married. It was only partially finished. The real story is everything you walked through in these past few years. Son, true love is not just a declaration of love, but the walking it out. And hey, if you write it, I'll read it."

I laughed and said, "great and you will probably be the only one who will read it."

He replied, "that's not true, I'm sure I can convince your mother to read it also," he said chuckling. "Joshua, sometimes what we are given to express through our hands and our mouths, our words and our thoughts, are only for the few. But you must always remember, you are a sower. It's not your job to grow a seed or multiply it, but it is your job to plant it. And who knows, maybe it will benefit you to get all those feelings out on paper."

So here I am with pen and paper. I never considered myself much of a writer, but I do like to journal, so maybe I'll just do that. Let's see:

Journal Entry 1.
The peril of the illness that swept through the depths of my lovely bride.

No, that's definitely too long of a title. Man, this is tough. Maybe I'll just write her another letter.

My dearest Bridget,

Do you remember the day when it seemed as if the pits of hell opened their gates to release an army against your health? I do. I wept that day in the Doctor's office and most of that night.

When those words left the mouth of your doctor. They landed right onto my heart with all the sting that news like that brings. But I knew deep down that the impact of this report would be far more impacting than either of us recognized.

I reached over and put my hand on yours and we walked out of that office with what seemed like a very heavy suitcase that I knew you weren't prepared to carry. The thoughts in my head seemed to run on repeat the entire drive home. You were quiet. I can only imagine what was going through your mind. I remember the whole conversation. I turned to you, "We're going to beat this Bridget," I said.

"How do you know?" You questioned as the tears began to fall down your face.

"Because I can't..." instantly I began to cry and then sucked all the snot and tears back inside. "Because I won't lose you. This is not your time to go. Every morning we are going to be thankful for another day, and we are going to beat this."

You replied longing for some sort of comfort, "Joshua, can't you make this all go away? What about the kids, they're so young?"

I knew that was one of your most plaguing thoughts that I could not make go away. I simply replied, "Bridget, every morning I'm going to look you in the eyes and remind you, you have a purpose in being here today. If you cease to have a purpose then that's the day you can be done here. But Bridget, you will never cease to have a purpose as long as I'm around. If I am your only purpose for being here, then let that be enough for you to keep fighting."

And that was the beginning of three long years filled with small victories, days of agony, hope lost, and hope restored. Laughter, and so many tears. Those three years were full of the things that make us human, as well as the things that allow us to touch the divine.

I put the pen and journal down in my lap as I push my feet off of the ground to begin the relaxing movement of my hammock chair. I look down over the lake and think back through those years. At times I'm blown away by the intensity of that season. It has shaped our relationship so much. Sometimes when I look back at our story and what we've been through it seems impossible. Like it's a made up story filled with tragedies and miracles. But you know what they say about miracles. 'You don't see them until you need them'.

I wonder what it would look like if Bridget wrote a book about everything that she went through? I wonder what she thought about me throughout those years. I wonder if she feels like Tory felt a few days ago when she thought I had left her alone in the woods to find her way home. I hope not.

100

Bridget was never alone. Even though she felt like she was the only one going through all of that, I was never so close to her. I remember so many nights while she lay on the hospital bed asleep. I would take her hand and tell her all the things that I loved about her, all the things I saw in her. The ways that her going through this would actually make her stronger and more beautiful. I'm sure she wished I would have told her all those things while she was awake, so that she would have felt stronger to keep fighting. But there's something about speaking to someone while they are sleeping. Their soul and perceptions don't get in the way of the message. It's like giving them a boost of encouragement without them even knowing where it came from. It's just in their pocket when they wake up, and they're not sure how it got there. Of course, she was wearing a hospital gown, no pockets, but a lot of open spaces. I'm sure there's some really funny stories out there about hospital gowns.

But back to the sleep talking. I really think there's something to speaking to someone when their brain doesn't get in the way. Now, I'm sure this could be done in a not so good way as well. But I would tell her about how courageous she was as she lay there, gaining strength from her sleep, and in the morning she would awaken with a smile. She would look at me sitting next to her and say, "I can do this today." That's pretty amazing. I don't have any scientific research on if this actually works or not. But I kept doing it, and she kept fighting, and she got better. That's good enough for me.

I remember the day she was finally released from the hospital for good. We were so excited. She had just had this tumor removed that had nearly killed her. Everything went better than was to be expected and before we knew it she was back home. It was like one day she was sick and we couldn't see where we were headed, and the next, the clouds lifted and she was on her way to a fast recovery. Even though she went through those three years of slowly fighting this disease out of her body, I still think it was a miracle. After a full day of testing, the doctor's told her she was good enough to go home. We were both in shock. We figured we still had a long road ahead of us. Bridget was still feeling symptoms from time to time, but the doctor explained that because the process of healing was so drawn out, her body became comfortable with some of the symptoms and even felt like they were normal. It would just take time for things to adjust to the way they were supposed to be, but that she was completely healed and shouldn't believe otherwise even if symptoms hung around for a little while.

I held her hand as we walked through those familiar hospital doors like victors across a finish line. I began to cry as we walked toward my Jeep. I couldn't believe we had made it. There were so many times throughout those years that I wondered if I would have to say goodbye for good. I believed with all my heart that she would be healed, but in the end, even with all of our beliefs, we can still lose the people we love. She looked like a new woman. With each step she took, strength seemed to rise up within her.

There are days when the sunset seems to hang in the air and every color in the world is represented in its perfect hues. It's one of those Kodak moments. Walking out of the hospital that day was one of mine.

Chapter 20

The dinner bell that Grandma still loves to use has been ringing for about two minutes straight, which either means there's an emergency, or she asked Ben to ring it. "Probably Ben," I laugh, as I start walking back to the house. "How was everyone's afternoon," I ask as I approach the back of the house.

"Great," says Tory. "We helped grandma with dinner, you're gonna love it."

Dad pointed out over the mountains. "Looks like a storm is coming. I wouldn't want to be out in the mountains tonight, could be a rough one," he said.

After dinner we got all of our storm gear ready. "Let's see," Grandma said aloud, "flashlights, candles, UNO, and some other choice board games, wood in the fireplace, blankets and pillows, and yes, snacks."

Storms have always been a big deal for us. We camp out in the family room which has a great view toward the mountains. We play games, eat snacks and watch as the lightning crashes like a fireworks show.

When dad built the house he used metal roofing over this part of the house. When it rains you can hear the pounding of the raindrops echo through the entire room. It's a different kind of music; you have to have an ear for it. But it is beautiful.

Most people don't like storms. I think a lot of people feel like they've been left out or unprotected and uncovered in storms. But when we are tucked away in the safety of this living room, it actually makes a storm something we can appreciate.

Grandma pulls the stack of UNO cards from its well-worn sleeve held together by duct tape, and challenges everyone to a game. She's pretty good. She always seems to win right when nobody's expecting it. And she somehow knows what cards you have. Must be a mother's intuition.

Three games of UNO in and she's won two of them. Surprisingly, Ben won a game. Not that I didn't think he could do it. I'm guessing she is probably teaching Ben all her strategies when no one is paying attention.

The fire is crackling and the rain is coming down heavy. Every few minutes we stop and watch the lightning show through the window. It is magnificent. The sky is a dark blue and then seemingly out of nowhere these explosions slice through the thick clouds and reach down toward the earth like a laser beam, coming closer and closer to their target. They are like heat-seeking missiles unsure of what to land on, but when they land, Wow! I've seen lightning split an 80 foot tall tree in half, right down the middle. That's some serious power.

"Knock, Knock."

We all look at each other trying to figure out if we all heard the knocking on the front door.

"Who in their right mind would be out in this storm?" asks dad. "Joshua, can you get that?"

"Sure Dad." I walk hesitantly to the door. There are many people or animals this could be. I begin to wonder if a bear can knock. What would that kind of knock sound like? They are smart animals. What if they knock and then when you open the door they get you? Or maybe the bear is just like us and really doesn't want to be out in the storm. I can't say I'd let the bear in the house, but I think I would let it stay on the porch till the storm blows over.

I open the door slowly. I don't recognize this person. They are obviously soaked from the rain and have the hood of their rain coat pulled over their head.

"Can I help you?" I say.

"Please, yes help me." A female voice responds through shivering. She pulls off her hood still looking down.

She's soaked but I can't tell what's from the rain and what's from her tears. She is sobbing, as she looks up.

"Bridget?" No other words are coming at this moment, not even thoughts.

"Josh, please, save me. I'm ready to come home. I don't even know if there is still a home for me. But if there is, I'm ready. This has been worse than going through those three years of almost dying. I honestly thought that if I could just find a place that seemed like it was more stable, that I wouldn't have fears. I was deceived. Ralph is not who I thought he was. And all the safety and comfort I thought I was gaining from him actually turned into him controlling me. I have lived in a worse place than I ever wanted to. And I gave up so much. Is there any way I can come home? Please say it's not too late Josh. I'm so sorry. I know what this did to you. I can't believe I did this to you. I don't deserve you, and you didn't deserve this. I was so wrong. Please forgive me," she said as she began to fall to the ground, worn out from the journey she had just endured.

"Bridget..." I said as I stepped forward to catch her from falling. "Call me Joshua." I held her tight, just outside of the reach of the storm. She was back in the safety of my arms, and I could feel her release every bit of tension in her body.

"Joshua, I do love you. Will you please forgive me?"

"Of course I will my Love."

We stood there for what seemed like an hour. Both of us refusing to let go. Words were not necessary, we were communicating with the inaudible music and lyrics that can only be heard in the redemption of love.

"Joshua?"

"Yes?"

"I think I finally know why you love me."

"Oh yeah, why is that?"

"It's because you choose to. Every moment you put my needs above yours and you see me the way I could be, not the way I am. And because your love for me isn't about what I do or who I am. It's really about who you are," she says with an understanding that she had not been able to grasp before. "Thank you Joshua."

I can tell something has changed in her, but I feel like there is so much that I just can't see yet.

"Do you think things will ever be like they used to be?" She says still holding onto me tightly.

"No, I don't. But I don't want things to be like they used to be. I want something new, something better than before. And honestly, I think that the journey we've been on is probably the very thing that will give us that chance. The kids miss you. You really do hold the key to bringing us all together. Come on in."

This moment was the most amazing time of restoration I have ever experienced. People talk about things like Reviving a city and Reforming a country, but what took place that night was unsurpassable by any of those things that we have ever seen take place on the earth. Tonight, I witnessed my Bride return into my arms after being led astray by her fears. After being held in bondage to lies and deception. She threw away all the comforts and chains that he held her with and chose to lay down everything to be with me. I don't know that there exists a word that could describe what took place that night.

Chapter 21

I wake up to an empty bed. I look around but there's no sign of Bridget in the room. Where is she?

I look out the bedroom window across the backyard and see her walking with dad around the lake. I can see the peace surrounding her as she seems to be just taking it all in.

I head downstairs pour a cup of coffee and take a seat at the table.

"Hi Joshua," she says as she walks in the back door, still feeling somewhat hesitant around me.

I stand up, pick her up off of her feet and twirl her around as I hold her tight. I know it may take a little bit of time for her to realize that she has not lost my love for her, but I want to do everything possible to help her regain that confidence.

I can feel her smile as I place her back on her feet.

"Joshua, can we talk sometime today?"

"Sure thing, how about now?"

"Ok, sounds good," she says.

We head out to my hammock chair and although normally I wouldn't share my favorite spot, I pull her onto my lap and hold her tight. This feels so amazing. I have waited so long for this.

"So, what's up?" I ask.

"Well, I was talking with your dad this morning and..."

She spent the next hour telling me all about what happened. She cried almost the entire way through and apologized repeatedly. I already knew most of this stuff, but I could tell she really needed to get it off her chest and bring everything out into the open. She then shared with me what dad had told her about Ralph and what needed to happen next.

"Are you sure you want to go through with that?" I asked, knowing that this would be incredibly painful.

"I have to Joshua, it's the only way I'll ever be truly free."

I knew she was right, but I couldn't make her do this. She was the only one who could make this choice.

"Ok, Bridget. Then I will stand right beside you."

"You will?"

"Sure I will," I said with deep compassion.

"But it's not your fault, you didn't do anything wrong."

"No, I didn't, but I told you a long time ago, that I would never leave you or turn my back on you, and that promise doesn't change in different circumstances. I love you Bridget, and I will stand with you."

As she reached her arms around me and laid her head on my shoulder, I could feel the purity of love once again emanating from her. I could tell she really was getting it. She can not earn my love.

"Bridget?" I asked.

"Yes, Joshua," she said sitting up to look at me.

"I think we should stay up here for a little while."

"Sure Joshua. If you think it's a good idea then I trust you," she said with a smile as she laid her head back down on my shoulder.

Trust is the key to relationship. The deeper the trust, the deeper the opportunity for the relationship. But without it, there is no chance of intimacy.

108

Epilogue

My journey is one of love not just because I have a great love story; but because I choose love in the midst of each circumstance. The choice of love is what makes for a great story. However, it's not just a feel-good kind of love. It's the kind that looks more like being willing to wait when it looks like the whistle has already been blown, and using all your strength to show kindness, especially when it's not deserved. It's the kind that doesn't get jealous and isn't walking around all like, 'Hey, look at me.' It's not defensive or only worried about what it will get out of the situation. It's not focused on how it's been offended and trampled on. It looks away from things that are bad, but celebrates and lifts up the true things in life. It's strong for itself and can also carry others. It never gives up hope, or it's beliefs. And it never stops, or quits. It never fails.

And if I had to do it all over again,
I would.

She is worth my life.

S

BOOK TWO

A girl named Bridget.

Chapter 1

A smile of release spreads across my face as I sit back in my seat and lean my head against the headrest. This is what I've been waiting for. The windows down, with the white center lines flashing past me like the memories of my life story. The soothing sounds of the radio mixed with the background of air flowing in and out of my car windows. It feels like a dance, and my heart is ready for a good dance session.

I left home 15 hours ago, pulled over for a short nap at a rest stop and am now officially five hours away from the new start I've been waiting for since I was six years old.

My mind turns back to that night, and off my tongue rolls these words like a poem,

"Six years old.

Six years old is too young.

Too young to lose everything."

It's funny that I've avoided talking about it for all these years, and now in the seclusion of my car as I'm about to start new, start fresh, this is what flows out of me.

It is the pain that shaped me to my very core. My parents had dropped me off at my friend Rachel's house to spend the night, so they could go out on a date.

We ate pizza for dinner and then ran up the stairs to Rachel's room to play with her new toy horses. After a little while I heard a knock at the front door and then some talking. The other woman's voice sounded like my Aunt Abbey, so I peeked out the door of Rachel's bedroom and down the stairs. It was my Aunt Abbey. I was surprised to see her there. I could tell she was crying, and as she talked, both she and Rachel's mom seemed to become more upset. Rachel's mom called up the stairs for me to come down. Something inside of me told me that this was the last moment I would feel the way I did. That everything in life would change the moment I reached the bottom of those steps. I had the thought of just staying up there in that bedroom and playing. Staying carefree to all of life's troubles, that I didn't realize could exist, would have been a better choice than what I was about to walk into.

I remember in that moment my thoughts being drawn to my parents and all of the love I had experienced with them. You know, a lot of people don't have any years that they can remember in their life with loving parents. I think that even those people have this dream somewhere inside of them that it's actually possible to have people truly love them. For some, it's buried deeply under the rubble of pain and tragedy, but inevitably it is still there. It's like instinct for us as humans, as if it was built into our DNA.

My dad was such a good man. So loving to me. I always had a place in his heart and his arms. I remember being so upset at times, but he could always get me to laugh in the midst of my anger or sadness. He would take me on dates, and for the night I was a princess. In fact, whenever I was with him I knew I was a princess. Some of it was his confidence in me, but most of it was the confidence he carried about life and himself. He didn't seem to have any fear about what others thought, and during those foundational years he instilled that in me.

My mom was more soft spoken, but when she truly believed something was in your best interest she was more than happy to share it with you in multiple ways. There was this time she was trying to encourage me to clean my room, but I was refusing. I was only four years old, but I had the will of a child much older and I was determined to hold my ground. Well, she convinced Aunt Abbey to dress up in a disguise and then told me that the room judges were on their way and that the cleanest room on the street would win a trip to the water park. I ran to the window, looked down the street and saw this lady dressed in all white walking toward

114

our house. The disguise fooled me, and I started cleaning up quickly. I won that trip, but I found out the next week about their trick. I knew to be on the look out from that time on. My mom was a little sneaky, but there was no doubt in my mind that it was because she loved me so dearly. I don't remember being very rebellious in those years. I had my moments, but I was so led by love, that I wanted to be in connection with them all the time, and I didn't want my bad decisions to cause a division between us. I just wanted to be close to them.

I was shaken out of my fond memories by Rachel's mom now trying to holler up the stairs in the midst of her crying. "Bridget, um, can you please come down."

I remember one last thought passing through my mind. I am so thankful for my parents.

I ran down the stairs not sure what I was walking into, but pretty sure it wasn't good.

"Hi Aunt Abbey, what are you doing here?"

"Bridget, can you get your things together? We need to get going. I'll tell you what's going on in the car," she said through sobs.

"Sure, Aunt Abbey." I think I knew that it was best to just follow her lead on this one, even though I felt like five more minutes of waiting would cause me to explode. I ran upstairs, hugged Rachel, and grabbed my things.

Staring out the window when receiving bad news seems like the most natural response you can have. It was raining as we drove toward the hospital. She explained all that had taken place. The accident, and the miracle that they were still alive. But that the doctors were unsure as to what would happen.

We arrived at the hospital and I completely forgot to pull my hood up. As I stepped out into the pouring rain, for some reason, I didn't mind. In a strange way it was comforting as my tears and the rain from above commingled down my cheeks. It felt like somehow I wasn't alone in this tragedy.

When you find yourself walking down the hallway of a hospital in a situation like this, your steps never seem to be quick enough. You don't know if waiting for the elevator for those two minutes is the difference between saying goodbye or not being there in time, and every doctor or nurse you see walking toward you makes you wonder if they are carrying your bad news.

Aunt Abbey was holding my hand so tightly. I glanced up at her. I knew this was just as painful for her as it was for me. My dad was like a father to her also. And my mom, well, they were best friends. I pulled her hand down so that she turned toward me and I held out my arms for her to pick me up. I was a child, and I knew at that moment I needed to be held like a child. It is crazy to think back on those moments and what was going on in my mind. I was only six and yet I was doing these things without realizing exactly why. It is as if human instinct brilliantly shows up and takes over, directing you even when your brain doesn't seem to have the ability to process an overload like this one.

A nurse saw us and seemed to know who we were. She walked to us and graciously directed us to room 2911. I buried my head in Aunt Abbey's shoulder as we stepped into the room. As we neared the side of the bed, I turned to see my mother lying there; she seemed at peace, but I knew things weren't the same. This whole thing was life altering, not just for me, but for her as well.

Aunt Abbey followed the nurse to the door and had a conversation with her that I was unable to hear. She hung her head then walked back to the side of the bed.

I was too enthralled with my mom to take the time to see if Aunt Abbey was okay. I leaned over the side of the bed and kissed her cheek. "I love you Mommy," I said whimpering. She smiled. I knew then that she would make it. I just knew it.

I glanced around the room, then blurted out, "Daddy?" I took off running. I just had to find him. As I reached the door, I heard Aunt Abbey call, "Bridget, wait."

I stopped at the door and turned to see her shaking her head as she placed it in her hands. "Bridget, come here sweetie."

"No, I'm going to see Daddy. I have to see him," I said as I began to fall apart.

"Bridget, I'm so sorry."

There are no proper ways of doing things in these moments. As humans we don't have the ability to handle these things, our souls are just not wired for them. I fell to the ground. I don't remember walking again till the day of his funeral. They must have taken turns carrying me around. When you are so broken by tragedy, it's impossible to recover to what you were. You simply find a way of existing that is different, and limping along, you find ways of living within the painful realities, until your callouses are thick enough or your wounds are uncovered and miraculously healed.

Chapter 2

I look down to find my favorite track and field t-shirt soaked from my tears. Written across the shirt is the name 'Warriors'. I don't feel like much of a warrior. "Maybe a wounded warrior," I say out loud as I let out a laugh. After that tragic day, I became known as the child who lost her father. (My wound became my identity.) I was handed pity wherever I went and from whoever heard my story.

I think some people relish pity. It makes them feel like people care about them. I would've traded all the pity in the world just to have him back again.

Things were not just different because I no longer had a father by my side, my mom was forever changed. She would never walk again in her lifetime. And because of the impact to her chest, her voice was never able to be heard above a whisper. Although this made things difficult, I was grateful for her whispers. I remember pushing her wheelchair out onto our back deck, and helping her into our hammock to look at the stars. I would lay next to her and she would tell me all about Daddy. We would both cry as she told stories that I never knew. She would always end those times by saying, "Bridget, you have a good father, you may not be able to see him, but his love for you will carry you through what his presence is not able to." And then she would ask me how I was doing with everything, and I would say, "I'm ok, as good as can be expected." She would smile at me with that smile that says, 'It's ok honey, it takes time.' And I would bury my head in her shoulder and let out another gallon of tears.

I was ten years old when I buried my mom. By that time I felt so numb I wasn't sure how to let out my emotions. My Aunt Abbey became my caretaker, and although she did her best to care for me, I didn't want another mom. Besides, for a large chunk of my life till that point, I was a mom to my own mom and I became really good at all sorts of life skills. I was a hard worker, and I didn't mind the responsibility.

I began to run when I was 12 years old. It started out as just something to get all those emotions worked out. I found that the more I pushed my body the more sorrow was released. At least enough for me to make it through another day.

Somewhere around the age of 14 the track coach at our school drove up next to me while I was out for a run and asked me if I had ever considered joining the team. I told him that running was a personal thing and I didn't really want to be on a team.

He actually missed his calling in sales, because by the end of the week I was wearing one of their jerseys and running my first race.

My favorite was the mile. It is the perfect combination of endurance and speed. You have to be able to push yourself continually for a long time. If you go too fast in the beginning you won't have anything at the end. My coach said I was a natural. What he didn't know was that each time I reached the last lap something in me would turn and I would begin to run to get away from my pain. Deep down I knew it was impossible, but it did make me run really fast. A long time

I quickly became a star athlete at our school. My aunt was so proud of me. She would run up and down the fence at the track like a crazy lady cheering me on. I think she believed this was the thing that was actually healing my wounds. It was certainly an outlet, but I was still so raw inside. Like a devastated city after a tornado has ripped through its structures. I remained a little girl, broken inside, who had never been rebuilt.

But that is why I am here, in this old Ford Escort on my way to a new beginning. At least I hope that is where I am headed.

119

As painful as it was for Aunt Abbey, she knew I needed to find myself and a clean slate somewhere. Heading out west is somewhat surreal. It feels like a well-worn storyline. It's where so many treasures have been found. There are stories of people leaving everything behind, some in search of something and others just being drawn. I feel more like I'm being drawn than searching for something, but if I can find some sort of a purpose in life, then I would be satisfied.

I smile as I pass a sign that says 100 miles to my destination, a small town in Northern California. A place where they say the mountains reach high up into the bluest sky you will ever see, and the rivers and lakes wrap themselves around hidden treasures like a bow around a gift.

Thankfully Lucy, my friend from high school, had relatives who agreed to take me in and help me get on my feet.

two hours later...

Driving through a new town can fill you with such wonder. I wonder who is the wealthiest? Who is the poorest? Who is the kindest? And who I should stay away from? What's the best coffee house? Or where is the place I can go and hide with a good book? Where do people go to get away from the busyness of the town?

It seems that whenever we find ourselves in a new place we naturally evaluate it based on the things we find comfort in. We rate places and situations according to the amount of good feelings they give us. I guess in a lot of ways it's a one dimensional way of looking at life, but it is what comes natural to us.

120

Chapter 3

As I pull into Dave and Mary's driveway, they open the door and walk out to greet me.

"Bridget, we've heard so many good things about you. We're so glad to have you stay with us while you are getting settled here," says Dave with a sincere kindness in his voice.

Mary steps forward and gives me a hug that reminds me of the embrace of my own mother. "Oh sweetie, we are so excited to have you here. Please don't be shy. Let us know if there's anything you need."

"Thank you, thank you so much, this is so kind and generous of you guys to let me stay here."

"I'll carry your bags in, just show me which one's to grab, and you'll be staying in Linds… I mean in our guest bedroom," says Dave.

I see him glance at Mary with a smile that looks like it has an ounce of pain in it.

He leads me upstairs to a bedroom decorated with flowers and pictures of ballerina's.

"This is it," he says as he sets my suitcase on the bed and turns to leave. He stops at the door and turns around. "Thank you Bridget."

"For what?"

"I'm not completely sure yet, I just think there's a purpose to you being here with us, even if it's just for a little while. Mary and I needed… someone else around," he said as a tear began to form in his eye. With that he turns to leave.

"You're welcome, Dave," I say as he walks down the hallway.

"You can call me Uncle Dave," he hollers back.

That was interesting. I'm really intrigued as to what is going on here. Lucy didn't talk much about Dave and Mary. Just that they would be cool with me staying here.

As I look around the bedroom, I can't tell if it was decorated in the hopes of someone staying here, or if it was for someone who had stayed here before me.

As I lay down on the bed a thought passes through my mind, 'Did I really just do this?' With the battle of anxiety and exhaustion raging inside of me, exhaustion finally wins and I give way into a deep sleep. The kind of sleep that feels like it could change the direction of your life forever.

later...

I'm awakened by a knock on the door.

"Hi Bridget," says Mary as she peaks her head in the door. "Dinner is ready, would you join us?"

"Oh, sure, that would be great. But you don't have to make me food. I'm just so grateful for a place to stay. I really don't want to impose."

"Trust me Bridget, you are not imposing one bit. We would love to have you eat with us. As long as you are with us, you are family," she says with a smile.

"Ok, I'll be right down. And Mary?"

"Yes dear."

"Thank you, I didn't realize how big of a transition this would be, but your hospitality is so helpful."

"You're welcome dear," she says smiling.

two weeks later...

I just got a job at a grocery store. It's not much but at least it's a start. Dave and Mary continue to amaze me with their generosity and kindness.

Last week Mary asked me to go out with her and ended up practically buying me a whole new wardrobe. She said it was just something she wanted to do for me. And a few nights ago, Dave asked me if I wanted to grab an ice cream cone with him. He took me to his favorite spot and we sat outside at a table overlooking the river. We spent over an hour just talking about life. He asked me all sorts of questions. The kind of questions that a father would ask his daughter. I haven't felt that kind of care and concern from a man since I was six.

After dinner Dave built a fire and we all sat in the living room with a cup of tea enjoying our patch quilt family.

"Uncle Dave, can I ask you a question?"

"Sure sweetie, what is it?" he said smiling.

"I'm all about being kind to people and helping people out, but you both just seem to be, don't take this the wrong way, but too nice. When I first got here you said something about there being purpose in me being here. I don't understand. I mean I'm eating your food, staying in your house, and if that's not enough you guys take me shopping and out for ice cream. How is me being here of any benefit to you guys?"

As they looked at each other I could see them exchange a thousand words, but I couldn't read one of them.

"You know Bridget, I uh, I mean, it's probably time we tell you about..." his voice trailed off replaced by the sorrow that only comes with death.

I know that look, I know this smell in the air. The pain in your throat that seems to pour down into your stomach. No, deeper than your stomach, your soul. On the verge of weeping he stands up, apologizes, and walks to the kitchen.

Mary looks at me with the same pain I saw in his eyes.

"Bridget, did Lucy ever talk about her cousin, Lindsey?"

"No, not that I remember."

"Well, it was a long time ago. Dave and I had a little girl years back. She was our precious gift. You should've seen Dave with her. He was, well, probably like how he's been with you. She was our only child. We had tried and tried to have a baby, but just couldn't get pregnant, and then this one little miracle was given to us, and she was born. She was perfect to us. When she was five she began to have some strange symptoms. We took her to the doctor and found out that she had Leukemia. Dave fought that diagnosis with everything he had. We did all that we could, and a year later, it just wasn't enough," she said, now staring through the window toward an oak tree in the back yard.

"I'm so sorry, Mary. Do you mind if I ask when that was?"

She looked into my eyes through the tears in her own. "Twelve years ago."

"Oh my," realizing what this actually meant.

"Bridget when Lucy told us about you, she also mentioned your parents, and well, it just seemed strange that your parents passed on around the same time that our little girl did. We just wondered if this whole thing was being orchestrated somehow. If there was some part of healing that was coming for all of us through you being here. We don't want to scare you with any of that. Just know that you are filling up a place in our hearts that has been untouched and well, wounded, for a very long time."

I stand up and walk to the kitchen to find Dave standing in front of the sink looking out at the same tree that Mary was just looking at. As I look closer I see a homemade swing hanging there. It looks worn, not from use, but from years of hanging.

"Uncle Dave?"

"Uh, yeah, what is it honey?" He says as he wipes the tears off his cheek and turns toward me.

"I'm so sorry," I say as I bury my head in his chest and begin to weep for both of our losses.

He wraps his arms around me like only a father can and we both cry.

A short while later Mary joins us and we all stand in the kitchen somehow finding more healing while embracing our pain. Strangers, bound together by a common pain within a moment of time that could not be orchestrated by chance.

Chapter 4

fifteen months later…

One of my favorite places at Uncle Dave and Aunt Mary's is the swing in the back yard. I spend hours out there just feeling the wind pass by me and watching beauty in motion. Every once in a while I'll look over toward the window and see them watching me. In some way the void that was in me is being filled, and I think the same is true for them.

Work is going good overall. I wouldn't say it's my dream job, but it is a good start to whatever is next. You know how you sometimes feel like there is purpose in something that you're doing even though it looks like it is directionless? That's how it feels there. Working at a grocery store isn't necessarily a ticket to the top, but I just have this feeling that it's a stepping stone to my future.

As I get my uniform on I glance down at the clock.

"Shoot, late again," I say as I grab my purse and run out of the house toward my car.

It's a cool fall day, and I wouldn't say it's a bad day, but I do feel a bit overwhelmed by my thoughts. As much as it is helping being here with Uncle Dave and Aunt Mary, I still have so many questions. There's still so much I don't understand about why my life has looked like it has. I find myself somewhere between this balance of gratefulness for what I have and confusion over what's been taken from me.

I walk into the grocery store one minute late for my shift. I think that's pretty good, but Maggie, my manager, has a look that says something else. She spends the next few minutes telling me about why punctuality is so important. She then goes on to critique me on my uniform being wrinkled and whatever other flaws she can find. She also references my bad attitude. I want so badly to tell her that my bad attitude is a result of her lack of people skills, but I refrain.

I thank her for helping me learn the right way and head to my register to begin my day.

A few hours pass and I find my mind daydreaming about what could be next, in between customers.

"Excuse me, Miss?"

I hear as I am looking down counting the money in the drawer of my register.

"Yes, what can I help you with?"

"Actually, I was going to ask if there was anything I could help you with?"

"Can you tell I'm having that bad of a day?" I say smiling.

"From about a mile away," he smirks. "You know, I used to tell people that there were no such things as bad days, just bad perspectives on situations within a day."

"I don't know about that one. I've had some pretty bad days in my life, and I'm not sure there is a possible perspective that could turn those days around."

"Ah yes, pain. Pain and bad are two different things. A painful day, now that is unavoidable. But a bad day means that it is void of anything good. It's like saying that there can be no light in the deepest darkest cave."

"But isn't that true, the whole light in the cave thing?"

"It sure is true. That is until I bring my flashlight down there," he says with a smile.

I let out a deep sigh and look into his eyes. Here it is, another moment where I'm six years old, staring into the eyes of my father. Something whispers to me, "I love you Bridget."

Instantly I'm back, days before the accident. My dad had taken me out on a special date. I had dressed up and was so excited. He took me out to a fancy restaurant and we dined like a king with his princess. That was the night he gave me the ring. I looked into his eyes and saw his love for me. "Why?" slips out of my mouth before I can stop it.

Joshua's dad looks at me and says, "My child, you have endured much pain in your lifetime. I can see it in your eyes."

My eyes were wide open at this point. Am I really that easy to read? No, I can't be. I've trained myself to not show emotion. After all, I know it is much safer to not wear vulnerability like a name tag.

"I'm actually doing really good. Yeah sure, I've had some pain in my life, but who hasn't? I'm just glad to be alive, you know?" That was a close call, but I covered myself pretty well and I'm sure he will be wishing me a great rest of the day any second now.

He looks at me with eyes that say, 'I understand'. How could he possibly understand? No one could ever understand what I've been through. No one has any idea what not having a father in your life sets you up for. The manipulation of people, the lack of identity you feel, the abuse. There's no way he understands.

"Bridget."

"How did you know my name?"

"I'm an angel sent from God," he says as a huge grin formed across his mouth, while pointing to my name tag.

I couldn't help but laugh. He must've sensed I was getting worked up.

"Bridget, could I buy you lunch? I've had plenty of times when I needed a listening ear, and maybe I can be that for you."

"Well, I'm not sure if..."

"How about I go pick out some food for us, and we can sit at the picnic table right over there across the parking lot?"

"Ok," I say, questioning my own sanity. I don't know this guy, but strangely, I trust him. Something inside of me wonders if he might be able to help me.

"Great, I will wait for you at the picnic table."

A feeling begins to open up within my heart. It is strange but familiar. The same feeling a little girl gets when she is waiting by the door for her daddy to get home from work. Anticipation of something good. I felt this a little bit with Uncle Dave, but not as much as right now. I didn't choose this feeling. It's as if it has somehow been planted inside of me.

As we sit at the picnic table I laugh as I look at the food he picked out. It definitely isn't what I would've chosen. But as I begin to eat I find out that I like a whole lot more than I ever realized. I had gotten used to eating the same old things and not wanting to have anything extra in my life. I wonder if that's because I grew up feeling like I didn't deserve anything extra?

"Well Bridget, let's talk about pain," he says smiling.

At this point I thought he expected me to spill my guts about all that I had been through in life. The years of agony and loss, and the years of foolish decisions that only added up to more loss. But he wasn't asking me to say anything. Instead he began telling me of pain after pain that he has experienced in his lifetime. About being betrayed by his closest friends. About broken commitments and promises people made to him. And about so many times that he had given to people only to see them turn around and use him for more. He told me how an employee started a revolt because of jealousy and led a third of his company to split off and start a new venture. He also told me about how he had almost lost his son years ago. At this point he stops. Up until now he had a smile on his face - a look that said, 'Can you believe these people actually did these things?' He didn't seem mad at all. In fact, he seemed somewhat amused by it. But when he told me about his son, his countenance abruptly changed. I could see a deep pain from the tragedy of it all.

"You see Bridget," he says drawing a circle onto the table with his finger, "pain cannot be avoided; but if you are to heal from it and move outside of it, then it must be embraced."

"But how do you embrace something that's lost?"

"My dear, nothing is ever truly lost. Sometimes things in life just take on a different form. Our loss of people isn't as much about the person as it is about what the person was carrying and placing in our lives. The love that is given through that relationship is really the thing that is so painful to lose and go without. It's not that losing people isn't painful, it's just that the key to healing from loss comes from an understanding of what that person represented. If we're paying attention, that love can actually be given to us through another avenue, or person. Your loss of your parents wasn't a death sentence to you ever experiencing that kind of love again. I actually like to think of those situations as opportunities to see a miracle happen. Not the kind of miracle where your car is totaled and you walk away without any harm done to your body. The kind of miracle where there was no hope of you receiving the thing you needed in order to have an abundant life, and then somehow one morning you wake up, take a deep breath and realize you have it."

"Wait, how do you know about my parents?" I ask.

"Bridget, I'm an old man who's been around quite a bit of pain. And I've been around long enough to recognize when a child has lost their parents. A lot of times the child had little to no healthy connection with their parents. I don't see that in you. It seems to me like your parents were pretty special people."

"They were," I say as tears try to break over my eyelids.

"Would you tell me about them?"

I spent the rest of my lunch break sharing stories that I had never shared with anyone before, with this old man who had been a stranger 45 minutes ago. Somehow, in a ridiculously short amount of time, he became like a father that I had lived so many years without. It seems so weird that I would open up like this, but when you are faced with goodness, it seems as if the only thing you can do is surrender to it.

He sat there with such care in his eyes. He was listening beyond my words. Somehow he was listening to my heart.

Glancing down at my watch I realize I need to be back to work.

"Thank you so much for lunch, and for everything," I said with a lightness now flooding my heart.

"It was my pleasure Bridget," he replied. "Bridget, would you do me a favor?"

"What is it?"

He went on to tell me about his son, Joshua, and how he would love for me to meet him. He even gave me a picture he had of him, from his wallet. He said that he would get Joshua down here to the store, but just wanted to know if I would be willing to meet him.

I agree and put the picture in my pocket. He does look kind of cute and, if he is anything like his father, at least I will have someone in my life that genuinely cares about me. I could use a good friend.

Chapter 5

Meeting Joshua was amazing. It had rained earlier that morning and there was a slight fog overlaying the parking lot. The air was crisp and so fresh. As I walked toward him I couldn't help but notice him shivering a little bit.

"Are you ok?" I asked.

"Oh, yeah, I'm fine, just enjoying the coolness of the day," he said smiling.

I noticed there were raindrops all over the table except right next to him. I smiled realizing he had dried off a spot for me by sitting there, which was why he was now shivering.

There is a confidence that he carries. Well maybe it's not so much like him carrying it as it is a part of who he is. His gentleness reminds me of his father and his compassion makes me feel like a treasure. How is it possible that with most people you feel good or bad after you spend time with them, but with certain people you feel something deeper than emotions? I wouldn't have considered myself a spiritual person, but that's the only thing that seems to explain our time together. It was kind of like when someone has an umbrella in a downpour, and they invite you to stand with them underneath it. For some people, they're just glad to be out of the rain, but for me it was the outstretched hand, that spoke to my heart saying, 'I will walk with you, and I'll even keep you dry along the way.' What a blessing.

I am not really sure that he will want to spend time with me again. I mean, I don't really know how I would benefit his life. But I do hope I get to see him again.

two days later...

When you think something is happening and then you have to wait for it, it shows the level of peace you have in your life. Joshua made me wait two days before he called. I know two days doesn't sound like a long time. But, when you get a glimpse of having something that your heart has been dead to for so long, it seems like an hour is an eternity. Multiply that by 48 and you can see that the past two days have seemed like a lifetime.

I've grown accustomed to not allowing certain parts of my heart to come back to life. I'm not sure if there is any other way to survive. Honestly, it hasn't been difficult. The majority of people that come into your life have their own hidden lives that they don't want uncovered, so it's like this unsaid mutual agreement that allows us all to be friends on a level that's comfortable for everyone. But that's not the case with Joshua and his dad. They are somehow different. The way they talk to me makes me want to lay everything out in the open. I actually want to be transparent when I'm around them. For the first time in a long time I want to be known.

Joshua is taking me to play miniature golf tonight. It sounds like fun. Most guys just go for the typical dinner and a movie, but I can see that he actually wants to spend time getting to know me.

He should be here any minute and I am determined to be ready on time for our first date. Being late can happen for dates four and on, but it's really important that you're ready on time for the first few.

The unique knock at the door startles me.

I can hear Uncle Dave greet Joshua downstairs.

"Hello there, you must be Joshua."

"Hello sir. Yes I am."

Haha, this is great, I'm sure Uncle Dave is enjoying this part of life that he didn't think he would ever get the chance to experience.

Last look in the mirror and here I go. Deep breath.

"Hi Joshua," I say trying not to sound too excited, as I walk down the stairs.

I grab my sweater out of the closet and we head out into a beautiful fall evening.

I start to think about how much I love the fall as I look at the trees passing by outside of Joshua's Jeep. It is, by far, my favorite season. Some people think that fall is just preparing you for the doom of the winter, which will bring in cold and dreary days. But I like to think of it as the grand finale in a fireworks show. It's cool enough for a sweater, but usually not too cold to make you want the heat of summer. The colors on each tree appear to be placed strategically by a master painter. And the best part… Fall drinks at my favorite coffee house.

"Bridget, would you be up for a coffee?" he asks.

What is up with this mind reading family? Seriously? I wonder what his mother is like.

"Sure, that would be great," I respond, trying to hide the smile on my face.

As we pull up to the drive thru window at the local coffee shop my best friend Gabi slides open the window. I met Gabi at the coffeehouse shortly after I got here. She has been one of those true friends. The kind that will laugh with you, cry with you, and tell you how skinny you look when you're having a 'fat day'.

"What can I get for you two? Bridget is that you? Is this the guy?" she says unashamedly.

"Hi Gabi, this is Joshua," I reply with an, 'I can't believe that just happened' glance at Joshua.'

He just smiles. I'm sure he'll bring that one up later.

"Two of your fall specials to go, please. Gabi is it?" he says.

"It is, Joshua," she says with a giddy voice that is completely unique to Gabi's personality. As she walks back to the counter I look over and see Joshua smiling.

I just continue the laughing inside of myself. Gabi really is special to me. Sometimes I joke with her that she was assigned to be my friend in order to keep me sane.

She arrives carrying two to-go cups with smiley faces drawn on the outside.

"Oh, and these are on the house," she says as she looks at Joshua.

"You don't have to do that, Gabi," he replies.

"I know, but I want to support your future together," she says smiling, knowing that only she can get away with saying something like that. "Bye, bye now you two. Have a great night."

"Thank you Gabi," Joshua says, as he puts his Jeep into first gear.

"Bye, Gabi," I say and smile as we pull away.

"Well, she seems like a very good friend," Joshua says grinning as he takes a sip of his coffee and shifts into second gear.

"Yeah, she really is," I smile.

I didn't realize what I was getting into, but Joshua is apparently an avid miniature golfer. He's also very funny. More like a cute funny. Most guys on the first date will try to have this cool persona that they portray. But I don't feel any of that from him. I don't think he feels the need to try and impress me.

"Alright," he says, "two more holes to go and winner buys ice cream."

"Nice. Well judging by the score, that will be you buying the ice cream."

"Never underestimate my ability to let you win," he says with a wink.

Two holes later and the final score is obvious.

"I told you that you were going to win."

"You just seem to know everything," he says with a grin. "C'mon, let's go get some ice cream."

"You have quite the sweet tooth, don't you?" I say smiling at him.

"Bridget, there are plenty of things in this world that taste bad. When you find something that is sweet you better grab a hold of it. In this case, I will be grabbing a hold of some Reese's peanut butter cup ice cream. What will you have?"

"Um, I'm honestly not sure what I'm in the mood for."

"You look like a Tuity Fruity kind of girl to me."

"What's that supposed to mean?" I reply.

"Oh, just that there's a whole world of flavors and you strike me as the kind of person who would like to experience all of them at once. Tuiti Fruiti is definitely the kind of ice cream that fits people like you."

"I see. I actually play it pretty safe and like to stick to the things I know."

"Maybe that's just what you are used to doing? I wonder if there's not a whole other side to you?" he says, smiling at me.

"Well, if you stick around long enough maybe you'll find out."

"Deal," he says with a smile.

As we sit at a table in front of the ice cream shop watching cars drive by, I find myself so relaxed. So at peace with being here; at being with him. I don't know that I've ever felt this comfortable with a guy friend before.

As we get out of his Jeep at Dave and Mary's, he walks me to the door and thanks me for a wonderful evening.

"Joshua?" I say as he turns to leave. "Do you really think there's more to me?"

"When I look at you I see an undiscovered world. I see a beautiful horse with a free spirit that is waiting for the ability and moment to break away from her past and run headlong into fields of freedom."

"Yeah, I have quite the past."

136

"So does everyone, but you are the only one who can decide whether or not to walk the road toward freedom and healing."

I sigh. "Thank you Joshua. I've been needing a friend like you."

"Me too," he says smiling.

That was such a fun time. I didn't feel any pressure to be something that I'm not. Although in some ways I had a tough time being anything. I think one of the problems with building all these walls in my life is that while I was keeping people out, I was also keeping myself in. I realized tonight that I don't even really know who I am.

I wonder, is this really safe? Will this end up like every other relationship I've had? Are his words what carry his integrity, or will his character show that what he says, is really who he is? I know that only time will tell.

I don't feel like I have much to offer him and I'm not really sure what he sees in me, or at least what made him pursue me, but I really hope he doesn't stop.

Chapter 6

It has been three months since Joshua and I met.
Although it is such a short time, I feel as though I know all
that I need to know about him, in order to make this decision.
I don't think it's always about knowing every detail or way
that a person is; it's more about knowing their character and
who they are no matter the circumstance. I have to say he's
pretty amazing.

Tonight he proposed to me. I know this is crazy. It goes
against all of my rational thinking to choose to commit my life
to someone after knowing them for three months. I remember
hearing people say 'they just knew'. I think I finally
understand that. I know that this decision doesn't just hold
my desire to have a husband, it somehow holds my path to
freedom. To coming alive. To finally being healed. Of course
I said, "yes!"

It was such a romantic night. He took me up to his
parents' farm and took me out on a four-wheeler excursion
through the woods and up on top of one of the surrounding
mountains. It was everything my heart had ever desired. As
we sat there looking out over the valley below and watching
the setting sun display its wonders against a blue sky canvas,
I felt at home. There have been few times in my life that I
have recognized or felt that feeling, that sense. But this was it.
This is what it feels like to be home.

He spoke to me about love. Love beyond how we feel.
Love far greater than a moment or a word. He told me that
love is a decision that flows out of who we are. He told me so
many things that he saw in me. Things that I have a hard
time seeing. I wondered if some of them were true. But
looking in his eyes, I know that somehow he can actually see
them. Being loved is an amazing thing. I cannot imagine life
without him. Why would anyone not want this?

"Joshua, I want to give you something," I said as we both gazed across the painted sky.

"What is it Bridget?"

He always seemed so excited by anything that I chose to give to him. He placed such a high value on my gifts. Much higher than I thought they were worth.

"Joshua, before my dad passed away, he took me on a date and before we left the restaurant he looked at me with such love in his eyes and handed me this." I pulled off the necklace that was around my neck and slid the ring that was now too small for my fingers off of it.

"He told me all the reasons he loved me, but as he handed this ring to me, he told me that there was one reason that was the most important reason for his love for me. Because I was his." At this I started to cry. "Joshua, I haven't felt like I truly belonged anywhere until I met you. You made me believe that I belong somewhere again. I am your's Joshua and I want you to have this ring so that you'll always remember that."

"Bridget, you are my treasure. I would sell all that I have for you, and I can not wait to start our lives together as one."

"Me too," I said with feelings of elation overwhelming my heart, as I leaned into his embrace.

two months later…

We decided to have the wedding up on the farm. Aunt Abbey came, as well as some other friends, including Gabi my maid of honor. She is the best person I could think of to stand beside me today.

What a beautiful winter day it was. Uncle Dave walked me down the aisle, which was so special to me. Even though my dad wasn't there to see this, I knew that I wasn't at a loss. As we stood there, face to face, I knew that something divine

139

was taking place. I can feel the weight of the promises that he is handing to me. I am so excited to be his. This is truly the new start that I had come out here looking for.

I could tell Aunt Abbey was so excited for me to find him and asked us to visit her soon. I think in some ways it was a burden off of her to know that I had found the thing that I really needed in life. True love. She told me that my parents would be so happy for me. I knew she was right. She and Joshua's Aunt Darra were like peas in a pod. Aunt Darra came up to me after the wedding and hugged me. She told me that if I ever needed anything I should just ask and that she would love to help. I find myself overwhelmed with gratitude at all that I've been given.

We had a literal feast after the ceremony and everything was absolutely delicious. Joshua's mom is an incredible cook and didn't spare anything for this day.

Most girls plan their weddings and have every detail of what they want it to look like and feel like, planned out. I honestly hadn't given much thought to it, until recently. Before I met Joshua, I didn't think that I would ever find someone that I really wanted to be with, but now I know I could never find some one else that could do what he has done for me. As for the wedding plans, I realized that I didn't need to have all of it planned out for it to be perfect. It was just right, not because everything was exactly what I had wanted, but because I was able to see the true meaning and purpose of it all.

Chapter 7

As the sunrise illuminates our curtains, I begin to open my eyes to a new day. Not just a new day, but a new life. This is one of those moments in your life where everything changes, in a good way!

I look over to find that my new husband must have snuck out of the bed before me. A moment later, the inviting smell of fresh brewed coffee hits my senses, and I am more than willing to get out of bed. I put on my fleece pants and a hoodie and venture out to the front porch to find my lover and my friend sitting in his chair sipping his coffee. It is a fresh winter morning, but by noon it should warm up a bit.

"Hey there, beautiful," he says as he stands up to kiss me. "I'll be right back."

I sit down and gaze out at the amazing view that he has prepared for us. Joshua is quite handy. The day after I said that I would marry him he began working on building this cabin on his parents' property. He spent so much time on making it the perfect fit for us. It was rustic, yet comfortable. The first time he showed it to me, he took me around to all the things that he had built, just for me. And it was wonderful. Little details that I didn't even know I would love to have. Like a large bay window above the sink overlooking the lake. A clawfoot tub in the bathroom. And he even built a small loft with a couple chairs placed in it, which made for the perfect get-away for getting lost in a book.

One of my favorite parts of this place is the front porch. It overlooks the east arm of the lake. It's very secluded from the rest of the property, which is especially important for the beginning of your marriage, but it's also a haven for wildlife.

"Here you are," he says as he hands me a cup of coffee.

I sit there for just a moment and breathe it all in. This is surreal.

"So what did you want to do today?" I asked.

"Well, why don't I take you someplace new?"

"Always with your secrets. I thought you had showed me everything already?"

"Think of them more as surprises for the journey of life. If I told you everything now, then life would be pretty boring. What would you like for breakfast?"

"Oh no, I can make breakfast. After all, I'm your wife."

"You can make breakfast tomorrow. Today I get to serve you. How does banana pancakes sound?"

"With peanut butter!" I said with a giggle and a full heart.

One of the things I love about Joshua is that he never expected me to do anything that he wasn't first doing. He loved me first, he wrote me a book first, and he made me breakfast first. There's something special about having an example to follow. Especially for me. So much of this relationship stuff is so foreign to me. It has been his gentleness and patience with me that has helped me learn how to love him and other people in a way that seems to come so naturally to him.

"As you wish," he said as he peered out the kitchen window to see if he could catch my smile.

After breakfast we walked up to his parents' house and hopped on the four-wheeler. He had a backpack that he had packed with what he called "provisions." He's such a stinker sometimes. Like when I catch him eating chocolate, and he says, "Uh, nothing, just eating some veggies." There's a childlikeness to him that you don't see often. He loves playing games and surprising people. So as I sit behind him on the four-wheeler, I unzip the backpack to find lunch and our bathing suits.

"Ha, caught you. You're taking me swimming." I slug him in the arm.

"Ouch, does love always hurt this much?" he smirks.

"Sometimes worse. But do you really think now is the best time to go swimming? It's pretty cold, and well, winter," I say as I wrap my arms around him and rest my head on his back.

"Just trust me," he replies.

We reach a clearing that just about takes my breath away. I have never been here before.

"Joshua this is amazing, how come you've never brought me here before?"

"We weren't married before. This is a family secret, and what if you dumped me before the wedding? Next thing I know you'd be selling tickets to bring people out here," he said smiling.

My eyes seemed as if they would burst as I gazed around this lush meadow filled with grass and wildflowers.

"Joshua, how do the flowers stay in bloom even when it is this cold?

"This whole lake is fed by hot springs, and it lets the water out through streams that run through the meadow. I guess it keeps the flowers warm enough to stay open all year."

As we near the edge of the lake I raise my gaze upwards trying to find the top of these granite walls rising like the spires of a castle fortress. My eyes finally reach the top as the strong and bold gray of granite pierces into the soft blues of a sun-filled sky. And in this moment I'm reminded of how small I am. Joshua points to midway down the cliffs and there is the most beautiful waterfall pouring into this small pristine lake like a stone pitcher releasing all that it has without fear of if there will be more. I wish I was that fearless. I'm always afraid if there will be more. More money, more strength, more time with the ones I love.

"Hey there. You okay?" Joshua says as he looks back at me and can tell I'm in the midst of some deep thinking.

"I have never seen anything this beautiful. Thank you Joshua, this is amazing," I say knowing that my insecurities and fears are my own, and all he needs to know about are the good parts.

"This has been a place of refreshment for me throughout my entire life. There were moments when I didn't feel like I could go on, and I would come out here for the day and jump in the water, and something powerful would happen. And now, my love, it is yours also. I know it will be refreshing to you just as it has been to me."

I squeeze my arms around him even harder. "Thank you Joshua, you're the best."

We spent the day swimming and relaxing in this paradise. This is one of those times when every muscle in your body finally releases its tension and the sigh that comes out of you isn't just a physical thing. I feel blessed. In fact, I feel like that lake; refreshment and warmth, peace and love, are crashing into my soul.

Joshua is laying on his side on the sandy beach and I am sitting beside him as he glances back at me, "Bridget, I'm so excited."

"For what, Joshua?" I ask.

"To spend my life with you."

"Me too." I can't help but smile. When you are living surrounded by love, it's easy to feel like a changed person.

The rest of the week is so relaxed. He calls this time together up here our honeymoon. It's different than what I thought it was supposed to be. Most people go to some exotic location and have moments during the week that seem like they should be in a travel magazine, but somehow this seems just right for us. He actually told me that he had enough money saved up to give us a honeymoon for a year up here. I'll be honest. The idea of not having to work for a year and being able to get to know my new lifelong partner sounds pretty good.

Chapter 8

My eyes open to a glimpse of sunlight cresting the Eastern mountain range. I glance over to see that Joshua is still asleep. Yes! I'm up before him. I slip out of bed quietly and head to the kitchen to make coffee for my prince. I stretch out my arms like a bear who's just awoken from hibernation. Ah, the morning stretch. I love it. I grab my coffee and head out onto the porch. It is so quiet out here, so peaceful. I could easily spend the rest of my life up here. As I glance down the hill toward the lake I see Joshua's dad walking. "This is a good morning for a walk," I say to myself. I put on my shoes and walk down the hill toward him.

"Good morning, Ed!" I say, hoping that I'm not interrupting a special time.

"Hello Bridget, my new daughter. Please call me Dad."

My heart sinks as I think about the last time I used that name.

"Okay, Dad," I say somewhat hesitantly. "Do you mind if I walk with you?"

"I would love that," he says with a smile.

As we walk around the lake I begin to ask him what he thinks about all sorts of life questions. He reminds me of this cross between a wise old sage and the cool old man who still rock climbs and seeks out adventure. But the thing that draws me to him the most is his gentleness. This is where Joshua gets his gentleness from.

I feel like I can talk to him about anything. As I ask him about my past and all the confusion and pain in the death of my parents, he reaches over and puts his hand on my shoulder, pulling me in close to his side.

"Bridget, explanations for pain don't always heal pain. Finding a reason isn't always the answer. Sometimes a single situation is too horrific to be covered by a simple thought or understanding. Bridget, I don't think your healing will come in an instant. There have been many years of you living with that wound. There may be many steps that need to be taken to come to a place of being truly healed and freed from the trauma of what you experienced. And even then, the pain may still remain. You see, pain is not the evil. It is simply a reality that is found in this world. However, the way that evil tries to control you by using the pain, now that is the problem."

"I'm not sure I understand. I mean, I'm sure I need to grow in a lot of ways, but just being here and married to Joshua, I already feel like I've changed so much."

"You have, my dear," he says as he chuckles and gives me that fatherly look. "I'm so proud of you for taking the steps that you've taken, and so glad that you are in our family now. Just don't allow yourself to be discouraged by the length of the journey toward freedom. It is a journey, but that doesn't mean it's a bad thing. You live in a world that is so much more comfortable with instant results than time and process. If you are going to get where you're supposed to be, it will take time."

"So, you don't think there's an explanation that will help me to understand why my parents died when I was a child?" I said hoping that the answer to my healing was something that I could understand.

"Bridget, do you see that mountain over there?" he says as he points north toward a peak with three spires rising from the summit like towers.

"Yeah, that's one of my favorites."

"I think that your process of healing from the pains that you've been through is like this. You began your life on top of that mountain. It was beautiful and stunning from up there. But then a life circumstance that was beyond your control carried you down here. If you will agree to the journey, then you will stand back on top of that mountain. It won't be easy, and at times you will question its worth. There may be times when you turn around and start hiking back down the slope. But if you refuse to give up, you will regain all that was lost. You see, the journey is what actually allows you to receive the reward. It miraculously gives you the ability to hold the treasure that's waiting at the end. Sometimes you'll find yourself running full speed and gaining so much ground. At other times you'll be crawling on your hands and knees. And there may even be times when Joshua will have to carry you. But I see in you such a determination, such a resolve to be up there again."

"But how long does something like this take?"

"Time is such a funny thing, Bridget. I don't like to live all bound up by time. When you get caught up in the 'when' of life, you will usually find worry sneaking around in your mind. The journey may take a month or it may take years. But you have to be willing to surrender to the process and trust that the journey has a necessary purpose.

By this time we have circled the lake and are back in front of the cabin.

"Thank you, Dad," I say with a smile as I give him a hug and a kiss on the cheek.

Is this too good to be true? The little girl that has been hidden behind her pain for so many years has longed to be called a daughter. I am that little girl and even an ounce of love in that empty bucket feels like I might just overflow.

"Oh Bridget, thank you," he says as I watch a tear form under his eye. "I've always wanted a daughter and you are such a special blessing to me."

As I walk up from the lake to the cabin, I see Joshua sitting on the front porch with his cup of coffee in his hand. He holds it up as I get close.

"Now this is good coffee, thank you." He smiles.

"For you my love, anything," I say as I sit down in his lap and wrap my arms around his shoulders.

"How was your time with my dad?"

"It was really good. As many questions as I have about life, I just feel like being around him is what really brings a peace to things."

"I understand. And I'm sure you'll figure it out along the way."

"That's pretty much what he said," I said laughing.

They are so much alike. And yet I feel like they are both so individually important to me and this journey I'm on.

"Bridget, is there anything that you feel apprehensive about with all of these changes? You know, getting married and moving and it's all so new for you."

"No, I don't think so. Everything is so exciting to me. I don't think I would change anything. Why? Is there something I should be worried about?"

"No," he chuckled. "I was just wondering where your heart is."

"Oh, that's easy, it's right here," I opened his hand and pointed to the center of his palm. Then I leaned forward and kissed him.

"You know, you are pretty special," he said.

"That's what they tell me," I say with a smile. "What are we going to do today?"

"I was thinking that we would drive into town and spend the day down there."

"That sounds great. I'll go get ready."

Chapter 9

As we drive down the dirt road away from the farm, I am once again amazed at Joshua's ability to navigate his way to the highway. Each time I've driven with him I've tried to pay attention to where he's going, but it's so confusing and my mind can't seem to keep up with it. He always seems to know just where he is. I'll either figure it out sometime or have to get really good at staying right next to him.

As we near the town, I can feel myself getting excited. I feel like a new person entering an old world. I'm excited to see my friends from the grocery store, and I can't wait to stop by and see Gabi at the coffeehouse.

We pull into the town square and park.

"Hey, are you up for walking through the town instead of driving?" He looks over at me and says.

"That sounds great to me."

I have so many memories of this place. It was my escape from a life I couldn't seem to find healing in. And it was also the place where I found a new beginning.

As we begin to walk we see a few people we recognize who smile and wave. We head over to the coffeehouse first to see Gabi. She squeals as soon as she sees us walk through the door. I love this girl. So full of joy and never embarrassed to show it.

"Oh my goodness! I am so excited right now. I can't believe you guys came to visit me. Listen, it has been so boring here since you left. Seriously, it's like you took the party with you when you left town. But enough about me, how are you guys doing? Newlyweds, ha, I bet you're doing great," she says, nudging Joshua with her elbow.

Gabi has always been a talker. Kind of funny that her name is Gabi. But she has also been such a good friend. Not the kind that just wants you to feel good, but the kind that cares about you enough to call you out on the hard stuff. I can tell Joshua feels a little awkward from that interaction, but I can't help but laugh.

"We are doing good, Gabi. The cabin Joshua built for us is perfect and yes, we are enjoying getting to know each other," I squeeze Joshua's hand and smile at him.

This is my new husband and I feel so proud to be his. Gabi seems so excited for me. She wishes us both the best and tells us to come back and visit soon. On our way out she offers us a cookie. I'm not very hungry I tell her, but Joshua just smiles and receives his with gratitude. I love this man, and all his little nuances.

We stop by the grocery store and say hi to some of my friends and then continue to walk around the town. Joshua tells me some of the history of the town and shows me some of the landmarks. It's funny to live in a town as long as I did and not know some of these stories. He tells me about the days when his dad was voted in to be mayor. And how everyone was so excited about it.

"I wish I could've been around then. It seems like it was a completely different town."

"It really was," he said. "There was so much more kindness among the people. They would help each other at the drop of a hat. It wasn't a perfect town, but it was a great one to grow up in."

"Do you think it could ever be like that again?" I ask.

"I don't know Bridget, it would take the people caring again. And I think it would take people changing their perspective on what good truly means. So many people equate good with how something or someone makes them feel. But there's so much more to goodness than that. It's about having pure qualities and characteristics. It's about people truly putting the needs of others above their own, and being willing to go out of their way to serve one another. Everyone wants to live in a place like that, but not many people want to do the work it takes to create a place like that. They want the benefit without the cost."

"That makes sense. Hey maybe someday they'll hire you to be mayor."

He just looks at me with that, 'yeah right', look.

"Seriously Joshua, I think you could help this town become something wonderful again. It could be just like what your father did."

"Well, nothing is impossible, but for now all I care about is being your husband," he says as he puts his arm around my waist and pulls me close for a kiss.

We get back to the cabin before the sunset so that we can watch it from our front porch. We eat a quick dinner and spend the evening sitting on the porch swing and reading.

As the sun goes down Joshua heads into the cabin and I can hear him rummaging through the kitchen drawers. He walks out with a box of candles and says, "Let's just do candlelight tonight."

I love the way he creates adventure within the normal things of life. It's the simple things that he does that turn a usual, and potentially boring situation into something so special. He loves creating memories: the kind that you know will stay with you throughout your lifetime.

Chapter 10

I wake up to the smell of coffee. He beat me again. It has become this friendly competition to see who will get up and make the coffee first. I honestly don't mind letting him win every morning. I just figure I better get up early every once in a while to keep him feeling like the competition is still going.

As I walk out onto the porch I'm greeted with a smile. I snuggle up next to him and breath in the feelings of all of this. I'm not oblivious to the realities of marriage. I know that there will be times that we disagree and even times that we struggle, but there is something so sweet about this season. I want to try and capture every ounce of it.

As I glance down the hill to the lake, I see Joshua's dad on his morning walk. Joshua looks over at me.

"Go ahead," he says with a smile.

"No, I'm good here with you."

"Bridget, there's something about spending time with a good father, and he just so happens to be one of those. We may not always live up here on the farm, so take advantage of the time you can have talking with him."

"Okay, you don't have to tell me twice," I say, smiling as I grab my shoes and run down the hill. He gets it. He sees I have this hole in my heart that should've been filled by my own father. And now I just feel so blessed to have the opportunity to spend time with his dad.

"Hi, Ed... I mean Dad."

He smiles. "I know, that's a tough one to get used to for anyone. How is my favorite daughter doing?"

"I'm your only daughter," I say smiling.

"Which is why I can say you are my favorite. No fear of making another child jealous," he chuckles.

I can't help but wonder what walks with my dad would be like if he were still around. What would my life have looked like as a teenager, and even as a young adult? I was so happy when Uncle Dave offered to walk me down the aisle. I felt sad that my dad wasn't there, but I was so grateful that it worked out the way that it did. I could see Aunt Mary crying through the whole ceremony. Again we found ourselves in a moment that there had previously been no possibility of.

Dad and I spend the next half hour talking about love. He explains to me so many things that my ears hear, but I'm not sure my mind has the capacity to fully grasp. I mean, he's talking about stuff that feels opposite to the way I've understood life. And definitely different than I see everybody around me living.

"Bridget, love isn't something that can be grasped by your mind," he says. "It's something that can only be grasped by something that is like itself. You have to be able to receive love first and that takes a capacity that you can't just will yourself to have or that you can earn."

I have such a tough time fully grasping what he's saying sometimes. I feel like someone just threw a whole bunch of seeds that hold the truth inside of my heart, and now I have to wait till they take root and begin to grow. I wonder how long that kind of thing takes?

He goes on to explain to me that love is not something that can be earned. It exists outside of the realm of an economy and has more to do with the giver of love than the receiver of the love. He also tells me about how intimacy is earned, but not by what we bring. He says that gaining intimacy is actually about what we surrender. The more we give up the more we receive of closeness in our relationships. But without understanding the truth about love first, intimacy cannot happen. It all seems so foreign to me, yet it makes so much sense when I think about it all.

Over the rest of our time in the cabin, I have many conversations with Dad about life. It really has been a season of growing for me. I already feel healed in so many ways. It's like my life got a do-over and I'm now experiencing the things that I thought I had lost forever.

I wouldn't trade this time for anything. It has been so wonderful. But I am confident that as good as this has been, our best years lay ahead of us.

Chapter 11

When we knew it was time to leave the cabin and move into town, we started looking for an apartment to live in while we saved up enough money for a house. We found the perfect place, and during that time Tory was born.

Tory was our first blessing and she was a feisty one. I remember Joshua picking her up and running around the apartment yelling, 'Quick she's about to blow', whenever she got riled up about something that was upsetting her. He never seemed bothered by the fact that she was so strong-willed. I asked him once if it frustrated him.

He just laughed and said "No way. I'd way rather have a daughter that has a strong will. It may be trouble for me now, but when she becomes a teenager it will mean pain for any boy who tries to mess with her."

As quick as we could, we saved up enough money to buy some land. Joshua started building our house right away. He worked so hard to get us moved in. The house was perfect for us. It wasn't huge, but neither of us wanted that. The views from the back deck were breathtaking and the style of the house spoke more of our personalities than a specific style of design.

After we had finished moving into our new home, we started spending our weekends up at the farm visiting Mom and Dad. They loved seeing Tory. Inevitably, Dad and Joshua would head down to the lake to go fishing, while Mom and I would stay back and play with Tory. This was really the season of my life where Mom and I began our friendship. It's not that we didn't get along before, we just didn't spend a lot of time together. But now, having more one-on-one interactions, I see things in her that I wish I had gotten to experience growing up.

She is so kind. I've heard horror stories of mother-in-laws, but I am so thankful for mine. It probably helps that I don't have a mother of my own. It makes me want her to be my mom all the more.

I tell her about all the things I'm learning as a new mom and she just listens and smiles. She doesn't try to control me, and even when she tries to give me some advice, it's never overbearing. And the best part of our time together is hearing the stories of when Joshua was a kid. He seemed like a handful. After hearing those stories, whenever Tory had one of her justice episodes I would glance over at Joshua and say, "Did you want to clean up your mess?"

He would just laugh. "Okay, I know she gets it from me. But that doesn't mean that I caused it."

After we had Ben, life became so different. We found ourselves getting into rhythms we had never expected. I wouldn't say we became the typical family with kids, but our life seemed a little less adventurous. Every month or so, something would stir in Joshua and he would announce, last minute, that we were to all grab our sleeping bags and head to the car. We would then drive in the dark to some spot way out in the mountains and set up camp. It seemed like he knew just when to throw one of these trips into the mix. There were times when none of us were very excited about it, but by the time we got to our camping spot, we would all be singing and laughing.

I started running again about six months after I gave birth to Ben. It was something I grew to love. I felt so good after a run that I couldn't help but do it. I would head out in the morning, run five miles, then get ready and take the kids to school. It just felt like the perfect start to my morning.

I became religious about running and I felt great because of it. I've been running for about eight years, but about a month ago, while running, I felt a sharp pain in my lower back. It seemed very strange to me, so I just walked the rest of the way home. The next day everything seemed fine. This went on for another few weeks or so. I would run for

156

four days and then, out of nowhere, this pain would force me to stop and walk. I began to experience the pain throughout my daily routines, so I decided it was time to tell Joshua about it.

"What do you think we should do?" I ask.

"What does it feel like?" he says with an obvious concern.

"I don't know, it's sharp but only when I am making a certain movement. It makes me think I just tore a muscle or something."

"Yeah, that could be. Why don't we give it a day of rest and then tomorrow if you still feel like it's not getting better let's go see Ron at the clinic."

"That sounds good. I'll just take it easy today then."

"Perfect, I'll grab pizza on the way home," he says.

"Thanks honey."

"You're more than welcome, I love you," he says as he places his hand on my back, and kisses me.

After about four hours of lying on the couch it seemed as if everything would be fine. I didn't feel any pain, and I began to think that a strained muscle could definitely cause that kind of pain. I then remembered working in the garden a few weeks ago and stretching in a weird way reaching for the shovel. Yeah, that was probably it. As I looked around the living room I took a deep breath, and thought about all the things I was thankful for.

Somewhere around two o'clock I realized the kids would be home soon and thought I should get up and get a snack ready for them. As I walked into the kitchen the pain shot into my back and straight up my spine. I barely made it back to the couch. After that I decided that I should probably just stay here for the rest of the day.

As I lay here trying to stay as still as possible I'm not sure what to do with all these thoughts. Or should I say, fears. Fear has been like a close friend holding a knife in my back, and I can feel it as I lay here, holding my hand and caressing my forehead.

"Ahhh," I yell out. "God, why now? Why me?" I release as I begin to sob trying my hardest not to move.

I hear the kids running up the sidewalk and laughing. I do my best to wipe off the look of crying from my face.

"Mom!" yells Tory

"Hi Mom," says Ben as he comes over and kisses me on the forehead. "You doing okay, Mom?"

"Yeah Ben, I just needed a day off my feet."

"Oh man, me too, they made us run the mile at school today. All that running stuff is for the birds, well, probably more like ostriches."

I begin to laugh. He can always get me laughing.

"So, how was school you two?" I ask.

For the next 20 minutes we talk about their day.

"Why don't you guys head upstairs and finish your homework before your dad gets home with the pizza."

"Pizza! Sounds great Mom." they say and head for the stairs.

I wait for Joshua as patiently as I can and when he finally walks through the door I feel at peace again.

"Hey honey, any better?" he says as he walks over and sits on the edge of the couch.

"Well," I begin to tear up. "No, I can't seem to move much without the pain, I tried walking to the kitchen and it was not good, and I um, I'm scared Joshua."

"I know baby," he says as he puts his hand on my arm and kisses my forehead. Sitting down beside me, he looks into my eyes and caresses my hair, and in that moment his love and peace overtake all the fear and dread that had just before been too much for me to handle.

"Hey, let's enjoy tonight and leave tomorrow to tomorrow, ok?" he says.

"Ok, I'll try my best," I say, but I know that will be easier said than done.

Chapter 12

"Thirty-two years old.
Thirty-two is too young.
Too young to lose my life."

...rolls off of my tongue as a whisper as Joshua turns the key, starting his Jeep.

Terror is a good word to describe my feelings as Joshua led me out of the doctor's office. I wouldn't consider myself a hopeless or fearful person, but when you receive news like this, it becomes really difficult to have any rational thoughts.

Joshua is trying his hardest to be encouraging, but I honestly can't hear it right now. There's too much noise in my head from the diagnosis I've just received.

"Bridget!" he says for the third time as he pulls out of the parking lot.

I glance over with tears about to overflow from my eyes. He pulls into the next parking lot and shifts the gear into park. He pulls me over onto his lap, wraps his arms around me and holds me as we both begin to cry. In moments like these it's not always about fixing the problem, or getting rid of the painful thoughts. It's about holding someone through the pain; helping them know they aren't alone. Thankfully Joshua knows this all too well. This isn't the first time he has held me through pain.

When I was pregnant with Ben, our doctor thought there might be complications. It had something to do with the abnormal position he was in. They weren't used to delivering a baby in this position so they handed us the fear that either Ben or I would not make it. Joshua, of course, handed the fear right back to them, thanked them for their concern and told them he was confident in their ability to handle the situation. I, on the other hand, held on to a little bit of that fear and it nearly ate me alive. It wasn't until a few days later that Joshua noticed something was going on inside of me.

"Bridget, what's wrong?" he said, giving me the chance to open up with what he already knew I was struggling with.

"Joshua, this whole death thing is... I can't do this. I lost the two most important people in my life when I was a kid, and now our son? This seems cruel. It's just wrong. I should never have gotten pregnant again, one child was enough of a blessing. Why, after all that I've been through? Why can't one thing be easy?"

Joshua doesn't make it a practice of answering my verbal processing. Instead, he likes to answer my questions with questions of his own. It drives me nuts sometimes. But I think he sees what my need in a moment is better than I can.

He sat down beside me, put his arms around me and looked into my eyes.

"What else are you feeling?" He pried, trying to make sure I got out all of my processing at once.

"Well, a lot of things." I went on to explain my feelings very convincingly to someone who seems unable to grasp the concept of worry.

I told him that I didn't think he was very concerned for me. He quickly called me out, and reminded me that showing concern for someone and allowing them to be overrun by fear are polar opposites.

We spent the rest of that night mending wounds from my past. He is one of the most patient people I know and I'm sure I've added some patience to his storehouse.

Ben came into this world without any complications for him or for me, and in the end there really wasn't a need to let fear be a part of the situation.

But this is different. This is more serious, and there's more at stake. I can't die now. This isn't supposed to be the end. We are still at the beginning. I've lived so much of my life in bondage. I can't die before I reach freedom. I just have to experience it on this earth. I have to know what it feels like to be healed in my heart and, now also in my body.

The doctors told us that they would be monitoring me every three days to see how I was doing. But, if my levels dropped below a certain point, they would have to admit me into the hospital.

one month later...

I'm sitting in our reading room. It's the one room in our house that Joshua and I both wanted the most. There's a wall of books with one of those ladders that slides across; that was my idea. It has five different types of chairs, including a hammock chair hung from the ceiling; that was Joshua's idea. There is a large window that overlooks the backyard and has a beautiful view of the mountains in the distance.

I can hear Tory and Ben playing in the family room. I can't believe Tory is going to be ten years old this month, and Ben will be seven in the spring. Wow, time really has a way of slipping between your fingers. I'm feeling good in my heart with this whole thing. But not so good in my body. I'm starting to have some pains that aren't normal to me. I'm sure it's just me fighting off this disease. The doctor's appointment went well this morning. They ran their normal tests and told me that if these results came back the same as the others they would move my appointments to once a week. I would be glad for that. It has only been a month of twice-a-week appointments but it's already wearing on me.

The phone rings, and I can hear Joshua answer it.

"Oh, okay. I will, uh, we will. Yes, goodbye."

"Is everything okay, honey?" I holler down the hall. He doesn't answer. Instead, I can hear his footsteps coming down the hall. I sit up in the lounge chair to see him walk through the door with a look that is full of emotion.

"This is it, huh?" is all I can get out of my mouth.

The tears flood his eyes as he falls onto his knees in front of me and buries his head in my lap. I pick up his head, and look into his eyes.

"I have to do this, Joshua."

"I know, but that doesn't make it any easier," he says.

There isn't fear in his voice. It's something else. We both knew the time would come when I would need to go into the hospital, we just weren't sure how long we would have or if some miracle would happen along the way. It's definitely not fear in his eyes, what is it?

It's sorrow.

"I'll go get my things and call Gabi to come watch the kids," I say.

The car ride to the hospital is quiet. Joshua turns on a CD of songs he wrote for me to encourage me through all of this. We sit there, hand-in-hand, and I try not to let my feelings in. I actually have all the tools from my past in order to walk through this. I became very good at building walls and shutting down emotions throughout my teenage years. I can feel that part of me rising up again. I don't know if that's good or not, but right now it seems necessary.

We arrive at the hospital and I get settled into my room. Joshua talks with the doctor and asks what we are to expect over the next few days. I actually don't feel that bad right now. Maybe this will be a quick in and out hospital visit, and I'll be back to normal in a few days.

Chapter 13

the next day...

This morning was rough. The medicine they have me on makes me feel so nauseous and there is this pain in my lower back that seems to get worse with each minute that passes. Just yesterday, when I got here, I felt like I could go out for a run and now I feel like I'm bedridden. Joshua is bringing the kids in at lunch time with one of my favorites: chicken verde burritos. He knows exactly what I like.

My two little rays of sunshine run into my somewhat dreary hospital room.

"Mommy! Mommy!" I love the sound of their voices calling out my name.

"Hi sweeties, come here."

They jump up on the bed and give me hugs, which sends a shooting pain throughout my lower back. I do everything I can to hold back the sounds of pain that are coming out of my mouth. Joshua hurries over and helps them off the bed while they look at me with the look that says, 'everything is now different'. I hate this. I remember that same feeling with my mother. I never wanted my children to feel that. It is a worse pain than what I'm feeling in my back.

"I'm okay kids. Really, I must have just been sitting funny."

They slowly come back to the side of my bed and I reach out my hand to touch Ben's face.

"My sweet boy. I love you so much."

"I love you too, Mommy," he says with that sheepish grin he often gives me.

"Tory, are you taking care of your father?"

"Seriously Mom, do you think we would be here if I wasn't?" she says with a grin.

I motion for her to come close so that I can whisper something in her ear, and then saying it just loud enough for Ben and Joshua to hear.

"Tory, hide the chocolate from your father!"

We all laugh out loud.

Joshua picks up Tory and spins her around and says, "Tory, don't listen to your mother. I'll share it with you," he smiles.

"Who's ready for burritos?" Ben says excitedly, holding up the bag of food.

"Joshua, can you help me up?"

"Sure thing."

I head to the bathroom to begin what would be a huge part of my sickness. I'm sure they can hear me throwing up in here. And I'm positive I won't be able to keep any food down today.

"Babe, is there anything I can do for you?"

"No, I'm fine. Can you take the kids out for a picnic and then come back when you're done?"

"Sure Babe. We'll be back."

"Come on kids, let's head outside for a picnic," he says trying to muster up a strength that I know he's not feeling right now.

"But what about Mom?" Ben asks.

"We'll come back after lunch, Bud."

"Okay Dad." I can hear the sadness in his voice.

I am not a victim. I don't want to be a victim. But everything seems to have been stolen from me in an instant. Can't I just have a meal with my family? Why does this stuff happen to people? Why is this happening to me? Maybe if I was like a murderer, this would make sense. I have lived most of my life helping other people and not doing the bad things that almost everybody else does. Sure, I'm no saint, but I don't think I'm so far from one that I deserve this. I spend the next half hour on the floor of the bathroom fighting with my emotions and a whole lot of self-pity.

As my nurse helps me back to my bed, I determine in my heart to not let my children see my struggle. As they come in the room they are hesitant. I can see it in their eyes. They are not sure how to be with me. Kids are not built for the change that is required in situations like these. Well, I guess adults aren't really either; but we seem to be able to manage and cover what we're feeling a little bit better than they do.

Joshua announces movie time and he plays one of our favorites on the television in my room. We all laugh together at our favorite parts and, of course, Ben narrates most of the way through. He is such a funny boy. I love that about him.

As I lay here with my kids snuggled up against me and Joshua sitting in the chair beside me, I begin to think about this room.

After we got married, Joshua told me that everything he had was now mine. That in a marriage we are one, and he didn't want anything separating us. I felt the same and so we joined our bank accounts and did everything necessary to start our new life together. I begin to cry as I realize for the first time, that this isn't Joshua's hospital room, and it's not even our hospital room. It is mine. This is not his or even our journey through sickness. It is mine. I know he will walk beside me, but it's not his. Tears fill my eyes and pour down my cheeks.

Chapter 14

I have been in this hospital room for three months now. Thankfully, the doctors think I may be able to go home in a few days if my levels stay where they are now. I will have to have a nurse come in and check on me every day, but I am so ready to be out of this room. I'm grateful for all that the doctors and nurses are doing for me, but this place feels like a prison most days.

Joshua should be here any minute. He has visited me every day. He is so faithful. I honestly don't know how he is taking care of the kids and the house, and working full-time. He doesn't seem overwhelmed, just in a constant state of concern for how I'm doing. But it's weird he doesn't seem near as concerned about how my body is doing as he does about how my heart is doing. On days when I've told him I'm ready to give up and I just want to be done, he holds me and weeps. He reminds me of all that's worth fighting for in my life.

As he walks through the door he tells me how beautiful I look today. Sometimes I have a hard time believing that he sees anything that looks good in me. I wonder, if I were him, would I be able to see anything good? Ever since we met, he saw more in me than I did in myself. I know it has been a struggle for me to receive it, but I also know that this is a part of my healing and freedom.

"Hi honey," I say with a smile on my face.

"Ah, a good day, I was just about to tell you that the weather report for today was sunny with a high chance of good. But obviously you already heard that." He smiles at me with that look that says, 'We can make it'.

The doctor walks in the door with his clipboard and a smile. "You Miss, are doing great. How would you like to go home today?"

"Really!" I can't hold back my excitement. "But what about waiting the three days and all?"

"Your tests from this morning are better than we expected and I'm not sure staying three more days is in your best interest. You will still have a nurse visit daily and will need to come in for treatments once a week, but I think this will suit you better. What do you think?"

"I think yes!"

Joshua is obviously in a state of shock, as am I. I'm not sure if it's excitement on his face or terror because he didn't get a chance to clean the house. We embrace each other and I can see the tears begin to well up in his eyes.

"Happy tears," he whispers and smiles.

I am elated the entire drive home. Like kids, we plan out how we are going to surprise Tory and Ben. Joshua comes up with a plan to go in the house and tell them that their Christmas present for this year is in the Jeep and if they go now to get it they won't have to wait until Christmas. I see them as they bolt through the front door and toward the Jeep. As soon as they see me in the passenger side seat their eyes widen.

Ben jumps into my arms as soon as he reaches me and starts kissing my face. Tory falls down in the grass beside the Jeep. She sits there with her face in her hands sobbing. I don't think I realized how this had affected her. She tends to keep things in, much like me. I squeeze Ben tightly then walk toward Tory and sit down beside her in the grass. I am weak and still in pain, but I muster the strength to pull her onto my lap and hold her like a mother should be able to hold her children. I comb through her hair with my fingers and whisper into her ear, "My sweet Tory. I am here. Just let go baby, let it out. Mommy's here." I can feel the tension that she's held from these last three months release and she is again at peace.

"Mommy, please don't ever go away like that again."

"I'll try not to, Tory." How do I answer that? I'm not in control of this. This is what I struggle with the most. It is absolute torture to walk through this pain, but it's even more painful to know what this is doing to my kids.

the next morning...

It feels so good to wake up in my own bed. I can't say I slept very well last night, but I'm so grateful to be home. And feeling Joshua lying next to me gives me such comfort. The nurse should be here in about an hour. I think I will try to get a shower and get ready.

"Joshua, I'm gonna jump in the shower."

"Uh, babe, you might want to step in, jumping isn't the best idea just yet."

"Very funny," I respond, catching my smile in the reflection of the mirror. I haven't seen myself smile in quite some time. Wow, I've lost a lot of weight. Unfortunately, I don't look very healthy. However, I finally feel strong enough to hold myself up, this feels so good. This pain in my back though, it seems to be getting worse. Oh No! Not now. I begin to lose consciousness and the only thing I can feel is the impact of my body against the floor.

"Bridget! Bridget!" Joshua is yelling right in front of me as I come to.

"Um, Joshua, yeah I'm here, I'm okay."

"Just lay still, don't try to move. Tory, call Gabi and ask her to come over right away."

"Okay Daddy," I hear her say before the weeping overtakes her voice.

"Bridget, you are going to be okay, just stay with me." I can hear him talking on his phone, but everything still feels so foggy.

"Yes, I need an ambulance at..." he says to the dispatcher as I drift in and out of consciousness. I only vaguely remember the ambulance ride to the hospital.

three days later...

"I've seriously been asleep for three days?" I ask Joshua. That doesn't seem possible. Questions flood my mind.

"It's okay, Bridget. There's nothing to worry about. I'm just so glad you're awake now."

"Joshua, what happened to me? The doctor said I was getting better, what happened?" I want to be angry, I want to cry, but I feel too weak to do anything except just lay here.

"Well, it seems that although you've been getting better, there has been a tumor this whole time that was wrapped around your spinal cord that they just were not able to see until now. This is what was causing the pain that they attributed to your disease at first."

"Oh." I pause for a second trying to figure out the ramifications of all this. "Well, isn't that good? They found it, now they can do surgery and get rid of it, right?"

"I guess..." he says before pausing.

I know this look. It's the same one my Aunt Abbey gave me at the door of my mother's hospital room. "Is this really hopeless?" I blurt out.

"No Bridget, it isn't hopeless; but the doctors can't do surgery yet because of the location of the tumor. If they did, there's a good chance that you would never walk again. But if they wait, they can actually begin to separate the tumor from your spine over time and then the surgery to remove it will be possible."

"Okay, well at least it's not hopeless. How long are we talking?"

Silence.

"Joshua, how long of letting this thing grow? Please tell me."

"Nobody knows for sure, but they think it could take two years to get to a place where they can safely remove it."

"Just kill me." I turn to the window as tears stream down my face.

"Bridget, you are not giving up, not now. Yes, it's a long time, I know, but I will walk every single step with you. Bridget, I can't lose you," he says as he begins to choke up.

"How bad is the pain going to get?" I ask, still staring out the window.

"I don't know. They said they will do their best to help you manage it."

"Do you have any idea how bad this hurts." I'm yelling, but I'm not angry at him, I hope he knows this. "Joshua, I was supposed to be better, and now you're telling me two years of enduring pain. Pain that might be worse than I've experienced already. I cannot do this!"

He walks around to the other side of the bed and kneels down in front of my view of the window and says the only thing that could possibly be said in a time like this.

"I love you Bridget."

As he gets up and walks out of the room I use the last of the strength I don't have to whisper, "I'm sorry."

Chapter 15

One year later...

When you find yourself in the middle of a hard road, everything seems insurmountable. I never tried to be a negative person. In fact, I would consider myself a pretty positive person with all that I've been through. But I find myself feeling like the more time goes by, the deeper I fall into desperation. How can you fight depression when it feels like a mountain that's too big for you to climb or even see the top of. The only thing that feels concrete in my life is the fact that I still have a long and painful road ahead of me.

Over the last year, Joshua and the kids have visited daily and I have noticed myself becoming more and more of a shell. The pain is so great most of the time that I have to stay on my pain medication. But that causes my thinking to be a bit cloudy.

At this point, I have one goal. Survive. There have been plenty of times when I've tried to throw that goal in the trash. But those are usually the days when Joshua shows up with flowers, or the kids bring a card they made that tells me how proud they are of me for fighting this fight for them. I can't imagine doing this alone. They are a source of encouragement that keeps me going.

I almost can't believe it's been a year. It feels like I've lost so much time. It's like I went on vacation for a really long time and I wonder what things will look like when I get back home. One year down. If the doctors are right, I have one year to go. I can do this.

I wonder what the damage will be to me after all this is finished? Everybody seems to think my body will be back to health after this tumor is removed. But what about my mind? There has been this constant stress on me. Some days I literally feel like I'm going crazy. I'm actually amazed that I can still have coherent thoughts at least some of the time.

I remember one day when I was in extreme agony, and my back was throbbing so badly that my whole body seemed to be echoing the pain. Joshua was sitting right beside me with his hand on my side.

He just kept saying, "Don't give up, Bridget. Don't give up. This will pass."

In the midst of the pain, when I could barely breathe, I yelled out, "It feels like I'm being tortured."

He just sat there at the side of my bed, as tears began to stream down his face. He knew he couldn't take this pain away from me.

But even in the midst of my worst pain, when I'm sure he feels my anger being directed toward him, he just stays right beside me, believing that the peace he carries will overtake everything that is against me and inside of me.

I know what it's like to walk through this from my perspective. But I often wonder what it feels like from his. I think this is why sometimes, I just want to die. His life would be so much easier if it weren't for me. Finally, after years of being married to him, I felt like I had something to offer him. I finally began to feel like I wasn't just a burden that he had to carry all the time. And now this. I just want to come to a place where I can say truthfully to him, "I know why you love me."

He is so much more determined to beat this thing than I am. He posted quotes and stories all over my hospital room about people who fought impossible battles and won. Somehow he knows I will make it through this. But I'm not sure he understands the mental and emotional damage I will carry as a result.

My days go on like clockwork. I wake up around 8:30 a.m. and eat breakfast. Well, I'm not sure that what I eat should actually be labeled as breakfast, but it is what my stomach can handle. Then a nurse helps me to the bathroom for my morning bath and somewhere around 10 a.m. the tests begin and go on until noon. I rest for a couple hours, and then Joshua usually shows up with the kids around dinner time. I ask Tory and Ben to tell me all about their day. Tory usually has to be asked specific questions, while Ben is more like a volcano of stories and details.

I have a roommate now. Her name is Sandy. She seems nice enough. I'm not sure why she is in here. I mean, I have this debilitating ailment and she doesn't seem like whatever she has is really hurting her that badly. Her husband came in to visit her yesterday. He seems like a nice guy, but nothing like Joshua. I can just tell from his interactions with her that there's not the same tenderness that I've grown to love and appreciate. However, he does seem to be pretty wealthy.

I've often wondered what it would be like to be wealthy. What if Joshua was some doctor or something like that? How would our lives change? I'm grateful for what we have, it's just that there have been plenty of times when I could've really used something, or even just wanted something that we didn't have the money for at the time. Like a massage, or a shopping trip. It's not like we were ever starving or without a home. I guess I just never felt free with money. It sure would feel nice to go to the grocery store without having a budget I have to think about. Carefree with money, now that would be nice.

I glance over to see Sandy fall asleep while he is there doing something on his phone beside her. He doesn't seem to notice until she has been sleeping for a good five minutes.

"Hello," he says, turning to me and smiling.

"Hi," I say.

"I hear that you are fighting some major stuff."

"Yeah, I guess you could say that," I say with a chuckle.

"Well, keep fighting. It seems like you have a lot worth living for, and who knows what the future holds?"

"Thanks, I will," I say.

He stands up, kisses his wife on the forehead and walks toward the door. As he reaches for the handle he looks back at me with a smile.

"My name is Ralph."

"I'm Bridget."

"Well, Bridget, I'm sure we'll see each other again soon."

Maybe I misjudged him? Maybe he's just preoccupied with all that's going on in their lives right now? I know how Joshua could probably appear to be not as nice to other people in this season with all that he is carrying.

I decide to talk to Sandy when she wakes up. She's not very talkative. It seems that she has some sort of cancer. She seems more preoccupied with the thought of Ralph promising to buy her a new Lexus if she gets better than she does with her sickness. I ask her about her symptoms and she tells me that she really doesn't have many. It's just that they wanted to have her in the hospital so that they could do all the treatments right away.

I asked her how she found out that she had cancer. And she told me that she had always had this fear that she had cancer, and one day her husband told her that he thought she might have it too. And so she went into the doctor and sure enough, her white blood cell count was high enough that they thought it was a good idea to do chemo.

"So here I am," she says with a sarcastic tone. "And I cannot wait to get out of my three-year-old Jaguar and into that new Lexus. I'm surprised my friends haven't disowned me already," she says with a laugh.

Wow, that is a different world than I know. She seems nice enough, but I'm not sure I could relate to her way of life.

the next day...

175

Ralph walks into the room and greets us both. He keeps trying to pull me into their conversations. I think he can see my loneliness. He is actually quite sweet. She seems a little less interested in talking and more interested in reading her fashion magazine.

"Honey, are you hungry?" Ralph asks Sandy.

"What do you think? I haven't been hungry since I started taking this awful medicine," she replies.

"Okay Sandy, I'm going to get something to eat and then I'll be right back."

"Whatever suits you, dear."

"Bridget, would you like anything to eat?" he asks me.

"Oh no, thank you. But thanks for the offer."

"You're welcome," he says smiling.

I feel cared for by him and bad for him all in the same moment. She doesn't seem like she has much interest in him at all. It's like he's a means to an end for her. It must be tough to be him, to have so much and be willing to give so much and yet not be appreciated or thanked.

Over the next few months my routine stays the same, except that I have more and more conversations with Ralph about his life. He tells me all about keys to success, and the hard decisions he's had to make to keep their wealth at a certain level. I guess I just thought when you were very wealthy you didn't have to think things through, but he seems very concerned about staying in control. He even offered to sit down with Joshua and me and help us with our finances and give us some direction in making investments. It all sounds very good to me. I would love to be able to retire at a younger age and not have to work or worry about money. That sounds like the good life.

One day, while Sandy was sleeping, Ralph opened up to me about their relationship and how things weren't so great. It seems to be the one aspect of his life that he is failing at, and it really bothers him. He told me that she's already

176

threatened many times to leave him and take all his money. He said that he would give up all his money to have someone who really loved him, who would give up their life for him. I can relate to so many of the things that he says. I think I'm at a different place on the journey, but all that he's feeling makes sense to me.

"Thank you, Bridget," he says as he gets up to leave.

"For what, Ralph?"

"For being a friend to me. I wish… I mean, you have just been really great over the past few months."

"You're welcome, Ralph. Goodbye."

"Goodbye," he smiles as he walks out the door.

It has been refreshing to be able to help someone else on their journey. And honestly, it seems easier to relate to him than… well, than other people. And I don't normally have these feelings about other guys, but he is kind of handsome. Not in a romantic way, just as an observation.

Chapter 16

some months later...

The doctors just came in and told me that in three months they should be able to do the surgery. That sounds amazing. It's the first glimpse of an ending I've had this entire time. I wonder what life will look like when I'm finally able to go home? Joshua and the kids still visit every day, but I can see it's wearing on them. I can't wait to give them the news that in three months I will be so close to coming home. They've waited so patiently for me, and served me through this process.

Sandy was given a clean bill of health a month ago and Ralph later told me about how excited she was to get home and get her new car. I didn't think I'd be seeing either of them since that day, but Ralph has stopped by a couple of times since she was discharged. He brought me flowers both times and a whole lot of encouragement. It seems like he really wants me to live. That's always nice when you get that from someone you don't really know. He also told me that things weren't going so well with him and Sandy. That's really too bad. I asked him about the cancer and how she was doing after the treatment. He told me something very interesting that I hadn't ever heard before. He said that there are almost always two types of treatments for any disease. There is one that they give to the average person who walks in through the hospital doors and it usually is a weaker version with more side effects. It's also less expensive. There is another option that is more expensive but will beat the disease quicker and cause less symptoms and adverse effects. I wondered which kind of treatment plan I was on. I never knew about this. He told me that he would never have let Sandy go through the lesser treatment. That he would consider himself a monster to not give everything to help someone get better quicker and with the least amount of discomfort.

one month later...

Having lots of time on your hands isn't always the best thing. I'm constantly thinking about all sorts of things from these last couple of years, and I have to say I'm a little confused. Is it possible that I didn't have to experience all the pain I just went through as well as what's ahead of me? Joshua and the kids arrive in the middle of my thoughts.

"Hi Mom," Tory says as she walks in the door and drops her book bag in the corner of the room.

"Hi Tory. How was school today?"

"Same old, same old."

"So, I'll take that as a best day ever?" I smile at her. She gives me a sarcastic look.

"Oh my dear Ben, please tell me that your day was better than Tory's."

"My day was great Mom, but I think it's all in your perspective," he says knowing that it's a direct jab at Tory. She shakes her head at him.

"I love you guys, and am so excited. Do you know why?" I smile at Joshua.

"No Mom, we don't know why?" Tory says.

Sometimes I wonder if there's any hope for our healing from the damage of this season.

"Tomorrow is my surgery!"

"Really, that's great babe," Joshua chimes in. "When did they tell you?"

"The doctors just came in about an hour ago and went over the results from my scan this morning. They said this is our window to move and we shouldn't wait any longer. I thought it would be another couple months, but speeding up the process is fine with me."

The kids seem a little hesitant.

"What is it, kids?" I ask.

"How dangerous is the surgery?" asks Ben.

"Oh honey, it will all be fine. This is the thing that will finally allow my body to be healed. I promise, it will be just fine."

I know I can't really promise that, but a new resolve has risen up inside of me now and I can finally see an end to all this.

"Okay Mom. Great, we can't wait. We really can't wait for you to come home and start cooking. No, I really mean it Mom, it has been bad," says Tory.

"Hey, guys," Joshua interjects, "I am not a bad cook."

"True, but not being bad at something doesn't necessarily make you good at it," Ben says.

We all start laughing. This feels good again. I can tell something is happening. It just feels like we are close to the end, and I'm so glad, because I don't know how much more I can take.

two days later...

The surgery went better than expected. The doctor told me it was as if the tumor wanted to come out of me. I laughed at that and told him that the tumor and I felt the same way.

"Bridget, you have come such a long way, but remember, you're not done yet," the doctor cautioned as gently as he could.

"I know Doc. I'm just so glad to have that thing out of me."

"Bridget, you've done a great job with this whole thing. I often found myself hoping that this would all be done in an instant for you, but your perseverance is absolutely remarkable," he said as he walked out of the room.

180

I whispered as he left, "Me too. I wish this had been over in an instant." I know there is something more to all of this, I just can't put my finger on it yet.

I am elated to see Joshua and the kids walk through the door. Ben is carrying flowers and Tory has balloons, but these won't be placed in my hospital room. They will accompany me to a celebration that awaits me in my own home. I made it! Well, I know I'm not done yet, but I made it through the surgery, and what could possibly be a greater fight than all of that?

Chapter 17

I wake up to the smell of coffee and lavender oil in the diffuser I asked Joshua to put on my nightstand. This is my bed, and there is nothing like it. I want to stay here for the next year to make up for all the time I've missed in it, but I cannot wait to see and hold my family. I stand to my feet, this doesn't feel great. There's a lot of stiffness in my lower back, but that's probably to be expected from the surgery and all. After a few steps I really do feel like I can sense that familiar pain coming back. I yell for Joshua. He comes running into the room.

"I think it's back." I'm starting to panic.

He leads me to the bed, places his hands on my cheeks and looks directly into my eyes.

"It is not back, do you hear me?"

His voice snaps me back into reality. I can see the kids standing at the doorway wondering what will happen this time. So much trauma they've already been through. Not again. They can't do this, I can't do this.

"Bridget!" Joshua raises his voice, not out of anger, but out of necessity. "Bridget, look at me. The doctor told us that you would experience these same pains. It was your body's way of working through the process of healing. It is not back. Trust me."

That's what I needed, to be reminded to trust him.

"Okay, yes, I am okay." Deep breath. "Kids come here, I'm so glad to see you, come give me some hugs." I motion them over to where I'm sitting. I can see their hesitance. "Ben, Tory, it's okay. We all have some adjusting to do, but please, I need you close to me."

"Mom," Ben speaks up, "I drew you a picture last week. Do you want to see it?"

"Of course I do Ben. I would love to see it," I say as he takes off down the hallway toward his room. He is back moments later holding his gift. He walks up to me and turns it around for me to see.

"It's a warrior, Wow!" I say. "It looks amazing Ben."

"Mom, look at her face. It's you."

That's enough to bring tears.

"Wow, Ben, this is the best drawing ever. Thank you so much," I say as my mind flashes back to my drive out here when I was just a teenager. I still feel like that wounded warrior.

"You're welcome Mom. Thank you for not giving up."

"You're welcome Ben."

"Come on guys, let's get some breakfast," Joshua says, directing us all to the kitchen.

We spend the morning lounging around the house. My nurse shows up around lunch time to run some tests and give me the medication for this disease that we can now fight full force. The doctors don't think it will be too long now until I get a 'clean bill of health'. I am waiting for those words more than any others. What will it feel like to hear those words echo throughout my body?

Joshua announces a movie night and the kids start jumping up and down. I wouldn't consider us a big television-watching family, which makes these times a real treat.

I cannot get over this feeling of being home. This is more than I could've asked for. Joshua picks out one of our favorites, which means that Ben will be quoting lines for the rest of the night and into tomorrow. Tory will be rolling her eyes at Ben, and Joshua, well, he will be squeezing my hand at all the parts that speak to true love enduring through impossibility.

After the movie, I kiss the kids goodnight and help Joshua tuck them in their beds. How I have missed this. The simple things in life that we get to experience each day are actually the real treasures.

Joshua makes two cups of Jasmine Pearls, our favorite tea then helps me out back to sit in our Adirondack chairs, and gaze at the stars.

"How are you doing?" he says looking over at me.

"I don't know," I sigh as I turn to him. "I honestly feel like I'm still trying to figure out what life is like. It's been so long since I've felt anything that seems like normal. I guess I'm just waiting for the excitement of being home to wear off to see what comes after that."

"Makes sense," he says. "So, what was one thing you loved about today?" he asks smiling.

He has always been the one to invite gratefulness into our home. He just asks us a question at random times and we find ourselves filled up because of what we've just expressed through our mouths.

"I don't know if I can narrow it down to just one. I feel overwhelmed with gratefulness for you and for the kids and being able to be here, and having that tumor out of me. I just feel really great and really grateful."

"I'm so glad. It's so good to have you back here. There were so many days that I wondered what it would feel like to have you back home. It's even better than I expected."

"I'm glad you feel that way. Honestly, I was wondering if I blew it this morning, with whatever that was. Joshua, what was that?"

"Honestly Bridget, I think that as much as your body is going to need healing, your heart and your mind are also going to require it. There's a natural time of adjustment that is going to have to take place. And that's okay. We're just going to keep moving forward."

"Right, sounds good."

three days later...

I find myself sitting down in the corner of our shower. "Joshua!" I yell.

He comes running into the bathroom.

"What is it, are you okay?"

"No, I'm not. I can't do this. How do I know I'm going to be okay? What if I'm never fully healed? I think the pain might be coming back, and what if the medicine isn't working? Joshua I..." I begin to weep as the water from the shower continues to pour over me.

"Bridget, I'm here." He wraps me up in my towel and carries me into our bedroom. He sits down on a chair and holds me on his lap and for the next ten minutes the only thing I hear is, "Bridget, I'm here."

My body finally relaxes and I feel exhausted even after just waking up. He lays me down in our bed and I fall asleep quickly.

I wake up a few hours later to a knock on the door. It's my nurse. Already? What time is it? Oh yes, it's that time again.

"Hold on one minute," I holler as I slowly get up and put on some clothes. "Okay, come in," I say as I sit back down on the bed.

"Hey there beautiful girl," says Lucy, my nurse. She is such a treasure, so bubbly and happy. She's been a light on some really dark days.

"How is my girl doing today?" she asks.

"Oh, I'm okay. I had some concerns earlier this morning, but I'm fine now."

"Good, I'm glad to hear you are doing better now. I have something for you," she says as she pulls out a card from her bag. She hands it to me with a little bit of hesitancy.

"What's this?" I ask.

"Well, do you remember your old roommate Sandy?"

"Yeah, how is she doing?"

185

"Good, she's fine, probably speeding around town in that Lexus," she laughs. "Well, her husband Ralph dropped this by the hospital the other day and asked me to give it to you. I normally wouldn't have taken it but he told me how your story was so inspiring to him and he really wanted to pass along some encouragement," she said as she hands me the card.

"Oh, well that was nice of him. Thanks, I'll look at it later." I set it on my nightstand and pull up my sleeve so that we can begin my daily routine of tests.

About an hour later I walk Lucy to the door and thank her again for all that she does for me. I really have been blessed throughout this journey to have such good people surrounding me and encouraging me. I know I wouldn't have made it on my own.

I'm actually excited to read the card from Ralph. In some ways I've missed talking with him at the hospital.

Dear Bridget,

I must say it's been sad for me to not be able to see you as I did before. Yet I am so glad to hear of your recovery. You are such a fighter. I admire that so much. I don't want to overstep any boundaries, but would love to be able to keep in touch and continue to hear how your story goes. I would also love to be of any help I can in your family's life and future. I know that you were concerned about stability in finances and how you felt subject to some uncertainties in life. I know nobody likes waiting for things. I sure don't! So, if there is any way that I can help you tie up some of those loose ends, I would be glad to help. You can email me anytime, ralph@torellolawfirm.com

I pray you are well.
Sincerely,
Ralph.

Wow! Ralph prays? I wouldn't have guessed that he was religious. He seems like he really wants to help us. What a nice man. There's this pulling in my soul toward him. It's like a magnet at a distance. I'm not completely sure why. I think it has something to do with the stability he seems to carry. Joshua has always talked about not having fear about things, and we've always made it, but Ralph seems like he has the answers, the things that would help me not to fear anything in life. But I trust Joshua so much. He has been with me through so much. I would never want anything else.

I hear Joshua come through the front door and greet the kids. I open the drawer of my nightstand and, lifting my worn copy of 'The Notebook', slide the card underneath. I ease the drawer shut and scoot a few inches away from where I had been sitting, as Joshua walks into the room.

Chapter 18

Over time I watch as this physical disease dies and leaves my body. But I become more and more overtaken by fear than ever before in my life. I can see it's starting to bother Joshua. We seem to have the same conversations over and over again. But nothing he says seems to keep the fear from coming back.

"I need something to make this all stop happening," I say to him after another panic attack.

"You are the only one who can stop it, Bridget, you have to trust..."

I interrupt him mid-sentence. "Great. Thanks. That's a huge help. Tell the girl who's always sick to just get better. You're so insensitive." I know this isn't true. Sometimes I wish I could rewind the tape and erase what I've said. The truth is that Joshua is the most sensitive person I know. But I am again opening my mouth when pain is overwhelming my heart.

My Aunt Abbey had a dog while I was living with her. Her name was Sunny, and she became one of my best friends. One day as Sunny and I were walking through the woods, she got her foot stuck in an old metal fence. She was so scared and couldn't get free. Each time she moved, it would cut her leg more. She was panicking and I wasn't sure how to help her. I tried to grab her leg and help her get out but in the midst of her pain, she snapped at me. I wasn't mad at her. I knew why she was doing that, but I also didn't know how I could possibly help her. Finally, I just sat down beside her and after awhile she laid down and rested her head on my lap. Then she was calm enough for me to get her leg free. I carried her home and cleaned and dressed the wound and she was back to running in a few days.

I feel like Sunny, except I seem to get my leg stuck almost every day. And Joshua, unfortunately, takes the brunt of my lashing out. I can't say I'm getting any nearer to the place where I feel like I understand why he loves me. At this point, I'm not sure I will ever figure that one out. Each time I lose it and he's there feeling my frustrations and fears, I come closer to not wanting to ever put him through this again. If I wasn't around, then he wouldn't have this burden. How could I not be considered a burden?

As I'm eating lunch on the back deck the craziest thought goes through my mind. What if Ralph could help us? What if I just met with Ralph and tried to figure this whole money thing out? That would help me, Joshua, and I'm sure our whole family out. It would be amazing to not feel like the one who has and is causing all the issues. I think I will email him today.

Ralph emailed me back in the evening and said he would love to help us out in whatever way I thought best. He asked if I could meet him for coffee at the end of the week. I'm so excited to finally gain some clarity on this life of mine. Maybe this is actually the key I've been waiting for.

three days later...

I start to get ready after Joshua leaves for work. I'm wondering what to wear. I don't want to look like I'm utterly helpless, but I don't want to come across as not needing anything either. I know that this could change everything for me. This could change everything for our family. I finish my makeup, splash on some perfume and I'm out the door.

As I sit at a table waiting for Ralph, I pick up a home improvement magazine and begin to flip through it. Before all this sickness thing happened I would balk at these pictures of extravagance. It seemed like such a waste to spend so much money on something just because of the brand it was, or because it was rare. 'Who would ever want that?' I would think. Honestly, I kind of want that now. Ralph's words echo in my mind from our conversation about the two different kinds of treatments, and what money can really do for you. I know money isn't the answer to all of our problems, but it does seem like it alleviates a whole lot of them.

I feel a hand on my shoulder.

"Hello Bridget," Ralph says.

"Oh, hi Ralph," I say as I stand up and reach out my hand to shake his.

He completely bypasses my hand and gives me a hug. Normally I would feel pretty uncomfortable with this, but as he hugs me he tells me how proud of me he is for fighting and winning against all odds. It feels more like a soccer coach giving me a hug after a game we won. This isn't weird; this is a friend I feel like I can trust. The only reason I haven't told Joshua about Ralph yet is because he wouldn't understand all of it. And I really want to be able to get a plan for us first, so that I can explain it to Joshua. I honestly think Joshua might be intimidated by Ralph.

"So let's get to it," he says as he pulls out a leather binder from under his arm and sets it on the table. "By the way, you look stunning, Bridget. I mean, you always looked so beautiful in the hospital, but wow, you are just stunning."

I can't hold back a smile. In fact, it feels like I am holding back five smiles at once. It feels so nice to be feeling better. And even nicer to know that people notice it.

"Thank you, Ralph," I say biting my lip.

"So what are your goals, Bridget? In ten years what do you really want to be able to say about your financial situation or life or housing?"

"Well, I'm not really sure any of that matters that much to me, I just really want to be at a place where we have enough money to pay for the things we need. I've been thinking about the two treatment plans you and I talked about in the hospital and I have been wondering what it would've looked like if we had the money to put toward me having a better treatment plan. Maybe I wouldn't have had to suffer as much. Do you know what I mean?"

"Oh Bridget, it took everything in me to not talk to Josh about what he was doing by not paying for the other option."

"Wait, you think he knew there was another option?"

"I don't know Bridget, it just seems to me that it's a pretty common scenario and that if I were in his shoes I would've been asking a whole lot of questions to find out if there was another way."

"I think he probably did ask that. Maybe the doctors knew we didn't have much money so they didn't even want to bring it up."

"You're probably right. I just wish I could've changed that for you. I don't think anyone should have to go through what you went through. But look at you now, you are amazing for fighting through that."

"I just don't want to ever have to go through that again."

"And you shouldn't. I hope that Josh can see what this has done to you enough to make better decisions in life and make sure that you are free from ever having to worry about all that."

"Thank you Ralph, I do too. How are things going with you and Sandy?"

He hangs his head, and I can see a tear start to form in his eye.

"Sorry Bridget, I'm not usually very emotional. Sandy filed for divorce about two months ago, and it's final as of yesterday. I had wondered if she was just after my money, and it appears that she was. I loved her so much. It hurts so bad to know that you gave everything to someone and they were so ungrateful. She's so different from you. I can tell that you are such a grateful person, and hearing about how you love your kids it just makes me feel so... I don't know what I'm trying to say, just that you are unlike anyone I've ever

191

met. You give me hope that there is someone out there that's perfect for me."

"Thanks Ralph, you seem like such a nice guy. I'm so sorry to hear about Sandy. Please let me know if there's anything I can do to help."

"Honestly, it's just nice having a friend to talk to."

"Of course I can be your friend, Ralph."

As we say goodbye at my car, he grabs my hand and squeezes it.

"I will talk to you later," he says as he turns to walk away.

"Okay, goodbye," I say as I sit down in the driver's seat.

I'm not sure what to make of all that. But I still have this lurking feeling that he holds a key to me being free from this whole fear thing. I think I just need to keep asking him questions about practical things Joshua and I can start doing.

Joshua pulls into the driveway and I am feeling a little hesitant to see him. It's not like I did anything wrong today. It's just stuff that he wouldn't understand and I need to make sure I understand it all really well before I try and communicate it to him.

"Hey honey, how are you feeling?" he says as he pulls me in close for a kiss.

"Good," I say. "I'm feeling really great today."

"Alright! I've been waiting to hear that come out of your mouth. How about we celebrate and go out for burgers?"

The kids are sitting on the couch doing homework, but when they hear, "burgers," they jump off the couch and race to get their shoes.

"Sounds good, honey," I say, trying not to sound ungrateful, although for some reason I'm in the mood for a fancy restaurant tonight.

We have a good time out together and I'm glad to be able to eat real food again. There's something normal about my family. I wouldn't call it the dream life, but I am thankful for what I have.

Chapter 19

nine months later...

Life has been such a whirlwind of events. After that meeting with Ralph at the coffeehouse, he asked me to give him some advice on what to do with his relationship with Sandy. He seemed so broken, and in so much pain over losing her. We met at a park and he went on to tell me of his struggle with it all and even began to cry. I can tell he is really a caring and sensitive man. I found myself wanting to reach out and just hold him. And so I did. I don't think I felt that feeling from an embrace since before my sickness began. Over the next few months our friendship grew. He would tell me how if the sickness ever tried to come back in my body, he would make sure what happened to me last time didn't happen again.

Then one day as we were out walking, he looked over at me, smiled and said, "Bridget, I've never met anyone like you. You are the woman I wish I would've taken hold of all my life."

"Ralph, thank..." I began to say.

But with that he took hold of me and gently kissed me. I felt overwhelmed with so many emotions. I guess I didn't really think this would lead me here, but after these nine months with him, I actually kind of want this. I can't believe I'm doing this. But I can now see why.

When I'm with Ralph I don't have any panic attacks. It's almost like he can just turn them off, but with Joshua I have to fight through each one. Ralph just seems to be able to throw a blanket over the fires and they are out.

What would anyone in their right mind choose? Do you stay where you are just because it's what people tell you is the right thing to do? Because you have a conviction or a value? Well, I am a real person, I have real emotions and feelings and real needs. And right now I really need to not have another panic attack. Joshua doesn't seem to understand that, but Ralph is like pain medication for my fears. I have to do this, I don't think I will make it if I stay on the path I am on right now.

one month later...

Ralph asked me to move in with him yesterday. I'm no longer shocked at each step I've taken toward him like I was in the beginning. It seems so organic and natural. I know there will be parts that are painful about leaving Joshua, but once Ralph told me that I could bring the kids with me, I knew this was the right decision. I cannot wait to see what it feels like to live in freedom. Freedom to choose what I want to do in life. Freedom to buy the things that I want, and freedom from worry. This is what life is supposed to feel like.

Now I just have to make it through another month here with Joshua so Ralph and I can have all the paperwork finalized for the kids.

It's not that I don't care about Joshua. I just feel so shut off to him. He still tries to spend time with me and it's like he's always there waiting for me to open up to him. But I know where that road leads. It's always been a hard uncomfortable road, and I'm tired of that. I have one life to live, shouldn't any part of it be about me?

Ralph and I have talked about this same thing so many times. I can actually hear myself repeating his little sayings in my head. "Bridget, if you don't take control of your life, who will?" And his personal favorite, "Would you rather have a lot of money or a lot of worry? It's your choice."

He really is like Joshua in a lot of ways, except that he is offering me a quick and easy way out of all the pain of life that actually makes sense. Sometimes Joshua's strategies are not as concrete. There have been so many times I find myself looking at him like, "How do I do that?" And his answer is always, 'One step at a time'. But how am I supposed to keep walking if I can only see the step in front of me? That doesn't make sense. Ralph has a five year plan. I can run through life if I want, because I can see what's up ahead. This just makes sense.

weeks later...

It's already here. Tomorrow I leave Joshua and I am on to my new adventure. I am somewhat beside myself. I haven't told the kids yet. I'm not sure that they would be able to process it and not tell Joshua before we leave, so it's probably better that he tells them. I know it's going to be an adjustment for them, but they are going to love living there. It's a huge house, with more room than anyone could need. There's also a maid, which is so nice, and it shows that Ralph understands my limits and wouldn't ask me to do anything that would bring too much stress to me.

I'm wondering how Joshua is going to take all this? I mean, he has to know something is up. We haven't exactly connected in a while, and although he's tried to ask me all his probing questions, I've just been visibly doing better and acting happier because of everything with Ralph, so I guess that is making him feel like everything is okay. I wonder if he will actually understand. He probably will. He's always wanted to make me happy, and finally I am. I know he would die for me, and it's not like I'm asking him to die; just to allow our relationship to. At the very least, we can still be friends. I do still care about him and appreciate all that he's done for me. I mean, he did walk through those awful years with me, but now I know he could've stopped them or at least made it so much less than what it was. And he didn't.

196

It's nine o'clock, and we just finished putting the kids to bed. Joshua walks into the kitchen and asks me if I would like some coffee.

"Sure Joshua," I say, trying to figure out when the best time to break the news is.

"Hey, why don't we sit on the back deck and talk for a little," he says.

"That sounds good," I reply.

I again find myself in one of those moments where my life is about to change completely, but for the first time I feel in control of the moment. This is my choice to change my direction in life and I can see how much better things will be.

Chapter 20

Well I wouldn't consider that conversation as having gone as well as I had hoped, but at least it's over. And I am on my way to the adventure of my lifetime. I feel so free right now. I decide to drive for a little bit to get rid of the bad feelings Josh put on me before I get to this new beginning.

A memory flashes across my mind. Josh and I were hiking through the woods right after we were married and we had to cross over a creek. As we began to walk across a log a few feet above the water I began to lose my balance. Josh immediately turned around and steadied me, which sent him sliding off the log and knee deep into the water. When we got to the other side I noticed he had blood coming through his pant leg. He had cut his shin pretty badly. I felt so bad, but he just smiled, wrapped a bandage around his leg and kept on moving.

I feel this shame wash over me. It's that feeling of finding yourself standing on a public street and realizing you're naked. It's not a good feeling. Time for some music. I turn on the radio to drown out all that negativity with some make me feel good songs. I love this song! You know how a song can just reach into a specific situation and make you feel completely okay about it. This is one of those songs. And I find myself pushing all those bad feelings off of me and out the open window of my car. I even give a couple fist pumps as I drive down the highway, singing along with the melody, "It's my life. It's my choice, and I choose to be happy." Yeah, that's right. It is my choice and I choose to be happy.

As I pull up to my new house, I find myself amazed that I would be able to have all this. There have been some tough choices along the way, but I'm sure they were worth it.

Chapter 21

months later...

There are a lot of adjustments taking place, but I'm sure once we get into a rhythm as a new family, things will be a lot easier. Tory and Ben are loving getting to do things they never had the chance to do before. Ralph bought them each a gift; a really expensive skateboard for Ben, and this little video game device for Tory that she can take and play anywhere. I normally wouldn't be too excited about her playing video games, but it seems like it's helping her adjust.

I haven't had a panic attack since I left Josh. It has been so nice to know that I made the right decision. I had lunch with Gabi yesterday. It was nice to see her again, but it didn't seem like we were seeing eye to eye on this whole situation. I could tell she wanted to talk about me leaving Josh, but I couldn't help but turn the conversation to all the things I've gained from the choice to be with Ralph. At the end of the conversation she asked me if I was sure this was the right thing. I paid for her lunch and coffee. I figure that should speak for itself as to whether it's the right thing or not. Just before we left the cafe she looked at me and said,

"Bridget, you know that money doesn't buy happiness, right?"

"Gabi, I don't want happiness, happiness is a byproduct of what I really need."

"Then what is it that you really need Bridget?"

"I really need to be free from those panic attacks."

Gabi is one of my best friends. She knows me better than anyone other than Ralph, well I guess probably Josh too. I know she will understand.

"Bridget, I can't help but feel like this is a mistake, but it's your choice."

Ouch, I really thought she would understand. I mean she knew about the panic attacks. She knew about all that I've gone through in my lifetime. I really thought she'd be happy for me to finally have a place of peace. A place that feels secure.

"Well, thanks Gabi. It is my choice, and I'm so glad I made it."

How could she doubt me like this? Friends are supposed to have your back and be able to understand you. They are supposed to encourage you toward your dreams, not hold you back from them.

As I say goodbye to Gabi, she hugs me and holds on to me.

"Bridget, I really love you. If I didn't, I wouldn't ask you the hard questions. Please don't shut me out."

"Sure Gabi. I won't."

"Thank you for lunch," she says.

"Hey, it's one of the blessings of my decision," I say smiling, as I turn to walk out the door.

I can see that comment hurt her deeply, but I'm not sure why. Does she really not get it? I've just been given the world at my fingertips. I've been given what so many people spend their lives striving for. Maybe she's just jealous. Yeah, that's probably it.

Tonight I'm making an award-winning dinner for our family. I know Ralph will just love it. I need to pick up a few final ingredients and then off to the kitchen.

Ralph texts me at six o'clock to tell me he got hung up at the office with a client.

"Kids, time to eat," I holler up the stairs.

They come running down the stairs and into the dining room. They love to run around the house when Ralph isn't here. He doesn't really like things being chaotic, which I completely understand. But when he's gone they seem to feel a little more free to enjoy themselves. I don't really mind, I just want them to be happy.

We sit there and they dig in right away.

"Where's Ralph?" asks Ben with a mouth full of food.

"Ben, no talking with your mouth full," I answer. "He's at work with a client, but should be home in about an hour."

Tory raises her glass and says, "Well, here's to family," with an incredibly sarcastic tone.

Ben starts to laugh as he shovels more food into his mouth.

"Tory, that is inappropriate," I say sternly, but she doesn't back down.

"Mom, it doesn't seem like inappropriate is a word that is a part of our vocabulary these days."

"Tory, go to your room," I snap at her.

She proceeds to slide her chair back dramatically, grab a piece of chicken and walk up the stairs.

"Tory, you know we don't allow food in your bedrooms."

But she doesn't stop, she just keeps walking. What is going on with her?

"Ben, how was your day?" I say as I try to regain some normalcy at our dinner table.

"It was okay," he says with his face now looking down at his plate.

"Honey, what is going on with Tory?"

"Mom, I think she just kind of feels like since you broke the biggest rule ever, then why should she have to listen to any rules at all?"

I thought I got rid of that shame out of my car window the night I left Josh. But here it is pouring through my soul like a flood. The biggest rule? What is the biggest rule? My mind races to try and understand what my now, eleven year old son has an understanding of that I seem to be blind to.

"Oh, well Ben, I think it's a little too complicated for you guys to understand. I wasn't leaving your dad because I was bored. It just wasn't a safe place for me anymore. Honey, you have to understand that you only get one life to live, and it's up to you to search out what the best road is for you to take. This is mine."

"Yeah, you're probably right Mom, we just don't understand," he says.

But I know he doesn't buy it. I know that in his mind he sees this all very differently. I'm not looking for friends or people to tell me I'm right. And I don't need excuses. I have a page of reasons.

"Ben, I'm going to go upstairs for a little bit."

"Sure thing, Mom."

"Ben, I love you."

"Thanks Mom," he replies.

That's the first time he hasn't told me he loves me back. What is happening? It feels like my decision left a hole in the atmosphere and now everything is changing without me seeing it until now. I head up to my room with one goal. I'm going to write out a list of all the reasons why this was a good decision to be with Ralph.

I begin to write:
-I couldn't bear anymore panic attacks.
-I have the things that I always wanted.
-I'm finally comfortable.

Look at that, three right off the bat. This is going to be easy. I sit there for the next hour with my pen resting on the paper, until I finally give way to sleep.

I wake up to Ralph's alarm clock. He is such an early riser and such a hard worker. I admire him for that. Sure, I wish he would've been home for dinner last night, but it's what is required of him.

"Hey there," I say smiling at him as he swings his feet over the edge of the bed and into his slippers. "You must have been out late."

"Uh yeah, Bridget, I was. You know work is demanding sometimes and those are the times when sacrifices have to be made," he says with an annoyance in his voice.

"Okay honey," I reply feeling shocked that he just spoke to me that way. He's probably tired and he did just wake up. I should make him some coffee.

I head downstairs and make him breakfast and coffee while he gets ready.

As he comes down the stairs he goes to walk out the front door.

"Ralph, I made you breakfast and coffee."

He walks back into the kitchen and picks up the coffee.

"Thanks Bridget. I'll just take coffee this morning. I've got a lot to do at the office and it's probably gonna be another late one tonight."

"Okay," I say as I walk around the island to give him a hug and kiss. He seems cold to me today. Probably just overwhelmed with work. I remember those feelings of being overwhelmed. I should try and help.

"Ralph, is there anything I can do to help you out? Do you want me to bring lunch in to work for you today?"

"No! I mean, no thanks. You know once I get in there and into the zone, it's so hard for me to take a break, and you know how you are able to get me distracted," he says with a smile.

"Okay, well have a good day." I smile.

"I will. You too," he says as he turns toward the door. "Hey, why don't you go out and buy an outfit for yourself. That always makes you feel good."

"Maybe I'll do that."

He leaves and I feel something that I've never felt around him before. It doesn't feel good. It's not like what I felt with the panic attacks, but it's similar.

I decide to spend some time this morning finishing my list of reasons, but each time I sit down with my journal my mind starts to wander off and I start doing something else.

I walk into the laundry room. I know we have a maid, but I don't like to not have anything to do so I decided that I would start taking care of the laundry. I start throwing whites in the washing machine. I pick up one of Ralph's white dress shirts and without thinking I put it up to my nose and smell it. That's weird. It smells like perfume. Nothing that I wear. I pick up another shirt. Same thing.

What is this?

Calm down Bridget, I tell myself. This is not what you think it is. I'm sure there's an explanation. My mind races and before I know it I'm on the floor in front of the washing machine. It's happened again. I cry out, but nobody is there to help me. I didn't think this could happen here. I have to be able to get passed this. I'm sure I'm just overreacting. I convince myself to not tell anyone. I'm definitely not doing any more laundry.

In fact, each time I walk past the laundry room for the next week I feel a wave of nausea. Over the course of that week I try not to let Ralph see my apprehension. I'm honestly not sure he would see it anyways. He seems very preoccupied.

Chapter 22

Josh is coming by to take the kids up to his parents' house for the day. I miss the time we had up there. It's such a special place. I haven't been back to the waterfall since before I got sick. I wonder how many times he's been up there since I left? I hear a knock on the door. That must be him.

"Hi Joshu... I mean Josh. Um, the kids are just finishing breakfast, do you want to come in?"

"I should probably wait out here, you know, I don't want to upset Ralph and his rules," he says.

"It's ok, he's at the gym getting in his daily workout. Come on in. Can I get you anything? Coffee?"

"No thanks, I'm fine."

"You know Josh, I've been thinking about the kids and some different things and I was wondering if you would be interested in being more involved? You know Ralph is such a great provider, but he is so busy providing and with his schedule he can't make it to a lot of the things that the kids are doing. I was wondering if you would want to help out with taking the kids to some of the extracurricular activities I had been wanting to get them involved in."

"Well, like what?" he asks.

"Well, Ralph thinks it would be good for them to get a well-balanced approach to life, so things like sports and dance and maybe some elective courses that the college is offering for younger kids."

"That sounds interesting. What are the courses about?"

"Well, there's one on maintaining your wealth that he really wants them to take, and another one on making your dreams happen. Oh, and another one on debating skills. He really feels like the younger that we train our kids to have and use these basic life skills the further they'll get in this world."

"I don't know, Bridget. I'm not sure I want our kids to be so focused on wealth or making things happen, or even

205

learning ways to sound right even when they're not. None of that seems like it's helping them to be real. But, if they want to play sports and dance, I'll definitely help with those things."

"I don't understand you Josh. Why is it so hard for you to just change? You know, to be what people want you to be, or at least, what could've kept us together?"

"So, I'm to blame for you leaving?"

"Well, yes in some ways. If you would've just provided a safe place for us, a place where I didn't have to worry about the things I was worried about, then I wouldn't have felt like I needed to go look for it somewhere else."

"Whatever happened to choosing not to worry about things, or fighting off the fears that come against you?"

"Josh, you know just as well as I do that whether you worry or not, there are still bills that need to be paid and things that were outside of our financial reach."

"Yeah, but life is more than just paying bills. It's more than a feeling of safety," he says.

In a moment tears flood my eyes, and as he continues, my thoughts return to the many days in that hospital bed. As my mind races through images and memories around that room all I see is his face. He was the one who was there every day. The one who was holding me up when all I wanted to do was give up.

"Do you really believe that you can't be touched by calamity? Do you really think that what Ralph offers you is more stable than a devoted love that will hold onto you while you're on your deathbed? Bridget, my love, wake up!"

That's too far. There is no reason for him to still be calling me, 'his love.' There is no way that he would still love me after all that I've done to him. This is too much.

"I have to go, and uh get ready. Uh... have fun with the kids today, I have to go," I stammer.

With that I run out of the kitchen and up the stairs to my bedroom. Where is it, where is it! I have to find it. I start rummaging through my nightstand, "There it is." I sit down on the edge of the bed and open up my journal to read the reasons why I left. Tears pour off my cheeks and onto the page.

"He's right," I say out loud as I begin to sob uncontrollably until I finally fall asleep, exhausted.

Chapter 23

I feel like I just bought a used car that looked like the deal of a lifetime. Only to find out that there is no padding under the leather seats, the air conditioning doesn't work, the radio is broken, and the engine is leaking oil.

I am an absolute fool. I cannot believe I gave up everything I had for this. 'Bridget, you're an idiot,' is the broken record that keeps playing through my mind.

Well, I won't be a fool twice. This was my choice and my mistake. Now it's my responsibility to stay in it and live with the consequences and shame. Josh didn't deserve this. As for me answering my lifelong question of why he loves me. I feel like I just maxed out the credit card on that one. Before I could've thought of a few things that might seem like possible reasons, but not now. There's absolutely no reason. He's probably just missing what he thinks I am, not who I really am. No, I'm determined to not go back. That would be just wrong.

two days later…

Gabi has been asking me to spend time with her. I didn't think it was a very safe place for a while, but I decided to meet up with her today.

"Hey there," I say as I walk up to the table she's sitting at.

"Hi Bridget, it's so good to see you. Thanks for giving me a call. I've been wondering how you are doing." Gabi says.

"I'm doing pretty good," I reply without a whole lot of confidence. "How about you? How are you doing?" I figure if I keep our time together focused on her life it will be much safer for me.

"Bridget, I'm just so happy to be alive. Life has had some painful parts lately, mostly friends and family related, but I'm hopeful."

There is something so refreshing about hearing her talk. It's like sunshine bursting through dark clouds. I didn't realize how heavy I felt until I heard the lightness in her voice.

"So, are things going good with Ralph, and how are the kids? I miss them so much."

I strategically skip the Ralph part and begin to tell her all about what the kids are doing right now and how they've grown. She is such a good friend, I'm not sure how I forgot that before. I ask her to meet us for dinner this weekend so she can see them and she excitedly agrees.

"Bridget, are you still happy with Ralph?" She says with some hesitance. Not because she lacks confidence or thinks she shouldn't ask, I think she's just expecting a certain response from me.

I start to cry. I can't hold it in. I tell her everything. From realizing my mistake, to suspecting that Ralph is cheating on me, to knowing I can never go back to Josh.

"Bridget, why would you not go back to Joshua? That just doesn't make sense. He still loves you."

"Gabi," I say through tears, "I don't deserve him. I've never deserved him. I can't think of one reason why he should love me. Since I met him, I've been trying to find a reason why, and there aren't any. My heart feels like a river; it follows a course that I don't feel like I have any control over. I will not go back to Josh. I don't trust myself."

"Okay Bridget. I'm sure you know what's best," she says as she reaches across the table and takes hold of my hand.

I love Gabi. She's never forceful with her opinions, she just has this way of lovingly sharing her concerns. I think she knows that if she just gives me enough space I will come to the right answer without her having to outright tell me. In this case, however, I really don't think the right answer is for me to go back to Josh.

Gabi gives me a big hug as we walk out the door and I am grateful to have a friend that loves me like she does.

Chapter 24

I can't help but wonder what my life is going to look like as I begin to try and settle in to all that I find myself in. As I think back through my life I realize that there have been three situations that I've felt enslaved to. My parents' death, the sickness and now this whole mess with Ralph. The only difference this time is that I chose this.

Most days I wake up and feel the shame and self-hatred waiting for me at the edge of the bed like a pair of dirty clothes that I am forced to wear. And each day I try to wear them the best I can. Because, I bought this outfit and if anyone has to wear it, it's me. And yet other days I find it easier to wake up and become someone I'm not. A woman who is content with her identity being wrapped up in things that really don't matter and don't ever seem to fully satisfy.

Ralph has become increasingly distant. I've tried to reach out to him and see if I can make this whole thing any better, but he is cold and harsh and doesn't seem to want much to do with me relationally. Yet, I can tell he would never let me leave. He's begun to treat me like I'm his property. He's also become especially harsh with Ben. It is not the father-son relationship I was hoping it would be. He's nothing like what Josh has been in Ben's life.

He doesn't seem to be bothered by Tory. In fact, I constantly find them talking together. I'm not sure whether or not I should be worried by that. It does seem like Tory has become increasingly negative and sarcastic.

I'm just trying to figure out how to manage all this and keep everyone somewhat happy. I didn't have to worry about keeping them all happy before. It was just a byproduct of our lives together. There was so much excitement and exploration. Life truly was an adventure. But the problem with an adventure is that you never know what is next. I guess I just got tired of not knowing what was next.

Josh invited me to go climbing with them a week ago. I had so much fun. It felt like the old days! I regret what I did, leaving him. I regret it so much. I wish there was some way to take it all back. I wish I could have seen how deceived I was.

I really didn't mean to do this. I honestly thought this was the only right path. Everything started out so innocently and felt so right. I would have never guessed that those choices I made to keep things from Josh and to follow what seemed like an easier way out of my fears would end up like this.

I'm reminded of the walks I would take with Josh's dad in the cool of the morning around the lake. As I think back on it all, so much of what he talked to me about, I've lived out. He would tell me about how the pain in life grows things inside of you. If you're not paying attention and carefully watching what is growing, one day you'll wake up to a garden full of weeds. As I look around, that's exactly what I feel like I'm sitting in. There is no path that could lead me out of this.

But if there was?

I would take it.

the next day...

Josh just did the most amazing thing for Tory. He really is so amazing. My heart sinks back into sadness as I think of what I used to have. Money couldn't buy what I used to have.

I can tell he's being really intentional about letting his kids know that he's there for them and loves them. He's even given me things from our past and said things that make it seem like he wants me back. But I built too big of a wall up between us. I know that if I let my heart open it will just lead me and I can't do that again, for my sake and his. It would be easier if he was a jerk or even a little insensitive, but the force that flows into my being when I come in contact with him could only be described as love. Unconditional love. It's so funny to think of someone who can actually love unconditionally. Ha, I obviously can't. He really does seem to love me outside of everything I've done wrong. I'm not sure how that works, but I still wonder from time to time if there really is a reason why he loved me.

Chapter 25

a few days later...

Josh and Tory should be home from their date any minute now. I can't wait to hear all about it. Tory has been such a different person since he surprised her the other morning. That must be them pulling in the driveway now. "Oh, never mind, it's Ralph," I mumble as I glance out the window and see his car pulling in the garage.

"Hey Bridget," he says entering his castle like a king. "Any dinner left? I'm really hungry."

"Uh, no, it was just Ben and I here so we just split a pizza."

"Ok," he says with a tone that reeks of disgust.

"Ralph, I didn't know you were going to be home this early."

"Yeah, well, I don't think it's too much to ask that a woman make dinner for her working man," he says laughing arrogantly.

"Sure thing, Ralph," I reply trying to appease him and end the conversation.

"Where's Tory?" he asks.

"She's out with Josh."

"She's what?" he says with anger rising in his voice. "This is unacceptable. He can't just show up whenever he wants. This isn't his house and it certainly isn't his family anymore. I'm filing a court order in the morning to keep him from stepping foot on my property."

"Ralph, don't you think you're overreacting a little bit? She wanted him to take her out for dinner and he cleared it with me."

"Oh so you're the one doing this behind my back," he shot back.

"If anyone is hiding stuff behind their back Ralph, it's you!" I couldn't keep that one in.

He stops, knowing I know more than I should, but wondering how far I will take this. There's a knock on the door. It must be Josh.

"Hi Bridget, thanks for allowing this, we had a great time," said Josh as Tory squeezed between us and headed upstairs to bed.

"Goodnight Daddy, love you," she hollers back to Josh.

"Love you too, sweetie."

"Bridget, what is it?" He says, sensing hesitation in me.

"Nothing Josh, thanks for taking Tory out," I say trying not to open up a window for conversation.

"Yeah sure, we had a blast. It's like I have my Tory back. She opened up to me just like the old days on our morning walks. What a blessing that was. Um, Bridget? Can I ask you something?"

"Sure Josh, what is it?" I say.

"What are the bruises on your arm from?"

"I told you already Josh, just me being clumsy."

"Bridget, please. If you need help, I can help, just don't stay in a bad situation. Not for yours or the kids' sake. Please, I can help but you need to talk to me."

I can tell he means it, but Ralph is on the other side of the door listening to this whole conversation.

"Josh..," I begin, as Ralph grabs the door and yanks it open the rest of the way.

"Hi Josh, what are you doing here?" asks Ralph, matter-of-factly.

"Oh, hi Ralph," Josh says looking a little surprised. "I was out with Tory, and we just got back."

"Josh, if I'm not mistaken, I don't think tonight is one of your nights to spend time with the kids." Ralph said with his, 'I'm in charge' voice.

215

"No, Ralph, it certainly is not. Tory asked me if I would take her out, and I understand that according to that paperwork you gave me, that if a child should request a visit outside the times stated, they will be granted the request with both parents' agreement. Yeah, I read over it just to make sure that there wouldn't be any issues."

"Well, there is an issue. We need to know these things ahead of time Josh, poor communication causes things to fall apart."

"Ralph, Bridget knew about this and didn't have a problem with it. Please don't mistake your role in my children's lives. And don't call control, communication."

I've never seen Josh talk to anyone like this. I can see fire in his eyes. Ralph slams the door and I watch as Josh walks down the driveway toward his Jeep.

"I cannot believe you," Ralph yells out. "After all that I've done for you. You ungrateful..." he says as he grabs my arms and shakes me, then throws me on the couch. This isn't the first time he's done this to me. I begin to cry, but hate that I'm showing any emotion at all. This is my fault, keeps repeating in my head. It will be fine tomorrow. As I begin to cry harder out from my mouth comes. "Please save me." I don't even know who I was crying out to at that moment, but in the next instant there is a crash as the front door flies open and slams against the wall.

The sound of it all must have startled Ralph a little bit because he came hesitantly over to the door to see what happened. His demeanor changed from anger to fear in an instant.

As soon as he sees Josh standing there, he yells at the top of his lungs.

"I'm going to call the cops on you. You're going to jail for this. You can't break someone's door down," he says with anger rising in his voice.

"You're not calling anyone. I have video of you abusing Bridget on my phone. Do you really want that in the headlines in the morning?"

"Get out of my house Josh, before someone gets hurt."

"There have already been too many people getting hurt in your house, Ralph."

Then Josh turned to me, "Can I take the kids with me?"

I nod in agreement.

"You're not taking my kids anywhere!" Ralph yells.

"They are not your kids Ralph, and if you try and stop us, the headlines will expose you to the world," Josh retorted. "You can come with me if you want, it's your choice," Josh turned to me and said with such love in his eyes.

"Bridget," Ralph piped in, "if you leave me you are leaving who you really are. This is everything that you wanted. The shopping trips, the freedom to make your life the way you want it, not wondering where the money will come from, and your protection from sickness. You will throw all that away and I won't take you back."

"Ralph, let me speak with Josh alone," I say.

"But..." he stammers knowing he has lost control of the situation. And he hates not having control.

"Ralph, I need to speak with Josh alone," I repeat with a firmness in my tone.

Josh and I step outside of the door.

"Josh," I say as tears begin to well up in my eyes. "I am responsible for so much pain. For all this time I thought pain just happened to me. And now I'm the one who has caused it. I feel like there are two roads for me and neither one of them seems easy. I just don't know which is the right one Josh. But I can't leave yet. I'm not ready."

"But what if he hits you again, or worse?"

"Josh, I don't understand it all, but I'm not ready yet and I'm not going to be back and forth with my choices anymore. I'm not sure how to help you understand."

"Understand what? I've shown you nothing but love, yet in the times when things were tough and uncomfortable, you actually believed that somehow my love had stopped. I know I didn't always have every detail of our life laid out, but we're still here. We always had enough. And look at you, you're better. I told you that you would get better, and you are. Bridget, what does it take for my bride to understand what true love is?"

"Josh, I'm just not ready," I say.

"Okay," he replies as his shoulders sink. He knew he could win a fight against Ralph, but this fight wasn't with Ralph, it was with my heart. And although he had poured out his life for my heart, it was still up to me to make the choice of where my heart would dwell.

"Bridget, we'll be up at my parents," he says.

"Okay, Josh. I'm so sorry," I pause, "it seems like I've messed everything up again."

"Well, then you're the only one who can clean it up, but if you want my help, I'm here."

"Thank you Josh, I'll get the kids packed up," I say. I walk quickly up the stairs and hurriedly pack their things. I don't want to leave Josh and Ralph down there alone for too long. I'm not sure how things would go.

Tory and Ben go running down the stairs with their backpacks on. "Dad, we're going to Grandma and Grandpa's?" Ben yells.

"Yeah bud, go ahead and hop in the Jeep," Josh says.

Ralph steps forward, "No way, you can't take them up there. It's... too far away, and we don't have a good way of contacting you up there." He looks at me hoping I will agree with him or at least be moved by his manipulative tone, "You can't let them go up there."

"Ralph, I can't change that. I'm sorry," I say.

He storms off into the kitchen sulking at his obvious loss of control.

218

"Goodbye Bridget. You know where to find me if you need anything," Josh says as he turns to leave.

"Thanks Josh," I say.

In my heart I want to jump in the Jeep right now, but I know it isn't the time yet. He stops and turns around and with a look I remember from our wedding day, he says, "The next time you see me, you can call me Joshua."

"Okay," I say, as tears begin to stream down my face.

I watch as they drive down the road and out of sight. I really am not sure of what is next for me. But I know I have a few things that I need to deal with, in order to find closure.

Chapter 26

Since Josh left with the kids, it has been quiet here. Ralph and I avoid each other at all cost. He's tried a couple times to be nice, but by this time I can see his motives and want nothing to do with it. I've been sleeping in Ben's room and Ralph is gone before I wake up. I'm not sure why I'm waiting to leave, I just feel like there's something that still needs to take place. I kind of think I need to tell Ralph that I'm leaving so that he knows I'm not coming back, but I'm a little scared as to how he's going to react. Maybe I'll wait a few more days.

days later...

Nothing has changed. If anything, I just feel like I'm losing more of myself with each day that passes. Ralph still hasn't been around much and I wonder if he would even realize it if I was gone. I've been thinking about just leaving a note, that way I can leave quietly and be able to explain all the reasons why this isn't right.

As I walk into the kitchen I see a letter on the counter with my name on it. Looks like Ralph beat me to the note writing.

Dear Bridget,

I know we have a lot of things to talk about, but it seems that you are so closed off to me lately. We've had so many good times, I feel like it would be a shame to throw all that away just because we had some misunderstandings. As I was thinking about your situation and all the choices you've made, I couldn't help but think that Josh would probably have a tough time forgiving you for everything you've done to him. I'm honestly okay with you still seeing Josh from time to time and continuing to live here. I don't think it makes sense to walk out on all that we've become. That seems like a worse decision than your first one. If anyone knows what it means to make some bad choices in life, I do. I can understand you way better than Josh can. We are so much alike, and I can't help but think that if you return to him you will regret it because of all the things you will miss out on. I honestly think it would be tough for Josh to look past all the pain that you've caused him. He will probably have a tough time ever trusting you again. But I trust you. I know that what you really want in life is to be happy and safe, and I can give you all those things. Let's not give up. Let's just figure out a way to compromise. I'm sure Josh would be okay with that.

Your lover, Ralph

He's right. I can't do this. I don't deserve Josh, and I would just make things worse. Just then Josh's words ring in my head.

"Bridget, I will never leave you or turn my back on you."

How can he possibly say that to me? After all that I've put him and the kids through? I deserve everything bad that has come to me. I don't even care anymore about the panic attacks. I know Josh is the only one that can help me get rid of those for good. Ralph has done nothing but lie to me, steal from me, and cheat on me. I can't trust him.

That's it!

His letter.

I can't trust his words, no matter how good they sound or how close to truth they are. I can't trust him.

I sit here pondering my options. I really need someone to help me think through what I should do next.

I'll ask Gabi what she thinks. She always seems to know the right thing to do even if I don't agree with her at first.

two hours later...

"Oh Bridget," Gabi says as she gives me a hug. "How are you feeling?"

"I'm doing okay. Actually I'm doing a lot better than before. I feel like a cloud has lifted off of me and I am thinking clearly for the first time in a while."

"Wow, that's great. I guess a lot has happened since the last time we talked. Tell me everything," she says.

I spend the next 45 minutes explaining and retelling stories and pouring out all that I've come to understand about myself and my situation.

"Well, what are you going to do?" she asks.

"I was thinking that I would just leave him a note and take off tomorrow while he's at work. What do you think?" I ask hoping she agrees.

"Honestly, I think you need to tell him face-to-face."

Oh boy, here we go again. Why can't she just give me an answer that is easy for once.

"Okay, why do you think I need to tell him face-to-face?"

"Well, if you leave him with a note, you are walking away while holding onto fear. I think there's something to you standing up to the thing that really makes you afraid."

I know why she's saying this. Because whether or not she realizes it, every single time in my life I've had to face a fear, I spent so much time trying to find an easier way out. I know she's right. I think this time I will just listen to her.

"You're right, Gabi." I say.

"I am?" she says astonished at my agreement with her.

"I'm going to face my fear head on. It's what I need to do to be able to move on."

I stand up, grab my keys and hug her tightly.

"You are a true friend, Gabi. Thanks for not giving up on me when I wasn't being one."

"You're welcome," she says as she starts to cry.

As I'm driving home I am trying to figure out how to talk to Ralph about all of this.

I think I have an idea.

Chapter 27

I get right to packing my things, as well as the rest of the kids' things into my car as quickly as I can. I make it a point to leave all the things that Ralph bought for us here. I'm not taking anything with me that has the stain of his existence on it. Except my car obviously. I mean, I have to be able to get out of here, and it's mine. Ralph gave it to me. I'm leaving no matter what, and I want to be able to walk out of this house quickly.

I then spend the next two hours preparing a feast. I make some of Ralph's favorite dishes and spread them over the table. I honestly don't know where this idea came from. I just felt like it was the right thing to do.

Ralph walks through the door in his usual arrogant manner.

"Hey Bridget," he says, as he walks around the corner past the dining room. "Whoa, what's the special occasion?"

"Oh nothing special, just felt like I needed to do this for you," I say.

"Well I'm glad to see you've been thinking through things rationally," he says as he walks over to the table to grab some food.

"Not yet Ralph," I say sternly.

"Fine, fine," he laughs.

I walk over beside the table and face him.

"Ralph I need to ask you something."

"Sure, but can we make it quick, this looks good and I'm pretty hungry."

"Did you purposefully lead me away from my family?"

"What? What are you talking about? I think you've got some craziness going on in your head," he snickers.

Don't get distracted, I can do this.

"Ralph do you see this table full of food?"

224

"Yes, and that's the problem, Bridget. I'm hungry, so what is all this about?" he says getting visibly angry.

"This table represents what I had before I met you. My life was full. It was wonderful, but when you came you feasted at a table that was not yours." With that I grabbed the table cloth and pulled as hard as I could, causing each dish to come crashing to the floor. "You took everything from me Ralph, for what? You don't love me, you're obviously cheating on me, and as for my poor kids, they are more damaged than I would've ever allowed had I known what you were."

"You are a fool, Bridget. You waste everything. Just look at what you did to Josh, you wasted all his love. He has no reason to love you. He'll never love you for anything you can do for him," he yells.

"Ralph, you are right. There are no reasons for him to love me. That's how I know he really does love me," and as those words left my lips the reality of what true love is, washes over me. I snap back into my surroundings. "Ralph I'm leaving, and I will never be back."

"Oh yeah? You'll come back to me once you start having those panic attacks again. You are a slave to fear Bridget, can't you see that? You need me. I'm your security."

"No, you're not!" I yell. "If I'm going to beat my fears I have to walk through them, and Joshua is the only one who can help me do that."

I turn and walk toward the door. I can hear Ralph yelling behind me. His voice is a blur but I can tell he's trying every last ditch effort to get me to stay. Fear was my prison. I just didn't realize that all this time, Ralph was my prison guard.

Chapter 28

The drive up the highway is a blur, mostly because of my tears, but also because of voices and thoughts running rampant around my head. I have thoughts of complete confidence and thoughts of utter hopelessness warring each other and I honestly don't know which is stronger right now.

As I approach the exit off the highway it's just starting to get dark and looks like it might start raining.

This should be fun, I say to myself. With the majority of the roads leading to the farm being dirt, it makes for quite an adventure to be driving on them in a rain storm. I stop at the gas station just off the exit and walk in to get a coffee. The attendant looks at me with a look of, 'You ain't from around here, are ya?'

"Will that be all Miss?" he asks with a hill-billy accent.

"Yes, that will be all, thank you."

"You ain't driving far, are you?"

"Just about another 20 miles into the mountains."

"Oh my, you may want to rethink that one. There's a big storm blowing through. They're saying downed trees and hail, and lightning. I reckon it'll be a doozy."

"Really? Well, I should be safe and sound in 30 minutes. Besides I have all-wheel drive on my SUV."

"Ha, you mean four-wheel drive? On that thing? That's funny, that looks more like it belongs in a showroom than on a dirt road," he says chuckling.

"Well, I'm sure it will do just fine," I say matter-of-factly. Honestly, I'm a little annoyed that he thinks my vehicle won't make it.

"Listen lady, here's my card. If you get stuck out there, Maurice and I will come get you and bring you back here."

"Who's Maurice?"

"Right out there to the left," he says, pointing out the front window of the store.

226

I look out and scan the parking lot, but no one is there; only an old beat up truck with big tires and rust spots. I laugh, but then try and cover it with a cough.

"Oh, thank you, I will keep that in mind," I say as I grab my coffee and start walking out to my off-roading luxury vehicle.

The rain starts falling as I start the engine. I pull out of the gas station and notice dark clouds that seem to be coming closer to the ground with each minute that passes.

fifteen minutes later...

I'm sitting here on the side of a dirt road holding a business card that reads, "Stuck? Me and Maurice will get you unstuck or there's no charge."

Catchy slogan. Should I call? I'm definitely stuck. I mean, there is no movement when I push the gas pedal.

I take my eyes off the road for a split second and I end up stuck in mud on the side of the road. This is not the way I was thinking I would show up at the farm, getting a tow.

I call the gas station attendant, but the line is busy. Great, I guess I'll just wait here.

10 minutes go by and I try the line again. No answer. "What am I supposed to do, walk?" I blurt out into the loneliness of my surroundings.

Another five minutes go by and I open the door. It is pouring. And that is not an over-exaggeration. I'm soaked by the time I step out and close the door. I pull the hood of my rain jacket up over my head, but my hair is already drenched. I know I have at least a two-hour walk in front of me. So, I better get to it.

Over the next hour I realize that the rain is actually soothing to me. Over the last few years I would've looked at this situation as a tragedy. I would've hated everything about it. But before leaving Josh, this would've been such an adventure, a story to tell my kids, a journey that would mark me for life. Although it came as a result of my bad choices, this is the only direction possible toward a good choice.

As I walk, I catch myself singing. It's been a while since I've started singing for seemingly no reason. Singing without music is a funny thing. I think most people only do that when they are either really at peace or really alone. What comes out of your mouth really does reveal your heart, and my heart feels like it is being washed right now. The stains that have set so deeply into it are finally starting to be released and they are dropping off of me like the water that is pouring off of my jacket.

Ouch! What was that? I point my flashlight down at the ground. Oh, gas station man was right, hail!

Well, here we go. Over the next 30 minutes I am pegged all over my body with hail that gets as big as golf balls. I duck under a tree during the golf ball drop and then continue on once it passes. But I don't feel the anger and resentment that I used to feel when something was painful. I keep coming back to the thought of standing in front of Joshua. I don't know that I would have or could have made this trip if I knew it would be like this. I probably would have just waited another day, but I know I needed to leave when I did. Another day of staying there might have killed me.

Finally something looks familiar, the old creek bridge. As I walk across it a feeling overwhelms me. It's the feeling that there are people around you cheering you on. I glance around at the dark forest surrounding me and see nothing, which in my case is probably a good thing, but I can't shake this feeling. I remember these feelings when I was a teenager running in track meets. I never ran for the cheering, but there was something so powerful about it. And now, I feel like I'm on my last lap. Probably about 30 more minutes and I will find myself in a moment where hopefully, my life will again change forever.

Over the next 15 minutes I begin to see more and more lightning. It even starts to get close. I look up at the dark clouds and start laughing. "Seriously, am I going to get struck by lightning now?"

In the moment the words leave my mouth a bolt lands on a tree within 12 feet of me and as I watch in what seems like slow motion, it's power and force surge through it, splitting it right down the middle. As soon as the energy reaches the ground the impact throws me off of the road. Slowly I open my eyes and everything appears blurry for a few seconds. It seems as if I've been knocked unconscious, but I don't have any idea for how long.

I lay here looking up into the sky that is pouring out it's tears onto my face.

I join in.

I don't even completely understand what my crying was for. But I could tell it came from somewhere terribly deep inside of me. There were groans from the depths of my soul that were being released for the first time ever. Memories flashed through my mind; all the painful situations I've gone through. But somehow this time was different. I didn't feel alone as I looked at myself in those memories. Throughout my whole life, every time I had a flashback it took me to a place of abandonment. It deepened my wounds of feeling like nobody out there cared for or loved me. But now those lonely and desolate places seemed somehow full. Just like the meadow by the lake that Joshua took me to. Those flowers should not have been alive in the dead of winter, but there was a warm spring of water flowing through the midst of them. And now, it seemed as though that same spring was flowing through me.

I continue to weep as I lay here on my back, and then out of instinct, I roll over onto my side and curl up. I continue to cry for another 20 minutes, feeling like I'm being held as this healing takes place in my heart that I don't understand or even believe is possible. It is the worst pain I've ever felt, but it is also the deepest warmth my heart has ever known.

I definitely never expected it to happen in the middle of a thunderstorm while lying in the rain-soaked grass. Unexpected miracles. You cannot control or plan things like this. It's as if moments step into your life like someone else ordered and planned them, and the only thing you can do is surrender to them, receive all they have, and hope that the change they create in you remains throughout your lifetime.

I stand up and I'm still crying. But even my crying has changed. My heart, my mind, my soul, and my strength is bent on one thing. I have to get to Joshua.

With each step I find a quickening. First within my heart and then within my stride. Until I am full out running. There is a difference between running in circles for a prize, and running toward a direction. The direction to the farm is north, and I am convinced it leads me to freedom.

As I approach the porch, a feeling of hesitation stops me, but I know now that I just need to keep taking steps. I push hesitation and fear to the side, step up onto the porch and knock on the door. I stand there amidst my own shivering waiting for what seems like an eternity.

"Can I help you?" he says in his gentlest tone.

"Please, yes, help me," I say with tears still coming down. I pull off my hood and look up into his eyes, those bright eyes, glowing with love like a fire.

"Bridget?" he stammers.

"Josh, please save me. I'm ready to come home. I don't even know if there is still a home for me. But if there is, I'm ready. This has been worse than going through those years of almost dying. I honestly thought that if I could just find a place that seemed like it was more stable, that I wouldn't have fears. I was deceived. Ralph is not who I thought he was. And all the safety and comfort I thought I was receiving with him actually turned into him controlling me. I have lived in a

230

worse place than I ever wanted to. And I gave up so much. Is there any way I can come home? Please say it's not too late Josh. I'm so sorry. I know what this did to you. I can't believe I did this to you. I don't deserve you, and you didn't deserve this. I was so wrong. Please forgive me."

"Bridget... call me Joshua," and with that he stepped forward and wrapped his arms around me. I could feel my body release all of its tension, all of its hesitation.

"Joshua, I do love you. Will you please forgive me?"

"Of course I will, my love."

We stood there for what seemed like an hour. Both of us refusing to let go. Words were not necessary. We were speaking with the unheard sounds and lyrics of love.

"Joshua?"

"Yes?"

"I think I finally know why you love me."

"Oh yeah, why is that?" he asks.

"It's because you choose to. Every moment you put my needs above yours and you see me the way I could be, not the way I am. And because your love for me isn't about what I do or who I am. It's really about who you are. Thank you, Joshua," I say as I rest my head on his chest and breath deeply. "Joshua? Do you think things will ever be like they used to be?"

He takes my face in his hands and looks down into my eyes, "No, I don't. But I don't want things to be like they used to be. I want something new, something better than before. And honestly, I think that the journey we've been on is probably the very thing that will give us that chance. The kids miss you. You really do hold the key to bringing us all together. Come on in."

Chapter 29

I wake up to the sun peeking through the curtains. Joshua is still fast asleep and I feel much lighter. I almost feel guilty for feeling good. I mean, to think that he would just take me back like he did. How does that even work? I don't want to trade it for anything else, but it seems a little unfair for him. I decide to enjoy the morning out by the lake.

As I walk into the kitchen Mom is standing at the counter smiling as she hands me a cup of coffee.

"Good morning, dear," she says smiling.

I start crying. "I can't do this. How are you all so forgiving after what I've done? The guilt of everything is too much. Mom, I'm so sorry. You've always been so amazing and kind to me. Never overbearing with your opinions, just gentle and comforting to me. And I go and do this to all of you and then you make me coffee and it's as if I've done nothing wrong. I don't understand it."

"My dear child," she says as she comes over and embraces me. "It's not about what you've done wrong, it's actually more about what you've done to make it right. You turned away from all those lies and all those bad choices and everything else and you came back to Joshua, and to us. Which is just what needed to happen for all of this to be redeemed. You see, we forgave you before you realized you needed it, but you turning and seeking forgiveness and restoration is what allows true redemption to take place. None of us wanted to go through that, but I think you will actually be stronger because of it and you'll probably see the world quite a bit differently. But as far as the whole feeling bad about stuff, that's probably a good one to go talk to Dad about. He's out on his morning walk," she says smiling as she points toward the lake.

"Thank you Mom," I say as I hug her again.

As I walk down toward the lake I am amazed that my decision to leave Ralph yesterday is changing everything so quickly. I'm met with such love and acceptance. I should be paying for this somehow. I should be staying in a guest room or someplace by myself until I can prove that I won't do this again. That's what I deserve.

"Hey there, daughter of mine," Dad says, grinning from ear to ear.

Okay, let's just face it. Today I will probably cry nonstop.

"I'm sorry Dad, it's just that I..."

"Bridget, I actually know how you feel. Some of those feelings are okay to have. But some of them will actually keep you from the ones you love and from the life you are supposed to live."

"But how could you know how I feel, you never did what I did?"

"Oh, my dear, it doesn't always take experiencing someone else's life to understand the pain that they feel. Bridget, I'm so proud of you."

Here I go with the tears again. I can't think of one reason why he should be proud of me. All I see are the reasons why he shouldn't be proud of me.

"Bridget," he continues, "You walked toward Ralph because of what made sense to your circumstances, because of the depth of your wounds from the sickness, and because of the bait that Ralph was putting out for you. It truly was the perfect storm. But you walked back to Joshua knowing full well, that freedom comes with a process and is many times painful and difficult. I actually think the main reason you came back to Joshua was because of what you chose to believe in your heart, that the journey of love is worth every pain you must endure. Which seems crazy to most people, but not to me.

The easy road is crowded with people, and there is an easy road for almost every circumstance in life. But the easy road never builds anything within you. It only ever takes from you. And when you get to the thing that you thought was the treasure at the end, you find yourself looking around at all the other unsatisfied people wondering what went wrong.

It was a really hard road for you to walk through the sickness and it was an even harder road to come back to Joshua after you had been deceived. I can't deny that your choice hurt all of us. That's a reality that cannot be changed, but what is done is done, and love truly does cover a multitude of sins.

Now about all those bad feelings about yourself, they need to be addressed, because you can't be moping around here with all that shame. Shame is like a door-to-door salesman to me. I don't allow either on my property," he said as he let out a big laugh.

"I know, Dad, but it feels wrong for me to be happy with all that I've done. I honestly feel better walking around with this shame. It seems like the very thing I deserve."

"Bridget, anything you deserved lost its power over you when you left Ralph and restored things with Joshua. That shame will eat you up and drag everyone else around you down. Instead, you should be celebrating that you found a love so powerful that would forgive you in your darkest hour and your greatest need."

"I guess you're right. But how do I get this feeling to stop nagging me?"

"Well, I've actually dealt with this kind of thing before. It's gonna take a lot of trust on your part, but I will help you if you want."

"I do," I said with confidence rising within me. "I want to get rid of it, Dad."

"Okay then," he said. "In three days we'll take a trip and this is what I will need you to do."

For the next twenty minutes he went on to explain all that he had planned for breaking me free from this bondage of shame. I can't help but want to try and find a different way around it, but I know I need to trust him. It does mean I will have to see Ralph again.

I really hope I can do this. I need to do this. I realize now how badly I need Joshua.

Chapter 30

two weeks later...

Although it doesn't seem like a very long time, so much has happened in the last couple of weeks. Dad was right about all that I needed to do to deal with the shame that was plaguing me and now I don't just feel free; I know I am.

There were so many things I knew with my mind before, but as I continue to work through all that has happened, I find I'm wrestling and reaching past knowledge and into belief. I also realized how wrong some of the things I had been believing were.

As amazing as it feels to be free from the bad decisions I had made, I still feel like there's so much that is still hiding inside of me. Maybe this is why they say life is a journey. It truly takes a lifetime to uncover and heal the wounds that live within a human heart. At least that's how it feels some days.

Joshua has taken me up to the waterfall multiple times and I can feel things inside and out being healed. We've also been able to spend some much needed time with the kids. I've cried over them so many times begging them to forgive me for all the ways that I had hurt them. They forgave me, but there's something in my heart that still longs to be able to keep them from making the same mistakes I made. I know it's their choice to do what's right, just like it was mine, but I pray that they will see it without having to walk through it.

As I sit here on Dad's favorite leather chair gazing out the oversized picture window that faces the lake, I wonder what is next for me. I wonder what goes beyond the moment I'm in right now. For most of my life I've been excited about taking the next step; excited about seeing what's around the next bend of my journey. But right now, with all I've been through, I just want to sit. I just want to be still. And I just want to take in each breath I've been given.

Joshua and I have talked a few times about staying up here for a little while and just focusing on our relationship and the kids. I think I really need that. He even started drawing plans up for adding a small addition to the cabin we had lived in across the lake. He and Ben have been like kids in a toy store dreaming up how they can build all sorts of cool things into the extra bedrooms and living area. Ben wants to build a slide that goes from his room the whole way down to the lake. I laughed when I heard about it, but I actually think Joshua might be considering it.

Mom talked to me the other day about starting a business with her. I think it would be a lot of fun. She loves to bake and thought that Tory, myself, and her could team up and sell baked goods at the farmers market.

Tory was so excited when she heard about it. She's been wanting the chance to spend more time with grandma. Tory always seemed to connect with grandpa so easily, but with grandma there just seemed to be this wall. I know she loves her grandma, I think she just wasn't sure how to talk to her, or what to talk about. But I can see a change in Tory already. It's this longing to be fully given to what's around her. She's growing up, and she's beginning to see that connection and relationship; unity and love are what really matters.

I smile each time I see her and Ben. They run around here like they're best friends. They still tease each other and love to play practical jokes on one another, but at the end of each joke they look at each other with such love and care. I didn't think it was possible for them to ever get along, but I guess when you walk through hell together, your friendships become about the things that matter. It's much easier to look past differences of personality and perspective of life. We could all really learn something from Tory and Ben.

I begin to write in my journal:

I'm convinced that this next season of my life will be exactly what I need. There have been times in my life when I have felt like I'm heading the wrong direction. It's that feeling in your gut that says, 'I missed my exit.' If there's one thing that I've learned throughout the years it's this. Sometimes it feels like you're stuck going south, when all you really want to do is head west. But if you find a true compass, you'll see that in time even the roads that lead you in a direction you would rather not go will eventually fill your life's canvas with beauty and clarity beyond what you could've painted yourself. It's not always about following logic of the mind, or what seems to fit with your desires, or even what adds up perfectly to what we feel like we can trust. It's about following what is beyond us. What has no beginning, and has no end. And this is each one of our journey's throughout this earth. What is this? Or better said, Who is this?

I am Bridget, and I am learning to trust a compass that I can not see with my eyes, and does not always make sense to my mind, but always points true north.

I put my pen in my journal and lay my head back as I pull a throw blanket over me. And in this moment of clarity in perspective I give way into a deep sleep. The kind of sleep that feels like it could change the direction of your life forever.

E

Book Three

His name was Ralph.

Dear Reader,

I've wrestled with what to share and what to leave to your own processing of the pages that lie ahead. But I will preface with this.

This book for some will be absolute frustration. For others, it will feel fitting. And still others, it will arise within themselves a question, 'Is there a Ralph in my life?'

We can run from these parts of a story, we can close our eyes and minds to the darker parts of life. However, if we refuse to face the reality of the storm, we will not receive the strength from enduring it. My hope is that as you engage with the words written here you will find all darkness in your hidden places brought to light and prepared for what lies ahead on your journey. Freedom!

"We cannot ignore the existence of evil, that is foolishness. We must expose it, grab it by the neck, and throw it into the fire to burn. This is the only right response when we come in contact with it."

-anonymous

Chapter 1

Some people are given the opportunity to change into the good that they discover within themselves. But what if the evil that you felt inside of yourself is who you really are?

When you have access to things that most people don't, you hold a certain power over others. It's not like I'm heartless. I'm just very aware of my goals and very intentional about accomplishing them.

I remember years ago when I was in high school. I wanted to take the head cheerleader to the prom. She normally wouldn't have noticed me, but I borrowed my Uncle's Corvette for a month and drove it to school everyday. Oh, she noticed me alright. And so did everyone else. They all couldn't believe that I had a corvette and since I had kept things pretty low key before that, no one was the wiser. I almost got her to ask me to the prom by the end of it all. It's funny, in high school, it wasn't about the money. Everyone has what they need given to them. It's really about the stuff. And not just any stuff, the right stuff.

I walked down the hall spinning my keys around my finger as I approached Cara at her locker.

"Hey there," I said, as I leaned up against her locker door.

"Hi," she said, with a smile that said, 'Whatever you want, just take me to the prom.'

"So you want to go with me to the prom?" I said with utter confidence.

"That depends."

"On what?" I said with a little less confidence.

"What car you'll be picking me up in," she said with a smile.

"Well, I think my friend is borrowing the Lamborghini, so it'll have to be the Corvette." I said, smiling back at her.

"Oh bummer, I was hoping for the Lamborghini. Just joking, I'd love to."

That was an amazing night. As good as it felt for her to be in the spotlight, it felt just as good to me to bring that feeling to her. I actually think I get more pleasure out of the feelings that others feel, than any that I have of my own. It's as if I get to live through what they feel.

I noticed this years ago when I was living with one of my foster families. I absolutely loved getting that man and lady to scream at me. Most kids try to avoid that, but I always felt in control when I could push them to that breaking point. There's something to a person's breaking point. It's that place in your life where you get beyond yourself and you begin to make movements that feel outside of your control. In some ways, it's absolute freedom. And inevitably, you feel better once you've let it all out.

In that house, I always felt better at the end of it.

"Ralph, I need you to take out the trash please," said Judy, my foster mom.

"Oh, so you guys just needed a servant, is that why you brought me here?" I knew this wasn't their motives, but it was so fun to see them squirm.

"Ralph, that is not why we brought you here, we brought you here to give you a new start on life. But there are things that we would like you to help us with."

"Sure thing, next it's gonna be do all the laundry and the dishes, so you can sit around, watch soap operas and eat bon bons."

"Ralph, that is not what our intentions are, we just need you to be a part of the family, and being a part of the family means helping out."

"Yeah, except that you always give me the dirty jobs, the ones that only dirty people should do. It's like you think I'm the dirty kid that you have to give a hand out to." I knew

244

at this point I was getting to her. I also knew my future as a prosecuting attorney would be a very prosperous one.

"Ralph," she said with tears welling up in her eyes, "please, we're trying to help you."

Just then the old man walked in and saw the damage I was causing to his wife for yet another time. He turned to me in the rage I had been waiting to see.

"Seriously!" he yelled. "Can't you just stop doing this to her, to us? Look at all we've given you, and all you want is more. You are never satisfied."

"I feel pretty satisfied right now," I mumbled with a smirk as I turned around and walked up to a room they had said was mine.

I heard them talking downstairs as she was crying and telling him that it was all her fault. He would interrupt her with his anger and start telling her that I was tearing the whole family apart and had to leave. I didn't really care. I go where anyone will let me stay. I've learned that it's a part of my being to control situations and lead people, even where they may not want to go. And I will do anything to not let people see who I really am.

Alright, it's probably time that I intervene. I splash water on my eyes and down my cheeks and run down the stairs. I run into her arms.

"Mom, I'm so sorry. Please don't get rid of me like everyone else does. I know I'm bad, but I want to be good," I said trying to show as much emotion as possible.

I can tell my foster dad is gritting his teeth, but I can feel the softening of her heart to me. She won't let go of me. She can't.

And so with that simple act I earn a place to stay for a little while longer. I think it was about three years longer that they put up with me, until she finally had a nervous breakdown and my foster dad really had the final say. By that time there were no pleasantries. He helped me pack my stuff, but that was probably to make sure I didn't steal anything. And with that I was off to a new house and a new family.

I actually didn't set out to be a terror to people. I know it seems like the worst thing to hear what I did to people, but when you have everything taken from you at a young age and you are forced to live like a wandering soul for what seems like an eternity, it just comes natural.

The next home I lived in wasn't much different. The mom was easily moved by her emotions of wanting everyone to be okay, and the dad was easily angered when he felt like things were getting out of control.

There was however, a weird thing that happened that I had never experienced before. It was actually the cause of me choosing to leave.

Chapter 2

My foster family only had one child, a boy who was about two years older than me. One night he went to some church meeting with a friend of his, and when he came back, I could tell something had happened to him. Before that night he was pretty uninterested in me. He would casually engage in the usual pleasantries, but didn't seem to care that I was there. Over the next few days he would keep me awake, even though I was in a different room. I could tell he was awake, and although I couldn't hear anything except what seemed like whispers coming from his room it was like someone was playing a trumpet in my ear. I barely slept for the next few nights and I grew increasingly agitated when I was around him. He began to ask me how I was doing and as I became more belligerent toward him, he became more kind. I needed to do something to stay in control, I just wasn't sure what. I decided it was time to visit Uncle Louie.

My uncle is the best. He is the only one who understands me. I didn't even know my parents, I was just an infant when they deserted me, but Uncle Louie was always there for me. Unfortunately, the system wouldn't let me live with him, because he enjoyed the drink a little too much. He would always tell me that the alcohol may be bad, but it's what it does to you that's so good. I never understood that, I felt more alive when I was feeling things, like anger and rage. I didn't want to numb those feelings. I wanted more of them. But either way, he was what kept me going, and taught me all I know about being in control.

"Hey there squirt," he said, as I walked through the front door of his single wide trailer.

"Hi Uncle Louie," I said, feeling glad to be in a place that felt somewhat familiar to me.

"What's the special occasion?"

"I need some help with something that's going on where I'm staying."

I then proceeded to tell him about what had been happening to me ever since my foster brother went to that church. He listened intently with a smile spread across his face. It's like he knew the ending of the story before I even finished.

"Well it sounds to me like this boy you're talking about just needs to loosen up a little bit. Try taking him out for some fun. You know, the kind of fun that will help him realize what life is really about."

"Alright, I'll try it," I said, not really sure what that even meant.

"Come back and see me in a few weeks if things haven't changed."

I went back to the house determined to figure out a way to get whatever he was doing to stop bothering me. I failed. After five sleepless nights I called my foster care advisor and told them I needed a placement. I made up some story about the family and they moved me the next day.

A few more years of the foster care system and I would be home free. Living life with no hindrances. I went through about four more families until I graduated high school and then it was off to college and then law school. I thrived in this environment. The competition, the arrogance and the partying were all the things I loved. Let's just say I created quite the list of memories during that time.

As far as the arrogance among my colleagues, it was the one thing that drove us to get to the top no matter the cost. Things like integrity are redefined in an atmosphere like that one. If I am perceived as having a level of integrity that is acceptable, then I'm automatically a person of integrity. But honestly, none of us cared about things like integrity. We just cared who was at the top of the class or on the winning side of the debate. By the time I was a sophmore I was leading the top students in our college at the mock trial competitions. I felt like my good deed in life was to help those poor saps learn how to win an argument. The key is recognizing that it doesn't matter if you're right or wrong. It only matters if you walk away having won. You have to be able to say I'm on top at the end of an argument. If you can't do that, then you need to bring in another argument to the mix and become king of that argument right away. Most people are debating an issue trying to find out who is right on that one thing. I was always establishing my authority in the knowledge of every thing, which would in turn, make me appear to be the expert. If people looked at me as the expert on a certain subject than they would already be at a loss if they tried to argue against me. I became undefeatable, not because of what I knew, but because of the perception I had created of myself for others. Nobody wanted to stand up against me. Even my professors learned quickly that being on my good side was a good choice.

Those truly were the glory days. After I graduated from law school I went on to work for a firm for three years. I quickly became one of their top litigators and doubled their number of clients within my time there. I knew I needed to leave and start my own firm when they refused my offer to become a partner. They didn't have any understanding of what I brought to the table, of how I had taken their firm to a place they never could have. After some choice words I packed up my office and walked out their front door toward my new destiny.

Chapter 3

Things picked up right away when I opened my own practice. Although it wasn't exactly ethical, I had taken all my client contact info from the other firm and had called all the clients I had won cases for, which was pretty much all of them, and asked them to come visit my new office. Almost all of them did, and I gave them a card and thanked them for their loyalty and the opportunity to serve them in the future as well as any friends of theirs.

After about two years of working nonstop, I had more money than I knew what to do with and I had to hire two other attorneys to take some of the case load. I kept winning cases and my name became the one that people called.

My slogan was, "If winning is everything, then I will do anything to help you." People loved me. I became like a god to them. There were so many times when they would start to tell me the "true" story, and I would stop them midsentence. I would remind them of my slogan and reassure them that the truth didn't matter. What really mattered is what they needed and wanted out of the situation.

"If you have goals, dreams, desires, then I can help you," I would say. And that was the most honest thing I've ever told people. Because I knew I really could do what I was saying I would do.

Not long after that, I was featured in two different magazines as the 'up and coming' in the region. I began to diversify. I had so much money I decided it would do me well to invest in some other things that I hadn't thought about before. I purchased low income housing units. A bunch of them right downtown. I had them cheaply updated and I began to rent them out. There was a twofold plan I had with this. Obviously, it would make me some money, but I honestly was more interested in the P.R. In my line of work there are many people who would like to expose all your not so good sides to the world. This wouldn't really deter most of my clients, because once you've tasted victory it's hard to give that up for something like the truth. But for future clients, I really needed to give my name a facelift, if you will.

As soon as the apartments were finished I began renting them out to poor people. I started them out with a better monthly rate than they had ever seen before and then every quarter I would raise the price by a small amount. This was a three year plan that was written into the lease agreement, and not to pat myself on the back, but it was utter brilliance. At first I would explain to them in order to keep the amenities I offered on the property I had to charge a little more, but after awhile they just didn't even ask questions.

I wouldn't consider myself a slumlord, I never liked that name, but if someone couldn't pay, then they were out right away. I had also written that up in the lease agreement. Being a lawyer has so many benefits. It allows me to back by the law anything I want. And I have yet to see anyone who is able to fight against my perception of the law and win.

The press made me into a king of the city. I had cleaned up one street and put my name on it. I became very influential in so many people's businesses. I was even asked to come and speak to a few networking groups in the city about how to be successful in a changing economic climate.

I would begin each of the meetings by reminding them that people will pay for what they want. So, if you can find out what the people want then you can always sell them on it. And if nothing you have seems to be what they want, than find a way to convince them they need what you have.

Every time I feel like I must be at the top of my game, I end up gaining more attention and more followers. This is truly the good life.

I still see Uncle Louie every once in awhile, but I haven't needed his advice in quite some time. I'm not much for all that relationship stuff, so I try to avoid being tied too closely to anyone. Besides, he's not really a go-getter like me. He's lived at that same trailer since I was born. He doesn't seem to care about taking more in life than he has. Other than that Corvette, everything else about his life is pretty junky. He's content where he's at, just living like a nobody. And his roommate, Bob, where do I start? That guy lives on a downward spiral. I'm surprised he's not dead yet. He drinks more than my uncle. I told my uncle to invest in a local brewing company once. I told him that with as much as Bob drinks, they could both be millionaires.

I really should go see Uncle Louie sometime. The least I can do is bring him a case of beer.

Chapter 4

When I met Sandy she was so hot and so innocent. So carefree and ready to explore. It didn't take long for her to fall in love with me. I was at my prime. I worked out everyday and had more money than I knew how to spend. I would be what most women would call their dream guy. I would buy her expensive gifts and take her on exotic trips. Her heart was easily won over, and it wasn't tough to see why things were in my favor.

It all started with this thought that maybe I should settle down, at least just a little bit. So, I popped the question after a few months of wining and dining her. And with a big rock slid onto her finger, she was all mine. I knew I had to keep her happy, so whenever she would start getting moody or try and tell me she didn't feel like I loved her, I would buy her something else and she would be happy for a few months. Money wasn't just a safety net for her, it was an identity. I've seen this happen with so many people. Once something becomes your identity it is next to impossible to change your perspective on your need for it. It's like being chained to something that you can't get rid of. It's an incurable addiction. Identity is everything. And Sandy was an easy one to figure out and to keep happy.

I remember when Tony, one of my top lawyers was in the middle of a divorce and asked me how I had such a good marriage. I laughed when he said that.

"It's simple, it's just like a business, give her what she wants and she'll forget what she thinks she needs. You just need to make sure you keep filling the pot of what she wants because if it gets too empty then she'll go looking elsewhere or start thinking and reading those magazines about relationships."

I then pulled out a thousand dollars and handed it to him. "Go buy her some jewelry, and go say you're sorry."

"But what if I'm not sorry, what if it's her fault?" he replied, while still reaching for the money.

"It probably is her fault; but remember, it's not always about being right, it's about winning, about staying in control," I said, smiling.

Here I go giving marriage advice. Who would've thought?

Sure enough, they're still together. I wouldn't say they are happily married, but who actually thinks it's possible to be happy in marriage? It's a worse bondage than anything else in this world. The only reason I'm married is because it keeps me sharp, and it looks good to clients and the rest of the public.

Sandy isn't what I would call the best companion. She's constantly complaining about things. I've become a master at what I call selective listening. Sometimes I wish I had hearing aids so that I could just turn down the volume, but regardless, I know just when to say, "yeah honey, wow," or "oh my."

She's pretty oblivious to most things in life. In my line of work there are many very grateful clients, and I'd be a fool to not take advantage of their gratefulness, if you know what I mean. So it's better that Sandy is who she is, that way it doesn't put the pressure on me to have to worry too much about hiding everything that I do. I'm sure it's no surprise to her that I'm not the most faithful guy out there. But she also knows what she'd be sacrificing if she left me. She tried to corner me on it one time. But I let her have it, and she knew after that point to never breach the subject again.

Women are funny creatures. They are manipulated so easily. Throw a little fear at them and they are bound up in no time. Then convince them that you can take care of their fears and they're yours. Dangle an appearance of love in front of their eyes, and they'll worship you. Tell them they aren't as beautiful as they once were or as some girl on a magazine and they'll become diehards at the gym and even give up food, just to attain that image they think is what they need to look like. They are so easily led away by the emotions they feel that it makes it almost too easy to take advantage of them.

I actually like to use their feelings to our advantage in the courtroom. I explain to them that whatever happened to them is deeply wounding. After over-emphasizing the wound it caused they begin to perceive the situation as worth so much, even if it wasn't that big of a deal. And once someone has a belief of something they will naturally be more ready to die for that belief. I helped a woman sue for a few thousand dollars because a person ran over her lawn. I won the case easily even though there was only a hundred dollars worth of damage, because by the time we got to the hearing she had become convinced that this action against her had actually ruined her well-being. She was so consumed with bitterness and despair over the situation that she was brilliant in the courtroom. As I walked her out of the courthouse she hugged me and said how thankful she was that she won. She got her money. There's obviously some unfortunate side effects of this, like the despair and bitterness that's now a part of her life. However, she did win, and in the end, what's a little turmoil for some cold hard cash?

Men are different. They are usually hardheaded. You have to search to find out what they really want out of life. Some just want to be left alone. They want to sit in front of a television and tune out. These are my kind of guys. All I have to do is paint a picture for them of how a large plasma screen on the wall of their man cave would look and they are in. Even lazy guys will work hard for a short time, if they can have what they think they really want. But when it comes down to it, all I do is give people what they want, and if they don't know what that is, I help them find something to desire.

I am incredibly good at what I do. I've spent years honing my skills with people, but even with all of this, there are times when things don't go the way I think they should.

I had a male client one time that I couldn't quite figure out. It was a small case. I kept telling him that we could get way more money than what he was asking for, but he kept telling me it wasn't about the money.

I smiled at him, "Sure, sure, I know it's not about the money, it's about the principle."

He looked across my desk with a look that seemed to pierce me as he said with a boldness nobody has ever talked to me with, "Ralph, I don't need your help winning this case. I am choosing to use you."

"I don't quite understand what you mean," I responded. "You came to me, obviously you need some help and..." I paused, regaining my composure, "I am just the guy to help you out."

"You are the guy to help me out, but this will be done my way," he said with such an authority, that for the first time ever I didn't feel in control of a situation.

"Okay, sure thing. Just tell me what angle we should use."

"There will be no need for angles. It's a simple case and justice needs to be served."

Well, needless to say, he won the trial, although it didn't seem like he got that much out of it. I, on the other hand, had a pounding headache. It reminded me of the time that I left that foster home because of that boy that kept me from sleeping. After that I decided to only work with people that I could understand. I felt like I was being used and manipulated, and I couldn't stand that feeling. I spent all these years learning how to be in control and I wasn't about to lay that aside for anything.

Chapter 5

Sometimes I can't believe all that I put up with. Sandy is driving me crazy. I don't mind her over the top spending habits, but she's been hounding me this last month about our relationship, and how she doesn't really know me. I keep buying her gifts but it's not working like it used to. She still gets that excited look in her eyes when I give it to her, but then she turns around 20 minutes later and talks about how she wants more time with me. This isn't working any longer. I need a new plan. I need some advice.

two days later...

"Uncle Louie, it's Ralph," I holler through the screen door as I step onto the porch.

"Hey there boy, come on in."

"Where's Bob?"

"Oh, he's passed out on the couch again," he said laughing.

"Don't you ever feel bad for the guy? He seems like such a waste of life."

"Nah, he chose his life. You know people die every day and whoever is left behind gets to choose what they do with that pain. When his wife and kids died he chose to come waste away up here, and it just so happened that I needed a roommate, so it was a good deal for both of us. Enough about Bob, though. What do I owe this visit to?"

"Well, it's just that Sandy is giving me such a hard time. She's hounding me constantly about our relationship. I've been buying her stuff nonstop and nothing seems to satisfy her. The other day she even talked about having kids," I said laughing out loud.

"Whoa, that's pretty serious. I didn't think you'd get to this point. Can you tell if anything has led her to this?"

"Well, the only thing I can think of is that she's been meeting with this women's group and they are all talking about bettering their marriages. At first it just seemed like a gossip group, which I actually liked because that meant she wasn't yapping at me as much; but after awhile she began asking questions about what being happy really looks like.

I tried to stop her from going cause I could tell it was making her think, and we all know how dangerous that is, but she kept telling me how good it felt. You can imagine how frustrating this is to me, since I'm used to being the one who leads her feelings. Regardless, I need help. This can't go on any longer. I need her to be back to who she was. Easily controlled."

"Oh my, that sure is a pickle you've gotten yourself into. But you've come to the right place. Here, have a seat," he said as we walked out to the porch and pulled forward a nearly dilapidated rocker. "What you need is a major distraction. You need something that allows you to be the hero again. You've been doing the same thing for too long with Sandy. You've got to spice up the game a little."

"Okay, what do you have in mind?"

He went on to explain his plan to me.

"Brilliance, pure brilliance," I said after he laid it all out so masterfully. I can't believe I didn't think of this. "You're right, Sandy has to see her life as hanging by a thread so that she will come to a place of neediness again," I said smiling.

later that day...

"Hi honey, how was your day?" I say as I walk into our house.

"Uh, hi," she says sounding shocked at my greeting.

I guess I don't normally show that much interest. I should probably tone it down a bit.

258

"It was good, nothing too interesting. How about yours?"

"Mine was great. I feel like I got a new perspective on some stuff."

"Well that's good. Are you ready for dinner?"

"Yes, I would love some dinner."

As we sat down at the table I couldn't wait to implement my new plan.

"Sandy, are you okay?" I say with care in my voice.

"Yeah, I think so. Why do you ask?"

I know this must seem so foreign to her for me to show concern like this. She seems incredibly guarded right now.

"Lately you've just seemed tired when I've seen you, and you look sort of pale right now."

"Really? I think I'm okay; but come to think of it, I have been really tired. I probably need to try and get to bed early tonight, maybe I'll head up now."

"Yeah, that's a good idea. Let me know if I can bring you anything."

"Okay," she says with a look that says 'who are you?'.

Over the next week I continue to couple my comments about her not looking healthy with a raised concern and care for her wellbeing. This may sound heartless. I mean it's not like I want her to die or anything. I just need to get back to that place of control. If I'm not in control, things get out of control, and I can't stand when things are out of control.

Finally, I convince her to go with me to see my friend Larry, who is a doctor. Larry runs some tests and shows us that some of her levels show that there is a slight possibility of cancer.

That was all that I needed. She cried the whole way home.

"I'm going to die. I can't believe this. My life is over."

"No, stop it. We are going to fight this and win. I won't let you die." I grabbed her hand and squeezed it. "Look at me, I'm not going to let you die."

With that she leaned her head over and rested it on my shoulder as she continued to sob. This was a great idea.

"How can you be so sure?" she asked whimpering.

"Because I've always taken care of you, haven't I?" I said with such determination. "Larry said that we can start treatments next week and make sure that this is taken care of."

"Really?"

"Yes, and I have you on the best treatment plan possible, as well as a surprise for you at the end of all this."

"What! What kind of surprise?"

"Well I was thinking that the Jaguar you're driving is getting too old. I mean, three years is a long time to have a car."

"I was just thinking about that also, you know, because of safety and all."

"Definitely. Well, remember how much you liked that Lexus two seater with the convertible top? I thought that might be a good celebration prize."

"Oh Ralph, you are my hero," she says as she sighs.

Like music to my ears.

Chapter 6

two weeks later, driving home from the hospital...

I know this seems crazy, but I cannot get her off of my mind. It feels like something has shifted in me. I've been so driven at work, so driven by accomplishment, and now all I want is to see her again. I've been with so many women in my life, but none have ever made me feel this desire before. I have to have her. She doesn't seem like any of the other women I've met. She's strong, even in the midst of her suffering. She's certainly not an easy target, but I am pretty cunning and determined.

Oh Bridget, there is something about you that just drives me crazy.

I decide to visit Uncle Louie again. After all, his plan with Sandy is working miracles for our marriage. Maybe he can help me figure this one out.

the next day...

Uncle Louie is sitting on the front porch as I drive up. "Back so soon? Didn't my plan work?"

"Actually, it worked a little too good." I smiled.

"Well then, what are you here for?"

"Well, I met someone at the hospital. She's actually Sandy's roommate and I've never felt anything like this before. She is so powerful and full of life. I can't even explain all of it, I just know I have to be with her. I need your help."

"Well let's see, tell me more about this girl."

"Well, she does have a family, which is obviously not ideal, but I'm willing to deal with the collateral damage. And she seems like she's not easily swayed by money or stuff, but I don't think it's anything I can't handle."

"Well yeah, that is not ideal. Do you know anything else about her?"

"Oh yeah, just that her father in law is the old mayor of the town."

"What?"

"Yeah, you know the guy they fired after that whole mess with the guy who was printing fake money."

"Yeah, I know the guy. Listen, just forget about this girl. There's a million just like her out there. Go find some other girl if you're bored with Sandy."

"What? I don't think you understand. I can't just forget about her."

"Well you are going to have to figure out a way to forget about her. Trust me, you don't want to mess with her."

"Can you at least tell me why?"

"Just trust me, you don't want to mess with that family."

"Fine. I gotta go."

"Sure thing Ralph, but I'm warning you. People like them will ruin you."

I spent the next week trying to get her out of my mind, with no such success. I finally concluded that Uncle Louie didn't know what he was talking about and that there was no way he could understand what I was going through or my abilities to make this happen. You can call this arrogance, but it's the exact thing that brought me into existence and got me everything I now have. And that's quite a lot.

I spent another week just trying to come up with a plan. I ran every scenario possible through my mind. But from what I knew of her, none of it would work. She didn't seem to care too much about stuff or wealth. I know she is sick, but even that seems to not be a huge issue for her. I have to figure out a way to her heart. There has to be some place of weakness in her.

As I walk into the hospital room I can hear Bridget crying. She is facing the window and, for the first time, I can see this has taken a toll on her. I can feel her weariness. Something like a confidence in me grows. This is what she needs. She needs to know she will never go through this again. We talked for awhile that day as Sandy was sleeping. The seed was planted in her heart. It was the very thing that would take time, but given her circumstances, would definitely grow. Now it was a waiting game, and although I am not very good at waiting, I am confident that this game is worth playing.

Chapter 7

Sandy got to the point where they couldn't keep her in the hospital any longer, and the doctor told her she was completely healed. She looked very relieved. Of course, as soon as we got back to the house she took a shower and got all dolled-up and then told me she was ready.

"Ready for what?" I said just settling down in my favorite leather recliner chair.

"Ready to get my car!" she squealed.

"Oh yeah, alright let's do that," I said, not even half as excited as her.

"I can't wait, you really are the best," she said as she sat down in my lap.

If she only knew what I was really like, and what I was planning she wouldn't be saying that. We drove down to the dealership and traded in her car for a brand new Lexus. I honestly wasn't that impressed with the car. But she was in love with how the car looked and how it made her feel. She really is vain. I, at least, am aware of my issues and choose to use them as strengths, but she is just ruled by her issues.

I decided to tear off the band aid on the way home and there's only one way to tear off a band aid.

"Uh, Sandy?"

"Thank you so much Ralph! This makes me feel so alive again! I mean, I felt awful in that hospital for all those days. I can't imagine what that girl in my room must've felt like. You know I can't get it out of my mind; for all the time I was in there I never heard her complain about it. She would cry sometimes because of the pain, but I never heard her complain. That's weird to me. Why do you think she never complained?"

I met her with a look that said, 'we just covered ten topics in two sentences.'

"What?" she questioned. "Why are you looking at me like that?"

Sometimes I think there's hope for Sandy to become a strong woman like Bridget, and then there's moments like these where I realize she is who she is.

"Sandy, the truth is that I'm not happy in our marriage. It really isn't about you, it's about a lot of things going on with me and I can see those things hurting you and I don't want that for you, so I need us to separate so that you don't get hurt."

There it is, I tried to get that all out at once so that she would be able to have a clear understanding of what I really meant. I always say honesty is the best policy, unless it costs you something. Then there is always a better way. She didn't have to know the whole truth on this subject, just the pertinent facts. I was done and moving on.

"You what? Why now? Are you cheating on me? I... I just don't know what to say. I mean, you just bought me a car."

"I know there's a lot of questions right now. As far as the car goes, I thought it would be like a parting gift. Something for you to remember me by. That way you can't say I didn't ever do anything for you."

"You really don't know how a woman works, do you?"

"Um, we've been married for quite a few years, I think I have a pretty good idea," I say chuckling.

"No, you don't! From the day we met everything has been about you, and about how you can have what you want. I have never once felt like you did something for me or gave me a gift that didn't come with selfish or ulterior motives. Your life is consumed with you and I honestly don't think it's possible for you to be anything else."

Finally, she gets it. This is who I am. I mean, I knew this all along.

She continued to berate me for a good ten minutes, and then when she was finished she looked over at me and said, "Fine, let's get a divorce, but I will be well taken care of if you expect me to leave quietly."

"Honey of...."

"Don't, just don't with your fake kindness," she interrupted.

"Okay then, we will treat this like a business deal."

"No we will not, you snake. You will give me what I ask, and I will keep your not so good reputation unknown to the rest of the world."

I sighed, "Okay."

As soon as we got into the house she headed upstairs to pack her things. I offered to help her with boxes or carrying things, but she wanted nothing to do with me being anywhere near her. I decided this was a good time to head into the office and catch up on some work.

"Goodbye, Sandy. I'm heading into the office."

"Whatever," she replied with disdain.

"Sandy?" I said gently.

"What?" she snapped back.

"Thank you." I could tell this stunned her, as she had rarely heard me say those words to her. She turned right around to look at me.

"For what?" she said hesitantly, half expecting to get slammed again with my words.

"For the pleasure you've brought me through the years. The way that you feel so strong about things actually felt so good to me. I felt so alive so many times throughout our years together. And you know me, busy with work and all, that doesn't happen too often." I really meant it. I was thankful for all those times.

"I guess you're welcome."

"I'm sure I'll be seeing you around. I mean, I'll be sending you a check every month," I said with a chuckle.

"Yes you will be," she said with a sideways smile, "sending a check, I mean. As far as seeing me, I'm going to stay with my sister, so I will not be seeing you Ralph."

"Okay well, bye then."

"Bye," she said becoming increasingly uninterested with my presence.

As I drove to my office I felt a sense of loss that I'm not used to feeling. This was very different from my experiences of leaving before. It's not like I really cared about her, but there was now this hole inside of me that I wasn't sure would be filled.

I worked late into the night and when I returned, the house was so quiet. There had been so many days when the house felt more full than I would've liked it to. So many days when I came home and wished she wasn't there, ready to bombard me with her ten thousand questions and thoughts. But now it just feels empty, similar to how I feel most of the time.

Well it looks like I need to get working on filling this place back up. Since Sandy is no longer at the hospital, I have to find a way to stay in contact with Bridget. Maybe I will visit her a couple more times.

Chapter 8

some time later...

I knew that card would work, but I did not expect it to take this long. It's funny, I've actually had to become a higher level of nice for Bridget. I guess whatever works is fine, but I'm not used to acting this sappy and kind.

Waiting is a funny thing. I always thought I would be okay with waiting for things, but I'm really not. I'm more of a pay as much as you need to, to get the job done now, kind of guy. This is new territory for me.

If I can just get this client out of my office quickly, I really need to get over to the cafe to meet Bridget. It's the first I will have seen her in quite some time. I wonder how she looks now? I wonder how she's feeling?

one hour later...

Beautiful. Even better than before. But I can sense there is something different about her. That resolve that I saw in her lying in that hospital bed. There's something different about that. She's carrying something that I didn't see in her before.

"Hello Bridget," I say

"Oh, Hi Ralph," she says

I decide this is the time to give her a hug. I don't want to scare her off, I just really want to let her feel that I care about her.

"So let's get to it," I say. "By the way, you look stunning, Bridget. I mean, you always looked so beautiful in the hospital, but wow, you are just stunning."

There's that smile. It's so easy to get a woman to smile. You just have to tell them what they are longing to hear.

"Thank you, Ralph," she says, still smiling.

268

"So what are your goals Bridget? In ten years what do you really want to be able to say about your financial situation or life or housing?"

"Well, I'm not really sure any of that matters that much to me. I just really want to be at a place where we have enough money to pay for the things we need. I've been thinking about the two treatment plans you and I talked about in the hospital and I wondered what it would've looked like if we had the money to put towards me having a better plan. Maybe I wouldn't have had to suffer as much. Do you know what I mean?"

I'm a bit surprised she believed this line I fed her in the hospital. I wouldn't exactly say that's the whole truth. It's more like, if you have money, you can get a more comfortable bed, and maybe some better food. That certainly would've made things more comfortable for her, so I guess it's not a complete lie.

"Oh Bridget, it took everything in me to not talk to Joshua about what he was doing by not paying for the other option," I said with the most compassion I could muster.

"Wait, you think he knew there was another option?" she said with a surprised and almost angry look growing on her face.

"I don't know Bridget, it just seems to me that it's a pretty common scenario and that if I were in his shoes I would've been asking a whole lot of questions to find out if there was another way."

"I think he probably did ask that. Maybe the doctors knew we didn't have much money so they didn't even want to bring it up," she said.

"You're probably right. I just wish I could've changed that for you. I don't think anyone should have to go through what you went through. But look at you now, you are amazing for fighting through that."

269

"I just don't want to ever have to go through that again," she said, almost pleading.

There it is. I was wondering what the chain was that she is now carrying. And now I can see it. Fear and abandonment, like two evil brothers stand behind her with their hands on her shoulders. She will do anything to avoid the pain and agony that she went through during her illness. I've seen this before. When people can't see any good in their journey through difficulties, they consider it a curse and do everything possible to never come under it again. But getting rid of something that feels like a curse doesn't happen by just trading it for something else. In fact, most people that try and trade their issues just end up with more issues in the end.

"And you shouldn't have to go through that again, Bridget. I hope that Josh can see what this has done to you and make better decisions in life to make sure that you are free from ever having to worry about all that."

"Thank you Ralph, I do too. How are things going with you and Sandy?" she asks.

I can't tell if she really cares or she's checking in on my status. I hang my head, and work out a tear that rolls down my cheek.

"Sorry Bridget, I'm not usually very emotional. Well, she filed for divorce about two months ago, and it's final as of yesterday. I had wondered if she was just after my money, and it appears that she was. I loved her so much, Bridget. It hurts so bad when you want to give everything to someone and they are so ungrateful. She's so different from you. I can tell that you are such a grateful person, and hearing about how you love your kids, it just makes me feel so... I don't know what I'm trying to say, just that you are unlike anyone I've ever met. You give me hope that there is someone out there that's perfect for me."

"Thanks Ralph, you seem like such a nice guy. I'm so sorry to hear about Sandy. Please let me know if there's anything I can do to help."

"Honestly, it's just nice having a friend to talk to."

"Of course I can be your friend, Ralph."

As we reach her car, I grab her hand just to let her know that friendship is the first step toward relationship. After all, I don't want my intentions to be too hidden.

"I will talk to you later," I say, as I turn to walk away.

"Okay, goodbye," she says.

Well, I would say that went pretty well. I can't believe how taken by fear she is. I can smell it all over her. She still has that appearance that everything is okay and she will make it, but I can tell she's looking for an answer, a way to control her circumstances and outcomes. She's tired of waiting and trying to trust in what she is actually unsure of. She's going to do whatever it takes to make an answer happen. And I know just the guy that can help her with that.

Chapter 9

For the past six months I've had to do things I normally would never do. I've helped people when it didn't benefit me in any way, except for one. I've gotten so close to Bridget I can feel her heart turning toward me and away from that joker she married. That guy has no motivation. He seems like he doesn't care about anything in this life. Every time I talk to someone who has met him and I ask about him they all say that he's genuine. What does that even mean? Genuine? That sounds like a word from 'Leave it to Beaver.' If anybody is genuine it's me. I know what I want out of life and I don't stop until I get it. Being genuine sounds like something that's worth a lot, so if anyone can afford to buy it, it's me.

Other than that, I can't seem to get any dirt on this guy. There's got to be something about him that she doesn't like. I mean, I can find plenty of things that I don't like about him. Sure, there's parts of what people have told me about him that seem nice enough, but in reality, nobody lives like he does. Who would want to? And besides that, who could live that way in this world? It is cutthroat and if you are not the one doing the cutting then you won't last long. That's why I'm determined to be the best and stay on top.

Maybe it really is just about her. If I can get her to see herself as the most important thing in her world, then anything that doesn't go her way will become a tragedy. Then she'll do anything possible to keep things going her way. I just need to help her to become more like me, a go-getter. I see what I want, take it and count the cost later. Bridget, the go-getter. That's my next assignment. To open up all sorts of dreams and desires in her heart that she believes will never happen unless she does something about it. Some people would actually have the nerve to call this a selfish perspective on life. That's ridiculous. The way I look at it, why else would we be here other than to experience the most pleasure possible in a lifetime.

Humans, by nature, are creatures bent on feeling things, so why not feel as much as possible? I've heard people say before that if you are led by your emotions and feelings you will be all over the place. Yeah, I guess that can happen for the people who don't have any goals, but I like to think of it like this, my feelings are driving me to get things that I normally wouldn't have the drive to get otherwise. Getting what you want out of life isn't cheap. There are things you have to let go of. Some things you may even think are good things. But you have to let go of them so that you can get that one thing that you know will satisfy you, even if just for a moment. And whatever you do, you never live for anyone else but yourself. That's just stupidity. Why would anyone want to serve someone else? I learned that from working at the firm right out of law school. Those guys were so shortsighted. It's a good thing for their sakes I left. I would've taken over that whole firm in a few years and pushed them all out of their own door.

three months later...

Bridget will be living with me in no time. As long as this has taken to get to this point, I must say, it is worth it. I've never had to work this hard for anything, but I've also never had such a strong desire for anything in my life. There's something pulling me toward wanting to conquer her that is unlike anything else. It's like those guys who spend years training to summit Mt. Everest. It seems crazy to most people, but it's the highest mountain in the world. It's the ultimate feat. I don't completely understand it, but I feel that way about Bridget. I can't wait to feel her lying next to me each night.

I really have to get this paperwork set up so that we will have no issues with Josh about the kids living with us. I can't say I'm excited about having the two runts live in my house, but I knew there was no way to get her without getting them also. I never wanted to have kids of my own. They seem like such baggage. They are so needy, and always asking for more. I figure I can just use all the tricks I used with Sandy on them. I mean, what kid wouldn't love having stuff? In fact, I should go pick up some presents for them now.

Let's see, I could get a skateboard for Ben; who knows, maybe that will get him some cool friends. I've only met him once, but he seems like he might have a little trouble fitting in with the popular kids. And for Tory, she seems like a book worm, but I don't want her reading too much. She needs some entertainment to take her mind off of things. Video games should do the trick.

I told Bridget to come over later today and decorate the kid's rooms just how she wanted. I gave her my credit card and reminded her that money is not an issue with me. I could see it in her eyes. That look that said, 'I think this is what freedom feels like.' I have no doubt the kids will be happy in this house. There's so much room here and all the highest quality electronic devices. I wish I had all this when I was a kid. And I'm sure they will love having the pool out back. They'll probably get more use out of it than I have.

Maybe it won't be so bad after all? This could actually be a new challenge in life. Think about all that I could teach them about getting the most out of life for yourself. I think this could be good to have a few little followers from the next generation. It's a good way to make sure your legacy continues.

Chapter 10

2 weeks later...

"Hey there beautiful," I say, as she steps out of her car. I can't believe it's finally here. She walks up the sidewalk and into my arms. After all that, she's finally mine.

"How did it go?" I ask, acting concerned about her feelings. I really don't care about anything other than her being here and me feeling once again like I'm on top of the world.

"It was tough, but like you told me, there are sacrifices that need to be made in life to get to where you know you need to go. I know I only have one life and I can't be trapped up in fear like I was."

"Yeah, definitely not. Fear is a monster, and what was happening to you with those awful panic attacks is just horrible. You need to be at a place where you can just rest knowing that whatever could come your way, I will just kick to the curb with the mighty dollar."

She squeezed me tighter as if to say, 'I feel safe here.' That's all that really matters in this life is that you feel good about your life. Feeling safe is what she really needed and whether or not I can do what I promised her, she feels the comfort of it all, and that's enough to keep her right here.

Tomorrow the kids come, so I'm sure that will be interesting enough. I'm hoping they realize how much I spent on their gifts. Hopefully it's enough to show them how they will be taken care of here.

I lead her into her new house. A place where she will stay consumed with all the good things of life. A place where she will find out who she really is and what she is really capable of. Throughout this long season of waiting for her, at times I would picture myself standing with Bridget on the top of a mountain and showing her everything around us and offering it to her. All she had to do was come live with me and give up that silly life of not knowing what's next.

I know how to get people to be able to satisfy the desires that grow inside them. And she is no different. For a while when things were going so slowly I wondered if she would be different from all the others; but I was right about her. It just took a little bit longer to help her see it from my perspective.

We spent the rest of the night settling her into the house. She had already seen the kitchen, but now that it was hers, she was ecstatic. She went through all the cabinets smiling ear to ear. I obviously had the best appliances available for her and couldn't wait for her to see all that was now hers by coming to live with me. We walked through the rest of the house as I showed her things she had never seen before or known that I had. This was a house of pleasures. If there was ever a place that made your soul feel good when you walked into it, this was it. From the moment you entered the front door you felt like you were entering a castle. As we made our way to our bedroom, I couldn't help but feel an overwhelming sense of desire for her. She seemed hesitant at first. But as soon as I told her all the things I had planned for us over the next few weeks, she became like putty in my hands.

And so it began, our connection became one that I was sure would last forever. She was now mine and I was sure I was teaching that poor sap who was her husband a good lesson. If you're not going to take what you want, someone else will. It just so happens that I'm that someone else and, once again, I win. I always win.

the next afternoon...

I'm waiting at the door as Bridget shows up with Tory and Ben. I must say I'm a little excited to see how they take to everything. I'm sure they might need some warming up to the idea of a new home and a new dad, but in due time I know that they will see all they are gaining here.

"Hi kids," I say as pleasantly as possible.

They walk right past me and into the house without saying a word. Okay, it will definitely take some time then. I turn around and smile at Bridget.

"I'm sorry, it's just..." she begins to explain.

"Hey, I understand. This is a lot for them. It's really okay. Why don't you show them around. I'm going to head to the gym for a little bit."

"Okay, thanks for being so understanding," she replies.

two hours later...

When I return, Ben is riding around on his skateboard in the driveway. It doesn't seem like he's very good.

"Well, keep working on it," I say trying to encourage him as I walk past him and into the house.

"Whatever," he responds.

I withhold any response that I would love to offer to this kid.

"Honey, are you here?" I holler, as I walk in the door.

Tory was sitting on the couch playing her video game, which she immediately threw on the couch as she ran upstairs crying.

"What's wrong with her?" I asked Bridget, who was sitting on a chair in the family room reading a magazine.

"She just really had a great relationship with her dad and this is pretty hard on her. He really is a good dad."

"Well, I'll be honest, he didn't seem like that good of a man to let you go through all that, and even the uncertainty he let the kids walk through. I would never do that."

"Ralph, you can't take away what he is."

277

I could see that she was getting upset at my slander. I'm not used to this. Usually when I get what I want, I'm not thinking about the best in someone else. I'm thinking about all the bad things in them.

"Listen Bridget, you chose to come live with me. That says something about me and about him, end of discussion," I said in my most authoritative tone as I walked out of the room and up the stairs.

Bridget walked into the room and sat down next to me.

"You're right, I did leave him for you. But the kids didn't choose this. It's going to take more time for them. Just wait, you'll see. They are really great kids and I'm sure they will like you once they get more comfortable here."

"Okay, I can wait," I replied. "Sometimes I just feel inadequate and when you say things about how good he is, it makes me feel like you don't really like me all that much."

I know she has a sensitive spot, so this little co-dependent line should work wonders on getting her to stop talking about him in my house.

"I'm so sorry, Ralph. I won't talk about him anymore unless if you bring it up."

"Thanks honey, that means a lot. Hey, why don't we take the kids out to eat tonight, and then to a movie? That might take their minds off of things."

"Yeah, that's a great idea," she says.

five hours later...

Note to self, never let Tory pick the movie again. No plot, no action, and nothing appealing to me. I think this was the first time Ben and I agreed on something. Now that the little runts are in bed, I finally feel like I have some peace and quiet in the house again. This may definitely take a while to adjust to. Not just for them, but for me. I can't tell you how many times I heard Ben running up and down the stairs and

278

through the hallways. I really need to find a way to get that kid to slow down. There's no need for anyone to act like a kid all the time. I need to start teaching him to grow up. I know he's only eleven years old, but soon he's going to have kids making fun of him for not acting the right way. I can see that I will have my hands full trying to teach him how to be accepted by his peers.

Bridget and I stay up late talking about our plans. I never pictured her as being someone who wanted to spend a lot of money, but maybe that was all just a cover. She tells me all of her plans to take the kids to all these places and do all these things that seem educational. Whatever it takes to keep her happy I'm fine with, but I kind of wish she would just buy clothes and shoes like Sandy used to. I'm not much for all this "purposeful" stuff, as she calls it. I really need to get her involved in something that will keep her busy. Maybe a small business or a women's networking group or even some social justice program. She seems like she really cares about people, so I'm sure I could get her to sign up for something that makes her feel good about herself and occupies her time. The last thing I need is for her to have extra time to think about her past life. I know she's happier now not having all that fear in her face, but I also wonder if she misses certain things about life before she met me? I can tell she's still holding onto things from back then. It's like I can sense that her heart isn't completely given to me. I honestly don't care about that, as long as I don't lose her. I have to make sure the hook remains deep within her soul. I have to keep her eyes on the things that I saved her from. Those are the only things that she needs to be thinking about.

Chapter 11

three weeks later...

What in the world is that noise? I can't take it anymore. I walk down the hall toward this awful blaring I can feel throughout my body. Oh great, it's coming from Ben's room.

"Ben," I say, annoyed, as I knock on the door.

"Yeah, what is it?" he replies.

"Could you please keep it down? I'm trying to sleep and whatever you're doing keeps waking me up."

Normally I would've yelled and made a big issue out of it. This is good. I don't need to do that with these kids, they seem to respond to me just asking.

"Sure thing, I'm heading to bed now anyways."

Well, that was easy enough. Back to bed.

three days later...

Again? I turn to get out of bed. What in the world is that kid doing making so much noise? I walk down the hall toward his room, but he must have heard me coming, I see the lights turn off quickly and hear him jump into bed. Fine with me, at least I didn't have to yell at him. I find that yelling just wakes me up more, which makes me even more angry. Hopefully I can fall right back to sleep.

The next morning at breakfast when Ben comes down, I ask him what he's been doing up so late at night.

"I've just been drawing pictures," he says. "I'm sorry if it's too loud. I honestly didn't think I was making much noise at all."

"Well let's just make a new rule. No more drawing after 10 p.m. okay?" I say in a stern voice.

"Okay," he replies hanging his head down.

I don't know who draws as loud as that kid. But whatever was going on was absolutely awful. I wonder if he just likes to listen to loud music while he draws or what? Silly kid. Well, I'm glad that's taken care of. It reminded me of that boy in that family that I lived with. That was bad enough to go through in someone else's house, I'm certainly not going to let that happen in my own house.

a few months later...

I'm beginning to recognize that the time the kids are spending with their dad is not a good thing. The more he comes around, the more he seems to pull them back over to his way of thinking. At first I was fine with a little friendly competition, but this is getting out of hand. I can even see Bridget starting to pull away from me. I think I have to change my strategy a little bit. If I can get Tory and Ben at odds with each other I'll have a better chance at keeping them all around here. It's funny, I don't even like them being here, but I definitely can't afford to lose to this Josh guy.

I think I will need to work on Tory. If I can get her to see what I see in Ben, then she will easily destroy whatever relationship they have.

the next day...

"Hey there Tory, do you want to go grab some ice cream?" I ask as I grab my keys.

"Uh sure, I guess. But what about Ben?"

"You know Ben, he's probably off in his own little world wasting time dreaming."

"Ha yeah, you're probably right."

I spent that evening telling her all the potential I saw in her. How every time I heard her and Ben arguing I could tell that she was right. I even shared with her some of my best tactics for winning arguments. She was hooked. It's the power that always gets to people. It's the chance to always be right that becomes a crown that no one ever wants to take off. And Tory is the perfect candidate for being a queen. By the end of the evening, she was on my side and I knew that her relationship with Ben was being filled with hairline cracks that would only grow with time and misunderstanding.

I watched over the next few weeks as she would say things so hurtful to him. I was always there to encourage her and tell her how she was right. I could see Ben becoming more and more closed off to her. They wouldn't even look at each other as they walked past each other in the hall. The only problem was that Bridget was starting to notice.

"Hey Ralph?" she asked one night before bed.

"Yeah honey?"

"Have you noticed anything weird between Tory and Ben?"

"No, not that I can think of. Why?" I say with the utmost concern.

"Well, it just seems like they are fighting so much lately, and becoming more and more at odds with each other. I can't help but think something is terribly wrong with them."

"You know honey, it's one of those things that kids go through. They are both getting into their teenage years and all sorts of crazy stuff happens during this time. They're probably both just going through natural changes."

"Yeah, I guess you're right."

"Of course, I'm right," I say with that smile I like to give in the courtroom that says, 'I did it again'.

"Ralph, can I ask you a question?"

"Sure, but let's make it quick, I've got a big day of meetings tomorrow."

"Are you happy? You know, with me and with us?"

"I'm not sure I understand what you're asking, but it seems like that's a good conversation for another time. Let's

282

talk about that tomorrow night, okay honey? I need to get some sleep. I have a new intern starting tomorrow and on top of that a huge case that I need to finish preparing for."

"Okay, goodnight."

Phew, that was a close one. How could I possibly tell her that I don't understand happiness the way that most of the world does. I'm only happy when I'm winning. And once I've won, the only thing that's important is finding the next mountain to climb. Some people would call that unfaithfulness. I call it a drive to excel beyond where you are. To always keep moving further, getting more and never settling for what you have. It's a good principle. It's what got me Bridget, and what keeps me going day in and day out. I am a conqueror. Like those Roman Emperors who loved to take more land and rule over it. There's something so satisfying about it to me. Bridget and her kids are now a part of my empire and I'll be damned if I let them out of my control.

Chapter 12

"Well hello, you must be Rebecca?" I say to our new intern that walks through the door wearing a stunning red dress.

"Hi, are you Ralph?"

"Yes I am. Come on I'll show you around the office."

"Ok, thank you, she smiles as she blushes."

I've had interns here before, but I have to say. She takes the cake. I glance back at her as we walk down the hall to what will be her office.

"This is Tony, he is one of our top defense attorneys."

"Hello," Tony responds with an obvious interest in our new teammate.

"And Doris works down at the end of the hall. She can be a bit grumpy," I whisper. "But don't pay any attention to it. And uh, oh yeah, Cory works in the office beside yours. He's across the state in a case that will have him tied up all month most likely."

"Oh, well thank you so much for allowing me to intern here. I'll do my best to serve any way I can."

"Oh, I'm sure you will," I say with a smile. "Why don't you start by touching base with Doris, she'll get you set up with an email account and all the other information you'll need to know while working here."

"Ok, sounds great," she responds as she walks down the hall, and walks down the hall is an understatement.

I see Cory glance out of his office to watch her.

"Get back in your office," I quietly scold Cory.

"Oh come on man. That girl deserves to be stared at."

"Yeah," I laugh. "I guess you're right."

I think she heard us, cause she looked back, smiled, shook her head and kept walking.

As I sit back down in my office my thoughts are overwhelmed with this woman. I just want to be near her.

The desire is similar to how I was attracted to Bridget, but Rebecca feels like my counterpart. I feel like she's this vacuum and I am not fighting back at all.

...end of the day

"Hi there," Rebecca says as she peaks her head into my office.

"Hi, so how was your first day," I say a little startled and feeling a little bit like a nervous boy in high school.

"It was really good. I think I'm going to enjoy it here."

"I know we'll all enjoy having you here. I mean I know I will."

There she goes blushing again.

"So, Ralph, do you mind if I sit down?"

"Sure, have a seat."

She sits in the chair across from my desk and crosses her legs. Looking up at me with those red painted lips and drawing eyes, she says. "So do you have a family?"

"Uh, yeah, I uh. Well it's complicated, but I do," I say completely not expecting that question right off the bat.

"That's great, I sometimes wish I had a family, but life can be so much more fun and free, not being tied down and all. You know?"

"Yeah, I know, I uh, well, this is crazy that I'm telling you this, but things aren't going very well and I," I say as I pause and look down at my desk.

"I'm sorry I didn't mean to pry."

"No, no you're ok, it's actually probably good to have someone to talk to. You know most people outside of what we do, don't really understand how hard it can be. Anyways, it's not going well, and I'm not sure how much longer we'll be together."

"Oh, I'm so sorry to hear that. That's never easy. Well if you ever need someone to talk to, just let me know."

"I will definitely do that. Thank you."

"You're welcome, have a good night Ralph, I'll see you in the morning," she says as she stands up and walks out the door. And again I am mesmerized by each step that seems more like a dance than it does a walk. This girl has got me hooked.

later that week...

"Hey boss," she says smiling as she leans her head in the door.

"Hey there, how are you doing?"

"I'm good. It's about lunch time, do you want me to grab you something?"

"Uh, yeah. Actually, we can both go. I could use a break. Give me five minutes, Ok?"

"Sure thing, I'll be in my office."

"Sounds good, I'll be there as soon as I wrap this up."

I'm not wrapping anything up. I was just looking at ESPN.com. But one thing I've learned is when you have a desk job, especially when you're the boss. You have to always make it look like you are busy and have so much more to do than you have time for. It creates this environment where people feel like they have to keep working to keep up with everyone else. Even though everyone else is doing the same thing. It's like we're all a part of a play and everyone is acting, but nobody tells anyone about it. Kind of funny when you think about it.

Five minutes goes by and I head down to Rebecca's office.

"You ready?"

"Yeah," she says as she stacks some papers into a pile and does one more mouse click. She knows the game. I smile.

"So where are we heading?"

286

"Well, there is this little Italian place across the street that I just love, how about that?"

"You mean, Finicci's?"

"Yeah, that's it. Is that ok?"

"Yes of course. It's very romantic, I mean, just the atmosphere is very nice," I say making it sound like I didn't mean to say what was on my mind. But in all reality I want her to know exactly what is on my mind.

She smiles. "Yes, it is."

We talk through lunch, she tells me all about her experience at law school and how she landed here. I enjoy talking to her so much. She reminds me of myself. Such a go-getter.

As we walk back to the office she looks over at me.

"So, I have a lot of case work to prepare for Cory, and I was wondering if it's ok if I stay at the office and work late tonight?"

"Yeah, I actually have to stay late and finish up some things as well, so that shouldn't be a problem at all."

"Oh, ok, good. Thanks."

"Yeah, no problem," I say as I open the door to the office for her and follow her down the hall. She stops abruptly looking down at the floor. I didn't have time to stop . I run right into her. In a moment we embrace out of accident, but completely on purpose.

"Oh, I'm sorry," she says laughing.

"No, I'm sorry, I didn't realize you stopped. I uh."

"Don't be sorry," she said as she continued walking down to her office. She glanced back at me smiling as she got to her door, then walked in.

I am so taken by this woman, wow. I'm pretty sure all she would have to do is ask me for anything she wanted and I would hand it right over.

I pick up the phone and dial Bridget. "Hey there honey, it's going to be a late one tonight, I just got a bunch more stuff to try and get done before a meeting in the morning. Don't wait up for me ok?"

"Ok, Ralph. Can I make you anything?" she says.

"No, don't worry about me, just need to stay focused here."

"Ok, thanks for letting me know."

"Sure thing."

"Oh, Ralph, can we talk about the kids and,"

"Oh, honey, I gotta go, I got another call, probably a client. We'll talk about that later ok?"

"Ok, bye."

"Bye."

Phew, sometimes I feel like she should be able to figure out what I'm really like but she is just so focused on herself that the truth becomes less and less of a desire, because of the cost of it. That is the funny thing about humans. They all have there limits. They can talk like they are a diehard about something but as soon as it gets close to their limit they'll toss it out of their car window. It doesn't matter if it's a favorite food, a football team, or even a religion. Mankind is weak, and I've taken the opportunity to figure out how people work so that I can use their weaknesses for my benefit.

It's 7:30 pm and everyone has gone home a couple hours ago, except for Rebecca and I. I hear her down the hall get up from her desk and walk towards my office. I quick check my hair, and shove a mint in my mouth.

"Hey there, mind if I come in."

"No, I was hoping you would."

later…

That felt so good. Needless to say these meetings would become a regular occurrence over the next month and it was obvious she was as hooked as I was. But our connection in our work was just as strong. She was brilliant in the courtroom as she would whisper strategies to me. She was even seeing angles that I was missing, which is hard to believe. It was obvious that her and I together made quite the team.

Chapter 13

"Ralph, come on. Just tell me when you are going to leave her," she says as she walks into my office and closes the door behind her.

"It's complicated, but trust me, soon enough."

"Ralph, I will not be some pet to you, you and I both know that working together we are unstoppable. But she is getting in the way. It's like this whole time you thought you were controlling her, and now all of the sudden you are the one being controlled."

"Excuse me? Listen, I do not get controlled by people. Everything is working out just the way I want it to, but I can't make my family go away overnight."

"Yeah, you can. You don't even love her, do you?"

"No, I don't. But a divorce does not look good to clients, so there is a process to all this that can make things not so offensive to people. It just takes a little more time."

"Ralph, I'm a smart girl. I know what I want and I don't like to wait. If you want what we can have together, you need to make up your mind."

"Ok, ok. Listen, I was going to save this, but I think now is as good of a time as ever." I say as I walk back to my desk open up my drawer and pull out a box. I walk over and hand it to her. She opens it and gasps.

"Ralph, it's beautiful," she says as she pulls the diamond necklace from the box."

"So, hopefully you have a little better idea of what my intentions are after this." I say as I take it from her and put it around her neck.

"Oh Ralph, thank you. I'll always wear it."

"You're welcome, love."

If only things were going as good at home as they are with Rebecca. It seems like each day Bridget is more distant and Josh is more of a topic. The kids are talking about him constantly. I just can't take it. I would gladly drop them for Rebecca, but the thought of losing control over Bridget is more than I can bear.

I grab my keys off of my desk and lock up the office. As I walk out to my car I think back through my life. All that I've gained from my time here. I mean I have accomplished so much. I've seen the rise and fall of so many people around me, and all the while I've been gaining more and more stuff, more and more status, and more and more of this world.

I glance in the rearview mirror as I start the engine. "You are a good man, Ralph Torello," I say as I chuckle.

What is good? People trying to solve world hunger think they are doing good, others devote their lives to stop crime and call it good, still others think that serving those who are ill or dying are doing good. That kind of good is just an action that we accomplish here on the earth and honestly, once we are done, or dead, it all just goes back to the way it was. Sure some people change, and some people have meals that they wouldn't have had, but the problems never seem to truly be solved by these 'good works'. And the religious people, they are the worst. Those people do all sorts of good things in the name of God, and don't even know who God is. It's sad really. To spend all your life going to church and praying at God and doing these good things, and then to go on living their lives as if they're in charge and God doesn't even exist. No wonder everyone thinks of them as hypocrites. I feel for all those poor saps, but what are you going to do. Some people just need that kind of stuff to get them through the day. It's kind of like having a special charm or trinket or something. I guess it just makes them feel better about themselves.

Chapter 14

This guy is becoming more and more of a nuisance to me. He took Tory out for dinner tonight, after surprising her a few days ago by bringing her flowers. She is really starting to change. She won't talk to me like she used to, and instead of the video games I bought her, she just sits around writing in that stupid journal she said her grandma gave her. Something has to be done to stop all this.

Bridget is at the front door talking to him as Tory runs up the stairs before I can get her attention to come talk to me.

I walk quietly towards the door. Bridget is standing there with the door half shut. I can tell she's talking with Josh, but I can't quite hear what she's saying. As I get close she notices me behind the door, and I can see her hesitate. She starts stammering as she talks to Josh. I pull the door open the rest of the way.

"Hi Josh, what are you doing here?" I say knowing that I've surprised him.

"Oh, Hi Ralph, I was out with Tory, and we just got back."

"Josh, if I'm not mistaken I don't think tonight is one of your nights to spend time with the kids."

"No, Ralph, it certainly is not. Tory asked me if I would take her out, and it's my understanding according to that paperwork you gave me, that if a child should request a visit outside the times stated, they will be granted the request. Yeah, I read over it just to make sure that there wouldn't be any issues," he says with a snarky attitude.

I do not like the way he is talking to me right now.

"Well, there is an issue. We need to know these things ahead of time Josh. Poor communication causes things to fall apart."

"Ralph, I'm pretty sure Bridget knew about this, and didn't have a problem with it. Please don't mistake your role in my children's lives. And don't call control, communication."

I can't take him talking like this to me. I slam the door right in his face. If ending the conversation is the only win I've got, than I'm taking it.

"I cannot believe you!" I say turning to Bridget. "After all that I've done for you! You ungrateful..."

I go on for a solid minute, berating her in every way I can think of. She turns her back to me and begins to walk away and into the family room. I reach for her to turn her around. She pulls her arm free of my grasp which only sends my rage to the next level. I grab her arms and shake her, then throw her on the couch. This rage that seems to come so natural in these situations has been quite common in our relationship. All the sudden she cries out.

"Please save me!"

And in the next instant there's a crash, as the front door flies open and slams against the wall.

Startled, I cautiously walk over to the door to see what has happened. I don't know when the last time was that I felt fear like this. In an instant I am the one being controlled. I have to regain my composure quick.

"I'm going to call the cops on you. You're going to jail for this. You can't break someone's door down," I yell at Josh as he steps through the doorway.

"You're not calling anyone. I have you abusing Bridget videotaped on my phone, do you really want that on the headlines in the morning?" He says.

What? I can't seem to find the words to explain what is going on in my head. If he lets that stuff out, then I will be ruined. I can't let that happen.

"Get out of my house Josh, before someone gets hurt."

"There have already been too many people getting hurt in your house, Ralph."

"Can I take the kids with me?" he says, looking at Bridget.

"You're not taking my kids anywhere," I yell.

"They are not your kids Ralph, and if you try and stop us, the headlines will expose you to the world," he yells.

"You can come with me if you want, it's your choice," Josh says to Bridget.

"Bridget, if you leave me you are leaving who you really are. This is all that you wanted. The shopping trips, the freedom to make your life the way you want it, not wondering where the money will come from, your protection from sickness, you will throw all that away, and I won't take you back." I can feel my grasp around her loosening. She can't leave.

"Ralph, let me speak with Josh alone," she says to me.

"But..." I try to think of something to say.

"Ralph, I need to speak with Josh alone," she repeats more firmly.

"Fine," I say as I throw my arms up in the air and walk into the kitchen.

For the next five minutes I pace back and forth trying to figure out another angle to use in order to regain control of the situation.

As soon as I hear Bridget walking up the stairs I make my way back to the front door. Josh is fiddling with the door frame he had smashed.

"You know Josh, this is really stupid. You're gonna regret all of this."

"Ralph, I'm not scared by your intimidation and I'm not going to be controlled by your manipulation. Don't you ever wonder what it would be like for you to be free? Free from all the ways you try to control your life and the lives of others?"

"Ahhh, shutup," I yell.

"Ralph, let me make one thing very clear. If you hurt Bridget, I will be back, and I'm positive you don't want that."

"Ha, Josh, you don't have the guts or the ability to take Bridget from me," I say with as much aggression as I could muster.

I cower as he steps up right in front of me. I can feel a lump form in the back of my throat. Nobody ever talked to me or stood up to me like this before. Who does this guy think he is?

"Do not question my abilities, for in just a short time all that you've stolen from me will be mine once again, and what is left to you will be your exposed deceptions and loneliness," he says with a ferocity in his tone.

"Fine Josh, have it your way," I say, trying to make a quick last ditch effort to make it sound like I don't care about what is happening.

"Thanks for understanding, Ralph," he says sarcastically.

Tory and Ben come running down the stairs with their backpacks on. "Dad we're going to Grandma and Grandpa's?" Ben yells to Josh.

"Yeah bud, go ahead and hop in the Jeep," he says.

"No way, you can't take them up there. It's... too far away, and we don't have a good way of contacting you up there," I say as I look at Bridget trying to get her to stop this from happening.

"You can't let them go up there," I say to her, half demanding it.

I know how things started to fall apart the last time they went up there. This feels too close to losing. I cannot lose.

"Ralph, I can't change that. I'm sorry," she says.

And with that he walks out of my house with Ben and Tory, and I am left alone with her. I have to find a way to keep her here as long as I can. The stuff I've been offering her just isn't enough anymore and now that she is starting to have the panic attacks about all different situations, I know my lies about getting rid of those are being exposed. I have to find something, anything that will keep her here.

I got it. I'll remind her that she doesn't deserve his love. I will remind her of all the reasons for her to carry the weight of her shame and she will never be able to get free. I will show her how evil she really is and she will have to believe something that's absolutely ridiculous about love in order to think that she still has a chance with Josh.

Chapter 15

This is impossible. Every time I try to talk to her she just walks away. How am I supposed to get her to understand how ashamed of herself she should be if she won't listen to me? There has to be some way to put a mirror in front of her eyes. That's it! I'll write her a letter.

Dear Bridget,

I know we have a lot of things to talk about, but it seems that you are so closed off to me lately. We've had so many good times, I feel like it would be a shame to throw all that away just because we had some misunderstandings. As I was thinking about your situation and all the choices you've made, I couldn't help but think that Josh would probably have a tough time forgiving you for everything you've done to him. I'm honestly okay with you still seeing Josh from time to time and continuing to live here. I don't think it makes sense to walk out on all that we've become. That seems like a worse decision than your first one. If anyone knows what it means to make some bad choices in life I do. I can understand you way better than Josh can. We are so much alike, and I can't help but think that if you return to him you will regret it because of all the things you will miss out on. I honestly think it would be tough for Josh to look past all the pain that you've caused him. He will probably have a tough time ever trusting you again; but I trust you. I know that what you really want in life is to be happy and safe, and I can give you all of those things. Let's not give up. Let's just figure out a way to compromise. I'm sure Josh would be okay with that.

Your lover,
Ralph

Now, that should do the trick. If I can't have her all to myself, I can at least keep some of the chains on her. All I really need to get her to believe is that with me she can have both of us, but if she decides on him, she loses her freedom to choose. I wouldn't say this is ideal for me, but in this situation I don't mind sharing. Besides, I don't think she really understands this, but I think I know him enough to know that he won't share. It's all or nothing with him. It seems a little ridiculous if you ask me. That someone would be asked to give up everything to gain confinement to one sole relationship. I would never agree to anything like that.

Think about what my life would be like if I thought about marriage that way. I wouldn't be able to survive. The only way this life works for me is if I'm in control. And if people get hurt along the way, that is their own fault. If everyone just worried about themselves and made better decisions that helped them stay in control of their own lives, then people wouldn't go through near as much pain. It's actually quite simple. I should probably write a book about it so that people could gain the wisdom that I live in. I think I'd call it, "This is your life, never lose it." Yeah, that's a good name for it. And I'm sure it could help a lot of people. It could definitely help Bridget. She is obviously very confused about what is best for her. She's not thinking about the here and now. I gave her answers for her life quicker than a fast food restaurant serves hamburgers and now she's ready to throw all of it away? I don't get her at all. Well this isn't over yet and I need to find a way to give her space, but also keep my arguments in front of her.

Thankfully she hasn't found out about Rebecca yet. I have to stay late at work a few times a week, but Bridget doesn't seem to have any clue at all.

Rebecca has become a little more pushy about me ditching Bridget, I'm not sure how to tell her that I just can't let Bridget go. I mean of all people, Rebecca should

298

understand. She got so mad the other day she threatened to come to the house. I honestly think if she had the chance she would go behind my back to get to Bridget. She's pretty conniving she would probably just try to deceive her into something that would mess her up.

What is a guy to do. It's actually a good problem to have. Two women. This is most guys dream. And I have to say, other than the pettiness they have a tendency to operate in. It's pretty nice.

Chapter 16

Driving home from the office I feel a confidence. I think that the letter was just what I needed to get her back into a place where she can recognize what's important in life.

As I walk into the house it smells delicious. I knew my plan would work. She made me a feast. She will tell me she's sorry for everything she's done, and once again I will have won. This is too easy.

"Hey Bridget," I say, as I walk into the dining room. "Whoa, what's the special occasion?"

"Oh, nothing special, just felt like I needed to do this for you," she said.

I reach for a chicken wing.

"Not yet Ralph," she says sternly.

"Fine, fine," I laugh.

"Ralph I need to ask you something."

"Sure, but can we make it quick? This looks good and I'm pretty hungry."

"Did you purposefully lead me away from my family?"

"What? What are you talking about? I think you've got some craziness going on in your head," I say, trying to think of some way to change the subject.

"Ralph, do you see this table full of food?"

"Yes, and that's the problem. I'm hungry, Bridget. So what is all this about?," I ask raising my tone a little bit to show her that I'm starting to get angry.

"This table is like what I had before I met you. My life was full, it was wonderful; but when you came, you feasted on a table that was not yours," she said as she stared at me with an intense anger in her eyes. I had never seen this kind of anger in her before. With that she grabbed the table cloth and pulled as hard as she could sending each dish crashing to the floor.

"You took everything from me Ralph, for what? You don't love me, you're obviously cheating on me, and as for my poor kids, they are more damaged than I would've ever allowed had I known what you were."

"You are a fool, Bridget. You waste everything, just look at what you did to Josh, you wasted all of his love. He has no reason to love you. He'll never love you for anything you can do for him," I yelled with an intense anger bursting out from inside of me.

"Ralph, you are right. There is no reason for him to love me. That's how I know he really does love me. Ralph, I'm leaving, and I will never be back."

"Oh yeah? You'll come back to me once you start having those panic attacks again. You are a slave to fear Bridget, can't you see that? You need me. I'm your security," I cried out knowing these words were my last chance and I had to make them stick.

"No, you're not!" she yelled, with such a strong conviction. "If I'm going to beat my fears I have to walk through them, and Joshua is the only one who can help me do that," she said defiantly.

I cannot believe this is happening. She is walking out of the door and I feel like I have lost all control over her. How could this happen? All I can do is yell. I continue to yell for the next 20 minutes even though she's long gone.

I decide to call Rebecca.

"Hey there."

"Hey, how's it going?" she says loudly.

I can hear what sounds like a party going on in the background.

"What are you up to?"

"Oh, I'm at a party with some girl friends of mine. Is everything ok?"

"Yeah, just wanted to know if you wanted to stop by."

"Sorry Ralph, I'll probably be out late. Isn't Bridget there?"

"No, she's gone for the night, I thought you could come stay over and see what it would be like to live here with me."

"Yeah, that would be fun, but hey I gotta go, I'll see you on Monday ok?" she says as she starts giggling.

I can hear some guy talking in the background to her. Even more anger billows up inside of me. I throw my phone across the room watching it smash into pieces as it hits the stone fireplace. I pace between the living room and the kitchen for the next half hour, stewing over all of these emotions, I've done so well at never having to feel before. Loss, rejection, loneliness, and the list goes on.

I finally passed out on the couch after trying to think of some sort of plan to get Bridget back in my clutches and Rebecca to obey me. I haven't lost yet. I just have to keep fighting.

Chapter 17

I'm woken up by a knock at the door. What time is it? I glance over at the clock on the wall. What? It's 10 A.M? I've never slept this late. Yesterday must've really taken its toll on me. I wonder who that could be.

"Yeah, what do you want?" I ask harshly as I open the door to a police officer.

"Are you Ralph Torello?" he asks in an authoritative tone.

"Yeah, that's me. What's this about, officer?" I say, in a bit of a nicer tone.

"I'm placing you under arrest. I need you to please come with me, sir."

"What? Yeah nice one! Did Cory put you up to this?" I ask, laughing, knowing that Cory, one of the guys at my office, would definitely do something like this.

"Sir, this is not a joke, and I need you to get in the car," he says with an increasingly stern tone.

"Alright, alright, but can you just tell me what I've done?"

"Sir, I can tell you your rights."

"This is absolutely ridiculous, do you know who I am? I will sue your whole police department, and don't be surprised if you show up to a pink slip in your box tomorrow morning."

"In the car, sir."

"Fine," I say with such an annoyance in my tone that I hope he can feel it.

We drive through town and to the police station. As we arrive I am greeted by angry looks from all the other officers as he places me in a prison cell. I've never been on this side of a cell before. I'm the guy getting people out of these cages.

"Where's my phone call?"

"In about 20 minutes you can have your phone call, sir."

"Whatever."

A man wearing a suit, who I don't think I've ever met before shows up in front of my cell.

"Ralph, would you like to provide your own attorney or would you like to have one provided for you?"

"Ha, that's funny. I will be representing myself, thank you very much. Don't you know who I am?"

"No sir, I don't know who you are, and I'm not sure that will make a whole lot of difference when it comes to the courtroom."

"Yeah, we'll see about that. Hey what room are we in at the old courthouse? You know I've been in every courtroom in that building," I say arrogantly.

"Sir, you will not go before one of the judges at the old courthouse. Because of the charges, the hearing will take place in a higher court."

"What? You can't do that. I'll appeal that decision."

"Sounds good," he says with heavy sarcasm that grated every bone in my body.

Who does this guy think he is? What is happening? 'Calm down, Ralph', I tell myself. This is nothing I can't get past.

"At least tell me who is prosecuting me?"

"I'm not able to release that information to you sir."

"C'mon! Fine then who is the judge?"

"I don't believe you know him, sir. He used to be the town's mayor. He handles all of these types of cases."

"What types of cases? I don't even know why I'm here."

"Sir, that is all the information I am able to give to you at this time. You will be able to make your phone call shortly."

I spend the next few minutes trying to calm down as my mind is swimming with all the possible scenarios that this could be about? Did they really find out about the insurance fraud? Or about the tax evasion? How is this possible? I've covered everything so well. Who should I call? I could call Cory at the office and tell him to start getting a strategy together for getting me out of this. No, I need a different kind of help. I need to talk to Uncle Louie.

Chapter 18

"Hello?" he answers in a guarded tone.

"Hi, Uncle Louie," I say, with the least amount of confidence he has probably every heard me speak with.

"Hey there squirt. How are you doing?"

"I'm... okay," I say quietly, trying to not be heard by the officer standing across the hall. I turn toward the phone that is hanging on the wall and cover with my hand the receiver and my mouth. "Uncle Louie, I need some help."

"Sure, what is it?"

"Do you remember the last time I came to see you we talked about that girl that I really liked?

"Yeah, I remember," he says, "I told you to stay away from her."

"I couldn't stay away from her, she was like a drug. And now I'm in a little bit of trouble and I need to know why you told me not to mess with her."

"Sonny, what happened?"

"I'm in jail right now. I don't even know what they are charging me with. All I know is that the old town mayor is the judge. Who is this guy? If I can find out about him, then I'm sure I can figure out a way to get out of this."

"Wow Ralph, I hate to say I told you so. This is real bad kid. I'm not sure what to tell you except, goodbye."

"What? Wait, Uncle Louie what do you mean? Why is this so bad?"

"Ralph, this is like a squirrel picking a fight with a lion. You're better off going quietly."

"Going quietly? No way, I have to fight, Uncle Louie. I can win this case. I can win any case. I always win."

"Son, I know you've always looked at me and thought that I should've done more with my life, but in all reality, I'd rather stay in the place I am than do what you did by trying to get everything in the world only to lose it all, which is exactly what you're fixin' to do."

"Fine, well if there is a way out of this I will find it, and before you know it, I'll be bringing you and Bob a case of beer to celebrate."

"Ralph, it's been good to know you. Goodbye," he says as he hangs up the phone.

What in the world does he know that I don't? I'm not scared. Seriously, if anyone can put up a fight it's me. I won't rest until I figure out how to beat this guy, and make him real sorry for putting me in this jail cell.

the next day...

"Seriously, can anyone tell me what is going on?" I holler out of the cell towards the officers.

"Oh yeah," the one officer who is sitting watching a television replies, "the Raiders just scored a touchdown."

The others start chuckling.

"I need some answers. Can anyone give me answers on anything other than the football game?" I yell.

"I can," a voice comes from down the hall as the man wearing the suit shows up in front of my cell.

"Finally, someone with pertinent answers. When is my hearing? I need to know all the charges, and I need to be able to meet with my defense team in order to prepare."

"Ralph, I don't think you understand the situation. The trial is actually just a formality. If we wanted to, we could just lock you away. But the hearing actually just allows us to tie up all the loose ends."

"Listen, I know how the law works, and it's not over till the court decides it's over. You can't just send me to jail. It doesn't work that way. Besides, I'm not going without a fight. And I never lose."

"Okay, Ralph," he says, but I know he's just trying to appease me, which ticks me off even more. "The hearing is set for tomorrow. That is all the information I have right now for you," he says as he turns around and walks down the hall.

"Wait, I need to meet with my team!" I yell. "Hey you, guy! Come back here," I yell as I grab the bars of my cell. This is just wrong. Nobody has control over me. So help me if this has anything to do with Bridget. I will not lose this one, just wait and see. In fact, I won't just win this case, I'll make Bridget suffer in the midst of it. Just wait till I tell all her dirty secrets to everyone in the courthouse. She'll be sorry she ever left me and even more sorry that she put me here.

Chapter 19

Living in a cell is absolutely horrible. Each day I find myself feeling weaker and more fearful. I'm not used to all these feelings, but I can't seem to shake them. The guards walk me to a transportation vehicle and we drive for at least an hour to a place I'm unfamiliar with.

As we pull up to a courthouse I've never seen before, I can't help but feel terror at everything that surrounds me. I still have some tricks up my sleeve, I just need to keep my cool and make sure nobody can see how I'm truly feeling.

"Get out," the guard hollers at me.

"Hey, you could be a little more kind, buddy," I say joking with him. He doesn't get my joke. In fact I'm not sure that he could understand any joke.

"Follow me," he says with the same amount of gruffness as his greeting.

We walk up the stairs to the entrance of the courthouse. On one side of the entrance is a statue of a lion with the word, 'Truth', inscribed on its base, and on the other side of the entrance is a statue of an eagle with the word, 'Justice', inscribed on its base. Funny how I've used those words so much in my practice. Mostly out of context, but when you're out to win, none of that really matters.

We walk through the doors into a grand hall and are directed to the first courtroom on the right. The doors open as we approach, and two guards are dragging a guy out. He looks like he is unable to talk and barely able to move. I slow my walk so that I can see where they are taking him. I watch as they drag him out the back doors which seems like an entrance into a dark warehouse sort of area. Good thing I won't end up like that guy, I think to myself.

The guard leads me to a chair behind a table. I sit down and relax a little bit. I look over to my right and see Josh sitting at the table beside me. No way! And there's Bridget right beside him. There are so many words that are coming to my mind right now that I would love to share with them. I can feel the evil smile spread across my face. "This should be easy," I whisper.

"All rise," the deputy says.

We stand there as in walks some old guy. This must be the old Mayor.

"You can't be the judge, you're..." is all I got out before the deputy took me by the arm and gave me a look that said, 'Don't you dare talk again without being asked first'.

I sit down, not sure what to do. Everything is stacked against me. Even all the jury members look like they are on Josh and Bridget's side. Well, if you can't beat them, take as many down with you as possible, right?

I look over to see Ben and Tory sitting a couple rows back from Josh and Bridget. This will make it even more interesting.

"The court would like to call Bridget to the stand," says the deputy.

"Ha," I laugh out loud. I really did try to hold that laugh back, but just couldn't help myself. The deputy stares me down. He does not seem like he's a very happy person.

She walks to the stand with her head hung low. Josh approaches the stand, and looks at Bridget.

"Bridget, would you please share your testimony with the courtroom?"

"Sure," she says hesitantly.

She then goes on to explain everything that she has done over the past two years. She tells them about us, and about leaving Josh and everything. I can't believe my ears. What is she doing? This doesn't make any sense at all. She is weeping as she pours all of this out. Well this should definitely work in my favor. This will easily take all of the focus off of me and I should be able to walk right out of this courthouse. I can see Josh is crying too. What a baby!

"... and it wasn't till much later," she continued, "that I realized that I had been terribly deceived." At that she stood up and looked at me with pure hatred in her eyes. I had never seen this look come out of her before. She raised her hand towards me and pointed her finger like a gun straight at my chest.

"He did it!" she yells, then slumps back into her chair. With her face in her hands, between sobs, she cries out: "I made all those choices. It was my fault and I deserve whatever punishment is coming my way, but he is the one who deceived me."

Well that won't hold up. They are really going to try me for deceiving her? That's just funny. I can't wait to see what dear old dad the judge has to say about that one.

"Jury, what is your verdict?" The judge asks as he looks at the jurors who are whispering back and forth.

This is the weirdest case I've ever seen. I can't tell if they are deciding her fate or mine.

"We the jury find the defendant, Bridget Vale, guilty."

"Ha, yes," I blurt out.

I watch as she hangs her head in shame. Yeah, she deserves this. After all, I never made her do what she did. I just provided the opportunity. The whole courtroom is silent. It's as if no one really knows what to do with all this.

I glance back to see the kids crying. I wonder if she has to do time in jail for this one? I never heard of someone going to jail for leaving their husband, but maybe there's some new law that just got passed? Either way, the weight is off my shoulders and I figure I can leave now. I stand up and turn to walk out, but I feel someone grab my arm firmly.

"Ralph, back in your seat!" orders the deputy.

"What are you talking about? She's guilty; that means I'm free," I say with an arrogance that even surprises me.

"Not so, Ralph. Take a seat," he replies.

I watch as Josh approaches the judge with a folded up paper. He hands it to the judge and returns to his seat. I look over at him, trying to see if I can get any sort of a read on what just happened. The judge spends the next minute looking over the paper. Then he looks up at Josh, then down at Bridget.

"Bridget," he says. "You are free. Free to leave."

"But I... I'm guilty," she says.

"Yes, you were, but you are no longer," he says as he shows her the paper.

She weeps out loud as she turns toward Josh. He simply nods to her.

What is going on? This whole thing is like some bad dream. Maybe that's it, maybe I'm dreaming right now.

"Ouch!" I blurt out, as everyone looks over at me to see my underarm pinched between my fingers. Nope definitely not dreaming.

"So, am I free to go now?" I ask, looking at the judge.

"Ralph! Do not interrupt again," the judge says, looking down at me with anger in his eyes.

The judge handed the note to the jury and they passed it around. The lead juror stood up and announced, "We the jury find the defendant, Bridget Vale, FORGIVEN."

This is the point where I start pulling my hair out. You can't just forgive someone and then suddenly everything is okay. Besides, how do they know she won't just do it again?

I turn toward Bridget and feeling pretty gutsy, let out, "Bridget, once a whore, always a whore."

Whoa, that one got to Josh.

"You!" he says as he starts toward me.

"Joshua!" the judge says sternly.

He stops in his tracks and waits for what comes next.

I sit back in my chair and put my hands behind my head.

"Jury, what is your verdict?" The judge says with an increasing agitation in his voice.

"We the jury find, Ralph Torello, GUILTY."

"What!" I yell, as I stand up disregarding the guard walking my way. "This isn't a fair trial. This isn't possible. I didn't even have a chance to share my defense. You can't do this." I'm flipping out now, jumping up and down and pounding my fists on the table.

"Ralph, you were condemned before you showed up in my courtroom. This wasn't about you being found guilty, it was about Bridget being set free," the judge says as he looks down at me. And with that he points his finger at me and all of a sudden my whole body goes limp and I can no longer speak. This must have been what happened to that guy I saw being dragged out of the courtroom before I came in.

How is this happening? I can feel my knees sliding across the floor as two guards drag me out. Oh no! they're leading me to the back doors. I have to fight, I have to stop this. But there is no longer any strength left in me. As soon as we get through the doors they throw me in amidst the others who are laying all over the floor. Everything is black. I know I'm in some sort of a transfer station with a bunch of others who've been convicted. No one is talking, and all of us seem unable to move. It's very dark. Terrifyingly dark!

W

BOOK FOUR

Chapter 1

As the glimmers of morning light travel across the flowing curtains, they dance in response to the wind that blows through a slightly cracked window, and I awake. As if from a dream I find my emotions and body feeling somewhat disconnected from my surroundings. As I roll over onto my other side, I have the strange feeling that something is wrong. Maybe those are not the right words. It feels more like the sensations of a distant memory in the past. My sight breeches my widening eyelids filling me with both wonder and horror.

"Where am I?" I blurt out.

I look around frantically. I know this place. But, how could I possibly be here. I get up and walk around the bed to the dresser. I look into the mirror and there she is, 18 year old Bridget looking back at me. How is this happening? This must be a dream.

I run back to the bed and try to fall back asleep, but that doesn't work. I try pinching myself, doing jumping jacks, and even hitting my head against the wall, but I'm still here.

"Hello?" Comes a voice from down the stairs. "You okay up there?"

"Uh, yeah, who is it?" I respond still unsure of all that's taken place and where I actually am.

"It's me, Uncle Dave," he responds with a little curiosity in his tone.

"Oh yes, of course, Uncle Dave. I'll be right down, just feeling a little out of sorts from just waking up."

"No problem Darlin, didn't mean to startle you."

I go into the bathroom and splash water onto my wrinkle-less face. All I want to do is sit down and cry. I don't know how I could possibly walk through a life that I think I've already lived. What do I do with all of these memories? I begin to weep as I think of Tori and Ben, and Joshua. Will I ever see them again? I sit on the bathroom floor and, as quietly as possible, I forfeit the reigns I have had on my tears.

My mind attempts to understand what is absolutely incomprehensible, but to no avail. I finally convince myself that this is a dream and that I'll eventually wake up.

But after awhile of this wrestling through all the thoughts, I decide to go downstairs.

As I walk into the kitchen, Mary greets me and notices right away that I've been crying.

"Oh Honey. Are you OK? I know this must be so hard on you moving to a new place and all. I'm so sorry. Is there anything we can do for you?"

"It's not that, I um... How long was I sleeping for?"

"Oh I'd say a couple of hours. You must've been exhausted from that drive. I'll have dinner ready in about an hour if that suits you."

"Sure that would be fine, I think I will go for a walk."

"Oh sure honey, if you take a left out the driveway, it's only about five blocks to the town square."

"OK, thank you."

I grab a sweatshirt out of my car and head toward the square. I pull my hood up and put my hands inside the pockets. As I get closer I try and see if I can recognize any of the buildings. It all seems similar but different, all at the same time.

I see a coffeehouse that reminds me of the one that Gabi, my best friend, worked at. I walk in longing to see her smile greeting me. She would be the very thing that could help me get through this. There is a guy behind the counter and I can see through a small window to the back that there is a girl with long hair back there. I can't quite make out if it is her or not.

I order a small Americano and sit down. Just then the girl walks out and glances my way. She smiles at me, but I can't seem to muster a smile back. It's not her.

I sit there sipping my hot drink wondering where to go from here. Part of me just wants to go back to Aunt Abbey. I mean, she is the closest thing to a form of normalcy that I could possibly hope to reach right now. I feel like I've gotten the wind knocked out of me.

I mean, seriously? What about all these memories with Joshua? I can't remember every single moment over the last 20 years, well I guess the last two hours, but I remember enough that shouldn't just fit that short of a dream time. What about Ralph, and all of that? And the farm, and the lightning, and the court hearing? How in the world is all of that not real?

"Oh, no," I whisper. I wonder if I have a split personality.

My thoughts are suddenly interrupted by the girl who is not Gabi now standing at my table.

"Hi, I'm Annis. Are you new to our town? It's a pretty small town and I know everyone here. And when you walked in, I was sure I had never seen you before. Do you have family here?"

Wow, she definitely talks as much as Gabi.

"I don't... have family here. I'm actually staying with a friend's Aunt and Uncle just up the road. I don't know if I'm going to stay here or not. I just have a lot going on right now that I'm trying to figure out."

"Well then," she says as she pulls up a chair. "I'm really good at figuring things out. Is it like detective kind of stuff, or boy kind of stuff? Either way I can probably help. I love Nancy Drew, and I like boys, so pretty much I got all your bases covered," she says with a genuine smile.

But I can't even begin to think about bringing someone into this. How could I possibly help someone understand that what I experienced before I just woke up felt more real, and was more real than where I currently find myself.

319

We talk for about 30 minutes and then I remember about dinner.

"It was great talking to you, Annis."

"You too Bridget, please come visit again sometime."

"I will," I say as I leave.

As I walk back to the house, I have this strange sensation blow through me. My mind races through memories of my other life, or dream as I am slowly accepting.

In an instant I realize that the experience I had in my sleep seemed somewhat spiritual. I have no other way to describe this sensation than something otherworldly. I continue to ponder why I would have a dream this specific, with this much emotion, and this much reality, and then wake up 20 years prior. Everything in me wants to go back. Even with all the mistakes I made and the pain I walked through. "I just want to go back," I release toward the heavens as I begin again to cry.

"I know you do," comes like a whisper through the trees beside the sidewalk straight into my soul.

I know this voice, or at least the way it is spoken. It is so familiar. It's Joshua! I stop and look around as if hoping to find him behind the trees. But I cannot see him anywhere. I hang my head and continue to walk. "Joshua, I need help," I say quietly wondering if there's any chance that I can hear his voice again.

The smell of home cooked food emanates from the front door as I open it.

"Wow, Aunt Mary, dinner smells amazing."

"Oh thank you dear. Now go get washed up and we'll be ready to eat in five minutes. Dave, get washed up for dinner," she hollers out the back door.

"Alright honey, I'll be right in," he replies.

They are so in love. Sometimes you can tell when people are just putting on a front and don't really care for each other, but I can just feel it in the air here. They are bound together by their love. I really want that again. Well, I guess I mean I really want to find that. This is so confusing. I'm not sure I will ever be able to shake this.

As we sit around the table I find myself feeling this whole scenario differently than I did 20 years ago, or before that dream. I still don't feel like I can just give in to it being just a dream. It feels like a part of me will have to die to say that or believe in it. I just....

"Bridget? Are you ok dear?" Aunt Mary says as she puts her hand on my arm.

"Yeah, I'm sorry I was just thinking," my words trail off as I try and think about how much I can or should share with them.

"You can tell us honey, anything you are working through we would be glad to be a part of."

"Thank you, it's just that. I don't really know how to," I say with a pause. Maybe I should just let them in? "Have you ever had a dream that seemed so real it literally felt more real than what your reality was?"

With that Uncle Dave let out a chuckle, "Well, I've had some doozies in my day, Bridget. Once I was being chased by a pack of wild chickens with teeth that looked like saw blades. For a week after that every time I heard a cluck, I took off running. Is that what you mean?"

"Well, not exactly," I smirk.

"Honey, tell us about your dream," Aunt Mary chimes in.

"Well," I begin to cry as soon as the words begin to pass my lips. I continue to talk about my life for the past or future 20 years, experiences I had, and the whole story with Joshua and on and on. I wondered through the whole thing if they were going to think I was crazy. But they just lovingly listened to me.

"Darra." They both say as they look at each other.

"What, who is Darra? I... I know a Darra, I met her at my wedding, well... nevermind."

"Darra is a dear friend of ours, and I think she might be able to help you with all of this," says Aunt Mary. "I'll give her a call tonight, and maybe we can go see her tomorrow sometime."

"Oh, thank you so much, that would be amazing. I feel somewhat lost on all of this."

"You know Bridget, I think you should spend some time writing down everything you can remember from your dream. I think it will help you process. It seems to me like you may have been given a gift in all of this. Even if it doesn't feel like it yet," she says smiling, with that endearing look only a mother can give.

"OK thank you, I will do that," I say as I slide my chair back and stand up to leave. I stop at the doorway and turn back around.

"I know why I'm here, well, at least a part of it. Uncle Dave, Aunt Mary, you lost your daughter the same year I lost my parents. I'm supposed to be like the daughter you didn't get to see grow up, and you are supposed to be like the parents I never had. The empty swing out back that you both stare at crying because of all that's been lost, will now be filled. And we will all now have the opportunity to feel what we had lost hope for ever feeling."

They both just sat there staring at me in shock, as the tears began to fill their eyes. I walk over to Uncle Dave and kiss him on the forehead, and wrap my arms around him. Aunt Mary walks over and embraces both of us, as we all cry for our loss. Yet somewhere in the midst of the tears, there is a hopelessness that is washed away. Once again, mercy springs up in our hearts like dew in the early morning.

I sit on my bed and begin to write. I laugh at all the funny things that I lived through and cry at all the things I wish I could've changed. But most of all, I simply long to have all of that back. I long for it to be a part of me again.

Chapter 2

As the light peeks in between my lavender and white curtains, my eyes open, releasing a sensation that travels down my cheek and onto my pillow. A tear. How many days have begun with that very sensation. I think the shock of everything is wearing off, because I now feel the dread and agony of never seeing my children again, never being held by Joshua again. And so begins the downpour of everything that is bound up in questions, fears, heartache and so much more that doesn't fit into a language. Maybe that is the greatest difficulty with death and loss. It can't be fit into our language. We have ways of describing things all around us. Experiences and joys, and even tragedies. And in our language we are able to bring conclusion to so many things. But when it comes to death, there are no words, just groans, and aches, and many, many tears.

I find my mind traveling back and forth between what feels like a death of my husband and children, and the death of my parents. How can this be? Anybody would look at me and try and tell me what I experienced wasn't real, that it wasn't a big deal, just a dream, and that I needed to get over it. I'm not sure how to do that.

"I know what you would say, Joshua," I manage to get out in between sobs. "You would tell me that I just need to embrace time. To let myself grieve the loss, and allow time to transform the pain into something beautiful. You would say that it's not about getting rid of the pain, but the change in me when I feel it. The change from a hopelessness spread across my face in the midst of the memory, to a smile and a thankfulness for all that I did experience. But Joshua, I need more time."

As I walk down the stairs to the smell of homemade breakfast and the sound of Uncle Dave playing the harmonica on the front porch, I feel so grateful to be here. I also feel fragile. It's almost as if your emotions all come to the surface in moments like this and you can't help but feel like with one word, or one thought, you will go back into a release of all the sadness that is pent up.

"Hey there honey, how are you this morning?" Aunt Mary says as she comes over and gives me a kiss on the cheek. "Did you sleep well?"

"I did. I really needed a good night's sleep."

"You look like you've been crying. Are you still working through everything that we talked about last night?"

"Yeah, I'm sorry, I know I must seem crazy for making this such a big deal and all, I just don't know how to let it go."

"Don't worry about all of that Dear. Time is the one you really need to embrace right now. Allow today to be today with all of it's emotions and thoughts, and leave tomorrow where it is. You'll be there before you know it," she says with a smile.

Just then Uncle Dave walks in and places his harmonica on the mantle. "Hey there Bridget, how's my girl?"

"I'm good Uncle Dave, how are you?"

"Oh just peachy. I just love sitting out on the porch and playing for the birds. Sometimes they sing along with me, but they sound much better than I do."

Just then the memory hits me from Dad playing for the sparrows, and the thought of never seeing him or Mom again, feels like another stab in my pain-filled heart.

"I'm sorry, Bridget. Did something I say hurt you?" He asks with care.

"No, it's just I knew someone who used to love playing his harmonica to the birds, and I really loved him. He was... like a father to me."

"Well, now I'm like a father to you," he says as he walks over and gives me a side hug.

"I know," I smile. "Thank you," I say looking up at him.

We sit down to eat a wonderful breakfast. The kind that makes you feel honored to be at the table.

"Thank you Aunt Mary," I say as I take my plate to the sink. "I'll be out back for a little."

"You are so welcome dear. Oh Bridget, I got a hold of my friend Darra. She said she would love to see you. Would tomorrow afternoon work?"

"Yeah, that would work great."

"Ok great, I'll let her know."

As I walk toward the swing in the back yard, I feel ready to experience the peace that only comes with the motion of a swing. I spend the next 30 minutes, swinging as high as I can, spinning in circles and drawing in the dirt with the tips of my shoes. I glance up to see Uncle Dave holding Aunt Mary as they watch me out the kitchen window. The healing for me is in the rhythm of this swing. The healing for them is watching my experience, as it is with parents and their children.

that afternoon...

As I look out the double window at the front of the house, I feel like a walk and a cup of coffee. I grab my coat and head out onto the sidewalk. I'm taken back to the time that Joshua and I came into town right after we were married. We walked through the town, and now however many years and miles away it actually is, I find myself opening my hand just wishing that I could feel his in mine again.

There are so many times in a marriage where you are so frustrated with the other person, so hurt and so angry that you don't want them anywhere near you. The thought of their touch makes you cringe. And then there are times like this when the smallest amount of affection would fill your heart to capacity.

And in this moment of my thoughts, I feel it, I feel it so strongly that I have to look down at my hand and then beside me to see if he is there. And with this sensation of his hand embracing mine his whisper again passes through me, just like the day before.

"Bridget, I will never leave you. I will never turn my back on you," comes like a gentle stream running along the caverns of my sorrow and emptiness.

"Joshua," I say in between my sobbing. "Why did this happen? Where are you?"

"Go to wisdom," is all I hear like an echo through those same caverns.

"What does that mean?" I whisper.

And just like that it is over. I no longer feel his hand holding mine, and I can't seem to get him to respond to any of my questions.

I continue on my way to the coffeehouse. As I open the door I'm greeted by Annis.

"Bridget! I was hoping I would get to see you again. Let me tell you, there is not a lot going on in this town, so when I meet a friendly face I do everything I can to get them to stick around. You are going to stay a little while, aren't you? I know yesterday you were unsure and seemed like you had a lot on your mind. Oh my. I should let you talk," she laughs.

"You know you remind me of a really good friend I had once. Her name was Gabi. I think I will be staying around here for awhile. It seems like a good place for me to figure things out."

"Oh, it definitely is. People come from all over the world to figure things out here," she says with a giggle. "Ok, well I might have made that up."

"So tell me, what do you like to do around here?" I ask.

"Oh my goodness, where do I start? Well, we have the annual fair that comes in around mid July. Everybody is there. And then we have the pumpkin festival in October. That one is a hoot. Oh yeah, and then the Christmas festival of lights."

"That sounds great. What is the Christmas festival of lights?"

"Well, everyone in the town comes out on a Saturday morning in early December and we all decorate the main street. Pretty much everyone is there that can walk and it's been a tradition for the town from before I was born. Then on Christmas Eve we have a big parade down Main Street."

"Wow, I don't think I've ever heard of people doing that. Maybe for a church or business or something, but not a whole town coming together to help."

"Yeah I guess it is pretty special. We might not be the most booming town in the world, but most people here have a pretty good idea on what makes life full."

"Fullness, that sounds like something Joshua would say," slips out before I realize what I'm saying.

"Who's Joshua? He sounds dreamy. Is he your boyfriend? Or your single brother?" she says with a smile on her face.

"Oh, Annis you are so funny. Joshua is," I hesitate to try and find a way to describe all of this. "He is my friend."

"Oh I see, well maybe he will be more than a friend someday," she giggles as she nudges my arm.

She is just like Gabi, I smile.

I am dancing between the memories of a past life and all that I'm experiencing right now. And I'm really unsure of what I'm supposed to be doing with all of this. On one hand my experience was more real than anything I now feel, and yet, what I now feel is the only thing my body can sense.

"So how about you, Annis? Tell me about yourself?"

"Well, I was just a baby when it all started," she laughed, as she slapped her knee. And then went on for the next half hour sharing her story.

There is something so beautiful about our stories. We tend to get bogged down with details that don't really add any color to the painting of our lives. But to step back and look at the journey you've been on. To see the highs and lows, the adversity, the guidance, the terror, and the elation of it all. What an amazing picture our lives paint.

"Wow, Annis. What an incredible journey you've been on."

"Really? I guess I just always felt like it was kind of mundane."

"No, not at all. I mean with all that you've been through with your love for horses, and competing, and then having to give it all up. And the craziest part is that you don't seem to be jaded by that. Most people would be bitter. After all, it seemed like it was the most important thing to you."

"It really was, Bridget. When my parents lost the farm and we had to sell my horse, I was devastated. I cried for weeks. But then one day I woke up and the sun was shining through a crack in my curtains and it's like this whisper woke me up. It said, 'I'm here'. Most people would probably have been freaked out by a voice in their head like that. But it was full of such peace, that I just knew I was going to be OK. That day I was working here and a lady walked in and asked if I was the girl who used to compete with horses. She asked me if I'd come work for her on the weekends and teach kids how to ride. I'll be honest, Bridget, it has given me more satisfaction to give out of what I've been given, than any moment of me using my gift for myself. I would've never thought about helping somebody else like that before. I was too busy, and everything was about me being the best. None of that filled me up. And so here I am, making coffee and teaching kids how to do the thing that I was created to do. I couldn't be happier, because I love what I do, and who I am."

"Annis, I've got a lot to learn from you. Thank you for sharing all that with me."

"Your welcome. Will you be by tomorrow?"

"No, I'm afraid not. I'm going to visit someone tomorrow."

"Oh that's great. Well, I will see you when I see you," she says with a smile.

"Sounds great Annis," I say as I grab my coat and stand up to leave.

"Hey Bridget," she says as I reach the door.

"Yeah?"

"Next time you're here, will you tell me your story?"

I chuckle, "I will, Annis. I will," I say as I turn and walk out the door.

Chapter 3

As I weave through the mountains on this road that feels like the journey of my life so far, I find myself holding onto an anticipation of what awaits me at my destination. I'm excited to meet Darra and hopeful that she has some answers for me.

As I knock on the door to this beautiful and quaint house that is seated high above the coast, I can only imagine what the view out the back of the house will be like.

"Oh hello, my dear Bridget," I'm welcomed with the spitten image of Joshua's Aunt Darra.

I'm stunned and taken back. Is it possible that she was in my dream and also exists here? I stumble over my words.

"Hi Aunt Darra, I'm sorry, I mean Darra."

"Oh Bridget, it's ok, it's me. Don't you remember at the wedding I told you if you ever needed anything to just come see me?"

"This is too strange I don't understand," I say as I take a step back. "But everyone else was just a part of the dream, how can you be here but also there? What is real and what is my dream?"

"Oh honey, you will have many questions that you may not get an answer for when you want. But finding the answer to how all the puzzle pieces in your life fit together isn't why you are living and breathing. The answers will come with time, but you worrying about finding them will only jumble things up. Come on in, let's sit and talk some more," she says smiling as she takes my hand and leads me into her home.

"Ok, but how are you real?" I say as I look around while walking through this custom crafted bungalow. My sporadic thoughts are calmed momentarily by the intricate design of this house.

"This is beautiful Darra," I say absolutely stunned.

"Oh thank you dear, every part was hand crafted by a really good carpenter friend of mine."

"I mean, wow, this reminds me of Joshua's..." My voice trails off.

She stops and turns to me, patting my hand with her's. "I know dear, you probably miss him a lot, don't you?"

In all the emotions spanning from absolute confusion to utter sorrow, I begin to cry. "I do miss him. I miss him and Tori and Ben, and Mom and Dad, and my best friend Gabi. I miss them all so much. Was it really you that I saw at the wedding? Is Joshua somewhere that I can see him?"

"Here, sit down dear," she says as she directs me to a lounge chair overlooking the ocean from high atop a cliff. Again my mind wanders from all that was enveloping it to the moment I am in, surrounded by breathtaking beauty. I can't help but stand up and walk to the large glass wall that faces the view of breaking waves and rock formations jutting out of the water, weathered and worn but not broken. We are in some sort of a cove and I can see out on the peninsula a lighthouse that appears to still be in use.

"Oh wow," I turn to Darra to see her watching me.

"Pretty incredible, huh?"

"Yeah, it's breathtaking, and the lighthouse is..."

"It's the last working lighthouse on this stretch of coastland. We knew we needed to keep it up and running since we have so many fisherman from our town. Most people think the only purpose of a lighthouse is to help a ship stay away from the land, and although that's a part of it, one of our main reasons is to show the sailors how to get back. You know, when you are struggling to know where you are in the midst of a huge ocean and it's dark and somewhat scary, you need a flash of light, a sign if you will, that you can still make it home."

"Wow, it's all just so beautiful."

"I think you should take a walk to the lighthouse. It's only about a mile and I think you'll really enjoy it. Who knows, maybe it will help?"

"Ok, that would be great," I respond. "So Darra, how do you know Aunt Mary?"

"First of all dear, you can call me Aunt Darra. It does seem more fitting. And second of all, I met Mary just after she lost her daughter. She really needed a friend, and I was glad to be that for her. It is always a hard road when you lose so much in life, just as you and Mary have, but I am convinced beyond a doubt that when you keep your heart open through every high and low of life, you will always find your way."

"I think I understand the whole keeping my heart open part, but what do I keep my heart open to when I'm not sure who I am. I don't know how much of my situation makes sense to you, but I just lived 20 years of life and then woke up without any of it being real. How is that possible?"

"Oh dear, that is difficult to bring understanding to. Sometimes you need to go back to the last thing that you knew you should do and do that."

"I don't even know the first thing I should do."

"Dear, why did you come to see me?" She said.

"I was told you could help me, and I wasn't sure where else to turn."

"Ok, so do you believe I can help you?"

"I think so, I don't mean to be rude, but everything is still spinning in my head, so I'm unsure about a lot right now."

"Well, if you think I can help, than what's the last thing I told you to do?"

"I uh... don't really know."

"That's OK," she said as she pointed to the light house.

"Oh, yeah. So, I should go now?"

"Sometimes the answer that you're seeking requires a very specific step to be taken."

"OK, I will go. I'll see you later."

"Sounds great dear. I'll have dinner ready when you get back."

Chapter 4

I'm not really sure how to take Aunt Darra. In one moment she is so sweet and kind; and in the next she is direct, seemingly narrow minded, and somewhat demanding.

As I walk along a path leading to the lighthouse, amidst tall grass that at times lazily arcs over the trail, the gentle breeze of the salty air and the beauty that only comes when rocks and oceans are joined, overwhelms me. I stop to gaze out toward what I cannot see the end of and inhale peace and tranquility.

I remember when I was younger I had a place that I used to go to in my mind. It was actually a picture that my english teacher had hanging on her wall. It was a beautiful black rock beach with the waves crashing in. It was cloudy and somewhat dreary, which fit my feelings about life, but it was also comforting. It was my own little getaway inside my head, and what I am feeling now reminds me of that place.

It's not always the sunshine that makes us smile. Sometimes it's about the place that makes us feel at home. Home has a feeling all its own, and when you are there you can't deny it, but in many ways it seems impossible to explain it with mere words. It is the very thing that we are all truly searching for.

As I get closer to the lighthouse I can see that it is made of stone. Every piece perfectly positioned. It looks as if it has stood the test of time. I stop to look at a placard on the side of the building that reads: "Built in 1823. For our fisherman, sailors and any who are lost, welcome home."

As I walk around the outside of it I see an old door that is closed. Like any human being would, I try the handle and sure enough, it opens right up. I glance around me to see if anyone is watching and then walk inside.

For as old as the outside looks it's surprisingly clean and fresh looking on the inside. There is a circle staircase that wraps around and a quaint little seating area with a desk here at the bottom. As my curiosity grows, I head toward the stairs. I begin to walk up these beautiful stone steps stopping to catch a glimpse at every little window opening on the way to the top. As I approach the top there is a door that is closed. I assume it goes into the room with the actual light. There is this pull inside of me to open it.

I turn the knob and slowly push it open. As I step into a cozy and quiet room, I'm startled as I notice a man sitting in a chair facing the ocean.

"Oh, I'm so sorry, sir. I didn't mean to intrude. I just saw this lighthouse and wanted to see the inside," I say, feeling somewhat embarrassed.

He turns to me.

"Hi, Bridget, I've been expecting you."

"Joshua?" I say in absolute shock.

"Hi," he says with a smile.

"I don't understand," I say as I run to him and embrace him, but in the instant that I reach him, he is gone.

"No!" I cry out as I fall to my knees. "Everything I had was a dream, and now I'm stuck in this nightmare. Where are you Joshua? Where are you?" I say as I begin to wail in the midst of my sorrow.

I feel the warmth of a touch on my shoulder. I look up through tear filled eyes. It is him again.

"Bridget, I cannot hold you the way that you long to be held right now. But I am here."

"Joshua please, I need you, don't leave me again."

"My dearest Bridget, I have never once left you. You may not have seen me or felt my presence, but I have never once left you."

"I don't understand any of this, how is it that I lived a lifetime with you and then you were just a dream, and now I'm not sure what you are."

336

"Just think of me as a reality. You get to choose whether I am the most real thing in your life or not, but either way I am a reality to you, and I will continue to be throughout your journey."

I refrain from reaching for him, not wanting to take the chance of him disappearing again. I just sit there with my tear stained face, gazing up into his eyes. Those eyes, like fire and love swirling around. How could anyone deny those eyes.

"Joshua, was it all a dream?"

"Yes, it was," he pauses, "and no it wasn't."

"Oh, here we go again. Can you please just give me an answer I can understand?"

"I'm sorry Bridget," he says. "I think that Darra will be able to answer most if not all of your questions, but for now just know that nothing that happened was without purpose. Trying to add everything up to make sense in your mind may not be the most worthwhile pursuit. Sometimes in the midst of the storm you just need to sit down and rest. Clarity can become elusive when we strive for it. Usually true understanding comes in the midst of surrender and peace. Find out how to do that and I think all of this will make more sense."

With that he leans over and kisses my forehead, and is gone.

I spend the next hour snuggled up in the chair he had been sitting in and gazing out over the ocean. Finally I decide to head back to Aunt Darra's house. I talk to him as if he is right beside me, while hoping that the next time I see him isn't too far away.

As I approach the house, Aunt Darra is sitting on the back deck.

"How was your time?" she asks with a huge smile.

"It was good, did you know he..." I begin to say but then realize there's no way that she could know about any of that.

"Did I know what, dear? That Joshua would be down there?"

"Yeah," I say stunned.

"Why else would I have told you to go down there?"

"This is getting really weird. Who are you?"

"I'm a friend, Bridget. Don't get distracted by all of the details that don't make sense yet. Just keep walking in the direction that you know you are supposed to go in."

"The direction I'm supposed to walk in? I feel like I'm a crazy person. I mean, just three days ago I was in my late 30's. I really was, and I had lived every day up to that point. And now all of a sudden I'm back to where all this started and I just saw a ghost, or whatever that was down there of my husband from that previous life. Darra, how can you say go in any direction? I'm just trying to survive and not have a panic attack," the words come out slowly from my lips. Why haven't I had a panic attack in all of this? If there was ever a reason to have one, this is it. I take a deep breath and sit back in a chair. "I'm sorry Darra, I guess I didn't realize how big of a deal this all really is," I say as I start to cry. "I... I had two children. I loved Tori and Ben, and I gave birth to them, and raised them and held them, and now they've vanished with the opening of my eyes. How can I endure losing everything?"

"I'm so sorry dear, I know this is a lot on you. I'm here," she says as she sits on the arm of the chair and pulls me over into her embrace.

"I just want to go home."

"I know you do," she says. "And that life was real for the moment and for the purpose, but this right here in front of you is now just as much your life, and you will have to learn to dance within two realities. Both are completely essential to the greater purpose of your life," she says as she squeezes me. "Dinner should be ready soon, why don't you go wash up."

"Okay," I say, as I wipe the tears from my face with my sleeve and walk inside.

I splash water on my face and look in the mirror watching it run down my cheeks. I am completely beside myself. I have no grid for this. I honestly don't know anyone that could have a grid for this. I mean, I feel as if I'm now in real life, but seeing Joshua and then him disappearing like that. That can't be reality. Maybe I am in a dream and I just need to wake up. I pinch my arm. Nope. Maybe I'm in a deep sleep like a coma of some sort. That's it. Was I in an accident? I strain my mind to try and think back to the last thing I remember from being up at Joshua's parents farm.

There was the whole court hearing, which was a little strange, but definitely did something as far as freedom in my heart and from Ralph. Then we were back at Mom and Dad's house for a few weeks. I remember sitting in Dad's favorite chair thinking back through everything and where I was at. That's it! That is the last thing I remember. I must've fallen asleep.

I dry off my hands and face and take one more look at my young face in the mirror. Well, my body definitely looks and feels better than it did before I woke up. I wonder if I will have to go through everything that I already lived through in my dream?

"Would you like to eat out on the deck, honey?" Aunt Darra calls.

"Oh, that would be great," I holler through the bathroom door.

As I walk back through the kitchen, I pick up my plate, fork and napkin and walk out the back door to the most beautiful sunset over the ocean. The feeling inside of me reminds me of the time Joshua took me to the waterfall for the first time. I am overwhelmed with beauty and in light of all that's taken place, I feel peace.

"Bridget, I know you have a lot of questions swirling around, and I know one of the main ones is, where do you go from here? I can't answer all of your questions today. It would overwhelm you, but that one I can answer. Your life, whether in another reality or this one, only works one way. One moment at a time. It is your job to find the purpose in each moment. You are on this earth for a reason. Now you have to figure out what that reason is. Because, I'll be honest, there is a whole world that desperately needs you to figure it out."

"That makes me feel like I'm some secret superhero or something," I chuckle.

"No, not a superhero dear, but you are chosen."

"What does that mean? That seems a little odd that I would be chosen or that I would have any influence over the whole world. I mean, we are all responsible for making the world a better place, everyone just needs to do their part."

She looks up at me with tears running down her cheeks.

"Bridget if you aren't able to see this..." She stops in an attempt to regain her composure.

"I'm sorry Aunt Darra, what did I say?"

"Your whole experience with Joshua and with your children was to show you who you are, to prepare you for what's ahead."

"I know, I feel so much more free now and I feel like I will be a better person in this world because of all that. Even though I don't understand it."

"Bridget, it wasn't about you being a better person, or fulfilling your part in the world." she says holding back her tears. "You are the hands and the feet, of something much bigger, what you do is an echo of all who have been loved by something so much greater than themselves. I know this is going to be hard to understand, but you are the culmination, the coming together of those carrying the light."

340

"I'm sorry, I don't understand."

She sighs, "I know dear, but in time I believe you will."

We finish dinner and I give Aunt Darra a hug and thank her for everything as I leave.

As I drive back to Aunt Mary and Uncle Dave's house I try and make some sense of what Aunt Darra was talking about. 'The chosen', and 'the coming together of those carrying the light'. It all just seems like another world to me. I know I don't understand that part yet, but I don't get why she couldn't just tell me why I had that other life or dream or whatever you want to call it.

In the midst of my confusion I also feel a confidence rising up inside of me that whatever lies ahead, I'm not alone. And in this moment I can feel his hand on top of mine on the shifter, and I cry because he has never felt so far away and yet so close at the same time.

Chapter 5

the next morning...

As I wake up from one of the most restful nights of sleep I've had in a long time, I am thankful. I sit up and stretch. Oh that feels so good. Instantly I'm taken back to a memory from our honeymoon. There I was awake before Joshua. It feels so tangible, even though it was a dream. I laugh as I think about making coffee as quietly as possible so I could surprise him. I remember sitting on the porch and looking out over the lake. And Dad, oh yeah, my walks with Dad. How I wish I could have one of those right now. I have even more questions now than I did back then. As I walk toward the window I see something dancing on the window sill. The most brilliant crimson cardinal. He sees me walking toward him and instead of flying away he just tilts his head to the side as if to say, 'hello friend'. I smile, as I kneel down in front of the window and for the next five minutes watch this beautiful creature as it watches me.

Like a whisper it comes again, 'I love you, Bridget'.

My new friend gives me one more head tilt and flies off.

I sigh and then get up and walk to the bathroom and begin to get ready. My mind turns back to my time with Aunt Darra. I laugh as I think of how she was supposed to answer my questions and now I have more questions on top of my old questions.

I turn on the shower and smile. There is nothing like a hot shower at any time of the day. I remember hearing about this boy in high school that liked taking cold showers. That's just nuts. I can't imagine doing that on purpose. Sometimes I just stand in front of the sprayer and let the water run down as the steam rises up past me. It feels so surreal. Just like the waterfall.

I get ready and decide to go see Annis at the coffeehouse.

Chapter 6

As I walk to the coffeeshop, I replay my experience with Joshua in my head. I still can't believe I got to see him and feel his touch.

I walk through the door, to see my new friend in this new life standing there behind the counter counting baked goods.

"Hey there, friend," I say.

"Bridget! I can't believe you came to see me. This is so great. What can I get for you?"

"I'll just take a pumpkin latte with whipped cream," I smile as I think about Joshua's sweet tooth.

"Coming right up. Listen I go on break in a half hour. Maybe we can talk then."

"That sounds great, thank you," I say as I take a seat in a worn wooden chair. I lean my elbows on the table and rest my chin on my folded hands, gazing out the storefront.

This is such a beautiful town. It's funny, I have this memory of this town, but it's so different from when I was here in the dream. As I think through the layout of the town in my dream it's similar, just different. Almost like if you were to take this town and turn it upside down it would be the same as the one in my dream.

"Hi there," a woman in a red dress with a stunning diamond necklace says to me as she stops at my table.

"Hi," I say politely.

"Are you new to this town?"

"Yeah, I am," I respond.

"Oh good, me too. I feel like a lost puppy. Do you mind if I sit down?"

"Sure, that's fine."

She goes on for the next five minutes telling me about how she ended up here and how hard it's been to meet any decent people.

I just try and listen without looking a little weirded out.

"So how about you? What's your story?"

"Oh me, ha. It's a doosey."

"Try me," she says with a smile and seeming concern.

"Well," I pause as the thought goes through my head 'Maybe if I just tell her the story she'll think I'm crazy and leave me alone.'

"Well, I had this dream. But it was real life for me for about 20 years. I can remember specific moments throughout, but also daily things. It was so real, I am still wrestling with which reality is the right one," I say as I stop and smile at her.

"No way. That is so cool."

"It is?"

"Yeah it is. I can't believe I am talking to you right now. I had the same thing happen to me. Well, not exactly the same thing. But similar. Anyway I found a way back into my dream."

"Really you did?" I respond in shock. "Hey by the way, what did you say your name was?"

"Yes, I did, and my name is Rebecca."

"Oh, hi. My name is Bridget."

"I know... I mean, you look like a Bridget."

"So, tell me more about this way you found back into your dream," I ask with excitement.

"Well, honestly it wasn't me. It's this guy named Brody. He has a shop downtown at the corner of Fifth and Main Street. If you're interested just tell him you had this dream, and you are trying to get back to it. He will help you out."

"I don't know Rebecca, what exactly does he have that will help me?"

"Bridget, you're gonna have to trust someone that has been where you've been. I know what it feels like to be alone and to want answers. Just go see Brody, I promise it will help. And Bridget, you need to go right away. If you don't, you may miss out on ever having the chance to go back."

"What do you mean? Why do I have to go right away?"

"Oh dear, once your memory of it all begins to fade there is nothing left for you to get back to," she says as she stands up and grabs her coffee cup preparing to leave. "It was so nice to meet you honey. And do have a great time getting back to the place you really belong. Trust me, I know how you are feeling and it is not fun."

"Thank you, Rebecca," I say.

"You're welcome dear. I'm sure I'll see you around sometime. And don't forget, go see Brody," she says as she squeezes my arm.

"Ok, thanks."

That was weird, I think, as she walks out the front door.

"Hey there," Annis says as she sits down across from me. "How are you doing?"

"I'm doing pretty good. Hey have you ever seen that lady that was just here?"

"What lady?" She says.

"The one who was just here, red dress, dark hair. You didn't see her? You had to have seen her."

"Sorry, I didn't see her."

"Oh, ok. That was just weird, and I, I don't know. Anyways, how are you doing?"

"Pretty good, morning rush is over and in a couple hours we'll get the lunch crowd in, so this is a perfect time for us to catch up. So, what's the latest?"

"Not much. Yesterday I went to see my aunt, well she's not my aunt, but..., I don't know what she is. She was supposed to help me understand some stuff, and now I just have more questions than I did before. But enough about me, what have you been up to?"

346

"Same old town, same little girl," she laughs. "Not much is new, except I started a new painting yesterday. I'm really excited about it."

"Wait, you paint? That is so cool, my Ben paints."

"Your Ben? How many boyfriends do you have?"

"I'm sorry, I mean, I am close to someone who paints, and he is so good at it. It's like a passion for him."

"That sounds like me. So, he's not your boyfriend?"

"No, no definitely not," I say laughing.

"Is he cute?"

"He is adorable."

"And single?"

"Annis, you can't date my so... I mean, my friend. Besides he doesn't even live here," I say hurriedly hoping that she will drop it.

"I'm OK with long distance, Bridget."

"No means no, Annis," I say with a smirk.

"Oh alright, but at least tell me about him."

"Well, OK. He has blue eyes that pierce like the sun glistening off the water. He's so calm and caring, much like his father. He sees every glass as half full, and lives in expectation of good things happening. He's creative and somehow his creativity connects him to something beyond himself. He loves animals and adventure. He doesn't seem to care so much for what other people think about him. Oh yeah, and his sister. He loves his sister, even when she is not the nicest to him."

"He sounds dreamy. So he has a sister, tell me about his sister."

"Oh yes, Tori. She has blonde wavy hair that looks like she just walked out of the salon. She is pretty normal as far as height goes and has the build of a gymnast. She is bold and courageous. She loves to study and read books, but even more so she loves to argue her way to understanding. She is full of love and passion. And although she loves to pick on Ben, we all know that deep down she loves him dearly."

"It sounds like you know them really well. You talk about them like how a mother talks about her children."

A tear forms in my eye. "Ha, that's funny that you say that."

She looks at me with a look of confusion. "How old are you Bridget?"

"I'm thirt...," I stop myself. "I don't even know how old I am," I begin to cry. "I think I'm 18, but I feel like I'm thirty eight. I..."

"It's OK, Bridget, you can tell me anything."

"I don't know Annis, this is pretty out there," I say as I grab a napkin and dab the tears that are starting to form in my eyes.

"Try me."

"Well, alright then," I say as I take a deep breath. "Right before I met you I woke up from a nap I had taken when I first got into town. The only problem is that nap seemed to last for 20 years. I had this sort of dream, where I lived my life out. I met this guy here in this town, well, it was different than this town, but still here. I don't know if that makes sense, but anyways. I met Joshua, we moved to his parents farm up in the mountains and were married, then moved back here to town and raised our kids and then I got sick. I got really sick, and it was so awful. Then I met this guy Ralph who totally tricked me and I fell for it. I left Joshua, and the kids came with me. That's who Tori and Ben are," I say as I begin to cry again. "So then I left Ralph and went back to Joshua, and he forgave me. I know it sounds like I was a total jerk, but I was having these panic attacks and was overwhelmed with the fear of getting sick again. Ralph convinced me that he could save me from that and I believed him. So, at the end of it, I had this crazy experience with lightning and crying in the middle of the woods and then this courtroom where they took Ralph away somewhere. I know it just all seems..."

"Unreal!" she said with eyes wide open.

"Yeah, unreal," I say hanging my head.

"Bridget this is incredible."

"How do you figure?"

"You got to experience life in another realm."

"I what? You're starting to sound like Darra."

"No really, a friend of our family's was over the other night. He's one of those traveling musicians. He has a band and they were playing in the area and crashed at our place for the night. Anyways, Rich and I were talking that night and he was telling me about how there's this whole other realm around us. There's good and evil and this whole war being fought for us. I thought it sounded a little crazy at first. But then I looked into his eyes. And I realized he knew something that I didn't. You know how you meet those religious people who talk about all their beliefs and how you should join their club because they have it all figured out. That's not Rich. There's something that he's got a hold of that makes you know it's actually who he is. It's the first time I thought about any of that faith stuff as true and real."

"Is he still here? I'd like to meet him."

"No, he left yesterday. He's headed east, but dad says he'll be back through in a few weeks."

"Can you make sure you let me know when he's here. I really want to talk to him."

"Sure I can do that. Now back to your story. Do you have any idea why this all happened to you?"

"Not really. My aunt Darra..."

"Wait, so she is your aunt?" she interrupts me.

"Yes," I say as I sigh. "She was my aunt in my dream, and she seems to have known about this dream, so she told me to call her, Aunt."

"Oh man, this could be a novel, keep going."

I shake my head and continue. "Well, she said something about me being an important part to this whole thing of the true light shining on the earth or something. And that I was the culmination of the light or something like that. I don't know what to make of it all. I don't even know what culmination means."

"Bridget, it means the coming together. It's like the crescendo of a masterpiece. It is the thing that everyone waits for. If she said that about you, then that means your life isn't about being a person on earth. It's about being a symbol."

"A symbol? A symbol of what?"

"Maybe Rich was right about that," she whispered to herself."

"Right about what, Annis?"

"One of the things that he was telling me about was how we tend to think of the earth as matter, like the trees, or rocks, or grass, or even buildings and animals etc. But that the earth is actually made of spiritual stuff first and out of those comes all the other stuff. And he said that love was at the foundation of it all."

"Love, huh. That sounds like a country pop song."

"Not like that silly. Like a spiritual love. A love that sees beyond our preferences. It doesn't have anything to do with sexuality, just a genuine, pure love. He kept going on and on about this kind of love that he had come in contact with. He described it as this blue flame that would've consumed his whole body if it came any closer. And then he started to cry and he couldn't speak for a couple minutes. It seemed weird to me at first to see a man crying about the whole love thing, but you should've felt the room. It felt like there was electricity in the air. I can't describe it good enough, but I just knew he was telling me what was true from what he had experienced, not just what he thought in his head."

"Wow, yeah, I should talk to him when he comes back through."

"Wait a minute, I didn't even think about that," she said hitting her forehead with her hand. "He was talking about you."

"How was he talking about me?"

"Well, he told me that he knew about one of my friends who was having a tough time with making sense of some things in her life. I couldn't for the life of me think of who he would be talking about. But it's you. How does he know you?"

"I don't know, that does seem strange. I didn't know any guys named Rich when I was growing up."

"Yeah, that is strange, but I guess not as strange as your whole other life," she said laughing. "I mean, 38 is pretty old, you could be my mother," she hits her knee and lets out another laugh.

"Very funny, Annis. Back to the symbol thing, I still don't understand, a symbol of what?"

"It's so easy Bridget. You're supposed to be a symbol of love on the earth. But not just any love. The kind that messed up Rich so bad."

"So, I'm supposed to be wacky like this Rich guy?"

"No, you're supposed to be the thing that connects people to the thing that makes them wacky like Rich," she says with eyes wide open.

"How do I do that?"

"I'll be honest, I don't even really know what I'm saying right now. I just get the sense that you need to figure out this puzzle, or else..."

"Or else what?"

"I don't know Bridget, but it can't be good."

"Well, at least it seems like it will be easy," I say sarcastically.

"Well, I'm here to help in any way I can."

"Thanks Annis, but maybe life is just more simple than all of this stuff. Honestly, it all feels so intangible. Maybe I'm just supposed to live a good life and work on fulfilling my dreams on the earth."

"Nope, I don't buy it. That sounds too cheap, and all this happened to you for a reason much bigger than that. Haha, listen to me. I'm talking like I actually have a clue what I'm talking about."

"Well, for now, I guess I'll just keep walking and see where I land. Thank you for listening."

"That's what friends are for. We can't always take away the pain, but we can be right beside you through it."

"Yeah, that is what friends do. That's what Joshua did for me. I wish I could see him again."

"I can't imagine how hard that must be to feel like you had all of that and then to lose it."

"It's excruciating, but sometimes," I lower my voice and lean in closer to her, "I see him and hear his voice. I know it's crazy, I don't even understand it, but as strange as it is, the hope that I will get one more moment with him keeps me going."

"Wow, what is it like when you talk to him?"

"Sometimes it's like a whisper in my soul, other times I can feel his touch. And there are times when I see something in nature that lets me know he is right there. Almost like he is using nature to speak to me."

"Wow, that sounds so cool."

"It really is, but it makes me want to get back to my other life so badly."

"I bet it does."

"Hey do you know a guy downtown named Brody? I guess he runs a shop on Main Street."

"Yeah, I know about Brody. What do you want with him?"

"I just heard about him and was wondering who he was."

"I'll tell you who he is: t-r-o-u-b-l-e," she spells out. "Seriously Bridget, you don't want anything to do with that kid."

"Why is that?"

"He's one of the biggest drug dealers in this town, and besides that he is super arrogant and thinks he is every girl's dream. Trust me, if you never run into Brody, you will be better for it."

"Ok, thanks."

"How did you hear about him anyways?"

"Oh, just in passing. Someone told me that Brody might have something that could help me with this whole dream thing."

"Nothing he has will help you. Trust me on this one Bridget."

"OK, thanks I will."

Chapter 7

weeks later...

Time passes and I'm finding a new rhythm inside a world I would rather not be living in.

I found a job at a local book store as the clerk, and have been enjoying being around all the stories. Mr. Jenkins, the owner, is a friend of Uncle Dave's and was kind enough to give me this job.

Most people would love to have a second chance at their life, to be able to change all the things they wished they had done differently, but all I really want is Joshua and the kids back again. I guess I'm glad that I didn't ever really cheat on Joshua and drag my kids through everything with Ralph. And that I didn't have to really go through the sickness and all the fear that came with it, but the crazy thing is that it all felt so real, and the memories are so vivid that my body and emotions feel as if I really went through it.

Each day the memories and the feelings seem to be a little more separated from me, but no matter how hard I try to move on, there is a part of me that still feels like that is my reality, and this is just lonely.

I still think, from time to time, about what Rebecca said and about going to see Brody. Part of me just wants to see what it is that he has that might be able to help. But the other part of me feels really hesitant. I have so many thoughts swirling around my head, sometimes I'm not sure which to hold on to and which to let go.

I mean, what if Joshua isn't who I thought he was? What if this is all just like a game to him?

I guess part of me is just frustrated because I haven't heard from him in weeks. Even the cardinal outside my window just flies off when I come near him. It feels so lonely, so empty without Joshua's little nudges, and what if even those 'visits' from him are just made up in my mind? What if none of that was real either? I think back to my time at Aunt Darra's and wonder if there is any chance that was a dream.

"I should go get some breakfast," I mutter as I close my journal and lay it on my nightstand.

"Hi Aunt Mary," I say as I step off the bottom step and turn toward the kitchen.

"Good morning dear. How did you sleep?"

"Pretty good."

"Have a seat, I made you some breakfast."

"Aunt Mary, you don't have to make me breakfast every morning."

"Bridget, please," she said as she turned toward the kitchen window and looked out toward the swing in the backyard. "For the first year after Lindsey passed I was in so much denial that I would make her a plate every morning and just let it sit there until Dave got home from work. He would clean it off and put it away and we'd do the same thing the next day. For years now I've wanted to make breakfast for my daughter. It is not a chore for me, or a task, it is so fulfilling to my heart. I know you don't want to be a burden to us, but it's these simple things that our father and mother hearts have been in such need of."

"I'm sorry, Aunt Mary. Of course I would love breakfast."

She turns and smiles and places a plate with a Mickey Mouse shaped pancake on it with sausage on the side.

"Lindsey loved it when I made this breakfast for her. I used to laugh. I'd say, 'Lindsey, it's the same as a normal pancake. It doesn't taste any different.' And she would respond. 'Mommy it's about the touch of love you put in them. That's what makes them so yummy, and I just really like Mickey Mouse.'"

"I'm so sorry Aunt Mary, there is no pain like losing your child."

"No there is not dear, and for as young as you are, I think you know what it is like. Am I right?"

"What do you mean?"

"I went to spend some time with Darra last week, and she told me about all that you've gone through. I'm so sorry Bridget. You must feel like a fish out of water," she says as she pulls a chair up next to me and hugs me.

I spend the next couple minutes just crying into the shoulder of a mom who understands.

"Yeah, I guess that analogy really fits," I say as I wipe my tears with my sleeve.

"Dear, just know that Dave and I are here for you, and we aren't going to think you are crazy or weird for any of this."

"Thank you Aunt Mary."

"Darra did say she'd love to see you again when you have time."

"Really?"

"Yeah, she said just let her know the next time you can come up there."

"Um, I have off on Thursday."

"OK, good. I'll let her know."

"That would be great, I could use some more time up there at her place," I say as I glance at my watch. "Oh no, I gotta run. I'm going to be late for work."

"Well, I will see you later, have a great day, dear," she says as she kisses me on the forehead.

I shove the last of Mickey's big ear in my mouth, grab my bag and head out the door.

Since it's only about a half of a mile into town, I walk most days. This town is starting to wear off on me. It is so quaint. It reminds me of one of those small towns in the movies where the girl lands after trying to get away from her past life and stumbles into the man of her dreams. I laugh out loud as I walk down Main street thinking about the differences of perspective on love and relationships between an 18 year old and a 38 year old. I mean, we all deep down want that movie-type love story that feels great from beginning to end, but time and experience tend to reveal a much different probability on actual love stories.

"Hi, you are...beautiful," says this boy that I've never seen before.

"No, I'm Bridget," I say laughing.

"I'm sorry, I'm usually more in control of myself, I just have never seen you here in town before," he responds.

"I'm new."

"Oh, I see. Well Bridget, I'm Brody. It's a pleasure to meet you."

"Oh, Brody, I uh. I've heard of you, from uh. Well, that's not important. Uh, do you know a lady named Rebecca by any chance?"

"No, I don't think so. Should I?"

"I don't know just, she said that I should come see you for something."

"Really? What was it for?"

"I honestly don't know."

"That sounds a little sketchy, Bridget."

"Ha, I know. I'm sorry. I had this crazy dream, and can't seem to shake it. So, she said maybe you could help me get back to it somehow."

"I'm sorry Bridget, I don't know who she is, or what she was talking about, but I wish I did know, if it meant the chance to see you again."

Oh boy, I'm torn between the life experience of a married woman with two kids, and an 18 year old girl's heart, just wanting to be filled up.

"Well, if you want to meet me after work, you can walk me home."

"OK, that would be great."

"3:30 at Jenkins Books."

"I'll be there," he says with a charming smile.

That was so weird. I expected something totally different from him. I mean, with what Annis said about him. I just don't get it. I was expecting someone else entirely.

Throughout the rest of my work day, my mind travels back and forth between Brody and Joshua. Part of me feels like since this is my new reality, I need to move on from Joshua and let that be the past; but on the other hand there is so much history there. Again I feel torn between two realities and unsure of how I'm supposed to live in both. Or am I?

3:30 p.m.

I smile when I see Brody walk through the front door of the book store.

"Goodbye Mr. Jenkins. I'll see you tomorrow morning."

"Sounds good Bridget, thanks again."

"Hey there," I say as I grab my bag and walk to meet Brody by the door.

"Hey," he says with a smile that melts my 18 year old heart, and causes my 38 year old mind to roll its eyes.

It's so funny to be in this moment and see charm for what it is, but still feel the effects of it.

He opens the door for me and we step out onto the street. As we approach the coffeehouse where Annis works I find myself a little concerned that she might see me. We pass the front of the coffeehouse and I think we are in the clear, when I hear the door open and...

"Hey Bridget, is that Josh... Oh, hi Brody."

"Hey Annis, how are you doing? I didn't know you knew Bridget."

"Uh yeah, she just moved into town and I met her not too long ago," she said obviously annoyed.

"Oh, that's great, yeah, I just met her this morning."

"Annis, I'll stop by the coffeehouse tomorrow morning to see you," I say.

"Either way is fine, Bridget."

"OK, well, I'll see you tomorrow then."

She hangs her head as she walks back into the coffeehouse. It seems like she feels as if I betrayed her, but I didn't even go see Brody. He totally found me. Ugh, friendship can be tough sometimes.

"You OK?" He says as he nudges my arm with his elbow.

"Yeah, just need to catch up with her at some point."

"Yeah, I'll be honest, she and I have a little bit of a not so good history."

"Oh yeah, why is that?"

"Well, it was a couple years ago, and I was going out with her sister, and she didn't think I was the best guy for her sister to be dating. Well, she sort of made up some stories about me, and her sister broke up with me the next day. I tried to work it out with her, but the damage was done. Ever since then I've kept my distance and she's kept hers."

"I'm so sorry to hear that."

"Yeah, it's a part of life though, you love and then you lose love, and then you learn how to love again."

"Yeah, funny you should say that."

"What do you mean?"

"Oh nothing, I just..."

"That was not an 'oh nothing' kind of statement. There's some weight behind that one."

"Yeah, I guess you could say that."

"So, go on," he says with a smile.

"I just had this dream, that seemed really real, and it was over a long amount of time, and then I woke up, and here I am, back at the beginning. Trying to figure out what happened, and how to go on."

"That's weird."

"I know, I'm not even sure why I told you."

"No, not the dream or any of that, it's weird that you and I met."

"Why is that?"

"Well, I had a similar experience a few years ago, and I've been trying to get back into it since. Well, this may sound too 'out there' for you, but I found a way back. I get moments back inside that world with those people. It's crazy, and I feel like all the sad feelings go away in that moment."

"Really?"

"Yeah, really."

"But how?"

"Well, you seem like a good girl, and I don't want to throw you for a loop on this one, but there's a specific type of herb that allows your brain to recall secondary memories, like the ones you have from dreams. Most people think it's a drug, but it's totally natural. For me it's the only way I've found to get back to those feelings. And honestly, all I want is to live there as much as I can."

"I've never done drugs before. I don't know how comfortable I'd be with that."

"Don't think of it as a drug, think of it as a natural herb that helps bring your memories to the forefront of your mind."

"Would I get to see Tori and Ben again?"

"I don't know who Tori and Ben are, but if they were in your secondary memory, then yeah."

"Yeah, never mind about them, but wow, that would be amazing. All I've wanted is to go back and see them."

"This is the only thing I've found that works."

"Is it dangerous?"

"I've been doing this for two years, and I'm still normal, ha, at least I think I am," he says winking at me.

"Ok, I'll try it."

"Sounds good," he says as he takes a small bag out of his pocket and hands it to me.

I look down to see two white pills inside the bag.

"This is it?"

"Yep, just take them after a meal and give yourself some space from people."

"I don't know, maybe I don't really need this. I mean I'm good and think I can get through this."

"Bridget, the question isn't if you can get through this, it's do you want to? I'm sure you can float through the rest of your life, but you would always be wondering about whether or not you should've at least tried to get back there. I know what you're feeling, and it's not fun. The least you can do is try it."

"Yeah, I guess I can do that."

"Sounds good," he says as he smiles at me.

We come to Aunt Mary and Uncle Dave's street and I turn and thank him for walking me home and for the help.

"You're welcome, Bridget. I hope this helps you as much as it has helped me."

"OK, thanks," I say as I continue walking.

What are these pills anyways? I mean I knew a bunch of druggies in high school and I never wanted to end up like them. It just didn't have the appeal to me. And I'm not trying to drown out my sorrow. I just really want to get back there. I really want to see my kids again and feel Joshua's embrace.

Chapter 8

"Are you OK honey?" Uncle Dave asks. "You've been quiet all dinner."

"Oh, sorry, I was just thinking about some stuff."

"Are you still liking your job?"

"Yeah, I really am. It's been so good for me to get back to work and I get to read when everything is caught up. I'm in the middle of this novel right now that is so intriguing. First I was like, 'Why in the world?' then I was like 'What?' and then I got to the middle and I was like, 'No way!' I'm just hoping it ends on a good note, cause nobody likes a story that ends bad."

"Ha, you're right about that one. I've read some really good ones in my day, and my favorites are the ones that tug on your heart so much that you have a tough time knowing if they're real or not," he says smiling at me.

"Yeah," I say, knowing that he is probably referring to my dream. "Uncle Dave?"

"Yes, dear?"

"If you left home when you were young and then realized that you missed everything, but had a chance to go back, would you?"

"Are you thinking of heading out of town Bridget?" He says with sadness in his voice.

"No, no, I just... I'm not sure what I'm asking. I just feel really alone now, even with everything I have here. Please don't take this the wrong way, I love you guys and am so thankful to be here, I just really miss my family."

"You mean from your dream?"

"Yeah," I say as I hang my head in shame. "I know this sounds silly that I would feel this way, I just really want to go home."

"You know Bridget, I like to think of life as a river. It runs in all sorts of directions. Although there are parts that

362

are straight and predictable, the majority of a river has twists and turns that nobody could've predicted. Many people try to get out of the river of life and try and settle up on the land somewhere safe where they can feel like they have control over everything. But in all reality, we were made to conquer the river, not avoid it. And the only way to conquer the river is to stay in it, to follow it, and to not be afraid, but keep your head above water, and at every moment possible..." he pauses as he reaches over and picks up my chin and turns my eyes to his. "Enjoy it."

"I know, I want to," I say, in between sobbing. "I just feel like such a mess trying to make sense of all of this."

"Bridget, you grew up in a world that is the opposite of what you're experiencing now, you may never understand all that has happened. Follow the river and keep your head above water. You'll make it, I know you will. And I am so proud of you, honey."

"Thanks Uncle Dave. I think I'm going to head up to my room for the night. Thanks again."

"You're so welcome."

"Oh Bridget, Darra said Thursday would work wonderful for her," says aunt Mary.

"Oh, that's great. Thank you."

"Goodnight dear."

"Goodnight."

As I walk up the stairs I feel this pull in my soul. I put my hands in my jacket pockets and feel the bag of pills that Brody gave me. I toss my jacket in my closet and walk toward my bed. I sit down and look up toward the window when the cardinal sitting on the window sill catches my eye. I stand up slowly and walk toward him. He just sits there watching me. He turns his head like he used to. I'm clutching the pills from Brody in my hand. I'm ready to see my kids and Joshua again. I reach for my water bottle and move my hand toward my mouth, when I hear his voice that sounds like a whisper but fills the entire room.

"Bridget."

"Joshua?" I look around the room quickly. "I'm coming Joshua," I say as I again put the pills to my mouth.

"Bridget, this is not the way. Please trust me."

"Joshua, please I need you. I need to see our kids. Come here please. If this really isn't the way then show yourself to me. Please Joshua," I cry out weeping on the floor. "That's it? Really? You say don't do this, and then you're gone? How is that showing me that you love me? All I want is to be with you. Can't you see that? AGHHH!" I yell as I pound my hands on the floor.

Instantly my mind goes through all the times he told me to trust him when I didn't want to, and how every time I trusted him it always turned out for my good.

Still crying, I walk to the bathroom and drop the pills from my clenched fist into the toilet and flush them. I head back to my room and lay down still crying, as this wave of realization washes over me. That may have been my only chance and I just gave it up.

"Why?" I cry out. "Why am I listening to these voices? Alright Joshua, I did it. I don't know why, but I did it."

And his response to me... silence.

I spend the next hour trying to journal some form of my thoughts but to no avail.

Finally I give way to sleep.

Chapter 9

I find myself in a familiar place, but I'm not exactly sure where. My vision feels foggy, but as I look around, things begin to clear up.

"The path around the lake!" I exclaim.

I keep walking and taking in every view I can. Oh, this feels so good to my whole body. It's been so long since I've felt this kind of comfort, it seems too good to be true. As I continue to walk toward the direction of Mom and Dad's house I have this feeling of expectancy. Good expectancy.

I look down at my body. It looks like I'm back in my 38 year old body. I lift up my shirt to see the scar from my surgery. Wow, this is weird. As I walk up the hill I look up toward the house and see him standing there smiling at me. I run toward him, but stop as soon as I come near him. Everything in me wants to embrace him, but I don't want to risk losing him like I did at the lighthouse.

"It's ok," he says as he reaches for me and pulls me into his arms. And in that moment everything fades away. This is love, it is far too deep to be called an emotion, far too pure to be called sexual attraction, it is the deep groaning of a heart that has found home.

"Joshua, why did this happen to me? What did I do to lose everything I had?"

"My dearest Bridget. I think it's time that I explain to you all that has happened."

"Please do Joshua."

"But first, thank you," he says as he looks deep into my eyes.

"For what?" I reply.

"For not taking those pills. I heard everything that Rebecca said, and even the way that everything went with Brody. I know that must've been confusing, but if you had taken the pills, you may not have ever been able to come back here."

"You mean one mistake and I never get to see you again?"

"What Rebecca and Brody offered you was a counterfeit. You would've met an image of me if you had taken those pills, and it probably would've convinced you to go back to the counterfeit over and over again. You would've become so confused and began to believe you were doing the right thing, but in reality you would've become more and more enslaved to this false reality. I can't tell you enough how thankful I am that you listened to me."

"You're welcome. Honestly, I didn't want to. It was hard to not take them, and then after I flushed them, I was so mad at myself, and thought I would never see you again."

"I know you felt that, I saw it. But your obedience to what you didn't understand but knew you should do, and your surrender to a path that didn't make sense, brought this opportunity for us to be together here."

"That's what it takes for me to be back with you? OK, what's next? Tell me what to do?"

"Haha. Bridget. I love you so much."

"Oh Joshua, me too," I say as I bury my head in his chest.

"Joshua?"

"Yeah?"

"Are the kids here?"

"Come with me."

"OK."

"So, there's some things I need you to understand about our time here. It is different than before. You see, I brought you here to help you understand some things for the next part of your journey."

As we walk toward our cabin he begins to explain more about why I was brought here in the first place, and why my life is important to my other reality. He shares with me how there is so much at stake in order for others to experience love.

"You've been given the gift and experience of it, Bridget. Now it's up to you to give out what you've been given."

"But give out what, Joshua? They'll think I'm the crazy girl who thinks a dream was real and real life is a farce."

"Bridget, in one word how would you describe what you experienced with me?"

"Love."

"It's that simple. It is what this world was created and formed with. You experienced it, and all the people of the world have that one simple craving. To know love. I just need you to share what you've been given. You experienced so much when you were here with me. You learned about deception, about fear, about shame and condemnation. But you also learned about trust, and hope, and faith, and love. You chose to walk away, but you also chose to walk back, and if anybody can share the story of love with the world, Bridget. It's you!"

"You really think so?"

"I know so. I know you feel like you live in a small town that nobody has heard of and how will you possibly influence anyone. But please hear me out on this one. I'm not asking you to save the world, I'm begging you to be available to the one person in front of you. If you will listen to my voice in the many ways it comes to you down there, then I will tell you exactly how to help each person you come in contact with."

"I think I can do that."

"I know you can."

"Come on in," he says as we reach the porch to our cabin and walk inside. "I know your heart has cried out for this," he says taking my hand and leading me into the family room. "We don't have much more time."

As I walk around the corner and into the beautiful rustic room where I have so many wonderful memories, I'm greeted by squeals, and "Mom!"

"Oh, Ben, Tori!" My heart leaps as I embrace my children. Ben I've missed you so much. Tori, I love you so much," I must have held them for five minutes feeling the warmth of their embrace as all the wonderful memories with them passed through my mind. And as I opened my eyes they were gone. But I didn't feel sorrow any longer. I looked up at Joshua with tears of joy flowing from my eyes, and whispered, "Thank you."

"You're welcome," he smiled as he came over to me, leaned down and kissed my forehead. "It's time Bridget."

"I know it is, Joshua. I lo..." was all I got out before my eyes opened to a ray of sunlight piercing through my curtains and my lips continued what I had not been able to finish in my dream. "love you, Joshua."

My mind races back and forth through the whole experience, as I hold my body pillow close and try not to move. Trying desperately to hold onto all the amazing feelings that I just experienced in my dream. Trying to grasp what is like the wind, powerful yet fleeting.

"Thank you," I say through tears of elation running down onto my pillow.

I walk over to the window and pull open the curtains to see my little buddy, the cardinal, staring in at me with his head tilted to the side.

"Yes, my little friend, it is a new day, and I am a new Bridget."

"Annis! Oh no. I need to go talk to her."

I throw on clothes, splash water on my face and run downstairs.

"Hi Aunt Mary, I gotta go meet a friend, I'll be back after work," I say as I give her a big hug and a kiss on the cheek.

"Okay dear, is everything OK? You seem different."

"I feel alive. I'll tell you about it later."

"Okay, well, have a great day."

"I will, it is a great day, and I can't wait to have it!" I say feeling a little overjoyed. It's that feeling of maybe I'm being over the top, but I really can't help it.

ten minutes later...

"Annis! Hi. I really need to talk to you."

"Oh, hi, Bridget. Well, I'm kind of busy, maybe later today I'll have some time."

"What? You're not busy, no one is in here and you've already cleaned everything."

"Well, I, I..."

"Listen Annis, I know you told me to stay away from Brody. I didn't go looking for him, I promise. I was walking to work and he saw me and started talking to me. And then I told him he could walk me home. For whatever reason I told him about my dream and that I wanted to get back and he told me about these pills."

"Ah ha. I told you he was a big drug dealer," she interrupted.

"Yes, I know. So, he gave me some pills."

"You took them? How could you? I can't believe..."

"Annis, just listen to me."

"Ok, sorry, go on."

"I didn't take the pills, I flushed them. It was like I heard Joshua saying not to take them. So, then when I fell asleep..." I went on to tell her all about my dream and Joshua explaining things to me and my time with the kids. "I just feel so alive. Like I haven't felt in awhile."

"Wow, Bridget that is amazing. So, you're not going to date Brody are you?"

"No, why?"

"He really hurt my sister, and when I finally convinced her to break up with him, he told everyone that I made up these lies about him and got my sister to believe them. It made him look like the victim and me the overprotective sister. He really isn't safe."

"I've been around those kind of guys before. Thank you for telling me about him. And Annis...?"

"Yeah."

"I do trust you, I just didn't know how to get out of the situation with him yesterday. Thank you for caring about me."

"Oh, Bridget. You're welcome," she says as she comes around from behind the counter and hugs me. "Hey, I almost forgot, well actually I wasn't going to tell you since I thought you were going to start dating Brody, but now that you are back in my good graces," she says with a chuckle. "I'm going out to our lake house this weekend and our friend, Rich, is going to be out there. Do you want to come?"

"Yeah! that would be great."

"Wonderful, I'll pick you up at 8am Saturday morning."

"Sounds great. I got to get to work. Thanks again, Annis."

"You're welcome, friend."

I turn and smile as I walk through the door.

I think about friendship the rest of my walk to work. I think back to all the fun times I had with Gabi. She really taught me so much about friendship. She wasn't afraid to tell me when I was doing something that was going to hurt me. She really loved me and wanted what was best for me, not just what she thought would make me happy.

I feel like something has turned for me. Before all I could think of was all that I was missing, and now I just see

370

all the things I'm grateful I got to experience. Something has definitely changed in me.

Chapter 10

I absolutely love this drive to Aunt Darra's house. Probably because it reminds me of the drive to Joshua's parents house. With so many turns and curves, no matter how many times you drive it, it is still unpredictable.

I arrive around 10am and am greeted at the door by Aunt Darra, who is wearing a look on her face that says, 'I'm up to something'.

"Hi Aunt Darra."

"Oh hi Dear, come in, come on in. How was your drive?"

"Wonderful, I just love the drive up here."

"Yes, me too. Sometimes I wish I lived down with everyone else, but then I look out off of my back porch, and I am once again convinced that Darra is made for the uncommon places."

"Haha, yes, she certainly is," I laugh as I walk through the door.

"Come back here dear, I have something I want to show you."

We walk through the living room and I slow down as I am mesmerized by the amazing abstract art decorating the walls.

"Are these paintings new?"

"Oh yes, I am friends with a bunch of artists and love to buy their work. Here, follow me," she says.

We walk to a closed door to what looks like a bedroom.

"OK, now before we go in here, I just want you to know that I've already talked with Mary and have cleared all this."

"Cleared what?" I say as she opens the door and walks in.

I follow behind her and there snuggled in a blanket on the floor is the most adorable little puppy.

"Oh Aunt Darra, he is precious," I say as I go over and sit down next to him and pet him.

"Go ahead, you can pick him up."

"How old is he?"

"9 weeks."

"Oh wow. What kind of dog is he?"

"He's a boxer. He'll get pretty big, but he is a great companion dog."

"I bet he is, oh he is just so adorable, you are gonna have so much fun with him Aunt Darra."

"Actually Dear, he is yours," she says as she looks down smiling.

"What? Really?"

"Yes, really. After our last time together I realized that what you needed for the next part of your journey was a companion. And well, I think North will do really good at that."

"Wait, his name is North?"

"Yes, do you like it?"

"I love it. Oh Aunt Darra, are you sure? I just don't know if I can handle a dog right now."

"My Dear, sometimes we don't realize what we need, sometimes we don't even want the thing we need, but in time we come to find that what we receive in life brings the blessing we are longing for. There is a world out there, all around you Bridget, that believes in getting the things they think will make them happy and as instantaneous as possible. And they are left unsatisfied every time. It's a shame really."

Aunt Darra and I spend the rest of the day playing with North and talking. I tell her all about the dream and all that I am learning.

It's interesting to me. Before I would've come up here with twenty questions that I felt like I had to have answers for. But now I just want to be with her. I just want to spend time enjoying life with her. I feel somehow as if being near her is changing me, giving me answers for my life. I honestly don't have a clue what the future holds for me, but I've never been so at peace with all of the uncertainty.

I lay North on my lap and begin the drive back home. We stop at a rest stop, and North quickly finds a spot to relieve himself. As we walk around on the grass I have a feeling I wasn't sure that I would ever experience again in this life. It feels a little bit like home. It's a passing feeling, but looking down at North I get this sense that he will help me more than I can understand.

"Come on boy," I say as I begin to walk back to my car.

He follows me along and as I place him back in my lap he lays his head down and falls back asleep for the rest of the drive.

one hour later...

"Hi Aunt Mary," I say as I walk through the front door with North in my arms.

"Hi honey, how was your time with Darra?"

"Oh, it was wonderful, and I have someone I want you to meet."

"Oh, I am so excited to meet this little guy. The moment Darra asked me about all this, I just had this feeling come over me. I knew this was going to be so good for you."

"Are you sure you guys are OK with it?"

"Of course, honey. In fact Dave has secretly always wanted a dog, but I would never let him have one. But I guess you could say I am softening in my old age," she says with a smile. "So what is this little guy's name," she says as she reaches to pet him on his head.

"His name is North."

She stops and looks up at me slowly, "Well isn't that fitting."

"What do you mean?"

"Honey, you've been trying to find your way most of your life, it seems fitting that you would have a companion that would remind you of the truest direction in life."

"Ha, I guess you're right. I didn't think of that, but that makes a lot of sense," I say as I put North down on the floor.

Just then I hear the back door open.

"Is that my girl?"

"Hi Uncle Dave."

"And who do we have here?" He says as he gets down on his knees and starts to talk puppy talk to North.

"Come here buddy, come here. I'm your new grandpa. Yeah that's right, we're gonna be pals."

Both Aunt Mary and I laugh.

"This is North, Uncle Dave."

He looks up at me slowly with that same look that Aunt Mary just gave me.

"Well isn't that fitting."

I hang my head and laugh. "Yes, it is very fitting."

"No, I just mean with finding your way and all."

"Yes, yes Uncle Dave I get it," I say still laughing.

And here in the middle of the family room with Uncle Dave and North on the floor and Aunt Mary and I smiling at each other, we have a family moment that will forever be etched in my mind. It's a memory, a Kodak moment, if you will.

Chapter 11

two days later...

I roll over and hit my buzzing alarm.

"North, buddy, today is the day that Annis is taking us to her family's lake house. Are you so excited?"

He stands up next to my bed and does his favorite dog stretch then licks my hand as I pet him under his chin.

I'm excited to meet this Rich guy. From how Annis describes him, he seems like one of those wandering musicians with unwashed dreads and a surfer accent.

Three honks sound from the driveway.

"That must be Annis," I say as I grab my bag and holler to North to come.

"Bye Aunt Mary. Bye Uncle Dave."

"See you later honey, have fun," Aunt Mary says.

"You too, North," Uncle Dave chimes in.

"We will," I say as I close the front door and head to Annis's car.

"I just love this car," I say as I open the door to her Volkswagen Cabriolet.

"Oh thank you, me too. Hi North, you are so precious," she says as she reaches over to pet him.

"Are you sure it's OK if I bring him?"

"Definitely, my folks love animals. Do you want to stop and grab a coffee? My treat."

"Well in that case, sure."

We get our Americanos to go and start driving west.

"So, how far away is the lake house?"

"Oh, about 2 hours or so. It's not super far, but the last bit of it is all back roads, so it takes longer."

"I love that. In my dream life, the drive up to Joshua's parents' house was like that."

"Really? Tell me more about it, please."

"Well, what do you want to know?"

"Anything, we have plenty of time."

"Well..." I go on telling her all about the lake and my walks with Dad. I tell her all about the cabin Joshua built, and even about the waterfall.

She looks at me with a funny look.

"Is that really what it's like?"

"Yeah, doesn't it sound amazing?"

"Actually Bridget, it sounds familiar."

"What do you mean?"

"Well, I guess you'll just have to see."

"OK," I say with a smile. "It's all just so beautiful out here Annis," I say as the road carves back and forth beside the rapids of a winding river.

"I know. As much as I would love to live up here. I think somehow I would forget how amazing it is."

"That makes sense. I look back at life with Joshua and the kids and how blessed I was and I can't help but think about how much I took for granted."

"It's easy to do. We look ahead and behind, above and below, but completely miss the moment and place we are in," she chuckles.

The rest of the drive is quiet as we enjoy our drinks and the beautiful views.

Chapter 12

As we pull up the lane to the lake house I see Annis's mom and dad out front talking to a guy that looks like he is in his early forties. He's got holes in the knees of his jeans, but they look more like they are truly worn than strategically placed by some fashion clothes company. He's wearing a blue and tan flannel shirt and has brown hair down to his shoulders. This should be interesting I think to myself.

"Annis!" he says with such excitement as he sees us get out of the car. He walks over to her and gives her a swing around hug, just like a good big brother would. I watch his eyes as he looks into hers with such genuine care and asks her how her heart is doing. She just smiles and says, "It's good."

"How's yours?" she says as she punches him in the chest.

He laughs, "Ughh, I think it just stopped for a second, but overall it's good." He stops and looks over at me.

In that moment I see the kindness and gentleness of Joshua.

"Is this...?" he says with so much excitement.

"Yes, this is Bridget," Annis says with a smile.

"Bridget, I am so honored to meet you," he says as he walks toward me.

"Thanks, me too," I say as I reach out my hand to shake his.

He completely bypasses my handshake and picks me up and does a swinging hug to me too. What is with this guy and hugs?

"Oh sorry, that might have been too much. I know we just met. You see, I was beat up by my dad quite a bit when I was a kid and so after a while I didn't want any sort of touch. But when I met my best friend and he helped me change everything in my life, he told me that the world is full of the wrong and hurtful and perverted kind of touch, but the

378

answer isn't to avoid. The answer is to run into the battle with purity and a lot of hugs. Sorry, that was probably a lot also for just meeting you," he laughs. "Well Bridget, it is a pleasure to meet you," he says with a British accent as he reaches his hand out to shake mine.

"You too," I say smiling. He's goofy but genuine.

"Come on in everyone," Annis's mom hollers.

I meet Annis's family and a few of their friends that have come up for the weekend.

"Who's ready for some tubing?" Annis's dad announces.

"Come on Bridget," Annis says.

"I don't know if I should bring North on the boat. It might be too much for him."

"I'll watch him if you'd like," Rich says.

"Really, you don't mind?"

"Are you kidding me. I've always wanted a dog, but with traveling like I do, I just can't. What did you say his name was?"

"It's North."

"Oh, I like that. Come here buddy."

He kneels down and North comes right over to him and nestles his head into his leg.

"OK thank you."

"You're welcome. Have fun you two."

As the boat pulls out I look back to see Rich on an Adirondack chair on the back deck with North in his lap.

"That would've been Joshua," I chuckle.

We spend the next hour or so getting whipped around the lake on tubes, screaming the whole time.

I arrive back on shore smiling as Annis decides to go for another round on the water.

"Where's North and Rich?" I ask Debbie, Annis's mom.

"Oh I think they are out front on the grass, dear. Did you have fun out there?"

"I did, it was a blast."

"Good, well we are so glad you could come up here with Annis, and so glad for your friendship to her," she says as she smiles.

"Thank you, I am too," I say as I walk out the front door.

"There you two are," I say as I step out onto the front porch.

"Hey there, North and I were just talking, and I was reminding him of why he is here."

"Oh yeah, why is that?"

"Because you needed a friend, Bridget, a companion. Someone to take care of you when you're feeling low."

"I guess I do, but honestly I think I could've used him more like a month ago than right now."

"Ahh, yes. Our self-determined time of need."

"Our what?" I say with a look that says, I have no clue what you just said.

"Well, it's like for me, I needed God to stop my dad from beating me when I was a kid. I wasn't even religious, but I'd cry out for help. And He never did. So, I figured He just wasn't real. Then when I was 16 and finally big enough to fight back, my Dad gets thrown in jail and spends the next 5 years not able to touch me again. I needed my dad gone when I was 3. That's when he hit me the first time. It sent me across the room. I spent years hating God and my dad. Honestly," he says as he looks over at me and quiets his voice just a little bit. "I had a plan and a gun, and the next time he laid a hand on me would've been the last. So then in my twenty's I was off living the dream. Making music and just enough money to live. I was traveling all around and having so much fun. I had everything I wanted, and I was so empty and still so angry. And one day I was sitting at the bar after a show and... I'm sorry, I'm talking too much again."

"No, no please, keep going," I say as I sit down next to him. North sees me sit down and comes over and crawls into my lap.

"Well, I'm sitting at the bar, and this guy comes over and sits next to me. He says hi and I say hi back, without even looking at him. Then he starts telling me about how God told him to come tell me that my dad going to jail was God's way of saving me. I just laughed and said. 'Listen pal, I don't know how you know anything about me, but my dad went to jail about 13 years too late. Either God isn't real or He's a really bad judge of timing.' I looked over at this guy to see tears running down his face. And then I realized it was my dad. But it didn't look like him and it didn't sound like him. He turned to me and said, 'Son, I know what I did to you, and I know what you were fixin to do to me, and I deserved it, but it would've stolen your life from you. God wasn't gonna force me to change, and unfortunately it cost you the most. But He wasn't late, you just haven't seen the whole picture yet. Me going to jail saved your life. Son, I don't deserve your forgiveness, but I'm begging you for it.'

And you know what I did?"

"No, what?"

"I stood up and walked out of that bar."

"Really? Didn't you want to forgive him, to give him a hug?" I said.

"No. You see when your heart is cold like stone, one breath of warm air doesn't penetrate it. Sometimes it takes a lot more. So that's what happened. I kept running into people that would look at me and tell me God loves me. I was getting so sick of it. I would yell at God. You don't love me! Love doesn't look like what you've put me through. And do you know what God said to me?"

"What?"

"Nothing. I spent a year hearing it from everyone else, but nothing from God. I didn't realize it then, but each person

381

was warming up my heart. It didn't matter that it was maddening when these complete strangers would say these God things to me. Each time my heart was getting warmer and warmer to His embrace. And that's when it happened," he said as he paused in silence.

"What happened?" I said softly, trying to be respectful.

"Ahh, I'll tell you some other time."

"What! No, you won't, tell me now."

"Haha, I'm sorry, I couldn't help it."

"Ughh," I say shaking my head.

"Well, I had an encounter."

"What's that mean?"

"If you stop interrupting me I'll tell you."

"You, are ridiculous," I say while slugging him in the arm.

"Ouch, fine I'll tell you. I met...," he paused, but this time I could tell he was getting emotional. "I'm sorry, please don't hit me again," he says laughing while tears start running down his cheeks. "I met Jesus."

"Jesus? You mean the sunday school character? Flannelgraph, white robe, and a blue sash?"

"A little different than that picture, but yes," he says laughing again with tears still running down his face. "I was playing a show in a not so good part of town. It was late and afterwards I was walking back to my car when I got jumped by a few guys. They just wanted my stuff, but when that first guy hit me, I had a flash-back to my dad and I went ballistic. I fought so hard and all the anger that was pent up inside of me came out like a tornado. I had just gotten done beating the second guy to a pulp when the 3rd guy came up behind me and hit me across the head with a crow bar. I was out like a light. I ended up in the hospital for three weeks. For two of them I was in a coma. They thought I would have brain damage from the intense swelling. I know I'm a little off my rocker, but I woke up completely fine," he says smiling. "But

382

those two weeks when I was dead to the world I was sitting talking with Jesus."

"Really? How is that possible? I mean, I know strange things happen, but do you think it was just your mind making it up?"

"Do you think your dream life was all in your mind?"

"Touché," I say smiling.

"You know we don't get to choose how God approaches us Bridget, we just get to choose how we interact with it. Do we receive it, and embrace it? Or do we try to make sense of it or see if it fits within our equations of life? It's only ever your choice."

"So, what was it like? You know, being with Jesus."

"Well, it was like I was on this farm, but not really. It felt like a place where food was grown and animals were present, but it wasn't like a farm here where there's just acres of open fields. It was up in the mountains and there was a lake that he and I would sit next to. We didn't talk, but just being beside him was so peaceful and the only thing I wanted to do. The first time we talked was when he took me to this place, it was a..."

I interrupt, "A waterfall?"

"Yeah, a waterfall, how did you know?"

"Just a hunch," I said smiling as I remembered my times at the waterfall.

"It was the most amazing place I'd ever seen. Full of life and beauty. Anyways, we walked there and as we approached the edge of a pool of water he motioned to me to jump in. It looked so appealing. I looked at him, he nodded, and I jumped in head first. The moment my head hit the water my ears began to ring. It was so intense it seemed as if it would be painful, but it wasn't, it was just overwhelming. And as I came back up to the surface. I began to hear like I had never heard before. I mean I heard the birds and the crashing of the waterfall. I looked up and heard him laughing, 'How does that feel?' he asked. 'Why didn't you talk to me before now?' I questioned him. He said he had been talking the whole time. I just couldn't hear him. I asked him if this was some sort of holy healing water. He just smiled at me and said that my surrender was what made it healing water. We spent the rest of the day sitting and talking. And that night he asked me if I trusted him. I said yes. He led me into this cabin and we sat down in 2 wooden chairs facing an old TV screen. He looked over at me with a look of apprehension as he turned it on. He then began to play every single scene from my childhood of me being beaten by my dad. But what was different this time was that he was in every single scene right there beside me, holding me through it. And as I looked closer at each scene, I could see he was crying. I put my head down into my hands. I wasn't sure I was ready. I stood up and looked at him sitting there. And before the words left my mouth, he was answering the deep confusion in my heart. He said, 'I know you feel like forgiving him is excusing his behavior. And I know that your pain was more of rejection and abandonment than it was from the physical abuse, but I promise you this is the only way for you to be free, and my friend, you were born to be free.' I lashed out at him screaming while I was crying, 'But why didn't you just stop it from happening? You're God, right? You're all powerful, right? Why didn't you stop it?' And he just looked at me as this look of sorrow spread over his face. He motioned to the chair. I sat back down still fuming as he turned the TV back on. I sat there in horror as I watched this man being beaten. Hit and whipped and spit at. I watched as pieces of his flesh were torn apart because of the whipping. I heard the sounds, the groans, the agony of it all. I cringed inside, and then I heard a voice in the background saying, 'If you're truly the son of God, then why don't you save yourself?' I began weeping for this man. I mean the pain that I felt, the beatings that I endured were nothing in comparison

384

to this. And then in the middle of it he looked up as if through the TV screen and straight into my soul. It was Jesus, the same Jesus who was sitting right beside me. I turned and looked at my new friend. I could see the look of pain in his eyes as if he was reliving that moment. As if his body could still feel the sensations of pain echoing throughout. I looked over and said, 'I'm sorry.' He stood up and walked toward the door, so I followed him. When we got outside he headed toward the lake. 'Jesus,' I said to him. 'I still don't understand why you didn't save yourself. I mean, I think I would've.' He looked over and smiled at me and said, 'Rich, sometimes the opportunity for the reward outweighs the cost of the pain. Unfortunately most people are so wrapped up in their pain that they never get to the place of being able to see their reward.' We reached the edge of the lake and stood there for what seemed like hours without saying a word. And then as I felt more and more at peace, he turned to me and said, 'Rich, if you want freedom, follow me.' He then hugged me and as he was hugging me it was if I was being pulled into him until I was just surrounded by light.

And then I woke up in the hospital bed. I opened my eyes and the first person I saw was my dad with his hands folded looking up to heaven crying out. Tears filled my eyes, as I whispered, 'Dad, I forgive you.' He looked down in shock then buried his head in my chest and wept for the next five minutes as he repeated over and over how sorry he was."

Rich looked over at me with true and pure tears flowing down his cheeks. "Bridget, I never found the right religion, I never found the right theology, or the right church. I found a friend…" he stops then clears his throat. "I found a friend who went through more than I ever did and did it for me and never once complained about the pain in his journey. He released the pain and embraced the reward, and I want everybody to know about him."

North gets up out of my lap and starts licking Rich's tears from his face. He just laughs.

"Rich?"

"Yeah?"

"Do you think that's what my dream is?"

"I do."

"Really?"

"Bridget, when Annis told me about it, everything she described seemed just like what I experienced. But you had a whole life that you lived there. It makes me think that you were made for something really important."

"You think so?"

"I would bet my bottom dollar on it. And I'm not a gambling man," he said chuckling.

"I'm just not sure where to go or what to do with all of this."

"You don't need to figure that out. You just need to keep the lines of communication with him open."

"Jesus or Joshua?"

"One and the same."

"Really?" I say, still trying to wrap my mind around all of this.

"Yeah, really. Bridget, he's not asking you to have all the answers or understanding on your next 20 years. He's only asking you to follow him on the next step. So, that's what we gotta figure out. What is he asking you to do next?"

"I don't have a clue. I mean, this all seems upside down to me."

"Haha. That is definitely what it feels like," he chuckles.

"Well, I guess I have a lot to think about then."

"Yes and no. If you spend too much time in your head, you'll be answering all the wrong questions. I think what you really need to do is ask Joshua to tell you what is next."

"You really think he'll answer me?"

"I'm pretty sure he will. Either way, it's worth the try, right?"

"Yeah, I guess it is. Thanks for the talk, Rich."

"No, thank you, Bridget."

"For what?"

"You'll figure it out soon enough, but I've found out that the more I pour out, the more I am filled up."

"That makes no sense."

"Yeah," he claps his hands together and laughs. "Upside down, right? The next time we meet I'll explain it to you, but I'm sure the next time we see each other, you won't need it explained."

"I'll just take your word for it. I'm gonna go check on Annis."

"Sounds good. See you later, North," he says as he pulls him onto his lap and hugs him.

Chapter 13

As I walk back through the front door, I'm welcomed by the smell of BBQ and all the mouth-watering sides a girl from a small town could dream of. North stops at the table and sniffs.

"Come on boy," I say as I keep walking toward the back deck looking for Annis.

"There you are, how was the boat?"

"It was awesome. How was your time here? What did you do?"

"I actually talked to Rich for awhile. He told me his story and, well, let's just say I have a lot to think about."

"Ha, yeah. He has that effect on people."

"Yeah, he does. I guess I just needed someone to help me see a bigger picture than I was able to see myself."

"Funny how that happens. That's why I think friendships are one of the most important things on the earth. I mean, if you just only do what you think is right all the time, than you are for sure to miss out. So friend, just let me know if you need some talk time," she says with a smile.

"I definitely will, friend," I say as I return the smile.

We spend the rest of the night eating and laughing. And as we finally pack our things and get ready to leave I realize something. I'm full. My heart, my emotions, my spirit, they all feel full. I'm sure I haven't felt this since the dream.

"So, you said you had a good time talking to Rich. What all did you guys talk about?" She says as she pulls out of the driveway.

"Oh, just about weather patterns and the affects it has on the African mongoose."

"The what? You what?"

I turn and smile at her.

"You stinker, come on, just tell me what you talked about."

"Well, in a nutshell, he thinks that my Joshua was actually Jesus. Kind of nuts, huh?"

"Maybe not."

"What do you mean?"

"I don't know Bridget, I was always fine with all the Jesus stuff being over on the other side of the road from me. I didn't feel like I needed it. And then when I hung out with Rich a couple months ago, I realized I didn't think I needed him, because I really believed I was OK. But when I talk to Rich and see the peace that comes out of him, the genuine love he has for people, and the kindness in his eyes, I realize I have a lot further to go on my journey. So, I started journaling to this 'Jesus' that Rich talks about, and a few weeks ago I found myself crying as I wrote. My pages were filled with more tears than words. It was the first time I ever really felt loved and alive and full. It was also the first time that I looked at and worked through a lot of hurts in my heart that I had buried. When I told Rich about it, he smiled so big and asked me if I was ready. I was like, 'Ready for what?' And he went on to explain that what I had experienced was the invitation. But I had to show up at the party and walk through the door. He then went on to tell me that I couldn't just show up at a church or read the good book and expect to be OK. That this whole deal was about Jesus' life for mine. And that from that point on I was his follower. Always doing life with him, never alone, and never leaving him behind," she says looking over at me as we cruise down the highway.

"So, did you do it, I mean did you make that decision?" I ask turning to her.

"You know everything in me wanted to fight it. I knew it meant that I couldn't just do what made me feel good in the moment or what I thought was best. In some ways you could look at it as bondage, but that would be a misunderstanding.

Bridget, when he began to touch my heart, I couldn't..." she stops and tears begin to drop from her eyelids. "I couldn't even put to words how knowing I was loved like that, actually feels. It's like other worldly. It's deeper than your head and your heart, beyond your soul. It truly is a spiritual thing, and the best way I can describe it is like being lost for a long time in a lot of pain and confusion, and finally finding your way back home. It's that moment when you walk through the door and there's a whole bunch of people who see you and start crying and rejoicing because you made it. He is like coming home. So, yeah. I came home," she says as she chokes up again.

"Yeah, I think I get that, but what about all the other ways there are to God, how do you know which is right?"

"Ha, I asked that one to Rich too. He said that Christianity has moved so far over the years from where it started. And nowadays Christianity is easy to compare to other religions, it's a set of beliefs that someone has from their interpretation of a source they deem as credible. The fight to figure out which one is right has become based on whose book is older or more accurate or who has more followers and makes the most sense. But we're talking about God, right? The one who created all of this, and us, isn't asking us to figure Him out. He's calling us to follow Him through our life's journey. I don't know if that makes sense or not."

"Dad," I whisper as my head spins through my dream connecting what Annis is saying to all of it.

"What? Your dad? Did he believe?"

"Annis, I met Him," I said as my body is overcome with something I've never felt before. It's similar to the waterfall that Joshua took me to, but more powerful.

"What do you mean? When?"

I begin to cry, but I can't for the life of me figure out why. It's as if my body is receiving sensations without anybody touching me.

"Annis, in my dream, Joshua's dad," I say as I continue to tremble. "I think that was Him. But, I don't know. When I was a kid I used to read about God in the Bible in the old part of it, and He didn't seem very much like Joshua's dad."

"That's interesting, what was he like?"

"I used to describe him as this cross between a wise sage and cool old guy who still rock climbed. But I don't think everybody knew him that way. That was more just my relationship with him."

"That's fun, I wish I could've met him like that. Hey, why do you think you got to experience God the way that you did? I mean, why didn't I get to experience that?"

"You got me there, I mean if anybody didn't deserve it and wasn't asking for it, it was me. I gave up on God after my real dad died, and despite my mother's efforts to try and keep me believing in something bigger than me that loved me, I was too hurt to receive any of it. I didn't have any way of understanding that in light of my circumstances. You know, before my mom passed she told me that she and my dad would pray for me every night about my journey with God and how important it was." I paused as a memory races back to my mind from when I was 10. "Oh yeah, there's some sort of a letter that she said I would get when I got older. I completely forgot about it. That's so weird, I can't believe I forgot about that. I'll have to ask Aunt Abbey about that." I shake my head as if to come back to our conversation. "But as far as the 'why me' question. I don't think it has anything to do with me. I think it has everything to do with Him and what He chooses. When Dad talked about me being healed from the pain of losing my parents. He said it was like I was on this mountain but circumstances carried me down to a valley. I could get back up there, but it would take process and a journey. And this makes a lot more sense now, but he said that Joshua would be able to help me on the journey. We don't get to choose our journey, but we do get to choose how we walk on it."

"Wow, can I be honest?"

"Yeah, of course you can."

"It's hard for me not to want what you had with Joshua and his dad and everything. I hate to say it, but I'm kind of jealous."

"You know, I never understood this before, but Joshua used to always tell me the reason we are given gifts is to come to the point where we can share them. If a gift stays with you, it becomes an idol, and idols are heavy. They don't give you anything in return and they keep you from going further in life. But a gift that is shared will keep you humbled, genuine, and free to go places you could have never gone to on your own. Like I said, I didn't understand it then, but now I think I get it. My experience wasn't for me, it's for everyone around me. It's kind of like a bridge that I got to help build, that allows people to get to a place they couldn't before."

"That's funny cause your name is Bridget, get it? bridge? Bridget?" she says as she slaps her knee.

I shake my head and smile.

"What does your name mean, anyway?" she asks.

I pull out the necklace from under my shirt that still holds the ring that my dad gave me. On the inside is an inscription. "It means strength or exalted one. But my dad used to tell me that there was a Celtic meaning to my name and that was why they named me that."

"What was that?"

"Bride," I say as I look down and think through my wedding day with Joshua.

"Wow, that's really cool."

"Yeah," I say as I chuckle. "It feels a little bit beyond me, if you know what I mean. What does your name mean?" I say, as I turn to her.

"Oh, it means, pure and holy."

"Wow, that's cool. That's a good name for you."

"What do you mean?"

"You're just not like a lot of other people I know, and you seem to really care about what is right. You just have this thing about you that is so innocent and pure, it's really refreshing. And really needed in our world."

"Thank you, Bridget," she says as she starts to cry again. "You know, I was made fun of quite a bit in high school. They would call me a prude and tease me about anything they could think of, but you saying that really means a lot to me. Thanks."

"You're welcome, Annis."

We spend the rest of the drive in near silence, enjoying the peace that is hovering over us and in a moment like this, our smiles are not from some happiness, or a wonderful day, they are from something deeper, I think you could call it joy.

Chapter 14

I'm greeted bright and early by my friend, the cardinal. North is passed out next to me. He had a very long day yesterday.

"Hi Red," I say as I walk toward the bathroom. I know it's not the most creative name for a Cardinal, but it works and he seems to like it. He tilts his head to the side as he watches me.

I get dressed and then head downstairs to grab a bite to eat.

"Hi Aunt Mary, how are you?"

"I'm doing wonderful dear, here have a seat, I made your favorite."

"Mickey Mouse pancakes," I say with the giddiness of a young girl.

"You betcha."

I think what makes these pancakes my favorite is watching the joy come out of Aunt Mary as she serves them. Every time she makes them, she watches my face as she puts the plate in front of me, waiting for my smile. It's the thing you hope for when you've made something for someone with more than just ingredients. It's when you make something with love.

"Delicious! Personally, I think the ears taste the best."

"Haha, yeah, they probably do," she says as she laughs. "How was your day yesterday?"

"Aunt Mary I don't think I can put it into words. It was eye opening, heart filling, and just plain fun."

"That's great dear, you've needed one of those days."

"I really have," I say as I take another bite out of old Mickey. "Thanks again, Aunt Mary," I say as I put my plate in the sink. "I'm going to take North for a walk."

"You're welcome dear, have a good time." she says with a smile that says she is filled up even more than I am from those pancakes.

On my walk I decide to call Aunt Abbey.

"Hey there, I miss you."

"Bridget? Oh Bridget, how are you doing? I've been wanting to call, but didn't want to be a pest."

"You're never a pest, Aunt Abbey. I would've called earlier but things have been, well, crazy."

"Oh really? Is that good or bad? Are you OK?"

"Yeah, I'm really good. I just have been seeing a lot of things that I never saw before."

"Oh well that's great dear, looks like the bird just needed to get out of the nest and spread her wings, huh?"

"Yeah," I say as I laugh, cause I know on the other side of the phone she is actually lifting her arms up and flapping them like wings.

"So, I have a question for you," I say in hopeful expectation.

"Yes dear, what is it?"

"Before my mom passed she told me about a letter that she had written to me, and that I would get it when I was older. Do you by any chance have it or know where it is?"

"I do. Your mom gave it to me just before she passed and told me to give it to you when your heart was ready."

"What do you think she meant by that?"

"Well, Bridget it was no surprise to any of us that you felt abandoned by your parents and by God and she knew it would take time for things to come around. She knew that although I wasn't your mother, I was the best caretaker for you in that season of your life and so she made me promise to her that I would let you walk through the process of healing, even if it looked like you weren't getting anywhere. And she asked me to give you this letter when your heart was soft again."

"I think I'm ready for it."

"You do? How do you know?"

"I um, I can't tell you the whole story, but I've met a bunch of people, and they helped me see what my experiences had clouded. I just really get the sense that the letter is a really important piece of the puzzle for me right now."

"Oh Bridget, I'm so glad to hear that. Did you find a church to go to? Is that where all these people are?"

"No, I didn't find a church yet. I will, I'm sure there's some good ones around here. But honestly, I just feel like I'm finally finding my home."

"Wow, Bridget, that brings joy to my heart. That is why I knew you needed to move out there. I could only take you so far. I'm so excited for you Bridget. I will put that letter in the mail today. You should get it in a couple days, OK?"

"Thank you so much, Aunt Abbey. And Aunt Abbey?"

"Yes dear?"

"What you did for me after my mom passed, taking care of me and all, I just really want to thank you."

"Oh sweetie. Thank you so much. I felt like such a failure so many days because I could see your heart just so far away, but oh wow, hearing that you are doing well just makes my heart so full."

"Well, I'm so glad. I'll call again sometime soon."

"OK Bridget, I love you, and I will send the letter."

"I love you too, Aunt Abbey, and thank you."

As I hang up the phone and put it in my pocket, I realize that Aunt Abbey was a puzzle piece for my journey, a very important part in my life.

Chapter 15

...three days later

The last few days have gone so slowly as I have tried to wait patiently for this letter to come. I've had so many memories resurface from times with my mom and dad. I guess I had literally forgotten how much God was a part of their lives. In my anger I must have blocked it out of my memory.

I have the day off of work, so my plan is to wait for the mail, then take the letter to this park down the road and read it there. There's a nature trail that winds all through the woods and at one spot is this picnic table right next to a creek. There's a small water-fall that makes the most beautiful song when coupled with the singing of the birds and the stillness of the forest.

...one hour later

As North and I walk through the woods, I look down at my hand holding an envelope that was forged in the realities of my past, is a treasure to my present and, in some way, holds the key to my future.

We make it to the picnic table and it is just as peaceful as the other times I've been here. North, of course, goes off exploring right away, and I take a deep breath as I slide my finger inside of the envelope and tear open what has been silent for the past 8 years of my life.

I pull out 6 pages of a handwritten letter and I can feel the embrace of my mother as I unfold the pages.

"I don't know if I can do this." I say out loud.

And then as quickly as the words leave my mouth, peace rushes into my soul and surrounds me.

I place the letter on the table and begin to read.

My Dearest Bridget,
Treasure of my life and daughter that I had dreamed of and prayed
desperately for, I love you and I miss you.

I push the letter away and put my face in my hands as
tears pour down my cheeks. And in this moment of sorrow,
North comes and leans his small body against my leg. I pet
his head, wipe my tears and pull the letter back in front of me
as I continue to read.

I cannot explain to you the pain that it is causing me to know what
you will have to walk through in your life. No child should have to
go through what you are going through. And yet, I have learned
this in life: The path of pain is the only true path to strength. It is
not as some would hope it is or believe it is, but you my dear were
made for strength and courage and most importantly, Freedom. I
would like to spend the rest of this letter explaining things about
you that you never knew. My prayer is that you are able to
understand why your life has looked the way it has over the last
years and that you are able to embrace your calling on this earth to
its fullest. Bridget, you are my wonderful beautiful child, but before
you were ever mine, you were God's. Here is the story before your
story began:
I was 17 years old and full of life. I was on the track and field
team and was a really good runner. My favorite was the mile, it
was the perfect combination of speed and endurance.

I stop, look up through the woods and smile. My mom,
all these years, I never knew she loved to run. That's why I
feel so connected when I run.

I made it to the state finals that year and when I was
warming up for the race I met your father. He was one of the
~ from a rival school. He was so handsome and sweet. And

he had this big smile on his face as he introduced himself. I just tried to be cool and act like I wasn't completely taken by him. But honestly, as I ran around the track 10 minutes later, all I was focused on was catching another glimpse of him. Needless to say, I lost that race, however, I did win his heart. And that was worth far more than a high school gold medal.

He asked me out after the race and I said yes. We dated for a couple years and then when he was in college we decided to get married. We dreamed of having a girl and a boy. We would talk about all of the details of it and were so excited. A couple years later we found out we were pregnant with a boy. We were beside ourselves with excitement. We got the nursery ready and planned out everything. Then came the day that our dear Benjamin was born. Sadly, he only lived for three days. We were devastated. There was an issue with his heart that wasn't detected earlier, and there was nothing we could do about it. I cannot describe in words the pain of that moment when the heart monitor flatlined and your dad and I looked at each other so broken. Bridget, I don't know what your life story has entailed up to the point when you find yourself reading this letter, but pain is real, and you cannot avoid it.

So, your father began to drink and I shut down to everything and everyone. And for a year that was our life. We were angry and bitter, but all of it stayed buried beneath the numbness that envelopes a heart so distraught with pain.

And then it finally took its toll. Your dad found me on the floor one day when he got home from work. I had cut myself and had bled so much that I was just about gone. I could faintly hear him crying out over me, something about God saving me, and that's when it happened.

All of a sudden I was at this farm in the mountains and it was so peaceful, I figured I must be in heaven. I was sitting by this lake and it was so calm and so beautiful. I heard a voice behind me and as I turned I looked directly into these eyes blazing with kindness. He told me he had a gift for me and handed me a small box as he sat down beside me. I said thank you and opened it. Inside was a small gold plate with the inscription:

Bridget, the bridge to Love.

I looked at him confused and he motioned to turn it over. As I did I saw on the back was inscribed the date, May 01, 1981. I looked at him even more puzzled. He pointed out to the water and said that the sadness in my heart would now be overshadowed by the joy in my womb. He then placed his hand on my stomach and I could feel this sort of peace and calm come over me. And then he said something that I hadn't fully understood until now. He said he would take care of Bridget.

I'm not even sure what all of this means to you dear, but I pray with all of my heart that it means something.

I then woke up in the hospital with your dad sitting right beside me. I saw the tears in his eyes and the tears began falling from mine. We embraced and I told him how sorry I was and that I had so much to tell him.

Later that week I sat him down and told him all about what happened when I was in the hospital. I asked him if he thought I was crazy, but he just smiled and hugged me and told me we better start trying again to have a baby.

We also started looking for a church, but neither of us felt led to a specific one and we were kind of confused by all the different types. We met this group of people who were doing church in their homes and it seemed like a good fit for us. We learned so much in that first year of being a part of that group. We were like sponges soaking up so much about life that we were blind to before. And every time we would spend time worshipping God, I would feel His hand on my stomach.

When we found out we were pregnant again I soon realized that your due date was the exact date on the gold plate that I had been given in my encounter. It blew me away, and I knew then that God had something very important for you to do. I just wasn't sure what it all meant.

You were born without any issues. My perfect daughter. Your dad and I spoiled you so much, until we realized that spoiling you was actually ruining you. So, we backed off a bit. But nothing could change that you were a gift that was given to us by God.

When you were two you began to get really sick, I know you don't remember it, but it terrified us. You ended up being in the hospital for three weeks as you fought this virus that was literally trying to take your life. One night I was so angry, angry at God. I stood beside your bed as you lay there with the stench of death all around. I yelled out, 'What are you doing? Are you really going to give me two children and then take them both away? What kind of love is this?' And in that moment he answered me, quietly and firmly saying, 'This is not of me and you have a promise.'

Oh boy was I mad. I began to yell at the devil and I let loose. And when all my energy was gone I laid my head on the bed and as I was sobbing I told you to get better, and your eyes opened. The next day we went home.

I have seen great victories in my lifetime and felt great loss. But I have found that God is in them both, right there beside me. If I can't see Him, it is my eyes that need adjusted.

My dearest Bridget, when I lost your father in the car accident I didn't think I would be able to keep living. But you helped me stay strong, you gave me a reason to fight for life. But I'm afraid that my strength is all used up. I would gladly fight for five more years if I thought I could, but I just can't. And it breaks my heart to know that you will grow up without either of us. The ones who treasured you so greatly. But I have been praying nonstop since the accident that because we will not be able to be there, that Jesus would show himself to you in an incredibly powerful way that redeems the past and heals your wounds. And I believe, with all my heart, that he will.

Your purpose on this earth is beyond anything that you can accomplish. You are to be a lighthouse for all to see, calling all who are lost into the harbor of love and protection. You are carrying the seed that must be planted in the souls of all men and women. It is the purest message from heaven, calling out to everyone 'Come Home!'

With this, I leave you until we meet again. If you chase the doing in life, you will only be left with the reward for your hard work. But pursue and search out the being of life and you will live above the economies of this world and so full of true reality that nothing could possibly overcome the love that rages through your very veins.

My love, Jesus is the only true love. Find Jesus, whatever you do, find Him! And learn what it means to love, from Him.

As I look up from these pages my eyes are blurred with tears, my cheeks are moist and my nose is running. I take a deep breath and my view clears back up. It feels as if my whole world has just shifted. The colors feel alive, the sounds and smells are abundant and I feel light yet satisfied.

I look up to the sky and with the simplicity of a child I speak to the one that I know is looking down upon me right now.

"Please forgive me. I will follow you."

A sensation washes over me. I know this feeling. In an instant I'm taken back to the moment I was knocked off the road by the lightning and lay there weeping in the wet grass. And I sigh a release as a smile fills up my whole body with a feeling that is beyond happiness.

I sit there for another hour just basking in the rays of sunshine that are piercing through the leaves. Not trying to figure anything out, just simply existing, and receiving all that has just happened.

North and I continue our hike around the loop and back to my car.

The drive back is quiet. I open my window, let my hand dance through the waves of 50 mile per hour wind and simply take it all in.

I guess I never expected my life to be or look like this. I start to think about Jesus and then Joshua and all that my mom said.

And so, I start to talk to Jesus like he is sitting in the passenger seat of my car and like he is my best friend, Joshua. And as I talk with him, I know he is there, and in my heart he responds with his whispers that feel like warm liquid love flowing through my veins.

As I reach over and pet North and look ahead at the road, there is a break in the trees and I can see our small town down in the valley, seemingly put together and with no visible issues. But I know the reality of what lies beneath the masks we all wear.

The road to freedom is full of demons from our past. And if freedom is where you are headed, then you must face your fears and your enemy head on. A smile spreads across my face as I glance beside me knowing full well that there does exist true love in this world. And the one who defines it, emanates with it, and lavishes it upon all who simply turn to his bearing point, is with me in my Ford Escort, and because He is here, life on this earth is no longer _____.

Dear Friend,

I wrote this for you because I love you. And my love is the invitation for any and for all to come and find the true treasures of life. What was the last word of the last sentence of the last page of this story that welled up in your heart? Bridget's story is not yours, and yet it is. And somewhere, between the symbolism and tears of it all, it was not your heart that was drawn in, it was your spirit. The very thing I've been begging to come to life within you. The very thing that has had an all out war placed against it. From every angle they've thrown shovelfuls of dirt down upon you as you lay in your open casket, wondering if what has been, is really what life is to be.

ARISE!

Take off your grave clothes and reach for my hand, it is now here waiting. The perfect moment of grace has been extended for you. I will help you on your journey out of this grave and back to the mountaintop, and together we will have the greatest adventure ever known to mankind. To be fully alive in your humanity, dancing through sickness, pain, loss, happiness, struggle, memories, hardships, friendship, agony, success, cloudy and dreary days, and the warm and comfortable sweatshirt that you enjoy snuggling up in on those days. However, it is impossible to experience the fullness of life in the good and the bad, without your spirit coming awake and alive to me.

Friend, it is time. Time for your choice. My journey continues and my hope is that yours will continue with me; but it will only ever be, your choice to make. This moment either begins our journey together through all of the rest of your time on earth, or it will be what it is for so many: a reaching, a grasping for water. Trying to fill your life with the things that appear in others to bring peace and happiness, but never truly satisfy.

There is so much more that I have to tell you and we will talk more on our journey if you choose to come with me. But for now I leave you with this: Life is a breath; breathe in deeply. Life is a gift; receive all of it. Life is a treasure; don't waste it.

With love as always and for always,

Joshua

(or as I truly am, Jesus.)

Some final thoughts from Bridget...

As I think back through all that I've experienced, I can't help but wonder what has kept you alongside of me this whole time. I'm sure you hated me when you heard Joshua's side of the story, and quite possibly cried with me as I walked through mine. Maybe you were maddened by Ralph's keen ability to deceive, and rejoicing, as I was, when I finally got it right and tore that table cloth to the ground. But the highs and lows, the pain and the joy were no different than what you've endured. Just a different time with different characters and different circumstances. The biggest reality to all of this is that you are just like me, and the deceptions brought on by fear can move even the strongest religious person to a path of destruction. Don't let your process overwhelm you, and don't leave the road of your process to try and find a quicker and easier way. It will most certainly lead you away from the direction that is trying to lead you to freedom and wholeness and peace. Stay the course that God is leading you on and in the end there will be no regrets. Do not let your mind, desires, and dreams determine your direction, let God. He is looking for followers that He can invite into friendship and then friends that He can invite into family and then family that He can release his inheritance to. Find Jesus, and in the moments when you feel like you've done everything to find Him and you can't seem to get anywhere, close your door, turn off the noise, sit in the silence and talk, not at Him, but with Him as He is present there in the room with you. Ask him how He is doing and sit quietly giving Him a chance to answer you. But most importantly remember, He is not interested in simply fixing all of your problems. He really wants to hold your hand and walk through them with you. Because that is what true love does, it looks out for the best interest of the other. Your best interest is to grow into being an overcomer, and He wants to help you with that.

You are at the beginning. And it is your turn to see the reality of your life with Jesus as more real than your life on earth. Treat Him more real than your greatest cares down here, and He will open His heart to you, and open your eyes to your truest existence.

...from Stephen,

The journey of literature that you have just completed was not crafted within the throes of creativity and sleepless nights. It was void of striving and the pursuit of the perfect verbiage. It was instead conceived in the most humble of places, far from civilization, in the middle of the woods of Northern California. There, on a single track hiking trail, a seed was planted in my heart. It was a seed that would begin to grow a week later in the middle of a noisy coffeehouse while sitting at a modern reclaimed wood picnic table. I would sit speechless, full of awe, as the story unfolded from my spirit, through my fingertips and onto a screen.

These words, intimate stories and books are a testimony of a Father and Friend, a Mother and a Love, that would have you know there is an invitation for all to, 'Please Come Home'.

Your direction is freedom, your map is your life, and your compass and your companion, is the best friend you will ever know on this earth, Jesus.

I am but a vessel that has poured out the wine that I've carried to your cup. Please do not waste this precious wine. May the truth and experience that you've had in these books not be buried and overshadowed by the screaming voices all around you trying to convince you to just lay down.

Stand to your feet, turn off the noise and take one more step. Freedom demands it, and the best friend you could ever have is waiting to lead you on. Through storm and trial, through war and peace, through confusion and fear, He looks into your eyes and says, "I will never leave you, or turn my back on you."

About the Author:

Stephen lives in South Carolina with his family and their dog, North. He has done everything from carpentry to writing music. From teaching children who did not have a stable home-life to washing the dishes at his own home. And from leading his kids on adventures in the woods to loving his neighbors, whoever they may be.

He finds great joy in sharing his own story with others; the one where he was led out of religion by Love.

At the end of his life he is looking forward to answering the one question he believes God will ask him.

"How well did you follow my Son?"

And to this end he writes books, he writes songs, he swings a hammer, he serves and loves his family, he encourages those around him and he prays for broken hearts and broken bodies. But more important and precious to him than any of that, he talks with his friend Jesus about all of it. He has become convinced that if he does everything while walking with Jesus, he will truly have the privilege and blessing of The Abundant Life.

My prayer is that everything that pours through me from God will be a help and a guide on your next step towards finding true freedom in Jesus.

Welcome to the journey, that I believe with my whole heart, will change your life!

To find out more about Stephen's
other books, music and writings, go to:

www.TheCompassSeries.com

THE COMPASS SERIES
Four novels
Four different perspectives
One story

Made in the USA
Columbia, SC
21 July 2024

39118333R00225